The Landlord's Daughter

Monica Dickens – the great-granddaughter of Charles Dickens – was educated at St Paul's School for Girls. She travelled abroad for a while after leaving St Paul's and then joined a dramatic school. In 1935 she was presented at Court and soon afterwards found a job as a cook – an experience described in her first book of autobiography, *One Pair of Hands*. She has since written two further books of autobiography – *One Pair of Feet*, which is about her work as a nurse, and *My Turn to Make the Tea*, a description of her life on a provincial newspaper – and many novels. She is married to Commander Roy Stratton and has two daughters.

Her novels include *Kate and Emma*, *The Listeners* and *Last Year When I Was Young*, as well as a number of children's books including *Follyfoot* and the 'World's End' series, published by Pan in Piccolo.

By the same author in Pan

Kate and Emma
The Room Upstairs
The Listeners
Last Year When I Was Young

In Piccolo

The House at World's End
Spring Comes to World's End
Summer at World's End
World's End in Winter
Follyfoot
Dora at Follyfoot

Monica Dickens

The Landlord's Daughter

Pan Books in association with
William Heinemann

First published 1968 by William Heinemann Ltd
This edition published 1970 by Pan Books Ltd,
Cavaye Place, London SW10 9PG,
in association with William Heinemann Ltd
3rd printing 1976
© Monica Dickens 1968
ISBN 0 330 02486 8
Printed in Great Britain by
Richard Clay (The Chaucer Press), Ltd, Bungay, Suffolk

This book is sold subject to the condition that it
shall not, by way of trade or otherwise, be lent, re-sold,
hired out or otherwise circulated without the publisher's prior
consent in any form of binding or cover other than that in which
it is published and without a similar condition including this
condition being imposed on the subsequent purchaser

ONE

WANTING HER to have what was right, after a life in which much had gone wrong, I would not let my wife go with the red-haired undertaker before Julia came home.

My wife's name was Charlotte, but everyone called her Charlie.

Julia is her daughter, not mine. She was brought up as Julia Morgan, the name Charlie was using when she came back with her to the village after she was born. Julia became rather briefly Mrs Stephen Lowe, and after her divorce in America, she changed her name back to the one on her birth certificate, her mother's maiden name of Lambert.

It seemed a weird thing to do, although there were people, especially in the village, who had never concealed their natural scepticism about Mr Morgan, so conveniently dead, sight unseen.

Julia had been told almost nothing about her father. But it might have been more fair if she had known that she had some right to the resentment, the sense of being cheated with which she soured her young life.

She carried the resentment into her five-year marriage, then carried it on afterwards, like a stuffed toy or an old guitar, to Provincetown on Cape Cod, where she now beachcombs among a crowd of eighth-rate painters and rope-sole layabouts much too young for her. In the winter, when there are no tourists for whom to parade like picture postcard peasants, with loony sunglasses and shrimps in their beards, they have grey little orgies with marijuana in clay pipes from the Surf'n'Sand gift shop, and Julia can tell them that none of it is her fault.

None of what? Nothing really bad has happened to her yet, although I fear it may, since thirty-five is a bit old for such gipsying. If she is found one day floating like a long-dead seagull in Provincetown harbour, I hope they don't send for me.

On the telephone, I told her, 'Cable me when you know your flight, and I'll meet you.'

She said, 'Oh,' and I knew that she had not thought of coming home for her mother's funeral. That seemed such an insult to Charlie, who perhaps was still hovering, tapping our trans-atlantic cable, that I told her curtly to get on the night plane from Boston.

'I'll pay you back the fare,' I added wearily. I had been trying to reach her for forty-eight hours. When her mother died, she was out on a boating party – in October! – and her voice when she finally answered my cable was as barnacled as the boat.

I was glad I had already decided that she should see her mother dead in the downstairs room where we had moved a bed months ago, when the stairs defeated her.

I would spare Julia none of it. If I could have made her see Charlie staring and mottled as I had found her, with her shoulders on the floor and her swollen feet on the bed, I would. But the surprisingly young undertaker, one of the new sucker fish incident to town growth, who was already behaving like a family lawyer and calling my sister Mary, although her name is Margaret, said that if I wanted to keep Mrs Kitteredge in the house, she would have to be embalmed.

He made a delicate stroking gesture to accompany the word, with the tips of his scrubbed fingers curved back, as if embalming were smoothing a counterpane. He was very seemly, in spite of the fiery hair and little Irish snout. When I telephoned him to tell him that my Charlie was now a customer – patient? – client? he had said, through a soft breakfast mouthful, either egg or porridge, 'Oh, Mr Kitteredge, we *don't* like to hear news like that.'

But if you didn't, you'd be out of business.

I did not actually say that. I thought of it afterwards when my mind was not stammering and trembling in the terrible chill emptiness that Charlie had bequeathed. I had understood for months that she would die. It was going to take time to understand that she had.

So the next day, Red sent the embalmer, who looked like his uncle, with tools of trade that included an enamel bucket. A bucket! He carried it away down the brick garden path with a lid on it.

Margaret, sorting clothes upstairs, for she could not stay long, and Julia would never do it, looked out of the window and said, 'What's that?'

'Well . . .' I dislike minced words, but there is no point in being pathologically candid. 'Whatever they do.' I was standing by the door at the bottom of the dark stairs that run from the sitting-room steeply up through the middle of this very small house. At night they shrink slightly away from the worn nails, crack, crack, crack, like the ghosts of old lovers going up to bed.

'Oh Gawd.' To Margaret it is not blasphemy if you mispronounce it. She came out of the room and stood above me, skirt too long, legs too thin, feet turned out. She looked at me for a moment and then asked, 'Don't you mind?'

I made some gesture. To mind about things like that would mean I thought that was the real Charlie in the room behind me, in which case I would not let Red in, much less his uncle with the bucket.

While he was in there, and Margaret was staying upstairs, and I was staying outside, looking in vain for tomatoes that had survived weather and weevil, an almighty crash had come from the sitting-room, followed by a sickening aftermath tinkle.

It was the door by the fireplace that looks on to the path at the side of the house. The french door, Mr Parks had called it grandiosely, when he glazed the top half to give the room more light.

I went to the door and saw the uncle's nose tilted defensively behind two broken panes.

'What the devil are you doing?'

'Bluebottle fly.' He sucked his lip. 'I got him.'

After he had gone, Charlie's face was much paler, waxen and bonier, the nose and brow more noble than when this had been the comfortably fleshed face of a middle-aged woman who had hardly noticed the loss of a figure which had never been the shape to send men into battle. Margaret had braided her dark grey hair into a sort of coronet on top of her head,

7

which added to the Roman emperor impression. This was not going to hit Julia hard enough. Charlie was less a dead mother than a tomb effigy, lacking only her old dog in stone across her feet.

Quite a few wreaths and sprays of flowers had come, and stiff arrangements in flat churchly urns from distant kin or acquaintance, discharging obligations by Interflora. There were letters and telegrams. Warm, spontaneous telegrams. Lovely letters from Barbara, Etty, dear old Quentin, written in haste, with more heart than style. The ones that would come in later colder blood would be more artistic gems of sympathy. I've written them myself, leaking at the eyes with the beauty of it.

The post office van had made a special stop at our house, its red roof shining like a tea-tray below the wall at the top of the bank, the driver a young coloured boy I did not know, who said easily, 'I'm very sorry for the loss of your wife.' George Baker, whom I know very well, footing it round with two bills and a catalogue the morning she died, had only been able to say, 'That's a bad job.'

We were arranging al lthe flowers and letters and the sympathy cards with lilies and praying hands to make a sort of shrine for Charlie in the room where she had sat many years ago with the whiskery dog and those dreadful fish. Sat with Peter, the curtains pinned across. Sat with me, both reading, in the trustful peace of our marriage.

Someone in the village had brought a great bonfire of chrysanthemums from his garden, and Margaret had put them in a copper jug near the bed. It did look too nice for Julia, although being more superstitious than sensible, she would still hate having to see her mother dead, and would not understand the ease with which Margaret and I were able to come in and out of the room, looking or not looking at the bed quite naturally, without strain.

When Mr Parks stopped in on his way home from work with a card from his wife, all silvery satin like a wedding congratulation, I told him what had happened to his french door.

'Too late to glaze this evening.' He murmured in the hall

with a furrowed brow, ear cocked towards the front room, as if Charlie might bark.

'Could you knock a piece of wood over just for tonight?' Time was when we would not have been seen dead locking doors and windows. Now, with Kingsgrove and the other country towns reaching out to meet the industry creeping on us from Oxford and Wycombe and Aylesbury, you might be seen dead if you didn't.

'You can't hammer a nail in a room where there is death,' Mr Parks said sharply, as if I should have known.

They have known Charlie much longer than me, the older ones. She came here long ago, in 1930. Came back again in 1932 as Mrs Morgan, widowed mother. She stayed until the war and then returned for good when the Air Force finally released her.

I only moved in ten years ago when we were married, because she had a job and a house, which were two things more than I had. They don't resent me in the village. I don't bother them. I sit on a few local committees. I have done a bit of teaching at Kingsgrove Secondary, and features and book reviews for the *Oxford Mail* when I get the chance. I announce at the local horse shows in a pork pie hat and Wellingtons, have learned to be polite to the children who take a short cut through my back garden, wear jackets that blend into the ploughed landscape, and don't expect a young man to come and do my digging.

I can't do it all myself, but I do understand, which people like Henry Clay don't, that I could not even ask one of the loping young gorillas in shrunken denims to come and double-dig the vegetable plot.

After Mr Parks had whispered backwards out of the door, as if the house of death were a throne-room, I could not find any plywood. We had burned everything on cold evenings last summer. So I tore up Margaret's grocery carton (like all women at a death, she had rushed off to buy food), and tacked that roughly across the broken panes.

Somewhere over my left shoulder, where Peter Clive's father kept his spirit conversationalists, Charlie was laughing because I pushed in the drawing pins quietly instead of knocking them with the tack hammer.

Julia arrived that night. Typically, instead of cabling, she took a bus from London Airport to Henley and telephoned me from there, so that I could not do her the favour of meeting the plane. I found her in a coffee bar near the bus stop, quite decently dressed, thank God, with her hair massed up in sort of Ionic scrolls on top, and shiny nylons on the sturdy legs I had not seen for years. She saw me looking at them and said, 'I bet you thought I'd come in jeans.'

'Why didn't you?'

There had been a sneer in her voice, so I was not able to say any of the friendly, stepfatherly things I had rehearsed on the road. I don't know why I had thought I could. Julia is not the sort of person to whom you can say, 'Thank you for coming,' or 'I'm so sorry dear,' or, 'She didn't suffer at all.' You have to keep quiet and see what she will say, and then try to match it.

In the car, the first thing she said was, 'I hope you meant it, about the fare. I had to borrow.'

'I meant it.'

She nodded, and did not say any more. She has a strong, heavy face, with an ugly nose but quite a well-made mouth with her mother's broad smile, though Julia's is rarer. Mostly she keeps her mouth clamped, as she did now, staring ahead in silence while I told her how her mother had died, whether she wanted to hear or not.

When we got home, I drove round to the shed at the back where I kept the car among the garden tools and the few hens who have not poked off across the road to better pickings in Gregory's barnyard, and we went in at the kitchen door.

Julia, who is tall, bent automatically under the lintel, though once inside, she looked round the shabby little kitchen with its makeshift flap-tables and vile antagonistic stove as if she had never seen it before. Margaret had swabbed it up a bit, but it is still the kitchen of Julia's childhood.

She walked through into the hall and stood with her suitcase like a stranger, like a new lodger, like someone come about a job; although she had betrayed herself again by ducking in the doorway. This house was home to her when she was tiny, and after the war when she was fourteen or fifteen and went to the local school, but because Charlie had always loved it, Julia must always reject.

Margaret came down the stairs and through the front room like a hostess, and put out both dry veined hands to take her by the shoulders for a kiss. 'I'm so sorry, my dear,' she said, bolder than I.

Julia avoided most of the kiss by leaning back. She said, 'Oh, don't let's have that. Why do we have to have that?'

'Why not?' Margaret lifted her nailbrush eyebrows. 'If you can't be emotional when someone dies, when can you?'

'Why be emotional at all? It's so damn insincere.'

This was standard. Julia always manages to insult someone or start an argument as soon as she appears. Margaret stiffened and said, 'There is nothing insincere about my feelings for your mother. Or James's.'

Having successfully got her goat, Julia dropped it. She patted her arm. 'Good Aunt Margaret.' She pronounces it Ant, another of her affectations when she comes home. In America, they tell me, she speaks exaggerated British, like a Hemingway peeress. 'I didn't mean it that way.'

When she smiles, she is quite different. Margaret softened. 'Come and see your mother,' she said in a holy sort of voice. Julia went stiff, but Margaret took her arm and led her into the front room to see what there was of Charlie. I went into the other room. I did not want to see Julia's face in there. Although I had planned this to shock her, now I wished she had not come. Whether she was shocked or sad or indifferent, I did not want to know it.

I went into the dining-room and stood looking out at the yellowing greengage tree. I had quite a real sense of Charlie with me now, not in the other room where her shell was embarrassing Julia.

Why do they call it spiritualism? When the dead return – no, not return, for they have never quite left – when they come close, they are themselves. Not spirits. Why spiritualism? Why must it be any ism, with all the closed-shop jargon? It makes people deny it for fear they will look like cranks.

I leaned my forehead against the window to ease my pain.

11

Damn the accomplices of Chinamen and little girls and Red Indians, who ignore the pure truth of death as a continuance of life. What should we think of our dead if we truly believed that they wasted eternity hovering about in some dingy Victorian suburb waiting for their loved ones to make a two-guinea appointment with a woman who picks her teeth behind a musty curtain? And damn, God double-damn people like Mr Clive with his shams and doorknobs! No wonder the dead mostly come back in dreams, when the coast is clear of farce.

Later when Julia had drunk what was left of my whisky and gone up to the room she had to share with Margaret, since it was that or sleep with me, Margaret told me how she had reacted.

'She was as stone.' A woman who can make any subject dull, my sister likes a turn of phrase. 'She looked at the bed for a while stiffly with her shoulders hunched, and then she turned away and lit one of her interminable cigarettes and started to read the letters and cards. She stood by the mantelpiece with that lumpish dead expression on her face. It's impossible to tell how much she minds.'

'She doesn't.' How could she? It had been absurd to bring her back, and now I was stuck with the fare. Serve me right for being whimsical. Even as I waited for the overseas operator, I had been picturing the graveside scene, and Julia there, head bowed, miraculously a gracefully mourning daughter instead of what she was, a sullen cow.

A stupidly cynical cow. She had spent the shank of the evening reading some of the kindly clichés from the letters.

'*She was a great character*. Poor Mum. Freehold brick house of character. *One of the dearest women I have ever known*. From that old queen, that's funny. *We're all thinking of you*. That's a help. *I shall miss her sadly*. Considering Etty hardly *saw* her in the last twenty years.'

'Shut up, Julia.' It's such an absurd name for her. A Julia should be a wand, with dark wet eyes and lips like Renaissance jewels. 'It's a gesture, something at least they can do for us.'

'It does nothing for me except raise bile.' She would have thrown Quentin's and Etty's letters into the fire if I had not grabbed them from her.

12

'She doesn't mind,' I told Margaret when Julia was up-stairs.

'But her own mother!' When our own unlovable little tyrant went, Margaret mourned for weeks, although it spelled free-dom. 'Everybody minds when their mother dies.'

'Assuming they were glad that they were born. With Julia, that seemed to be her major grievance against poor Charlie.'

'Of course, if her father hadn't died ...' Margaret was still trying to fit the situation into a recognizable pattern of family relationships. 'It was before she was born, wasn't it?'

I nodded. After Julia had put the whisky bottle outside the back door, from habit of setting out the empties at the Pro-vincetown bar where she works in the summer, I was drinking Mrs Meagan's elderberry wine, which Charlie and I had kept for diarrhoea.

'So very sad. Poor Charlotte, she never talked about him.' Pause. Sip tea with long lip vacuuming.

I sip elderberry wine, my equally long lip puckered neatly at the small glass.

'Nor have you, James.'

'I never knew him.'

'Oh?' The crew-cut eyebrows up again. 'I always thought you—'

'I didn't know him.' I was in no state to parry probing, as I had parried it off and on for thirty years. Thirty-five years to be exact. August. I know the date because it was the month the two old ladies said they saw the Loch Ness monster crossing the Glen Urquhart road with a dead baby in its mouth.

'Let's go to bed.' I stood up and stretched and heard my bones crack, and pulled in my stomach when Margaret looked at me. She does not accuse me of going to seed. She reassures me that at sixty-five one can't expect, etc, etc, which is worse.

'I was going to heat some milk for you,' she said, as if I were a dotard.

Although I knew I was going to be lonely as hell, I was already looking forward to the time when good soul Margaret went home and left me to roam about the place in peace. She will come back often, with tins of shortbread and an eye for my buttons and socks, and she will occasionally pry me loose

13

to stay with her and Tom and the dachshund in what is called Greater London, but is only a particularly characterless sprawl of dwellings, neither urban nor rural nor even suburban. Mostly I shall be here alone, with Mrs Meagan bringing my half pint of milk and once a week 'sweeping me through', which means literally right out of the back door in a great cloud of dust and tobacco shreds and flapping mats.

I pushed the old dog out into the garden, where he stood shivering in his old fur coat, testing the night with his faded leather nose. His eyes and ears have gone before his sense of smell. He was with Charlie twelve years (he wore a bow at our wedding). I expected him to howl when she died, but he went on about his business, ignoring the shell I called Charlie, which increased my conviction that it was not her.

I went into the sitting-room to lock the french door without even turning on the light.

'Are you all right, dear?' Margaret called down the stairs, knowing I was there in the dark.

I did not call back, because if you can't hammer in a room where there is death, you can't shout either. I murmured, and she went into her room, thinking perhaps that I was praying.

Being a non-praying woman, thanks to our mother, who would not have it in the house, like May blossom or an open umbrella, Margaret gingerly respects prayer, in the same way that children of the Reformation respect the goings-on of Catholics. They don't believe in it themselves, but then again, you never know, and so they assume a special enthusiastic voice for planning to get weekend guests to Mass, in case they might get a little sanctification by osmosis. Since *jour maigre* was abolished so incontinently that it now must feel like a sin to eat fish on Fridays, the hostess has been cheated of the facile halo of remembering Fridays, and making sure the Papists noticed she had remembered, and was not just having salmon because it was in season.

I had prayed for Charlie, of course, but not since she died. I am self-centred, but not as arrogant as that. Either she had found out that there is no God after all, in which case I'd look very silly, or she had already caught a glimpse of His glory, in which case I'd look sillier still, down on my cracking old knees beside her bier, instructing Him to have mercy on her soul, and no messing about with Purgatory, you hear me, Sir?

After I had locked the side door, I stayed a while in the room, pottering in the small light from the hall, putting back the letters Julia had taken up to mock, shifting vases, and smiling at the notion of putting the flowers out in the hall from sick-room habit. I was smiling as I stood by the bed and laid one of the fiery October chrysanthemums on the sheet over my wife's breast, only three days ago so cushiony, now so flatly sculpted. Red's uncle had left her hands folded outside, but I had hidden them as she always did, sitting on them or keeping them in her pockets or in the lap of her skirt, the good hand covering the other one.

When I was a little boy, I had been ill for days, actually running a temperature, after I was forced to see my grandmother dead. I saw Julia's father when they fished him out of the water, and had to take sleeping pills for weeks. In the war, I helped to dig a woman out of a pile of bricks in Great Portland Street. I fainted when she came out without a head, and the lady with the mobile canteen, who had just done her First Aid lectures, was delighted to find a casualty to whom she could actually administer hot sweet tea.

But now there was no terror in this room. Not only because I *am* much more aware of Charlie over my left shoulder than on that bed by the smouldering chrysanthemums, but because I can easily visualize myself on the bed, and Margaret, who will outlive me, bleaching out the kitchen sink and buying lard and cornflakes (who for?).

The nearer you approach death, the less the fear, obviously, or you would go starkly mad as you grew old, not calmly senile. Even had I seen my own corpse lying on that bed, I would perhaps have merely nodded and passed on to lock up the rest of the house. I have always thought Scrooge overdid the hysteria. '*Am I that man who lay upon the bed? No, Spirit, oh no, no!*' The old boy had only a few more years to go, at best.

The old dog slept with me, on Charlie's side of the bed. She always had these common bristly little dogs like stairbrushes, neither attractive nor attracted to anyone but her. In the middle of the night he woke me by scratching at the blanket and whining. I thought he wanted to go outside, so I put on my dressing-gown and padded down without my teeth or slippers. I had reached the turn of the stair before I saw he had not followed me. He was sitting on the top step, still whining. There was light round the edges of the door at the bottom of the stair, and I heard Julia sniff. How strange that she should have come down to keep vigil. Would I now have to start dredging up sympathy for her?

I opened the door. A short slight young man with long bobbed hair and white trousers like dirty wrinkled skin spun round from the mantelpiece, shining his torch on me so that he was instantly blotted out.

'What are you doing?' Bad choice of words. You get no attack on a T or D without your teeth.

He still stood behind the glare, paralysed by the sight of this harmless householder in a Paisley dressing-gown not properly tied. Would he shoot me or throw a knife? I put out a hand and turned on the light. He pointed the torch at me like a weapon.

'Put that bloody thing down,' I said, trying to work some saliva into my mouth.

'You stay where you are, mister.' He had big dewy eyes in a flat pale face within the girlish frame of chestnut hair.

'Of course. I'm not going to hurt you.' I put my hands in my pockets, nonchalant, although my heart was bumping up against the place where my back teeth should be. 'I thought you should save your battery. You might need it going home.'

'Yeah.' He threw the torch wildly towards me and ducked for the door. I saw that he had pushed in one of my pieces of cardboard to turn the key.

'Don't go,' I said quickly.

To my surprise, he stopped at the door and turned round, standing against it like a starfish, hands out, legs spread wide from the tight crotch. Did he think I had a gun? I had not even pointed my finger at him through the dressing-gown pocket.

I had always wondered what I would do if I woke and found a burglar. Barbara and Charlie both said that they would lie

16

back and accept rape, and I always thought that I too would cravenly let him take anything he wanted, even my wife under my very eyes. But now I was master of the situation. I had not thought of an intruder being more afraid of me than I was of him.

'Who are you?' I held up my chin, the grand inquisitor.

'None of your business.'

'Oh, look here, I'm not going to turn you in. I've got better things to think about, can't you see?'

He nodded. He could have cut and run any time, but he stayed, jammed against the door. Although he was a secret night prowler, I had the curious impression that he wanted my company.

'Come into the other room,' I said. I was not embarrassed in the room of death, and he did not seem to be either. Although Charlie had seemed quite close to me yesterday, she was not discernible now, behind my left shoulder or anywhere else. However, I had not quite lost all sense of what was fitting.

'No.'

'Tell me your name then.' I jutted my chin. *Ihre name sofort!* Had they ever had a toothless Gestapo?

'Terence Haig-Davenport. That's not my real name, of course.'

'Of course. Where do you come from?'

'Up the Estates.' He jerked the bell of hair towards the valley beyond Kingsgrove where toybox houses and zigzag blocks of flats and schools and supermarkets and sanitary brick pubs creep over the rich meadows below the chalky hills.

'Why did you come here?'

'See what there was.'

'To steal?' Padre Jaime in the confessional. Ask pardon for your sin against the tenth commandment, my son.

'I was trying doors.' His face had a squashed look. A dab of nose, retreating mouth and dented chin, as if someone had put out a hand and pushed in all the features with gentle fingertips. 'I do that sometimes, for kicks. Don't often take nothing.' He was more relaxed now, leaning against the door, not poised for flight. His eyes were wide, with childish lashes, not crafty, surprisingly candid. He was twenty, twenty-one, perhaps less.

17

Padre Jaime was losing his grip. I rather liked him. 'Cigarettes sometimes, to give away. I wouldn't smoke a cigarette.' He muffed his Rs. Not a babyish W sound, but catching his teeth on his lip. Cigavwettes. 'Half-cvwown milk money from a mug. Saw someone's rent money once, in the book. I never took it.'

'Then why do you—?'

'Silly, innit? It gives me like, a kick to get in where I don't belong.'

'What is this – kick you keep on about?' I asked irascibly, testy old dugout, pretending not to be *au fait* with jargon.

'Well, it, you know, gives you a thrill to be in where they don't want you.'

Julia's voice, lazily American, said on the stairs, 'A substitute for sexual assault?'

His dark blue eyes watched her unhappily as she thumped down the last three steps. He swallowed air down his young vulnerable throat. He was only an Estates boy, import not native Oxfordshire, only a boy who tried doorhandles and window catches, with perhaps a spot of Peeping Tommery thrown in. Nice clean stuff. Julia had thrown a false note into our conversation. The boy put his hand on the doorknob, ready to go now that she had spoiled his evening.

'Must have been quite a shock for you, coming in here,' Julia told him coolly. She was wearing her khaki raincoat, crumpled cotton pyjama legs showing below, make-up clogged on her nose, a witch's straggle of hair that stank of cigarettes. She had lifted the scrolled coif off at supper intact, like a hat. 'Or are you a corpse watcher?'

He glanced quickly towards the bed. It was the first time he had looked at Charlie. 'Well—' He licked his lower lip and shifted his feet. 'I had the car out, you know. Buzzed the village, and then thought I'd do a few houses. I've been round here before. Never took nothing. Just came in once with a coat hanger on the back window catch and tried your biscuits.'

'For kicks,' I explained to Julia. If I went up for my teeth, he might go, and I wanted to hear the rest of it.

'Right. So I see this cardboard, you know? I pushed it in, get me hand through – she's turning very sweet.' Warming to

18

his tale, he lifted his pinched boot forward, pantomiming, very theatrical. 'I step in' – he raised his knee – 'almost too easy. I look round' – a crouch, pivoting, then a hand flung out – 'and what do I see?'

'You tell us.'

He shook his head. Some won't hammer a nail. Others won't say dead body. Corpse. Stiff.

'Well.' Julia sat down with her back to her mother and lit a cigarette. 'You came for thrills.'

He nodded. They understood each other. Telling his dramatized story, he had forgotten fear of us. For all his horrid accoutrements – the hair, the rubbed jerkin, string tie, spotted shirt and gimcrack death's-head belt buckle – he had a small poise. At least he was on his freakish own, not in a snickering gang.

'I wasn't scared,' he boasted. He tried to put his hands in his pockets, but his trousers were too tight, so he put them on his narrow hips, with just the thumbs in the pocket slits. 'I mean, I seen people like that before. Bit of a surprise, of course. I thought, come on, what's this? I shone the light.' He pointed an imaginary torch at Charlie, holding the other hand before his eyes, peeping through the fingers as if he were at a horror film. 'But I wasn't scared. She looks quite nice,' he told me politely, as if I had made a cake. 'I was just looking round a bit. That's what I do, you know. Just look round, and no one knows I've been there, into their personal things. The Eye was here. Sometimes I leave a note. They go frantic, looking to find what I took, but I was just . . . there.'

You could not mind him. He was no modern delinquent. He was Robin Hood, Raffles – the Peter Pans of uncriminal crime.

'Why weren't you scared?' Julia was laughing at him, cigarette tilted up between closed lips.

'All right. I was.' He grinned. Because of the clothes, or the hair, or the pretensions of protest against something or other, they could be allies. 'But I had to have a look round. That's what I come for. The flowers are vevwy nice.' Another polite nod to me. 'Then I had a look at the letters.' He held up the palm of his hand and made scanning movements back and forth. He looked at me. 'My mother died last year,' he said conversationally, and glanced at the bed, as if he expected to see her under the sheet, instead of Charlie.

'You get many letters?' Julia hung a leg over the arm of the chair, swinging a bare foot not clean, but seaside healthy, not misshapen like a town foot.

I crossed the room and stood by my wife, as if I could protect her from this surrealist scene, although I was proud of myself for being able to swim with it. I felt that she would rather I swam than was conventionally outraged. As long as Margaret did not come down in her steamer rug dressing-gown and the quilted slippers. I could hear – or feel – the vibration of her catarrhal breathing through the boards and lath and plaster between us.

'Shut up,' said the boy. 'She was killed on the road. Ford Cortina. On holiday, it was. She and her friend, they'd won this prize, picking out fashions in the newspaper. First holiday she'd had for years and they run her down in Shanklin, Isle of Wight.' He slashed his hand down like a scythe and glared at us through his thick lashes, daring us to belittle. 'We buried her down there. No one on our road really knew she'd gone. She didn't go out much, being foreign. She didn't speak to people. Her friend, Mrs Zanzetti, she didn't either. That's why they were friends.'

'I'm sorry,' I said stiffly. Colonel Bogey, *sans dentures*.

'Yeah.' He thought for a moment, trying to remember how he had felt. 'My father cried. He'd got after her for winning the competition and going off on holiday, but then he cried. I told this girl I knew, and she said we should get married and she'd cook for me and my Dad. They'll move in on you, you see.'

'Who does cook?' We were getting much too involved.

'I do. Or him, if I have a late round. I drive for the linen supply service.' He upgraded the vowels, as if the laundry van were a royal Daimler. 'Doris, she gives us a hand sometimes.'

'The girl who wanted to marry you?'

'Not her. Dovwis is the kid I work with. Guitar stylings.' He plucked strings of air, eyes faraway. 'Doris sings. She's only a little girl and she's in a wheelchair, you know, singing. Winged Pigeon, it's called.'

'Pigeons don't sing,' Julia said.

'This one does. You ought to hear her. Sitting in this chair with a rug over her legs. Pretty sick, eh?' He scanned our faces, mine blank from surprise, Julia's from lack of it. 'I'm her manager. That's how I got my name. Terence Haig-Davenport.' Tevwence was how he said it. He spoke it as if he had not had it long, although it was the sort of name one might never get used to saying casually.

'Oh no, come on.' Julia yawned. 'What's your real name?'

'Ben Japp.'

'I like it better.'

Without any warning, I felt that it would be easy to cry. I wished Ben Japp would go, but had no energy to tell him. I sat down and blew my nose on a piece of old sheet Charlie had torn up for night handkerchiefs.

The boy took a comb from the pocket of his dotted blue shirt and ran it carefully through the gruesomely groomed locks. 'You her daughter then?' He nodded towards the stone crusader on the bed, unfocused watchman of our ridiculous charade.

'Yup.'

'She must have been a lovely lady,' he said as soppily as a Victorian gatekeeper.

'Don't be stupid,' Julia said. 'You don't have to be so stupid. What's the point of the clothes and the hair and the night prowling and the sick bit with the guitar and the girl if you're going to be just as stupid as everyone else?'

The boy shuffled his feet uncomfortably. 'We're all human,' was all that he could manage. 'You oughtn't to talk like that. Those letters I read. Vevwy' – his epiglottis struggled in his throat like a marble in an old lemonade bottle – 'vevwy nice I thought they were. I'd be proud if they was written about anyone in my family. Or me.' His eyes looked inward to savour his own death scene. *'A vevwy fine person has left us ... I am proud to have been her friend.* That's what it said, in one of the letters. Here—' He picked Etty's mauve notepaper out of the pile on the mantelpiece and handed it to Julia. *'I am proud to have been her friend.'*

Julia was growing angry. She snatched Etty's letter and

21

stood up, crumpling it, her grubby raincoat creased up at the back over her broad haunches. 'She didn't know my mother. What did she know about her? None of them knew her, what she was like.'

The boy stepped back in alarm as she shouted at him, his eyes like squashed pansies.

Julia dropped her cigarette on the rug and trod on it with a weathered heel. 'She wasn't even married!'

This was so comically yah-boo that I was suddenly stabbed with the loss of Charlie, the appalling vision of all the empty days when I must laugh alone.

'Now, you shouldn't speak like that,' Terence Haig-Davenport tried to swallow the glass marble again. He looked at me for help, and I heard myself tell Julia dully, 'I wish I hadn't made you come.'

'You didn't. I came on my own. It's my mother.'

Now I felt my anger rising to meet hers. I did not get up, because I was tired, and anyway she is taller than I am. I gripped the arms of the chair with my freckled bony hands and said, 'I think I have more claim to her than you do.'

'I am proud to have been her friend.' Julia threw poor Etty's letter into the fireplace and stood there on the worn hearthrug with her short arms hanging and her face blank. 'I am proud to have been her daughter,' she said bitterly. 'Why should I be?'

Then she began to sob in a very ugly and noisy way. She cried standing up, with her shoulders hunched like a bull and the back of her cuff for a handkerchief, affronting me with the saliva stringing her square mouth, and her lumpish, unwomanly body. I could neither speak to her nor look at her, but the boy, who seemed to have become as inextricably involved with our family as we were with his, stepped up and patted her briskly on the back, as if her trouble were a fishbone.

But death does bring these incongruous kinships. Red, the old family undertaker I'd never seen before. Terence Haig-Davenport whom I would never see again. That reporter at Peter's funeral thirty-five years ago who broke his wrist and his clumsy box camera when I pushed him over a headstone, so that I had to pay for his doctor and his new camera and answer letters from one McIndoe (solctrs & est agts) for months afterwards.

'Of course it hurts,' Terence told Julia kindly, his eyelashes dewed like a cow after a frosty night. 'I cried all the way going down in the train to where they had my mother. I know how you feel.'

'How can you?' Julia gave a long sobbing gulp and straightened up, throwing him aside. 'How can you or anyone know what I feel? Don't you understand?' She padded over to the door, giving me a rotten look as she passed. I knew that she had always thought very little of me as a stepfather, or even just as a person, but I had not realized just how little.

'Don't you understand?' She turned her damp red face and shouted back at the poor harmless boy, as if she disliked him as much as me. 'She didn't even know my father's name!'

'Oh, I say.' He looked at me after Julia had stumbled upstairs, his mouth quivering, his eyes reproachful. I stood up and jerked my head towards the french door.

'Get out,' I said curtly. I should have said it long before.

'Get back to bed,' I told Margaret almost as curtly, when she came questing down after he had gone to say that she had heard people chatting (chatting!) and found Julia sitting on the steps to the attic with her face a sight.

'It's all right,' I said to the sharp cold nose whose kiss I avoid, and the anxious eyes under the low-slung hairnet. 'Go back to bed.' I had to be alone. I could not stand any more talk.

'Should I go to Julia?' No one but Good Ant Margaret would even suggest it.

'She'll be all right. She was upset, that's all.'

'I thought you said she didn't care.'

She didn't. When I woke late in the storm-drenched morning to find Margaret, already in her funeral hat, dusting the dining-room table and setting the chairs straight with admonitory jerks, Julia had gone.

She had taken my car to Kingsgrove, got Dick Meagan's taxi to the airport, and was now somewhere over the Atlantic on her way back to Boston.

Margaret's comment: 'So there was all the expense of the embalming for nothing.'

Charlie's family kept on about Julia, although they should know what she is like by now.

'Can't understand her not coming over.' It was the theme song of the wretched day, intoned against great howling sheets of rain which drove across the churchyard like the risen damned. 'Why didn't you make her come?'

Margaret and I had decided not to tell them she had come and gone. We did not want them to know how much she had hurt us.

Margaret did not know how much.

Never knew your father's name, eh? All right, Julia Morgan, Lowe, Lambert, whatever you call yourself among the lobster pots and New York State chianti. I was never going to tell you the truth. Now I believe I must. That's why I am writing this, my pen plodding down the long ruled pad, the fields beyond my window saddening damply towards winter.

They will be green before it's done, or even golden, and I shall send you the whole thing airmail, at enormous cost. Or leave it in a hollow tree and shoot myself. Or put it in a bottle and float it across the ocean.

Never knew your father's name ... All right, Julia. All right.

Charlotte Lambert met Peter Clive on a Sunday evening in September 1930. She was driving her blue two-seater back to the village, to this same square brick and flint cottage at the top of the bank on the Kingsgrove road, which had only recently become hers. It still had no curtains, no rugs on the floor, very little furniture and no domestic comforts beyond oil lamps, a rainwater pump in the kitchen, a well outside with a bucket and rope, and an earth closet down a damp black path between the privet hedge and the shed.

She was returning from a weekend house party at Garfield Hall in the north of the county, which was both more rural and more chic than the south of Oxfordshire, where villages like this were already beginning to feel the profitable irk of London weekend cottagers, like sand in oysters.

The weekend house party at Garfield Hall sounds as if Charlie was quite gay and sophisticated, which was far from the truth. She was rather gauche and lubberly, still with the farouche uncertainties of adolescence, which no experience of her twenties had so far dispelled. She had always had to fight out of the shadow of her good-looking mother and her theatrical brother and her gorgeous younger sister. At school she had been slow to read, which in those pre-dyslexic days gave you a label of stupid that did not wear off for a long time. In a family like hers, not quite ever. She was buxom at fourteen, but bosoms were between seasons, no longer proudly boned and not yet an official sex zone; so she hunched her shoulders and folded her arms and fell in love with the captain of cricket.

She grew up tall and strong and her feet and hands grew big and her face had a country health, although she lived in London, where the face of the day was gamine, with nightlife circles under the eyes. It was her bad luck to have grown up in that time. Twenty years earlier, she could have given herself to some undemanding young man with soft whiskers and had four children and no questions asked about fulfilling her destiny as a woman. But now, you had to prove yourself a vital force, which was quite hard on girls like Charlotte Lambert, who did not want to be one.

That September, she was twenty-five years old, big-boned but nicely rounded, an athletic, ungraceful girl with a bright, healthy skin, steady chocolate eyes and long, clean, dark hair that she often wore in pigtails or tied back with anything handy, like a shoelace or a piece of tape.

For the weekend, she wore it plaited across the top of her round head, like Lea Seidl in *White Horse Inn*, but driving home on Sunday evening, wisps of it were hanging down, a hairpin dangling inside her collar. It did not matter. Nothing mattered except getting back to her cottage, her cave, her shell. Uncaring, she drove past the blaze of colour at the corner of the little wood, then stopped and backed and got out of the car to pick an armful of the red and yellow leaves.

Not for herself. Having a peasant heart, in spite of her urban upbringing, Charlie was a looker, not a picker. But when the fierce colours caught the corner of her brooding eye, she remembered that Miss Perrott had asked her to look out for unusual autumn foliage on which to hold autopsies with the Lower Fifth.

Miss Perrott was the botany mistress at St Gabriel's School in Stokenchurch. Charlie was the gym and games mistress. That, of itself, had caused the final shredding of an already tattered weekend.

The host and hostess were friends of her parents, which was unpromising for a start. As Mr Lambert's building ventures prospered, their friends grew grander, and it was the sort of house party where you changed your clothes three times a day and everyone was expected to go cubbing, if not on a horse, then on foot, which was worse.

Charlie had a rotten time. I know she did, because I was there. I was in those days hopelessly in love with her younger sister Barbara, although Charlie was nearer my age. She and I had grown up together, off and on. Our families had been friends long before prosperity set in and the Lamberts moved to the pinnacled abode in Hampstead. Together we had endured vast Christmas parties, where great-aunts were whiskered and children acted playlets. In linen hats and bloomered sunsuits, we had dug moats on Belgian beaches, the nurses calling like seagulls as we pottered far over the shining sands at low tide.

In 1929, Clarence Hatry 'honestly' confessed that he had swindled stockholders and banks and the Borough of Swindon out of some twenty million pounds. A little of the money was my father's, and he shot himself with his service revolver in the dining-room of our house in Lancaster Gate. Running from bed, we found him slumped across the table, a note propped against the fruit bowl, neat and conclusive.

My mother was sick on the carpet. I never liked her so well before or since. As the shock of the trial wore off, people began to say that Hatry's victims had got what their greed deserved, and Pope Pius observed that they were money mad. My mother agreed with all of this. She had never trusted my father, and his ruin put her once more in the right.

Small and ironclad, indomitable widow, she wrenched me from my art school and compelled Charlotte's father to employ me in the drawing office of his construction firm. He was builder and landlord of small blocks of flats in the growing suburbs, and along the wider roads which were beginning to carry the new race of wheeled Londoners in and out of town. I learned to design doors and windows. It was surprisingly enjoyable.

Charlotte had always been my friend, but now my blinding love was suddenly the sneaky baby sister who had spoiled our games and blabbed our secrets. Charlotte was Charlie and Barbara was Bubbles, since every person, animal or thing in the Lambert household had a nickname, including the car and the cook. All cooks were humorous, like vicars, and their sayings were quoted in comic cockney.

Bubbles Lambert had bleached her hair into a dry platinum cloud, and painted her nails and lips like luscious plums. In later years, her chin squared off and her nose sharpened and her cold eyes told the truth. But at twenty, she had the kind of illusory celluloid glamour I had long lusted after from my two-and-sixpenny seat in the darkness. She had what we called sex appeal, which was not necessarily the same as sexiness, as I discovered when I married her.

Charlie had been dragged before King George V, sat out one debutante dance in the ladies' cloakroom and then scuttled away to the refuge of the physical training college. Bubbles, of course, was a famous debutante of 1928. Her picture was always in the *Tatler*, at dances and weddings and race meetings with people called Rags Montcalm and Diddy Lycett-Hays and Bonzo Law, either with titles, or so grand they did not need them. I was only on the fringe of her sort of group, her father's employee, extra man when all else failed, always a little poorer than everyone I knew, a little worse dressed, my golf bag lighter, with no car, and no acquaintance among headwaiters or bandleaders.

I had only been invited to the house party at Garfield Hall because Bubbles, on a whim, had asked the hostess if I could come, and then hardly spoke to me the entire weekend. No one spoke much to Charlie either, even I, miserably Bubbles-watching, but somebody's nephew kissed her wetly and rather brutishly in the butler's pantry on Saturday night.

On Sunday, she overheard him telling Bonzo Law, as a sort of scientific curiosity, 'I never kissed a gym mistress before.'

So it was small wonder, driving home along that narrow white Oxfordshire lane between the Cotswolds and the Chilterns, that she was almost too wretched to make the effort to stop and collect Miss Perrott's autumn foliage. She only told me her version of that weekend years afterwards. When she was young, the worst humiliations might somehow not be true if she kept them to herself. It was only after her small world had reeled and tipped her spinning into the grand unguessable that she could smile at the early Charlie, and even caricature her bruises for my benefit.

Only for *my* benefit. Am I betraying her now? If so, forgive me, Charlie, forgive me for this. But I have to tell the truth, because of Julia. And because it is all in my own head, where you heaped it over the years, detailed, confused, repetitious. Sometimes contradicting yourself, or even lying, because you could not bear me to know the whole of it. Sometimes so uncannily clear that I could live it with you, know the stones under your feet, the print before your eyes, Peter's hand, the small foot of Mr Clive, stepping carefully over a line of ants.

I say it is for Julia, but perhaps that is only an excuse, and I shall burn it when I've done. Perhaps it is quite simply for myself. It will keep me out of mischief, Mrs Meagan said, after she found me at the table under the window in my pyjamas at noon, and asked. 'What in the name of all that we hold dear are you doing?'

'Writing a story,' I said. 'Please don't tidy this table.' Although she never had, and has no idea of starting now, with the mistress of the house departed and everything gone quite to pot.

The window looks out beyond my garden wall and the blackberry brambles across the sunk road to Gregory's meadow, then elms and a chestnut tree threaded on a rail fence, a stubble field, then the stream marked by shaggy willows, not pollarded for years. Beyond, the vari-coloured arable rises to the smooth hill with a clump of wind-scarred beech trees where the Danes camped a thousand years ago. In the war, the Germans saw 'Danish Entrenchment' on the map, so they dropped a stick of bombs there and killed a cock pheasant.

To the left of my view, the eyeless brown stucco of the end council house, with chestnut paling fence, so controversial, and the latest grandchild's vestments ever on the line. To the right, the dark copse and the top of the silent steeple, where the birds fly in and out.

My view will change as the leaves fall and the stubble is turned into dark furrows, and I shall sit here, out of mischief, trying to recapture my Charlie.

Charlie in the green dinner dress she wore at Garfield Hall, her face a little mulish from boredom, arms turning blue in that Siberian dining-room. Charlie in Air Force uniform, drilling those poor bedraggled girls who had never walked half a mile in their lives unless they missed the last bus home to Camberwell. Charlie in a bright blue gym tunic with the whistle between her teeth, trotting up and down that quagmire of a field on the border of Oxfordshire and Bucks, crying, 'Shoot, shoot, Fiona!' while the rooks swayed about on top of the elms like sightseers on the top of the Empire State Building.

Charlie as she was in that September of 1930, with the whistle and the mud and the rooks and the smoke going straight up in the pale afternoon air from the brick cottages at the end of the playing field of St Gabriel's School for Girls, Stokenchurch, Bucks.

'Come on, you lot of slackers!' Charlie trotted out of the damp pavilion on to the muddy grass like a boxer in training. 'You've wasted so long getting changed, it will be Time before we start.'

'Cheers,' someone said quite loudly. They did not care if old Lottie heard. She did not really care either.

She was Lottie to the school, as naturally as she had been Charlie to her family from the day she was born in the big bed in Bayswater, with straw down in the road when her mother threatened to haemorrhage. 'Come and see little baby Charlie!' And her brother wept because he thought they meant a boy. It was a waste of a beautiful name to christen her Charlotte.

She was quite happy in a dormant way, trotting about the hockey field and slapping the leather vaulting horse, hup, hup, hup, to keep the slackers coming. She did not mind that most of the older girls rebelled against gym and games and sat out with 'colds' far more often than once a month. It was a waste of time to talk about sporting spirit to these great girls who knew that it got a woman nowhere. Look at Lottie Lambert.

The Lottie Lambert they looked at from the privilege of sixteen was a shelved spinster of twenty-five, surprisingly well preserved and more amiable than most of the other hags who ran this prison hulk. But that hair. And the clothes. And ye nose that yshone. A peasant verily. She gave her life for a hockey stick, they quoth, and hath never known man.

The Lottie Lambert they did not see was a blundering dreamy creature who had never come completely awake. The girls were right about the man, but not about the hockey stick. Gym and games were merely the only things she knew she could do. She had not given her life to anything. She had not really started to live at all.

Tall and strong and smiling, two long dark plaits bobbing on her back, she trotted on to the field because it was the winter term, and you only walked out in summer, for cricket. The girls straggled out behind her, the older ones giggling, or grumbling at Charlie, and hitting each other on the ankle with

30

hockey sticks, the younger ones galloping round her with cries of, 'Please Miss Lambert, oh Miss Lambert, you said I could be centre half today, you *said*!'

From a distance, it was hard to tell Charlie from the girls. Once, at the drill display, she heard a parent say to the Head, 'That girl with the medal looks rather mature.'

Miss Baxter, who wore purple stockinette tubes and dyed her hair and eyebrows orange in a last stand against superannuation, had answered vaguely, 'We bring them along as best we can,' so as not to contradict.

The big bronze medal, from the British Empire Association of Athletic Training, was the only difference between Lottie Lambert and her girls. Like them, she wore a butcher-blue gym tunic with a belt about seven inches from the hem, brown woollen stockings with seams like hawsers, blue bloomers underneath, and white cotton knickers under the bloomers.

Bulky, but Charlie was glad of it, slogging up and down the hockey field on a raw winter afternoon, with the fog beading her white pullover and smoking in her throat like the chimneys of the indoor people in the lane at the bottom of the field. If she ran with the whistle in her mouth, she could scarcely breathe at all, but most days, it was hardly worth taking it out, since she had to blow it constantly for fouls and lack of finesse.

St Gabriel's was a day school, with no reputation for anything much. When their first eleven played the second eleven of Wycombe Abbey, or even the third, if St Gab's was having a bad year, Charlie had to beg her girls before the match to try at least to pretend to a team spirit.

Charlie's girls were better at things like swimming and races, where you won or lost for yourself and did not have to keep passing the ball just when you were going well. It was not that there was a bad atmosphere. There was no atmosphere at all, no cohesion. The girls only thought of St Gab's as an Alma Mater after they left, and then only if they were unnerved by the world and needed to invent themselves a stable background.

They came every morning, by car or bus or bicycle, fatnosed and small-eyed from bed, and dispersed every evening to Wycombe and Stokenchurch and Risborough and their satellite villages. The staff went home to husbands or parents or nobody in houses or flats or furnished rooms which they called digs, to make themselves feel like bachelor girls. Charlie went home to her dog and her fish and her whispering staircase in the brick and flint cottage on the edge of the village.

It was always called the Village, even in the little market town of Kingsgrove, which fed and supplied and collected rates and taxes from a dozen other south Oxfordshire villages which were known by their names – Ewelme, Brightwell, Swyncombe. The cottage had once been called Bankside, but Charlie found it as Calloways, and now it was already 'down Lambert's'.

She had found the house last spring. Before that, she had lived for two years with Etty, who taught the kindergarten, in a beige stucco bungalow thrown down in a chalky field on a road that led to nowhere.

One Saturday, her brother Philip – always called Reggie, after a bald, red-faced comedian he had resembled as a baby – had stopped at the bungalow on his way to London.

'Wanted to renew acquaintance with my little sister,' he said indulgently, although really he despised Charlie for her way of life, and thought her a handicap, when he thought of her at all, and had only stopped to impress Etty, who was not bad looking in a vulgar way.

He had a new car. It was a Riley sports, red and white, with dazzling tin hub-caps and a bonnet twice as long as the engine.

'Oh glory, how ripping!' Although she was engaged to a steady young solicitor in High Wycombe, Etty exuded at any man, and Reggie was a god from another world. She had his picture on the inside of her stocking drawer, where she did not know that Charlie had seen it.

She swung round from the window and knocked a china cat off the sill with her eager hips. 'What'll she do?'

'She'll be good for a modest sixty.' Slapping two leather gauntlets together, he stood on the vantage of the steps that led into the sitting-room and smiled at her through short chestnut eyelashes which he lengthened with mascara on the stage.

'Gosh, did you hear that, Lottie?'

'Yes, I heard that, Etty.' Behind her brother's slender back,

Charlie threw a simpering grimace at Etty's rapturous smirk. Reggie was conceited enough without this. So conceited that even with the fair success his light pleasant voice and easy way on the stage had brought him, he must still woo the adulation of Etty, whom he called 'Your tarty little chum with the bedroom legs.'

The car was open. It had a leather strap round the long bonnet to stop it flying off at the modest sixty. Reggie had goggles and a leather coat with a fur collar, and he laid the windscreen down flat so they should think he was going faster than he was.

Etty had manoeuvred to sit in the front. Her eyes were streaming and her nose and cheeks mottled scarlet and blue, but she kept laughing and chattering into the wind, for who would ever imagine that she was out in a car with Philip Lambert? She would let it slip tomorrow both in class and in the staff-room. The class would say, 'Philip Lambert, who's he?' although they knew perfectly well, and someone in the staff-room would say. 'Well, he's only Lottie's brother, after all', but that would not disguise their envy.

Philip had never been seen at the school. Miss Baxter had once asked Charlie if he would make a speech on Prize Day, but she had not even told him.

Wrapped in a rug, she crouched in the narrow back seat of his roaring little car, which was so low you could feel the gravel attacking you from below. Her hair was whipping about her face and her teeth were paralysed, but if Reggie took you for a ride, you did not say, 'When are we going home?' Even his two tiny children knew better than that.

The exhaust was a volcano under her seat. As he racketed round a sharp corner on two wire wheels, he shouted back to her, 'Fun, Char?' and she yelled back into his ballooning tweed cap that it was.

Whatever his reason, even if it was for Etty and to boast of the car, he *was* nice to come and see her and take her out. Whatever the years had done to make him now almost a stranger, spoiled, superior, out of her ken, she *was* proud of him. When she sat in the stalls last month and heard him cry, 'Bernice!' as the girl left him for ever, lurching down to the

33

footlights with a sob in his voice to break into 'She was my love', Charlie had to stretch her mouth and open her eyes wide, because she could not use a handkerchief without her mother seeing.

He slowed down in a flurry of chickens to go through a dead afternoon village between Benson and Kingsgrove, and Charlie suddenly said, through lips made shaky by the rush of air, 'Stop the car, Reg.'

'Going to heave, ducks?' Etty asked. She was never ill. When everyone at school had been laid low with trichinalis or psittacosis, or whatever the topical scourge was, she had bounced about the staff-room swishing at bodies with a ruler and saying, 'Come on, you lot of sissies.'

'Shut up.' Charlie was staring across the road. 'I'm going to buy that house.'

Her brother tugged the car into gear impatiently, and Etty said, 'What a feeble joke.' But the reliable young solicitor was due to bear her away in his sidecar next autumn, and so Charlie could say, 'I want to live here,' without hurting her feelings.

The village was right. Three gritty streets patched by muddy cart-wheels, set in a triangle among wide arable fields and small pastures below the Chiltern hills. Few people about, moving slowly, in clothes that were neither winter nor summer. Small children in dry manurey dust playing something with little sticks. Boy with terrier and dead rat. Post office in someone's front room. White Hart on the corner with pub door on one street and sweetshop door on the other, offering Mazawattee tea. One sizeable stone house in a little railed park, the rest low-windowed cottages and small farmhouses with barns and middens and orchard paddocks contained within the pattern of the village, as if for a siege.

The cottage was right. Square flint with brick patterning, four empty windows and a peeling door, moss blurring the edges of the tile roof, the whole thing appearing to lean very slightly backward at the top of the bank above the road. Two crooked fruit trees had stepped out of their blossom on the long grass, and toadflax and seeded silvery pinks and small scrolled ferns grew in the wall which separated the dishevelled

34

garden from the footpath. The house-agent's rain-warped board leaned out on a rotten pole, at its last gasp, beseeching.

'I'm going to buy it,' Charlie said. She had been mad even to think of staying on in the crouched bungalow after Etty left. 'This is just what I want.'

'A farmworker's cottage?' Her brother screwed up his neat, handsome face as if he had bitten an aspirin. Etty said, 'But look here, dear girl, there won't be any light or running water or drains or all that.' Since she went to France last year with a group of teachers in a bus, she always called it the twalett, but in front of Philip Lambert, she could not even call it that.

'I don't care,' Charlie said recklessly. She climbed over the side of the car and scrambled up the grass bank on all fours to stand at the tilted gate and stare at her own front door. It had once been painted a soft grey blue, like the window frames. It would be again. She would have dogs and cats and smelly things like hens, and she would live here, safe as an island, where no one could both her about dancing or clothes or bobbing her hair, or quirk a humorous eyebrow when she talked about her job.

She turned round to look down triumphantly at her brother and Etty, who was dabbing white powder on her ruined nose with a piece of cotton wool. 'It looks as if it has been empty for ages. They can't want much for it.'

'You haven't got much.' Reggie sat with both leather paws on the steering wheel, anxious to feel his tyres once more licking up the gritty road.

'Uncle Walter's money.' Charlie's godfather had been killed at Ypres. An uncaring, unpatriotic sacrifice, his rabbit wife, whom the family had underestimated, already gone off before the war with a dancer. Damn gigolo. When Charlie was twenty-one, she received three hundred pounds, a sacred trust from Uncle Walter, betrayed and martyred.

Not to be spent lightly. The following week, she came back by bus to Kingsgrove, and was told that the price of Bankside was two hundred pounds.

'Offer 'em one-fifty,' her father said, even before she took him inside, poking at the spongy doorstep with his stick. 'It's robbery,' he told her, after a grumbling, suspicious tour, pulling away torn plaster from the lath, kicking at a rotten wainscot, 'but if it's what you want . . .'

He had wanted wild things in his life – money, a battlemented house, a wife who was the model for the Academy picture of the year, *The Yellow Satin Dress*. Sometimes now he forgot he had not always had them, but he did understand wanting, and single-minded pursuit.

When Charlie lived at the bungalow with Etty, they had bicycled to work, heads butting into the wind, coasting down the dip of the lane with their feet up like schoolgirls. But the cottage was six miles away from St Gabriel's, so she spent the rest of her legacy on a bull-nosed Morris Cowley two-seater with celluloid windows, a dickey with no stuffing in the cushion and a throbbing gear lever you had to catch and subdue before you could change gear. Charlie could never double de-clutch without a grinding of metal, nor start on a hill unless she was propped with a stone, but she taught herself to steer in the back lanes and the disused Army camp, and joined the sporting camaraderie of the roads with a college muffler and her hair stuffed under a beret.

The car was called Mick the Miller, after the champion greyhound. Charlie's mother had christened it that when she first saw it, panting slightly and bubbling at the radiator cap after its climb in low gear to the Lamberts' house at the top of Fitzjohn's Avenue.

The real Mick the Miller could run faster than the little blue car, and you could not always get in or out of the doors, but it was the final seal of Charlie's independence. Each afternoon, as the school day wore out, she began to look forward to the drive home. Down treacherous Aston hill, which she once had to climb backwards when the engine was ailing, through the late shoppers of Kingsgrove, a mile between cut-and-laid hedges and a swing round the corner of the back lane to bump the sawhorse at the end of the shed like a train fetching up at the buffers.

This Friday in September, she must hurry to get into the car and home, because she had to change and pack and drive unwillingly to join her family and heaven knew who else at

36

Garfield Hall, seat of the St Irwins, gentleman farmers for opinionated generations.

Five minutes early, she blew a long blast on her sucked whistle, with Olive Bartlett dribbling furiously down the right wing and the doctor's daughter stumbling beside her piping, 'Pass! Pass!' But Olive would not pass to her if she could help it. Tubby Taylor in goal, padded on stomach and shins, three people's jerseys round her neck, made off for the pavilion at once like a shambling bear. 'Shoot! Shoot!' Cara sprayed through the wires on her teeth, and Olive side-stepped dreaming Betty and shot cleanly into the empty goal.

'Goal, our side, we won.'

'Cheat. Not fair.'

'Fair.'

'Not fair.'

'Fair. Sucks.'

'Nyah.'

They argued without energy or rancour, galloping back to the pavilion, not caring who won.

Cara did care. She marched by Charlie with her stick over her shoulder, looking up tensely. 'It was a fair goal, Miss Lambert, say it was.'

'Well, I had blown for Time.'

'You were still blowing when Tubby walked off.' With an immense contortion, Cara took the restraining mechanism out of her mouth and rubbed it on the front of her tunic to clean off the mud. She put it back with a sucking sound, champed her jaw on it and walked by Charlie in silence, glancing at her without moving her head.

She was passionately in love with Lottie Lambert. 'Twill pass,' Etty assured, but Charlie did not necessarily want it to. She liked the eager, spidery child. No one else had a crush on her. 'A crush on Lottie?' the girls jeered at Cara. 'How pointless.' Crushes were for glamorous people with cherry lipstick and uplift brassieres, like Etty, or domineering sex-substitutes like Mrs Northcote, dictator of the Middle School.

Sadistically, Charlie made the child wait until she reached the end of the field and picked her college blazer off the back of the goal net before she asked casually, 'Want a lift home?'

Cara's bony cheeks flared red. From her eyes, she might have been offered an Arab stallion, instead of a quarter-mile ride in a chugging biscuit tin with a hole in the back window and your feet under a cascade if it rained.

Her house was on the Oxford Road, on the way home. Charlie could have taken her every day, but she made her wait and wonder. Often when she went to the yard at the back of the school where the car stood like a Shetland pony next to Mrs Northcote's lumbering fifteen-horsepower Austin, she saw the child lurking. Sometimes she pretended not to see. Sometimes she called, 'Going my way?' in a breezy gymnastic voice. If she took Cara every day, the acrid cry of favouritism would rise like bonfire smoke. That was an excuse for her enjoyment of power. And as Charlie knew well, having been in love with a few unattainable people, male and female, the uncertainty was half the thrill.

'Meet you at the car,' Cara hissed, and sped into the pavilion, swinging her stick to get bodies out of the way.

In the staff cloakroom under the school, where a miasma of shoes and women in the pre-deodorant age hung under the low ceiling like marsh gas, Etty was flouring her nose with a lot of flying powder.

Charlie sat down on a bench and took off her brogues, which were so perpetually caked with mud that there was no point cleaning them. But she would have to take them to Garfield Hall, in case there was golf. For cubbing, there would be Wellingtons to borrow, ranged in a tiled back hall that smelled of dog. She had never been to Garfield Hall, but she had been to other house party weekends, and that was how it was.

She hoped there would be golf. Too late for tennis, since the St Irwins would be sure to have a grass court, best in the country, but if there was golf, no one need mind being landed with Charlie as a partner. For dancing or indoor games they could mind, but not golf.

Scraping her shoe with the back of an old knife, she looked up at Etty, licking a finger to slick the powder off her startled brows. At the bungalow, the flesh below used to bulge raw and shiny on plucking nights. Charlie would never let her come near her with the tweezers.

In the mirror, Etty's engrossed face was an enamelled doll.

'How do you get the powder to stay on so smoothly?' Charlie asked. 'If I use it' (she hardly ever did), 'it's like tapioca in five minutes.'

'You're such a child, Char. Haven't you ever heard of vanishing cream?' Etty had only heard about it herself when it was first advertised a few months ago.

'I've heard the joke about the girl who rubbed it on her stomach to make the baby disappear.'

'So has everyone else for the last hundred years. Here, I'll put some on you.' She took a small jar from her bag. Charlie sat like a child being washed, screwing up her eyes while Etty stroked sweet-scented cream over her nose and broad cheeks and round chin with delicate fingertips.

'There! You look almost human. Now powder.' She floured her up. 'A bit of lipstick.'

'I've got some somewhere.'

'Tangee,' Etty scoffed, digging in her bag again. 'You can't see it from two feet away. And men don't like the taste of it.'

'How do you know?'

'I used to use it, centuries ago when I had that boyfriend from the kennels. Here, try mine.'

'You put it on.' Charlie pursed her lips.

'No. Draw them back against your teeth.' Straddle-legged to get to Charlie's bench level, eyes fierce, tip of tongue protruding, Etty carefully painted on a mouth and stepped back, the fat lipstick poised like an artist's brush.

'It looks lovely,' she said.

Charlie dropped the shoe and got up to look. Bending to the low mirror, she saw a morose clown with two scarlet sausages in a white face.

'Leave it,' Etty said, as she put up a hand. 'You'll be just right for the grand weekend.'

It worked on Etty. It worked on Bubbles and her noisy friends when they rouged and powdered and spat into their cakes of black mascara. Charlie stared at the mask of herself for a moment, then went to the basin and began to lather soap vigorously on her face.

'I give up,' Etty said quite crossly. 'You never should have moved off on your own. A nanny, that's what you need. Or a keeper.'

'Ha, ha,' Charlie said, through a towel which she would have to take home and scrub, or Mrs Rivett would pin up a notice about misuse of school property. But when she looked at Etty, she saw that she meant it. 'What's the matter?'

'Nothing you'd understand. You don't understand anything.'

Wasn't it any fun after all, being married? Were the sloppy, giggling bungalow days already the Good Old Days?

'Sorry, kid.' Etty beamed quickly and swooped on her, all crochet bosom and warm rounded arms. 'I feel rotten today.'

'Are you going to have a baby?'

'I don't know,' Etty said vaguely, and they laughed and pinched each other.

Watching the back of her silk legs going up the stairs, Charlie thought of the young solicitor with his eyes set close as a newt and his dimpled hands. But Etty had slept with him before she married, or said she had. She must have known.

Charlie shook her head like a dog to clear the pictures, ran up the steps and went whistling out into the grey netball yard, where three or four cars were parked by the wire gate. A ground-floor window shrieked up and the head of Miss Perrott looked out, pollen on her glasses and the sacks of her bosom resting limply on the sill, flanked by peach-stone seedlings and saucers of mustard and cress growing on wet flannel.

'Hullo, dear,' she called. 'You're off early. The bell hasn't rung.'

'I'm in a hurry,' Charlie said, although she had been quite ready to delay with Etty in the cloakroom. 'I'm going up north of Oxford for the weekend.'

'Oh, you are so gay.' Miss Perrott's head bobbed and wagged. An intermittent tic closed the loose folds of her left eyelid. She had once gone into a fit during Assembly. The girls in her botany class hoped it would happen again. 'We shall just be quiet, Mother and me.' She leaned farther out as Charlie waved and started to turn away. 'No chance to go gadding all over the countryside like you. Do be a dear, and if

40

you see any interesting bright leaves, do gather me some. We're going to do glycerine preserving on Monday as part of our autumn project. Acorns, etcetera, and crab apples. I've asked the girls to go nutting.'

What a hope. Charlie said, 'I'll try,' and started to walk away. Cara was standing on one leg by the car with an attaché case and a blue raincoat with an uneven hem.

'I see you're taking the little Miles girl again, mm . . . mm . . .' Miss Perrott made a strange humming sound, waggling her head like fury, because Cara's father had fobbed her off last time with a bottle of medicine which Miss Forster had analysed for her in the lab and declared to be mostly peppermint and sugar. 'You're very kind to the poor child,' she said, nodding and shaking her head at the same time, and shut down the window.

Cara was not a poor child. She was quite happy at home with her quiet doctor father and a serenely joyous mother who tamed squirrels and cared for crippled birds and knew the name of every wild flower on the Chiltern hills. At times the mother looked like somebody's charwoman, and girls at St Gabriel's had heard their parents say the doctor was out of step with the march of modern medicine, and so what with refusing to say she hated her parents, plus having a crush on Lottie Lambert, Cara's status at school was quite low. Obsessed with Charlie, watching for her at every corner, taking roundabout routes to music or chemistry in case the gym door was open, she hardly minded, or even noticed.

'Get in,' Charlie called, for it was beginning to rain.

Cara tugged at the door. 'It's stuck again.'

'Get in the other side.'

'That's stuck too.'

When one door was stuck, you could usually open it from the inside. When both were stuck, you had to find a metal rod on the floor of the dickey, put it under the handle and bang the end with the mallet that was used for knocking round the nut wrench when you changed a wheel.

'Quick then, before Mrs Northcote comes out.' Last time, she had caught them at it, and asked Charlie why she did not leave the poor old car where it was and jump in her Austin, since she was going down the hill and could drop her at the Lambert Arms (a four-mile walk from her village).

They got one door open, scraping away a bit more of the chipped paint.

'One day, I'm going to paint the Miller,' Charlie said.

'I'll help you.' Cara looked up quickly, toothplate agleam.

'All right, we'll do it together some Sunday.'

'Honest?'

'Honest.'

Cara threw in her case and climbed in over the gear lever and the handbrake. Charlie bent to the handle to start the car with a cough and a choking gasp and then a welcome rattling roar, just in time as Mrs Northcote appeared in a tarpaulin cape at the staircase door, her humped nose scenting through the rain for trouble.

Charlie ran back to get at the accelerator before the engine lost interest, banged the door very hard to keep it shut, which was one reason why it often jammed, crashed into first gear, spun the wheel like a tram-driver, and they lurched out of the gate, dropped back on to four wheels and trundled gently off down the middle of the road.

Charlie's dog, who had a whiskered face and harsh brindle fur like a hedgehog, was watching for her through the bars of the front gate. When he saw the patched roof of the car go by at the bottom of the bank, he rushed round the house to be found crouched on the kitchen doorstep, as if he had been there all day trying to get in.

When she took him into the house, he drank water as desperately as if there were none for him outside, sprang up and down when she picked up his dish, then flattened as she took it empty to the door. He knew what that meant.

When Charlie went away, to her parents in London or occasionally to a married friend, patronizingly fulfilled with milk-sodden babies, the dog stayed with Quentin and Bob at the other end of the village. The fish went too, a small sour tankful of pouting goldfish who gave no pleasure even to themselves.

With the dog on the seat and the tank on the floor, Charlie drove cautiously to the hairpin corner where the Kingsgrove

42

road met the village street. The triangular garden was heavy with fruit trees and overblown flowers. A willow brushed over the gate where a board from the side of a blue wheelbarrow said, 'End o' the Road'. The long, low cottage, recently white-washed, had enough beetling thatch and lattice and wrought iron for a pantomime house in the scene where the lost princess knocks at the door – rat-a-tat on the drum box – and who should come out?

Quentin came out as Charlie went up the cobbled path, light as a fledgling in a loose shirt and green corduroys tied up with gardening twine. Quite a lot of water had slopped out of the tank on to the car and Charlie's gym tunic, and he pursed his lips with a little cry and rushed it into the kitchen. His cottage had running water and a bathroom, like the Jaffrays' weekend place near the pond. Most of the newcomers, except Charlie, had taps and baths. Eventually, it was said, there would be electric light. The people at the big house, who made their own with a dynamo in a throbbing shed, warned at Council meetings about 'Pylons marching across our beautiful countryside'.

Quentin settled the fish on their usual shelf, gave the dog a playmate biscuit, and kissed Charlie with his cool dry lips.

'Have a lovely time, Charlotte.'

She made a face. 'I'd much rather stay here.'

'Why don't you?' Quentin had been doing what he wanted ever since he was sent down from Cambridge.

'My mother says I've got to go.'

'Ah, mothers.' He understood. His own, an erstwhile diva gone to ruin, was always cropping up in his novels and the lightweight pieces he did for newspapers and magazines on things like paper milk bottles and the threat of the zip fastener. She would have been living with him at the white cottage if Bob had not put his foot down.

Bob had a job and a wife somewhere, but he came every weekend and pottered in the garden, read the Sunday papers by the fire or in the sun, and fetched draught cider in a brown glazed jug from the White Hart, where he tried unsuccessfully to talk to the silent local drinkers. Quentin was more success-ful with the village people. He held long rustic conversations which went into his writings, quainted up, along with his mother.

They were Charlie's best friends here, gentle and unexacting. They laughed at her jokes and listened to her tales of St Gabriel's and praised her for small triumphs like painting a bookcase or making a cake.

'Be happy!' With the dog struggling in his arms, Quentin stood tiptoe in moccasins by the white gate and waved her away, his thinning honey curls boyish in the evening breeze.

Charlie packed a suitcase quickly. She did not have much to pack. A green chiffon and an ugly red taffeta, to prove she had more than one dinner dress. A pleated skirt and a cardigan. A maroon stockinette dress centuries too old for her which she would never wear, but it looked new in case she had to let someone unpack.

She took off the school bloomers and the woollen stockings and garters, and put on thick shiny silk stockings and a pink corset out of which she had pulled the stays, like drawing turkey tendons. She put on a locknit petticoat and stood by the mirror to unbraid her hair.

It was a grey afternoon which could lead to a weekend of rain (bridge, billiards, jigsaw puzzles, mah-jong). There was not much light in the room, but it was not worth fetching a lamp. She stood and brushed slowly at her long dark hair, stroking it down in front of her shoulder, tossing it back like a scarf, gathering it up and letting it fall again, soft and heavy on her bare shoulders.

In the dim mirror, her eyes looked large and her face mysterious. Dropping the brush, she hung her head and put her hands up into her hair. It fell in front of them in a curtain across her face, and she hung her head lower, bending out of a window for a man to grasp and kiss the heady, acrid fall of it. He kissed its waves in the moonlight. She dropped her hands and gathered the end of her hair and smothered it over her lips. Oh sweet black waves in the moonlight. He was covered and hidden by her hair, caressed by it, his head against her breast.

She jerked up her head and threw back her hair to stare entranced at her dark dreaming eyes. Staring, she pulled all

44

her hair over one shoulder, and her fingers moved in it automatically as they had for years, weaving, plaiting a dark red love knot – what was a love knot? A rose, a ribbon, a streak of blood – into her long black hair. She smiled, watching her mouth soften and lift. Her fingers still busy in her hair, she leaned forward again and looked down into her heavy breasts, and the pungent sweetness of her skin.

Outside the window, a branch of the greengage tree dipped, shaking its leaves at her like shocked old ladies. Anyone looking in would think she was mad.

One night, a tramp had come to the door, very dirty but not old, a Lancashire man, out of work, walnut brown with harsh red lips. She thought that she opened the door and he came in, under her long black hair.

She dreamed that, not asleep, for long after he had gone away with a shilling from her door, dreaming, her hands in her burning hair, hardly knowing if it were true.

In twenty years time, she would be as mad as a hatter. Village children would stand outside her front wall and stare and point and dare each other to knock and run.

She fixed the thick plait over the top of her head with many pins in an old-fashioned Austrian way that they could like or not as they pleased, climbed into an oatmeal jumper suit with a long belted jacket which they could also like or not, but the dotted scarf might do it, trod into strap shoes, and took her beret in her hand since it would not go over her coronet of hair.

She looked at herself again, sturdy in the waistless suit. That's better, Lambert. Good sensible girl. The healthy sort. I like that. No nonsense about her. These girls today – cars, films, wireless, dancing. All gone amusement mad, if you ask me. This is my daughter Charlotte. Charlie, we call her. Oh, how jolly.

How can I write this? How do I know these things about Charlie? I know. Or think I know, which is nearly the same thing. I've written enough fantasies in my life – those television documentaries in which we presented YOU with the FACTS in a one-sided load of pulpitry – to understand the indistinguishability of knowledge and belief once they are down on paper. I imagine and invent, of course – this isn't a police report – but already there are no edges between imagination and memory and truth.

I remember a Christmas party, centuries ago, when we were at our most inhibited. Some ass of a grown-up cousin who did monologues cried out that all the young ones must do a turn. Smug little girls in organdy recited, with gestures. Lay sleepy head on hands. Point at star. Hand to ear for fairy trumpets. Annabel danced, in those boots her mother made her wear. Reggie sang, of course. His voice broke late, and he was still drawing unreligious tears from parents in the school chapel. I ran away and hid in a cupboard, but Margaret told me later that Charlie, pushed stomach first on to the performing rug, had launched stolidly into Alfred Noyes's 'Highwayman', and droned through the whole thing from end to end. They couldn't stop her, and serve them right.

'You're so alone,' Mrs Meagan said, after Charlie's dog died last week, as I knew he would, although he had appeared not to notice she had gone. 'What about a little fluffy kitten or a jolly little pup, faithful doggy eyes? My dear Mr Kitteredge, man was not made to tread this earth alone.'

Bang, clatter, in an apron and a hat she sweeps me through and does not know, while I make tea or find something to do until she's gone, that I can't wait until her dust settles again and I can go back to what she calls writing in my book.

I am not alone. Writers pretend it's a lonely profession, but I have discovered, sitting at this window with the blackberry hedge across the road full of boys these afternoons, that writers cheat. They cheat on God and on life by shaping it the way they want, and find that more real. I cheat by bringing Charlie

46

back. Not the companionable, amused middle-aged woman of whom Mrs Meagan and I sigh ruefully, 'She always loved the smell of a day like this.' But the girl she was, clownish, unused, bumbling towards the edge of a ravine whose depths she had never even heard of.

In the fields at which I stare (yesterday I stared straight into the china eyes of a small coloured boy popping up from the garden with an apple ballooned from his mouth like bubble gum) the wind is beginning to gather more strength in the shedding trees. I know the truth of her at twenty-five, although I didn't at the time, being obsessed with her sister. And Charlie didn't show it. Who does show it? People who look passionate are often as frigid as mussels. Look at Bubbles.

She came to the funeral two weeks ago looking less hatchet-faced and rather charming, with that red-faced husband I never thought she did deserve. Barbara has improved since the days when we were married, and we are better friends than we were then. If you marry your first wife's sister, you can't keep up the disgust.

Reggie came with his daughter and two of his grandchildren. The girl is sober and purposeful, with stained laboratory fingers and a face like Joan of Arc. The boy at nineteen is already on the stage, but nothing like his grandfather. Some of the pictures of Reggie in tennis flannels, and in the white aviator's suit for *Flying High,* and in the endearing tweeds he wore when he went to Australia as Inigo Jollifant in *The Good Companions,* have been exiled to the gents' lavatory of the Camden Hill House. Reggie does not mind. He too has improved with age. Have we all? I don't think I have. I used to be so spry and involved. Now I barely know or care who is at war with who.

The boy does not sing. He acts, with his back to the audience. Not all the time, but I am forced to admit, and so is Reggie, who never really acted at all, that he is fifty times more arresting with his back to the audience than his grandfather ever was head on.

The funeral was quite nice, if you like that sort of thing. Young Red managed the whole thing with a finesse beyond his years. He fetched away Charlie, and then came back with two

47

cars for all of us, because he would not allow us to go to the church in my red Volkswagen or Reggie's Jaguar.

He was still calling Margaret Mary, and moving about this house as if he had been in and out for years, so that he should not seem as intrusive as death is. His family had been in the business for three generations. When he was only a lad, he used to fill in if a coffin-bearer didn't show up, the load dipping a little at his corner. Today, because you can't count on coffin-bearers and the lads are otherwise engaged, Red has a sort of gliding bier like a hospital trolley. When he had shepherded us through the rain and into the front pews of Kingsgrove church, he trundled Charlie up the aisle on rubber wheels and rubber soles, with the proud, solicitous face of a nanny perambulating the first male baby of the Dutch royal family.

After the service, he eased us out by the side door, so that we need not face the staring congregation. I knew the little church was full, but it was not until we were standing under the chestnut tree while Red held a black commissionaire's umbrella over Mr Hartigan for the dust-to-dust bit, and Reggie's granddaughter stepped forward to throw a handful of Oxfordshire loam, that I saw how many of the local people were there.

With egotism, and to keep my mind off the image of Charlie's face close under the coffin lid, I wondered how many of them would have come for me. Should I start now cultivating people like Henry Clay and the brewers who bought the Jaffrays' place and made the duck pond into a swimming pool, so as to ensure that they will take the morning off to see me under?

'Where's Julia?' Etty came up and kissed me, her face damp and warm under her cushion of blue-white hair, for she had been crying.

'She wouldn't come across the street for her mother, let alone the Atlantic,' Barbara said edgily, tired now, needing a drink.

Red's impresario arm coaxed us towards the cars. As we moved away into the wet wind, a few people shook hands and murmured, but most of the churchyard mourners shifted away before us in their blacks and macs and rubber boots, as if I had embarrassed them by losing my wife. It was only then that I saw, standing afar off, a slight figure hunched against the rain with his long hair plastered over his face like a surfacing swimmer. He had gone before I reached the gate.

But a few days later, after Margaret had gone, Terence Haig-Davenport came to see me again, and brought Doris, the Winged Pigeon.

'Can't you both come in?'

I had gone out to the road to be introduced to Doris. Tiny, with eyes blacked in like bull's-eyes. A load of false lashes. Sabrina hair. A white blanket over her knees.

'Want to?' he asked her.

She shrugged. 'I don't mind.'

'Is it worth getting out the chair?'

'Please yourself.'

'I could carry her,' I suggested, to get back into the conversation, but Terence laughed, although he is slighter than me, and will be a bony wisp at my age.

'She's vevwy particular who picks her up.'

He drove round to the back of the house, and lifted her out of his white mini car quite easily and carried her into the house. He set her on a chair and tucked the blanket round her knees with an assiduous face, as if she were his crippled child.

She is not much bigger than a child. She sat in the chair and drank a glass of marsala, demure as a little girl visiting a parent, while Terence and I renewed acquaintance in the room where we had first met.

The bed has gone. He glanced quickly at the place under the window where it had been. When he saw my untidy writing-table there, he jerked his hand as if to acknowledge Charlie's ghost, and then was able to sprawl relaxed in an armchair, one ankle high up on the other knee, white jeans straining at the crotch.

I offered him beer, but he looked doubtful, so I suggested whisky, although in my day, as they say (I try not to), he would have been much too young. He took it neat, from bravado I suspected, rather than habit, and swilled it thoughtfully round the glass while conversation lagged.

'How did you know the funeral was on Monday?' I asked him.

'I have my spies.'

'Was it your day off?'

He shook his glossy head. He probably worked or not as he pleased, and people waited for their laundry when he didn't please.

'Where's your daughter then? Very upset, she was,' he said to Doris. 'I told you.'

'Yes. You told me.' She had a trick of repeating gently what he said, which gave her an air of docility, if not of intelligence.

'My stepdaughter. She doesn't live here. She's in America.'

'We're going to America,' the Pigeon said, putting a strand of amber hair back behind her ear for the twentieth time. 'Ben's going to take me.'

'Tevwence.'

'Terence.' She appeared to be somewhat under his thumb. After they had relaxed a little, and Terence had watched me pour him another whisky, without demur or thanks, I risked asking her, 'Where you – I mean – have you never been able to walk?'

'It was an accident,' Terence said curtly.

'Like your mother?'

'Yup. Car got her.' He spoke of cars as if they were predators.

'That's tragic at your age.'

She looked at Terence, and he pushed his squashed mouth in and out and said. 'She doesn't like to talk about it. I see you never had that window fixed.' He changed the subject, grinning at the piece of cardboard I had tacked back over the broken glass because I could not bother with Mr Parks fumbling about the place in his carpenter's apron with glazier's points in his mouth like a dressmaker.

'I keep it like that in memory of you,' I said. 'Been doing any more visiting?'

'Not since that night. Frankly,' he leaned forward, turning his glass between his knees, and looked up at me with those wet candid eyes, 'I got a bit of a shock that night. Though I

50

didn't show it, of course,' he added, either for my benefit or the Pigeon's.

'You were very cool. How did you know I wouldn't turn you in? I still could.'

'Oh, I don't know. I'm a pretty good judge of people, you know. Insight. Most artistic people have it. I didn't think you'd cheat.' He spoke as if I were the miscreant, redeemed by honour. 'I quite like you, Mr er—'

'Kitteredge. James Kitteredge.'

'I like you, Mr James,' said the boy. 'Don't ask me why. Never had much time for old people really.'

'Perhaps,' I said, 'you are sorry for me.'

'Yeah. I expect that's it.'

'So you're like the ladies from the church visiting the old people in the almshouses.'

'Eh?' He was slightly deaf, from a bash on the head as an infant, which seemed unusual for a musician. Perhaps he only imagined that the Winged Pigeon was a lark. But when she sang for me on their next visit, she was surprisingly good.

Even more surprising, they have become quite frequent visitors, turning up at odd hours, sometimes in the laundry van, and once at midnight after a show, picking a window latch to prove Ben still had the touch. It was the Ben Japp side of him that did the breaking and entering, in secret power. Haig-Davenport had the girl, and could impose his personality through a clangorous electric guitar.

I got up and we all had cocoa and Irish whiskey, and the Pigeon sang for me, 'You've gone, it's over.' All her songs were about rejection or loneliness or lost love. Her voice was very true and sweet and much larger than herself, as if the strength from her legs had gone into her throat.

'She's really good,' I told Terence.

'Natch.' They had just cut a record. Terence knew someone who had connections with a disc jockey. It might get on the air.

'I used to be a BBC announcer,' I said.

'Get away.' He didn't believe me, so I didn't press the point.

As a matter of fact, it was that wretched weekend house party at the St Irwins that started my career with the BBC.

Not a bad career either, I'm proud to remember. A well-known voice for a while, if not a face. Part of the gentlemanly underpinning that helped to shore up class barriers for yet one more decade. Now, you can hardly get a job in wireless or television unless you speak with some kind of regional accent, native or acquired. In 1930, when I began my years of quiet popularity, bringing civilized news of civil war in China and the Wireless Military Band, conductor B. Walton O'Donnell, you could not hope for any job above tea-boy unless you spoke with that voice that comes from where the throat meets the jawline, fluid, literate, just hesitant enough to be slightly insulting in its implication that you are not really trying. Nowadays you only hear it from foreign interpreters at the United Nations.

'You have a very lovely speaking voice. I could arrange an audition, if you'd care.'

When the middle-aged man with the silky grey hair told me that, over the hot breakfast dishes on the sideboard at Garfield Hall, I thought he was making a pass at me. I blushed, being rather naïve for twenty-nine, and thought no more of it. But a few months later, I was off Mr Lambert's drawing board and into the newsroom at Broadcasting House.

I had gone up to Garfield on the afternoon train. Two or three other people got off on to the windy Cotswold platform, whence we were collected by a chauffeur with the Humber, and arrived in time for tea in the great hall. A huge fire, thank God, at each end of the stone-flagged raftered chamber. Five different kinds of fruit cake. Children in riding breeches whispering on the window seat. Teacups like soup bowls. A staircase where an ancestor fell dying after the Battle of Bosworth Field. And Barbara.

Luminous, exhilarated with her own looks, she gave off radiance like a shout. Because she was talking to a man with demonic eyebrows whom she had already marked down, like a cow pony, for cutting out of the herd, she jumped up and kissed me.

'Darling James! This is James, everyone. He is absolutely my best friend in the whole world.'

52

A few people looked to see this phenomenon. They saw a lean, diffident young man with brown hair and a magnificent pair of Oxford bags bought especially for the occasion, a blazer with the crest of a fairly decent college (Mother was already hinting that its exorbitancies had hastened my father's ruin), and an amiable throwaway manner that hid an inner struggle between wanting to be liked and wanting to be above caring.

'Darling James!' She kissed me with cherry ice-maiden lips. My heart leaped and sank at the same time. Why had I come? I had known all along it was going to be a hopeless weekend.

Charlie told me years later that she had driven up to Garfield at fifteen miles an hour, pretending to enjoy the scenery, and then driven round the back roads of the village before she could summon the nerve to turn into the long straight drive, the great house watching the approach of the Morris like Mussolini behind his desk.

Because of this, she arrived at the wrong time, too late for tea and too early for cocktails. She left her car near the front door, whence it was removed later by an unseen agent, to appear again on Sunday afternoon along with two shiny saloons and a tourer and a spanking brown horse and trap in which the doctor had driven over for lunch.

Everyone but the dogs was upstairs dressing for dinner. Charlie was taken up to a room overlooking a well behind the kitchen where a drainpipe let out intermittent Niagaras of steaming suds under her window.

She wanted to find her parents. While a maid unpacked for her with a drugged face that would not have been excited by the Hope diamond, much less Charlie's single string of coming-out pearls, she sat in a convex chair and rehearsed sentences in which to ask the maid – who might be deaf as well as drugged – to take her to her parents' room.

'Could you please show me where Mr and Mrs Lambert are?' she asked, as if she had just thought of it, as the maid was leaving.

'I'm sorry.' Decontaminating, she dusted her hands in the doorway. 'They are in the other wing.' As if this were an isolation hospital.

It was not really that kind of house. Not formal. But informality can be just as unnerving if you are not on the inside track of it. And there were hidden rules here. Things you were expected to do, like it or not, such as animal slaughter and paper games. Things you had better not do, such as refusing St Irwin's claret or reading a book in the drawing-room. Casualness here was on its own terms, rich, unthreatened. There were animals and servants and guns all over the house, and two prankster sons who drove recklessly round London on treasure hunts, used Oxford as an annexe of home and let a fox loose among the guests at the hunt ball.

Venturing from her room to see if she could find her mother or father, Charlie met one of the boys hurtling round a corner with a great dog baying at his heels.

'Hullo ducks,' he said in a friendly way, and hurtled on down a short back stair, crash bang into a sort of housekeeping person with an armful of towels, whom he squeezed round the waist, while she made a face that said, 'Get along with your nonsense, Mr Roddy.'

Gilded youth. When he and the dog had gone, Charlie called down gently to the housekeeper.

'In the tower room,' she answered, as if Charlie knew the house like the frequent visitor she should have been, instead of the stranger she was, invited by one mother to another, 'You must bring *both* your daughters!'

'Oh lovely, Alice, I will.' The Lamberts were great ones for herding everywhere. Huge Christmas parties, with great-aunts preserved from the grave for this, like Karlsbad plums. The whole front row of the dress circle. Belgian coast holidays with a swarm of cousins and friends and nurses.

So Charlie had been conscripted for the weekend, and Reggie and his wife would be here tomorrow night, driving down after the theatre. Quite a catch to get him all this way.

Possibly that was why Mrs St Irwin cultivated the Lamberts, who were, after all, though not *nouveau riche,* nothing much *as* family.

There was no tower room, nor even a tower, as Charlie found afterwards when she looked at the house from the outside. The only person she met was a beautiful girl with chestnut hair in a satin petticoat and bare feet, leaning in an open doorway talking to a man who was lying on the bed smoking, with his shoes on. The girl stopped talking while Charlie passed, which was as insulting as if she had stared.

A bell sounded somewhere in the great stone house. Fire? Escaped convicts? The bull got loose? Back in her room, Charlie tidied her hair with more pins and stepped into the green chiffon dress which hung in pointed pleats to the knee in front, almost to the ground at the back. A bow dropped somewhere, pointlessly. The neckline drooped beyond the V of browned skin. The sleeves did not quite reach the place where her shirt had been rolled up for tennis.

Her shoes were green, canoes on her large feet. She had a green bag too, and the pearls, and the apricot Tangee lipstick. She did not look in the glass again, for fear of being discouraged, but when she finally plunged down the haunted staircase into the hall where elegant people stood or perched like Act I, Scene II in one of Reggie's plays, her mother enfolded her with claret velvet batwing sleeves and cried, 'But dear old chump, you look very nice!' in some surprise.

'This is our Charlotte. Charlie, we call her.'

Colonel St Irwin – all the St Irwin chiefs were called colonel or major, although they never spent long enough with the Army to spoil their farming – was not there yet. Out with the heifers, or shoeing a horse, or beating the bounds; Charlie forgot to listen to what his wife was saying. Mrs St Irwin was a small hunk of gristle with a veined fox-hunting nose, quick of eye and tongue, auburn cropped, tacked up for dinner in lace and emeralds. She introduced Charlie to the other guests, but lost interest before she was all the way round. There were one or two people whom Charlie never did meet all weekend.

She met the petticoat girl, who was Binkie something. Bonzo Law, terrifyingly familiar from the *Tatler,* friend of the

Prince of Wales. A grey-haired concave man in a blue dinner jacket who was in the BBC. Somebody's cousin, about thirty-five, who panicked her by putting a little pressure on her hand and saying, 'So you're Charlotte.'

Invited for her? Squinting very slightly, not from short sight, but for something to do with her face, Charlie saw a well-fed man with plastered hair and flat, assessing eyes. What did he see? A tall, bright-skinned girl in a green dress all wrong for her, dark hair done all wrong, but soft and clean, clean, everything clean as a milkmaid, a willing mouth hovering on a smile if wanted.

That was what I saw from my place on the cushioned seat that ran round the great hearth. Taking her hand away from the cousin, who had continued to study her, amused, without comment, Charlie greeted me with relief.

'Dear James.' She breathed warmly into my neck. 'There's a spot on your shirt. I'd die if you weren't here.' She stayed by me, but I was watching the stairs for her sister, and no use to her.

Barbara came, in a hard red dress and a mouth like blood, down the wide stairs with her father as if he were giving her away. I had a flash image of myself sweaty-palmed before an altar, half turned to see her shimmering towards me down the aisle, before she was absorbed, the group waiting only for her, and handed a sidecar and a slap on her satin bottom from the other St Irwin son, a retarded buffoon of twenty-five.

Mr Lambert came to Charlie and patted her in a way that was more reassuring than her mother's flamboyant embrace. Mrs Lambert was a caricature of that lovely smiling girl in the Picture of the Year who had sat so demurely with her unread book, challenging you over the shoulder of the billowing yellow dress. She had been beautiful then, darkly glowing, her lips alive with innocent promise. Now all the fine features in the painting were disenchanted by exaggeration: the nose grown bony, the brilliant eyes deeper sunk, the smoky black hair harshened with streaks of white, the mouth stitched with the lines of constant animation.

Ugly, analysed feature by feature, but the whole effect attracted. She was stimulating, flat out to charm, roaring into any conversation with a knowing laugh or a witty insult. So amusing, people said of her. So much fun. She was of the generation of women who were not allowed to have enough to do, so they had to make a career of being themselves.

When her husband began to make money, he bought the Yellow Dress picture from his father-in-law, the Academician who had painted it. This man had never given away anything valuable in his life, and did not intend to start with his son-in-law, a man of trade, redeemed only by success. Dudley Lambert hung it in the drawing-room to honour his wife, but she had it moved away to his study.

'Can't stand the contrast,' she said. She overcame chagrin by freely admitting it. Catching herself in a mirror, she would shriek, 'What's that?' She called herself a hag, an old hen, the prehistoric woman, to forestall anyone who thought it. Her anecdotes were ostensibly against herself, which brought her out of them with victory banners waving.

Charlie's father was a hard-working man with heavy tortoise-shell spectacles to strengthen a harmless pink face under a freckled dome that wore its dun-grey hair like a skull cap on the back of the head. He was quieter than his wife, less admired, content to let her carry the colours of success while he did the real work. Outside his special artisan's gift, I always thought he was a bit dim and humourless. He liked Charlie more than his other children, who had gone beyond him. 'I want the best for you,' he would tell her, without suggesting how she might get it, or even what it was. All his imagination and interest was absorbed by the work he loved, those outer London flats of which he was designer and landlord. All his romance and poetry went into their design. Even my doors were encouraged to be rococo.

Each small block was a unit of about a dozen flats, the outsides stucco and plaster, set with patterns of brick or tile, turrets and suggestions of battlements appearing here and there, a Spanish curly roof, a little scrolled ironwork, a vaguely Flemish gable, a dab at shutters, Tyrolean carved. The insides were good for about thirty years of semi-gracious living before the rot set in.

The groups of flats had names like Chambord House and

Chenonceaux Keep, which the people who lived in them could not pronounce. Other blocks were named after poets or painters. Keats Mansions. Tennyson House. Rubens Court. When I was at Lambert's we were working on Botticelli Close and Alma Tadema Gardens at the end of the new Underground extension (above ground) at Hendon.

Some of the flats were bombed in the war. Some fell apart by themselves. Some still stand, uncomfortably occupied, crumbling, seedy, their lifts awash with urine.

When Chambord House was bombed, I drove Mr Lambert out in his ARP siren suit to view the ruins, like Churchill or the Queen Mother, and he wept with the homeless.

Before dinner, we had cocktails: white ladies, bronx, side-cars, mixed in dashing figure-of-eight shakes by young Mr Roddy. It seemed to be the only thing he had learned at Oxford. Colonel St Irwin came from the midden in a braided red smoking jacket, square and boisterous, drinking for two, arguing with anyone who had a good word for the Government. Ramsay's a traitor. Put the buggers to digging a Channel tunnel, and so on and so on.

One of the guests was a Socialist. He would not be asked again – Nor would I, it was clear at dinner, if I did not quickly stop discussing trade unionism with him.

Bubbles called across the table. 'Don't be such a bore, James,' and threw a piece of bread at me without even turning her face. She had Bonzo Law on one side and young Mr Roddy on the other, both making her laugh. I could have shot either. I was a bore, was even a bore without opening my mouth, merely by being a salaried worker in contact with people like plasterers and bricklayers, the greatest bores of all, with their marches and their demands and their queues outside the Labour Exchange.

'Look at me. Look at these hands.' The Colonel crashed two vast red fists among the plates and silver, and claret went over the dress of a lady who was so intimidated already by being placed next to him that she dabbed at it secretively with her napkin and made no fuss.

'Soak the idle rich, says Snowden. If any one of those buggers who shuffle down the Strand with mouth organs had ever worked one hour in his life as hard as I do to help feed my countrymen—' and so on and so on. His eyes were bulging bloodshot marbles. His face was purple. Would he have a stroke?

When he got on to the male servant tax, it seemed inevitable. 'And now they tell me – they have the bloody nerve to tell me I've got to pay fifteen bob for every man I – I personally save from the dole—' and so on and so on. The butler bent over him with the decanter, his long moose face masking the seething plans for his own night of the long knives.

Dinner went on for hours. Charlie sat somewhere in the middle of the table, rubbing at gooseflesh on her arms, eating more than she talked, trying to make an intelligent face to things that were said to her, or when nothing was said to her lapsing into a sort of moon-faced narcosis. When Mrs St Irwin took the ladies away, she could not find one of her shoes. I saw her limp out with one bare foot, hoping nobody would notice, but the elder St Irwin boy brought it up with a yell and threw it across the table to his brother who caught it and ran for a touchdown under the sideboard. The butler stepped inscrutably aside.

The Colonel told terrible stories over the port, about the matings of swine, and calves being pulled out of cows by tractors. My employer talked to me about his new dream of gardens and balconies and buildings staggered to catch the sun, when the Great West Road went through. He was always nice to me, not only because he had been my father's friend. When Bubbles finally allowed me to be engaged to her, he was genuinely pleased.

Soon after we joined the ladies, everyone went to bed, because everyone was getting up at crack to go cubbing.

'I don't want to go, do you?' Charlie got me in a corner.

'May as well.' Bubbles was going to ride.

Next morning, I sat on a gate dangling my muddy boots for what seemed an eternity, while Bubbles and the rest cantered squelching up and down through the cobwebby mist, and nothing much happened, thank God. Nobody seemed to mind not killing anything, even the hounds, who leaped in and out of the thickset wood and quartered the fields, noses down, tails unfurled, enjoying the exercise of their smooth muscular bodies.

A man in knickers with a placard about blood sports went home quite soon on his bicycle. I saw the same man, or his son, at a meet of the South Oxfordshire last week. They'll never stop foxhunting here, because the English don't feel cruel about it, and therefore not guilty. Bubbles rode with the eyebrows man all morning, and went off with him after breakfast to see a ruined monastery. I had the weird conversation over the chicken livers and scrambled eggs about my beautiful speaking voice.

'We're looking for younger people with the right sort of — aura,' said the BBC man, no white disarrayed by his session in the mud with Newmarket boots and a shooting stick. 'You possibly have no idea of the kind of influence we wield in matters of taste, culture, political thought, and so on.'

'I know everyone listens to the wireless,' I said, cutting him a delicate lamina of ham.

'It's got to stay that way, do you see? Newspapers will eventually be obsolete, but we've got to be sure of capturing the younger generation for life — now, before this television thing takes hold of them.'

'But surely, sir,' I remember saying crassly, 'no one's ever going to take that seriously.' The Baird Process, it was called in those experimental days, with the perennial joke already outworn about hooking it to the telephone and seeing your friends in the bath.

We poured coffee. At Garfield Hall, no servant was allowed at breakfast, which was a mute and monkish meal. The BBC man was showing bad form by murmuring to me at the sideboard.

'Don't fool yourself.' He added yellow Jersey milk to my cup. 'It's a very real threat to us old wireless pioneers. That's why we need the new young voices. I was on to you as soon as I heard you speak. There's a great clarity of charm there. Great charm.' His eyes dwelled on me. His mouth was like a rose. That was when I blushed, and forgot the brief vision of myself and my voice wielding influence.

Charlie did not appear, either for cubbing or breakfast. She went to sleep again after the drugged maid brought in her tea, and when she got up, she found that everyone had gone long ago. She met a manservant polishing brass who did not seem to know anything about breakfast, nor even what such a meal was. She met a jolly country maid who offered to try to get her some tea and eggs, but she heard herself say that she never ate breakfast.

She got out by a side door, cut through a shrubbery and a soaking pasture and walked a mile into the village, where she bought potato chips and a twopenny packet of biscuits and cheese, which she ate sitting in a cattle shed on the side of a hill until it was safe to go back.

Her mother, who did as she pleased in this house or any other, did not get up until noon. Her father had gone up to Birmingham to see a plumbing factory, and so nobody noticed that Charlie was missing until she turned up flushed with ends of hair in damp wisps while everyone was drinking sherry, and said she had been for a long walk.

'Why?'

'I like to walk.'

'You should have been out with us,' her hostess said. 'Get all the walking you need, and jolly good sport into the bargain.'

'I don't like it when they kill the cubs.'

'We didn't,' said Mrs St Irwin, as if they had not meant to, and someone asked Charlie, 'I say, are you one of those cranks or something – nut cutlets and all that?'

'Yes,' Charlie said, partly from embarrassment, partly bravado, and so had to pass up the roast beef at lunch and eat vegetables. At dinner, she risked going back to meat, and nobody noticed.

She was in better shape by then. Two foursomes had gone out on the rough nine-hole golf course that ran round the deer park (two stroke penalty for picking up out of a cloven hoof-print), and Charlie had shone. She had been playing golf since she started caddying for her father at the age of twelve, and could hit the ball as far as many men, and farther than some, with her muscular brown arms. She partnered the cousin, whose name was Alaric, wearing her divided tweed skirt, a shirt and tie, and her beret. She added the white school jersey for warmth, let down her pigtail and looked about eighteen, and more attractive than in the droopy green dress and prim Austrian sausage of hair.

Cousin Alaric was pleased with her. They came hand in hand to the tea-table, which Alaric thought would make him look boyish, although the years and the booze were bagging under his basilisk eyes. He fed her hugely, and animated her with quite a little attention on the window seat, and when Colonel St Irwin turned up from rallying the combine harvesters (one never saw much of him except at meals), he said, 'Who's this?' although he knew quite well.

'Don't be silly, Harry,' Mrs Lambert called through a waggling cigarette from the bridge-table. 'That's my daughter Charlie.' Everything went on in the great hall, either round one fireplace or another, or in the draughty middle, if you were unlucky. There was a perfectly good drawing-room, with chintz and a thick pale carpet, but that was only used when the judge stayed during Assizes. The Colonel was Lord Lieutenant of the county, as his father and grandfather were and his elder son would be, God help us.

'Charlie, eh? Fine looking gal.' He made his bulldog face at her, opening eyes and mouth wide, and then clamping down, with brow in folds and jaw pugnacious.

'She's a damn good golfer too,' cousin Alaric said.

'Is she, b'jove?'

It was her hour of glory. She sat beaming. Colonel St Irwin took her off to see a room full of guns and dead horned animals, which was quite boring, but a signal honour. In a vaulted passageway, he took her hand and scratched his calloused fingertips in her palm. She did not know what it meant, except that in some way it was a signal honour too.

When the dressing bell sounded at seven o'clock from the cupola above the stables, Charlie went upstairs quite happily. The drugged woman was off duty, or had died of her addiction, and it was the jolly young maid who came rustling in her gingham print down the angled staircase that led to Charlie's oubliette to say that her bath was running.

In her woollen dressing-gown, swinging a sponge bag, Charlie followed her along passages up and down steps to the bathroom, which was larger than her bedroom, with high flaking ceiling, clawed vat of a bath and vast sash window open to the elements.

A wind had risen during the afternoon. Dark loaded clouds had rolled in over the park, the first drops falling as Charlie ran for tea, with Alaric a step behind her, trying not to pant. The house was now under a full storm, and as she sat in the bath, the wind drove in the rain, chill against her steaming back. Being cold was no novelty. In her cottage she was already sleeping in a jersey and socks. Last night at Garfield Hall she had put the bedside rug on top of the covers. But this evening she was a success, desirable, a courtesan in the hot water, and the rain destroyed her mood.

The window was open at the top. She got out of the bath and tugged at the ropes on each side, but the heavy window did not move. Fresh air and bathrooms went together. It probably had not been shut since the plumbing was put into the ancient stone pile. By standing on the box of the wooden lavatory, Charlie could step on to the basin and from there reach up with the heels of her hands and with a giant effort unstick the window and push it shut.

She fell off the basin, sprawling wet and naked on the linoleum, and climbed happily back into the high bath. Adding hot water, caressing her soapy skin, she lay with her eyes shut, thoughts about Alaric passing idly back and forth like a punkah. In the bath, he was younger, cleaner cut, without the nicotined nails and the lurking impression of having a wife somewhere.

When Charlie let out the water with a sound like thunder and went dizzily back to her room, she found the maid laying out the green chiffon and the jolly-boat shoes as kindly as if it were a Paris ensemble.

She smiled at Charlie. 'Would you like me to put up your hair for you, miss? I could arrange it lovely. I'm good with hair.'

Charlie sat at the dressing-table (Here sate she, while her maidens tired and curled) while the maid brushed her long damp hair, murmuring at its thickness, and then swept it up and pinned it in a clever way that Charlie would never achieve again, nor even attempt.

'You look ten years older,' the maid said proudly, when it was almost done.

'Do I want to?'

'Oh yes. It doesn't do to let yourself be taken advantage of because you don't look your age.'

What did she mean by that? Had she been watching Charlie and thinking that she ought to be in the nursery with the children instead of in the dining-room with the grown-ups?

'How old do you think I am?'

'About twenty-five, I suppose, same as me.'

'I wish I was you,' Charlie said unguardedly to the rosy intent face at work in the mirror. If she were behind the face, with just a job to do, she could turn down beds and fill hot water bottles and then go away and take her shoes off in the kitchen and laugh and say terrible coarse things about the guests.

The face split in a grin, showing bad teeth. 'Don't have me on, miss. Forty pounds a year and all found? *When* you can find it.'

'Don't you like it here?'

'It's all right.' The girl looked surprised, as if she had not thought about that. 'I've had worse places.' She bent to pick up a hairpin. 'And some better ones, I suppose. Mrs Wilson, you've got to watch out. She's a tartar.'

'The housekeeper? Oh, I saw *her*.' Charlie entered eagerly into backstairs gossip, as she used to when she lived at home, playing cards in the kitchen, gabbing with the maids while her mother looked shrilly for her upstairs. 'I thought she looked a bit of a devil.'

But the grin had faded, the maid withdrew, shutting Charlie out of her world again. 'It takes all kinds, I suppose.' She fixed in the last pin and dispatched the piled mound of hair with a pat. 'There. That looks more like it.' The rest was Charlie's affair.

When she came downstairs, balancing her newly-shaped head as if it might fall off, her sister, narrow hips shimmering in gold lamé, told her, 'I know a marvellous new man in Hay Hill who'd cut it all off and give you a perm for five guineas.'

'Peroxide thrown in?' Charlie accepted a rosy-coloured

drink from Roddy's shaker. The sisters were always quite rude to each other. Not as a joke. They meant it.

'When Bubbles was only a few weeks old,' their mother told Bonzo Law, 'Charlie tried to stuff her down the lav.'

'Oh, shut up.' He laughed in his high-bridged nose, enchanted.

'And pulled the chain. I mean it. We had to give her artificial respiration.' She laughed back into his sophisticated triangular eyes, compelling him to find her fascinating, although she was wasting her time, since Bonzo Law was that kind of British neuter, guest at everybody's party, usher at everybody else's wedding, suave organizer of everybody's funeral.

Dinner was rather dull. Conversation always centred round whatever was on the Colonel's mind. He announced that ruin lay close ahead, and would hear no good of England. He would take his cattle and possibly his family and go to South America.

Charlie's cushion of hair was slipping. When she went up afterwards to look at it, she heard a hullabaloo at the bottom of the little back stairway.

'How dared you defy my orders?'

'I didn't, Mrs Wilson.'

'You did indeed. That bathroom is in your charge.'

'I never shut the window.'

'Do you take me for simple? This will mean your notice.'

'It's not fair.'

'I'll say what's fair and what's not fair.'

Charlie stepped round the corner and said loudly, 'I shut the window.' She smiled down at the red-faced maid, a real ally at last, in league the two of them. The girl would see that all guests were not worthless just because they were guests.

But the maid and the housekeeper only looked up at her briefly and then went on arguing as if she were not there. What she had done or not done had nothing to do with their quarrel. The housekeeper would go off miffed to her room and brew tea and read her old love letters from a man in puttees who was killed in the Great War. The maid would go down and play whist, slapping down the cards as if they were her grudge.

Later, she would meet someone behind the stables, or in a hayloft if it was still raining, with the uncomplicated smells and the small stampings and blowings of the horses below.

Dancing. Paper games. Charades. Even Sardines. Charlie's hair broke loose again. Her golfing fame was quite obliterated. Alaric took no notice of her. Bubbles told her she had lipstick on her teeth. Whisky and soda. Cups of tea. Dumb Crambo. Hide and Seek. No one was allowed to go to bed until Reggie and his wife arrived.

He came at last, a slim tired god with his make-up still on, and Charlie found him stagily at his ease by the fireplace when she came into the great hall, red and breathless, wanton-eyed, a swatch of hair down one shoulder like Marie Antoinette.

'Good God, Charles old dear, you look like the collapse of civilization.' Reggie stretched out a hand to call her to him.

'We've been playing Sardines.' She stayed where she was, one hand to her burning neck to push back her hair, wanting him at the same time to guess and not to guess that the loose wet lips of cousin Alaric had covered her mouth, his tongue thrusting, his knee between her legs as she stood pressed up against the early morning tea-trays on the counter of the butler's pantry.

How can I write this? I can't, not very well. It has been a time of plodding and stupidity, my hand driven like a prisoner to the bottom of each long page, tearing it off and crumpling it on to the floor without even reading it. Mrs Meagan sweeps the pages up and lays the fire with them.

Mrs Meagan has a friend who writes poetry. She sits in the branches of a tree and lets it all come to her, and when she climbs down, she commits it to paper and sends it off to a firm who makes Christmas cards.

'Do they buy it?'

'My friend is not in any way, shape, or form commercial.'

'You mean they use it free?'

'I've not said that, Mr Kitteredge. I've only told you her methods of work. I thought it might be of some help to you.'

'I don't need help,' I growled, cramped and chilled, with lead in the fold of my stomach from bending over the low table half the morning. I put books under the legs, but Mrs Meagan put them back in the shelves yesterday because the new couple at the school were coming to dinner, and I got so tied up with Charlie in the butler's pantry that I did not stop to put them back again.

How can I write about it? How can a man know how a woman feels? Well, you can tell from the way they behave, can't you? Especially when they are young, and not bold at it.

And don't forget, I was there. I was in the hall chatting to Reggie, because it was Bubbles who suggested Sardines and she was in a cupboard with someone, I was past caring who. I saw Charlie as Reggie saw her, half flaunting, half furtive, the cousin's whisky breath in her open mouth, flushed, sluttish, a village girl knocked willingly back into the bushes.

And when she and I were discussing that ludicrous weekend from a distance of years, laughing ruefully at our hurt young selves, she confided to me that she lay awake for most of what was left of the night, magnifying that one sottish kiss into a grand affair, a seismic passion that would transform her life.

What would tomorrow bring? She lay in her inconsiderable room, and watched the angle of the roof and the drainpipe come into detail against the lightening sky, seeing him better than he was, seeing them go off together, climb a hill, lie in the grass, find a hay barn. What would she do about her car if he wanted to drive her back to London? What would she do about her job, her house? Her idiot mind raced hectically ahead. If he did have a wife somewhere, would he leave her now for Charlie?

Next morning, he did not look better, but rather worse. He did not speak to her, and when she was sitting on a damp wooden bench at the side of the house, pretending to admire the day, she heard him in the library behind her explaining as a sort of scientific curiosity, 'I've never kissed a gym mistress before.'

'What did it taste like?' Bonzo Law asked, high in his rooster nose.

'The inside of a drill sergeant's shoe.'

It was a variation of the current joke: 'inside of a chauffeur's glove', 'bottom of a parrot's cage', but it made it no less unbearable.

She got away somehow after lunch, crushed, deadened, making her goodbyes politely, smiling dutifully at her brother's joking: 'My hat, Char, you look worse than last night. It *must* have been a party.'

He was always in fine fettle on his Sunday off, ready to charm everyone to pieces, wooing the children, mauling the dogs, dazzling the servants, telling stories well, being sweet but just a little whimsically patient with his gentle wife. She gave him no annoyances to be patient about, but the mere fact of her being a wife, a woman, was the feed for the punch lines of his appeal.

'Don't tease her, darling.' She put her arm around Charlie. They had been friends ever since Reggie had first brought her home as Marjorie, and Mrs Lambert had declared her name was Midge. 'She's tired. She works harder than anyone in this family.'

'There she goes . .' That was the clue for Reggie to be off. Misunderstood, prophet without honour, women lined up six deep outside the stage door and wife at home telling the baby, 'Daddy's gone play-acting.'

'What's the matter?' Midge, who was little and frail, looked up at Charlie with concerned blue eyes.

Charlie looked away and pulled herself free as she felt the salt come into her mouth. 'I've got to go,' she mumbled ungraciously.

There were no servants about for people like Charlie departing, though a battery of them for people like Bonzo Law and

Mrs Lambert, like the staff of a French hotel where tips are supposed to be on the bill. I carried her suitcase out to the car, struggled with the door for her, and nearly got my wrist broken winding the beastly thing up.

I was going to lean in and kiss her, but she had the talc window up. Before I could even yell goodbye over the clatter of the jerking little car, she had scrunched into gear and jumped forward with a small explosion from the exhaust that made the doctor's brown horse snort and step sideways. The man who was holding it swore at Charlie as she trundled away down the drive on her narrow wheels. It was cold. I turned up my coat collar and went back into the house.

Because she did not like driving on main roads where other motorists whizzed past her crawling Morris at forty miles an hour, she took a back road she knew north of Oxford, which would take her round the town. It was somewhere between two little farming villages that she saw the leaves in a corner of the wood and remembered Miss Perrott and her autumn project. The sun was briefly out between the rolling clouds, and a fresh wind was tossing the bright branches like flags above the ditch at the side of the road.

Charlie drove on in her stupor of misery. (Life in ruins. Never marry. Through with men. Live and die a gym mistress.) Then the leaves registered in an image of Miss Perrott clapping her hands and crying, 'You *are* a jewel!' her whole face in motion. She stopped, fought the worn knob of the gear lever into reverse, and backed a few yards on to the grass.

She got out. The air was lovely. The wind and sun revived her deadened face. She climbed through the ditch and over a low hedge – to hell with her stockings now, no one would ever invite her anywhere again – and reached up among the orange and yellow leaves. In the road, she heard Mick the Miller's engine cough, give a couple more half-hearted turns, and backfire into silence.

She broke off an armful of branches and brought them back to the car. She tried the door on the passenger's side without much hope, but because the car was tilted at a slight angle towards the ditch, it opened for the first time for days.

She put the branches on the seat and banged the door hard.

It had opened with her once in Wallingford, and swept away a bicycle standing at the kerb and a basket of rotten cabbages. As she banged the door, she reached out with her other hand to push in a nodding leaf, and the door shut on the nail of her right thumb.

She yelled, and wrenched at the handle again. The door would not open. The handle would not even turn. She was trapped in the wet grass by the side of the road, the end of her thumb held tightly by the metal edge of the door.

In the first shock of surprise, there was no feeling. It was only when she looked at her hand and realized what had happened to it that the pain stabbed into her, up through her shoulder and right into the pit of her stomach, doubling her up with a cramping gasp that left her retching, eyes streaming, wiping her mouth on the sleeve of the trapped arm.

The car was tilted slightly towards her. Although she was standing a little below it on the sloping grass verge, her thumb was caught low in the door, where she had leaned down to push back the leaves. She was bent over in awkward supplication, tugging futilely at the unyielding handle, sobbing and crying to the car, 'Please! Please! Oh God, oh God . . .'

She dropped on to her knees, her left hand still hanging on to the handle, and leaned her forehead on the dusty metal, her thumb and hand and arm a throbbing agony.

Please. She hung there and beseeched the car with despairing sobs that brought no tears. Mick the Miller had never let her down before. The car had been her friend, partner in a secret life that no one shared except the dog, braced on the front seat, staring ferociously ahead.

Now the Miller was an enemy, implacable, teetering evilly over its kneeling victim on the side of the road. She dragged again at the clenched doorhandle and felt the car shift weight a little. It would fall on her and crush her into the ditch, her thumb still trapped.

She let go of the handle and beat against the chipped panel of the door with the flat of her hand. Bang! Bang! Bang! Someone would hear.

'Help me!' she called. 'Help!' and went on shouting weakly with her head against the car. She had no idea whether there were any houses near, or anyone working in the fields. She had been driving along the narrow chalk road without looking to right or left. The coloured leaves had only come into her vision at the corner of her eye. Damn them. Damn Miss Perrott. She flushed into scalding anger at the thought that it was all her fault. Her fault. Look what you've done to me. Now look what you've done. I hope you're satisfied.

'Help! Help!' She banged on the thin metal of the door again, then let her hand drop to the dried mud on the running board. Her hair hung down over her face. She leaned against the car to try to ease the weight off her thumb, paralysed now into a leaden agony.

The sun had gone. Her coat was in the car. It was quite cold. There was no birdsong. No voices. No clink of spade against a stone. No foot on gravel. No clatter of a bucket, creak of gate. Nothing. The rustle of the wind in the trees of the little copse. Somewhere very far off, a train whistle.

A dog barked, and she shouted again, quite weakly. It went on barking in a mindless rhythm, as if it were tied up in a farmer's yard.

Before dark, the farmer would come down the road with his cows or his manure cart. The big slopping feet of the horse would stop above her. 'Hullo there.' The man would drop down from the shaft and come to her.

A boy would come down the road on a bicycle. A woman would come by with a milk can. Somebody would come at last in a car, a car, a car. There had been no cars, no bicycles, no carts going either way on this narrow back road since she passed the last cottage. She had been here – how long? – half an hour, an hour? No cars had come because nobody travelled this road but her. Nobody. She was alone for ever with the wind and the silence and the enormity of the empty country-side.

With an effort, she raised her hanging head and looked through her hair at the hand. It was swollen, the curled fingers a yellowish colour, like horseflesh, the upper side and the wrist a bluish purple. It stuck out of her brown jersey sleeve like a piece of dead meat. It did not belong to her at all. The pain of it was separate, like a stench or an excruciating noise

71

made by somebody else. After a while, the end joint of her thumb would fester off on to the seat among the leaves, and she would drop on to the grass, free.

But it was not jammed sharply enough for that. Before it could fall off, the bone must be cut through. It felt as if it were broken, but the edge of the door and the frame were holding flesh. They were not meeting through bone. If she had a penknife in her pocket, she would cut off the end of her thumb and either bleed to death, or make a tourniquet of her belt and stagger down the road for help.

If she had a penknife, or even a pocket, if she were a true Girl Guide leader, sports coach, gym teacher... For the first time since the door slammed, she thought of cousin Alaric. She sat once more on the bench outside the mullioned library window and heard his tacky voice as she would hear it endlessly, unchanged, jeering through the empty chambers of her brain, every time she was compelled to summon it. She would go back and back to it like a drug, to the voice, to herself listening on the wooden bench. Each time, it would drop into her heart like a stone, endlessly down into fathomless cold.

Although the wind was still busy in the trees, the road and the fields were so quiet that she heard the sound of the car a long way off. It came to her and went, as the wind rose and fell, now a small steady thrum, now a brief faraway roar. It might not even be on this road.

She began to shout again, although it was still too far off. She tried to stand up and wave above the roof of the car with her free hand, but she could not get up from her knees. She banged at the side of the car and waved her arm as high as she could. If there were a turn in the road – she could not remember and could not see – and it was going fast, it might pass without noticing her crouching there behind the tilted car. Another old crock pegged out, they would think, with brief pity for its owner slogging off for help along this deserted white road.

The car was on this road. It was coming up behind her. It was coming nearer. She turned her head over her poor tortured right arm, straining to see, but the road was too far above her. She felt the car's wheels on the earth. She smelled it. She heard the engine very loud, felt the ground shaking, and the rush of air, saw the wheels turn past, scattering stones into her face.

There was a squeal, and the car stopped out of sight. The door banged. Feet took quick steps on the road, and a man was kneeling beside her. His thick white jersey smelled of soaped wool and something else, warm and animal. His skin was brown. His voice was deep and a little rough. Her eyes were blurred with tears in among her hair, and she could not see him properly.

'What's happened?'

'My thumb. I can't open the door.'

He pushed her fingers from the door handle, and tried it with a grunt, his trouser leg pressed against her head. He strained at it again, and swore.

'Wait a sec.'

He disappeared. She heard steps to his car, click of a door, clink of tools. He got into her car from the other side, and she felt his weight on her arm as he leaned across among the leaves. As he worked on the handle from the inside, the pain came back with such terrifying intensity that she would not be able to bear it now when the door opened and the pain changed its shape. The door creaked. She screamed, 'No! No, don't!' The door came towards her, bringing her thumb, and as she fell backwards before it, he caught her wrist and held up her poor ruined hand, staring at her with eyes that were a bright coppery brown, not pitying but watchful, still intent on what he had done for her.

When she got her balance, he let go of her hand, and she sat in the grass and nursed it, moaning over it, holding it in the pleats of her skirt.

'All right?' He had a slight accent, not local, not quite London, not quite educated.

She nodded. Her hand did not look so bad. The nail was blackened, dark blood oozing out, the flesh swollen and discoloured. Now that the sickness of despair was gone, a little pride crept in. She had lived through it. It had happened. She had borne it. She looked at him and found that she could smile.

He came round the car and crouched beside her, chewing a foxtail grass with short white teeth. His light brown hair curled onto a forehead wrinkled with concern. His mouth was long and flexible.

'How long you been here?'

'For ever. I shouted and yelled, but there was no one about.'

'It's Sunday.'

'Oh.'

'We ought to get you to a doctor, I suppose.' He looked at his watch, frowned, and glanced over his shoulder at the road, as if he were thinking of something else. Then he turned back to her and took her hand up gently in his brown fingers, which were scrubbed under the nails, surprisingly clean. 'That must have hurt like the devil.' He tightened his lips judiciously, diagnosing.

'That's the least of it. I think the end of the bone is broken.'

He made a wincing sound, bending a little in the middle, as if it made him feel sick. 'Poor kid,' he said. 'That's tough on you.' Crouching, he pushed his hand into his trouser pocket and brought out a cigarette case, opened it and put a cigarette in his mouth. As if she were quite helpless, or as if they were quite intimate, he lit the cigarette, took it from his mouth, and put it into hers.

He lit one for himself. 'Better?' He smiled at her as if a cigarette could cure the ills of the world.

She nodded. 'It doesn't hurt so much now. It's numb again. I'm sure I could drive, if you'll start my car for me. If we wrap my hand in something, I can rest it on the wheel when I have to use the other hand for gears. I think I can drive home and get to my own doctor.'

Dr Nixon would be at his Sunday supper. Cold lamb, pickles, beetroot, sardines in a china dish the same shape as the tin. Bruised lettuce with too much vinegar. Apple pie left over from lunch. Cider from a bottle, Camp coffee, thick and syrupy, other people's lipstick on the napkins. Charlie had been invited twice. Mrs Nixon did not like her living alone. When the surgery bell rang, she would come to the door on her duck's legs to protect Dr Nixon from the hysterics and shams who could wait until tomorrow, and she would say to the thumb, 'Oh, Charlotte, I knew something like this would happen,' as if the car door had jammed because she lived alone.

'Are you sure you're all right?' The young man looked up at the road again, then back at Charlie, undecided. He took a big handkerchief from his trouser pocket and wrapped it round her thumb and tied the ends round her wrist. There was hardly any blood. The flesh was bruised and pulpy, but not cut. The blood from under the nail was slow and clotting.

'The beggar of it is,' he said, 'I'm in a hell of a hurry. I'm late already, and if I sign in late again, I'll be in real trouble.'

'Oh dear, and I've made you later.' What for? It sounded like prison. Was he a trusty out on parole? 'You've been so wonderful.'

'Oh, that's all right,' he said quick and shy. 'I didn't do much.'

'Except save me. I'd have died if it had got dark and I'd had to stay here all night.'

'I don't think so.' He smiled at her for the first time. His face had been concentrated and serious before, like a man with his mind on a carpentering job. 'You don't look that type. You've got a lot of pluck.'

'Thanks.' When she got up, she staggered backwards towards the ditch, her legs unexpectedly weak. He grabbed her arm and helped her up on to the road and round to the other side of her car, a friend again, its sins forgotten, like an immediately forgiven puppy.

She felt dizzy and sick, but the man looked restless, fretting to be gone. When he said again, 'Are you sure you're all right?' it was a rhetorical question, expecting the answer Yes.

'Yes. You must hurry. How far do you have to go?'

'The other side of Bedford. Place called Cardington.'

'The airship place?'

He was tugging at Mick the Miller's other door. 'Yes. This door's no picnic either, you ought to—'

'Are you something to do with the airships?'

He nodded, still tugging.

'What do you do?'

He got the door open. She climbed carefully into the car,

75

resting her wrist on the steering wheel, hand up, holding her breath in dread of knocking it.

'I'm in the flight crew,' he said.

'How marvellous.' She looked at him, standing in the road with his brown face and thick white jersey, waiting to shut the door. He looked like a man of adventure, a man who did something different and exciting. 'Are you going on that flight?' The R101, biggest airship in the world, was about to make its epic flight to Karachi.

He nodded, pleased that she had found out. The officers and men of the wonderful dirigible, buccaneers of the new air age, were national heroes already. The newspapers had been full of stories and pictures for weeks.

'That's why they're so hot on overstaying leave. We're due to fly any time after next weekend.'

'I shall read everything that's written about it, and listen to the wireless all the time, and think about you,' Charlie said.

'I'll think about you thinking.'

He shut the door. 'Slam it!' Charlie called. 'Good luck!'

He waved, and ran to the front of the car. It started at his first strong turn of the handle. When she touched the accelerator, the engine roared as sweetly as if Mick the Miller were in racing shape. She waited while he got into his car, which was stopped just ahead of her at the side of the road. It was a black Vauxhall, with a self-starter. He must be an officer to have a car like that, although he did not talk like one.

The self-starter, said the critics of progress, was all very well as long as it worked. When it did not work, it was just one more example of invention gone mad. We are becoming the slaves of gadgetry, they said. Shall our servant the machine make serfs and fools of us all?

Charlie heard the starter of the Vauxhall click feebly a few times, and then not at all. The airship man got out of the car and opened the back door (people who had self-starters always had a starting-handle within reach). He bent to the car, and wound and wound, until his brown face was brick red.

Charlie got out into the road again, holding her arm under the elbow. 'Take my car!' she called. 'I'll walk back for help.'

'I can't leave you here.'

76

'Please take my car. It goes all right. I'd die if you were late and got into trouble because of me.'

'Well, I—' He looked less confident now, biting his lip, looking up and down the road as if he hoped to see a bus come along.

'Might they stop you going on the flight?'

'Might. I don't know.' His face was creased unhappily.

'You *must* take my car.' The fate of the R101 was in her hands.

'There's a farm or something up ahead,' he said. The dog was still barking, and a loose trail of grey smoke was just visible above a hedge before it lost itself in the clouds. 'I could stop there and send someone back to help you.'

'I'll get your car going, and bring it to Cardington tomorrow and get mine.'

'They won't let you in. I'll have a bit of time off in the middle of the week. I could bring yours down, if it's not too far.' He came back to her, looking in his trouser pocket for a piece of paper. He wrote down her name, and where she lived.

'Come in the evening, because I'm at school all day.'

'Teacher?'

'Yes.' She had never thought of not saying gym mistress before this morning.

'You are a sport, Miss Lambert,' he said. 'I don't know how to thank you.'

'Don't,' she said. 'Just hurry up and go. I told you. I'll be all right.'

'I've got a bag.' He pulled out of his car an old leather bag with straps round it, a cross between a large suitcase and a small trunk. 'Been up to my mother's to get some winter gear.' There was just room for it in the front of the Morris, half on the floor, half on the seat. He put Charlie's case into his car, hung her coat round her shoulders and gave her arms a squeeze.

'Thanks, chum,' he said into the back of her neck. He jumped into Mick the Miller, slammed the door, raced the engine and was off.

'Good luck!' Charlie called to him. 'I'll be all right.' Her voice trailed after him in the chalky dust.

77

Mad, quite mad, her mother would say. But her mother would never know. He would return her car in a day or two. He said he would. She had his car, and it was a better one than hers. If he never returned the Morris, she would keep the Vauxhall. She could not think beyond that. Her head felt more numb than her hand, which was beginning to hurt again, pulsing under his handkerchief.

'You know nothing about him at all,' her mother's voice said. 'Dear old chump, you don't even know his name.'

'He's in the airship, Mummy. I can find him.' She sat in his comfortable car with her head against the window, and argued wearily with her mother. After a while, a farm tractor came slowly up the road and a leering youth with a carbuncle on his neck jumped off the iron seat and came up to her.

'You the lady wan shelp?' That was obvious, since she was sitting there in a dead car at the side of the deserted road.

She opened the window. 'Could you tow me to a garage?' she asked.

'On Shunday?' His laugh was a cavernous horror. He had had all his teeth out at this early age, and no new ones put in.

'Then could you get a taxi for me, or tell me where I could telephone?'

'Telephone?' He had never heard of it. His right eye dropped in a wink that was no less offensive for being congenital rather than lecherous. 'Wash wrong with thish here?'

'I don't know. How should I know?' Charlie spoke angrily, to keep back the tears. She could not stand much more.

'Lesh have a look.' He lifted up the side of the bonnet and poked his long nose inside. He could not possibly know anything about cars. He did not look as if he even knew about chaff-cutters. He fiddled inside the Vauxhall, whistling through the ransacked mouth, then came back to the window with a gaping grin. 'Dirty Poinsh.'

Dirty points was one of the few disasters even amateurs recognized, like Big End Gone, and Overchoked. He was a boy of his times, born to tinker with engines and master them, as his forebears, no less unprepossessing, had mastered horses. He took out of his pocket a rag or a handkerchief, wiped and whistled, then called out, 'Starterup!' The starter was dead, but he turned the engine over easily, leaping back to pull at the throttle lever, his carbuncle on fire with joy.

'We got er.' When Charlie gave him a ten-shilling note, he hardly wanted to take it. She had given him his pleasure for the day. He looked at the note as if it were foreign currency, put it in his pocket and got on to the tractor again. He rode it backwards without looking, all the way to the farm round the bend of the road. Charlie had to drive slowly after him, nodding and smiling wearily as he leered and winked at her, and waved his piece of rag.

When he backed into the farmyard, she increased her speed cautiously and headed towards the Oxford road. No more side roads. She had never driven a car like this before. She had never driven any other car but the Morris, except once when Reggie had let her drive his sports car and she had backed into a lamp post and he called her a clumsy cow.

Her hand resting on the wheel was a dragging weight of pain. Her head swam with vague unrelated images. She tried to shake it clear. She took her good hand off the wheel and hit herself on the side of the skull. Get some sense into you, girl. If you pass out now, it's all up.

As she came into Oxford on the Woodstock Road, primly housed and Sunday quiet, she knew she might pass out. Heaviness shifted down inside her, and her ears sang. I'm not helpless. She had been proud of saying that, but if she had been helpless, he would have said, Damn the airship, and stayed with her. He would have left his car and taken her to Dr Dixon. But Charlie had let him drive away and leave her. Dizzy and sick, she navigated the Oxford streets where bicycles came at her like schools of fish, and undergraduates strolled in the road. There were ten miles between her and the doctor. She would never reach him. Desperate, she swung the car wide like a battleship and crawled towards the hospital, chugging in top gear since she could not change down.

You've got a lot of pluck, he said. You are a sport. But men didn't want sports and girls with pluck. They didn't want gym mistresses ... Inside of a drill sergeant's shoe, she heard the jering voice say, as she reeled through the Casualty entrance and collapsed, with the nurse running towards her.

TWO

YEARS LATER IN 1948, Charlie went back to that hospital, not as a patient, but to help with exercises for the fractured femurs when one of the therapists was away.

Going down to Casualty for some case notes, she looked on the floor of the entrance way for the raised nail head which had dug into her knee when she collapsed on all fours. All threes really, crouching over her injured hand, and rolling over as she passed out.

When she came round on the operating-table, just in time to be put out again, the small hole in her knee hurt more than her hand. They were strapping her arm to a splint, and she tried to tell them it was the wrong limb, but they put the rubber mask over her face and shut her up.

Eighteen years later, the wooden floor was covered with linoleum, but she found a slight bump where the nail was still raised underneath.

'Did you drop something?' A very young nurse came pushing an old man, who lolled over the side of the wheelchair like winter celery in a shopping bag.

'It's all right, thanks. Thanks so much.' Charlie straightened up and marched off to the desk, trying not to swing her arms. She had not been demobilized long enough to lose the voice or the walk.

It had taken her three years after the war to get out of the Air Force. As long as all those girls were still in the WAAF, someone had to drill them and organize netball, restive though they were for the fuller life. They could not unleash all the WRENS and WAAFS and ATS any more than they could let go all those flint-hearted women at the Ministry of Food, because what would they do with them? We'd had our fill of unemployment after the First World War. We weren't going to be caught that way again. So we had food rationing until about 1949, and austerity until at least 1952 and even longer, right up to the time when Macmillan suddenly told us we never had it so good. In 1952, I went to America to make my fortune, and I remember staggering out of a supermarket with bagfuls of things like tinned tongue and mayonnaise and great blocks of chocolate, because I was still in the habit of grabbing and hoarding if a delicacy appeared on the shelves, whether I needed it or not.

I also started smoking again in America, since cigarettes were so cheap. Mrs Meagan, banging cheerily about in her hat and apron, makes a great fuss about the ashtrays, and the stubs and spent matches that don't quite reach the back of the fireplace.

'Why shouldn't I smoke myself to death?' I asked. 'What have I got to live for?'

'Yours is the earth and everything that's in it,' she quoted as if it were an original remark. 'They've proved that lung cancer causes nicotine.'

Terence is shocked because I smoke so much. To him, that's worse than alcohol. He is extraordinarily proper. Although he is still breaking into houses once in a while, and comes afterwards to tell me what he finds in the larder, he is very austere about our local delinquents who slash the cinema seats and tear out the plumbing.

The Winged Pigeon is now working in the laundry – she irons sitting down – and seems to have moved in with him on the housing estate, but they are chastely respectable, although they are living quite openly together. Or are they? I can't avoid the common prurient speculation about people in wheelchairs.

After she got her discharge, Charlie still had to wait to get her house back from the Army. These things take time. After all, Mrs Morgan, this country has been at war. When she was finally able to move back, she almost broke her heart over the damage done by the Land Army girls. It may be as you say, Mrs Morgan, but you can scarcely expect us to investigate every claim as soon as it is made. There are others worse off than you.

Her father's death had left her enough for repairs, and even for living, but she put Julia into the Kingsgrove school, and

81

went back to work. At forty-three, she was too old for the new St Gabriel's, which had gone classlessly boisterous since the State took it over, but she got into rehabilitation at a local convalescent home for Service casualties, with a few odd therapy jobs in Oxford.

Always healthy, it was the first time she had been in that Oxford hospital (except to have Julia in the cottage hospital in Devon) since she was picked up off the Casualty floor with her thumb wrapped in Peter's handkerchief.

They set the distal phalanx bone of her thumb on Sunday night, and splinted it. She lay quietly in the private room, which her mother had demanded over the telephone, although Charlie might have preferred the mateyness of the ward, and thought about the young man bringing back her car.

He would come on Wednesday or Thursday evening, stopping in the road below the bank to check the name on the crooked gate. The dog would bark. Charlie would see the seamed roof of her car from the window. She would come out with her arm in a sling and call to him to drive round to the back where his own car was. After that, it would be natural enough to offer him supper, or at least a cup of coffee. Beer? She had better take the jug over to the White Hart as soon as she got back from school.

'You won't be going back to your school,' the doctor told her on Tuesday morning, 'for quite a while. I'll telephone them.'

Charlie lay flat on the bed and looked at him with feverish eyes in a burning face. 'I'm going home today, you said I could.'

'I didn't know you'd get yourself into trouble,' he said, as if it were her fault that her temperature had risen with the rising sepsis.

'But I must go home. You must let me.'

'We'll see.' He chewed the ragged end of his moustache and

went away. She slept and woke and dreamed and woke in a panic and slept again in nightmare, and did not know whether she was asleep or awake, most of that day. By evening, her racking hand was part of the nightmare. When she raved at the doctor, 'I must go home!' she could not remember why any more, only that she must.

People were in and out, voices near and far. Her mother came. 'Where's Daddy?'

'Won't I do?' Mrs Lambert was never insulted. She was too quick to see a joke against herself and laugh at it before anyone else.

'I want to see Daddy.'

He would get her out of here. He had got her out of the school play when they tried to make her be Titania.

'You'll have to make do with me,' her mother said, 'and this poky room, I suppose, since they *say* there's no other.' She was extremely suspicious of the hospital, since it did not contain My Bone Man, or Umphie Sears, My Man in Harley Street. She roamed the hospital, poking her strong nose into forbidden places where sputum mugs were kept, and senior nurses drank tea. She wandered round Charlie's room, touching things, dropping jars in the basin, tapping at a pigeon on the sill, ringing the bell every ten minutes to say, 'This child is *ill*!'

When the doctor came, she paced the corridor outside while he examined the thumb, looking in on other private patients with jokes and bits of clinical advice. Through the haze of pain and fever which imprisoned her, Charlie could hear the braying of her voice. Then she could hear her arguing with the doctor, but it did not matter any more.

Shortly after that, they took off the last joint of Charlie's thumb, and by the time she was able to think coherently again, it was the end of the week, and he would have come with her car and gone away – with or without Mick the Miller.

As soon as they would let her up, she went down the corridor and telephoned the village post office to ask Mr Eldredge if he would give a message to Quentin. Mr Eldredge was very unreasonable about it.

'How can I leave the post office?' he grumbled, although there was never much business, and he did not keep more than a few pounds worth of stamps and postal orders behind the chest of drawers and fireguard that stood between him and the public.

'When you close up. Please.'

'It's not on my way. I don't go down that end of the village.'

'Then ask Florrie to. It's urgent.' Florrie was as disgruntled as her father, though she did not have his ulcer, so less excuse.

One of them must have gone, because Quentin arrived by bus next day and sat on the side of the bed since the nurses had taken the chair for a patient with more visitors. He was very light on the bed. He hardly made a dent. He held Charlie's hand while she told him the story and asked him to go to her house and see if her car was there.

He understood. He did not think she had been foolish. He said, 'An adventure, oh *good* for you, Charlotte, that's the spirit.'

Her mother did not understand. 'You gave him your *car*?' She had dug most of the story out of Charlie, who had not intended to tell it all. 'My dear child, that's the giddiest thing you've *ever* done.' As if Charlie were a madcap, constantly escapading. 'Dudley, you must go at once to the airship place and see this man.'

'We don't know his name.' Her husband winked at Charlie. He had no intention of going.

'Get on to the Air Ministry. Demand to see the CO. Have them all lined up.' She knew he had no intention of going, but she was giving herself the illusion of action.

Midge came, bringing smoked salmon and a bottle of wine. One of her children was ill with scarlet fever. She had been up two nights with him, and her small neat face was shadowed, and older than its youth. Charlie sat in the chair and put Midge on the bed, and she closed her eyes and went to sleep. When Sister Drummond looked in – she always socialized with the private visitors, but was quite rude to the parents and husbands whispering round the ward beds – she said, 'I can't allow it,' as truculently as if Charlie were a charity patient.

'She's going to have a baby,' Charlie lied.

'Not on my ward.'

Midge slept on, as lightly as a child.

Etty came, with genuine news of pregnancy. She was glad about it. The solicitor was not so sure. A man with a programed career, he had not planned it this way.

'How does one plan?'

'Honestly, Lottie, you are frightfully naïve for twenty-five.'

'Tell me.'

But Etty herself had not understood all the divine revelations of *Married Love* that came to Marie Stopes under the yew trees in Leatherhead. Only that it had not worked.

Mrs Baxter came, in emerald knit, with news of a lost netball match, and something boring about Marcia Stone and School Certificate. Charlie was not listening. St Gabriel's seemed a continent away.

'I'll be glad to get back.' She would, once she was there, but hospital was limbo. You looked no further than the next meal.

'I hope you'll be able to – er, to – er, play tennis.' Mrs Baxter avoided looking at the castrated thumb.

'I can learn to play with my left hand, I suppose.' Were people going to treat it as a mutilation, and deliberately not look? All the rest of her life, Charlie had the habit of putting her right hand in her pocket, or sitting on it, which may have dated back to Mrs Baxter's embarrassment in the hospital.

Now that she was recovered, a fraud with a bandaged hand, whose temperature and pulse the nurses could record without taking them, Sister Drummond gave her pillowcases to mend and bandages to roll, and showed her how to twist cotton wool on sticks to make ear swabs.

When Quentin came back on Monday, she was in the kitchen cutting bread and butter. Sister Drummond was quite annoyed with him for wanting to talk to Charlie before the tea trolley had gone round. They sat in coats on the balcony, where Mrs Sprague lay under red blankets and ate her tea with mittens.

Quentin reported that the bullnosed Morris had not yet come home. Had the man brought it and gone away again? Perhaps he had not been allowed to leave Cardington. Meanwhile, she had his car. She felt a traitor to Mick the Miller, stranded in Bedfordshire, but meanwhile, she had his car. He had to come.

She had spent most of the weekend, when visitors did not interrupt, listening to the wireless in Mr Trent's room across the corridor. Mr Trent was a fat thyroid patient under sedatives, who slept most of the day, right through the dance bands and church services and gramophone records by Christopher Stone. Charlie woke him up for news, for if he was not excited about the R101, he should be. Everybody else in England was excited except Sister Drummond, who said that if God had intended man to fly, he would have given him wings, and she, for one, was glad to say that her wards kept her too busy to bother with such follies.

Although airships had been lumbering across the Atlantic since 1919, sometimes crashing and sometimes not, this flight to India was the zenith of lighter-than-air achievements. It was to be the first leg of a route that would eventually reach Australia and New Zealand, and bring the outposts of Empire to Britain's door.

It was only people like Sister Drummond who saw this as a folly. The rest of the public agreed with the Air Minister that it was 'as safe as a house'.

Safety First had become a national slogan, since the internal combustion engine had revealed itself as yet one more way of killing people. The R101 had been built to a safety-first policy, the experts publicly announced.

In private, the experts were inclined to agree with Sister Drummond. The designers of the R101 knew that it was not as good as its sister ship, the R100, which had recently been stripped half naked in a storm over Montreal, but after five years of sibling rivalry, they were not going to say so. The crew of the control car knew it was too heavy for its power. The engineers at Cardington knew it was not ready to go to Karachi or anywhere else, but the Air Minister wanted to go to India, and he wanted to arrive in grand dirigible style.

Charlie and Mr Trent, listening to the wireless with its gothic loudspeaker and intermittent whistle, knew only that it was the biggest and most luxurious airship in the world. Its five engines were fuelled by oil instead of petrol, so for the first time in airship history passengers could smoke, although everyone would wear rubber soles, to avoid sparks. There were newspaper pictures of the smoking room, with wicker chairs and tables and stewards in tail coats serving tea, and the observation lounge on the bottom of the hull where people lounged in deck chairs, with fields and hedges passing beneath the celluloid windows at their plimsolled feet, far more at ease than the jet passengers of the future.

There were pictures of the crew, young and athletic in overalls and tennis shoes, trotting along steel catwalks and climbing the open ladders to the control cars, overalls bellying and hair blowing in the wind, nothing between them and the landscape.

There was a picture of all the officers and men grouped together on the grass in front of the shed which housed the monster dirigible like a pod. Charlie scanned it long and earnestly, while Mr Trent dropped off to sleep again. There were two people who might be him, one with an officer's gold on his cap, one without. The features were not very clear, so she expended an equal amount of thought on each.

Mr Trent was woken to have his back rubbed. He wallowed snorting in the bed, as cumbrous as the R101 itself. Charlie held the picture over the spread blancmange of his face.

'Which one is the chap you know?' His snail's eyes goggled, unfocused.

'That one.' Charlie pointed to the officer.

'Is that your young man? I say,' the nurses said to each other, craning to see, 'that's Miss Lambert's young man.'

Charlie went out as they rolled up their sleeves and spat on their hands for the formidable effort of rolling Mr Trent on to his side. She borrowed Mrs Sprague's magnifying glass and found that neither of the men she had been looking at was the man with the concentrated brown eyes who had knelt by her in the grass at the side of the road.

Where was he? She looked at every face in the group. Surely he could not be such a liar, whatever he was (what was he?). Only a child or an idiot would have invented themselves into an exploit which the whole country was watching.

On Wednesday, the airship was taken to the mast-head for its trial flight, and Charlie was released from the hospital without the top joint of her thumb.

One of the porters came with her to help her start the black Vauxhall. Her father had had the battery charged, and it started at once, which the Morris never would have attempted after standing outside for ten days in the rain.

She drove cautiously through the town, weaving among the bicycles and pedestrians, at civil war with cars. Motoring laws were still considered faintly un-English. Everyone had a sporting chance at the right of way, and motorists were cavalier with traffic officers, and said, 'Call me sir,' although they themselves called all policemen George.

In the village, she collected the dog and left the fish with Quentin, because she had agreed to go to London for two nights, although not to letting My Bone Man look at her thumb.

Quentin had written a nice little article for the *Morning Post* about a cat who ate all the goldfish but one, because it stared at him. He had not got a cat, but if he became famous, he would get one. He expected that his collected pieces, published each Christmas, would eventually bring people to 'End o' the Road' to see for themselves the angling cat, and the flower that blushed for shame, and Mrs Ram's lardy cake whose recipe had been passed down through the generations by tongue, like antique choreography.

Charlie's cottage looked dear and shabby, the leaning shed empty, no fresh tyre marks in the muddy yard, notes on the door from Florrie Eldredge and the baker: 'Fetch parcel from PO' and, 'Last wks money owing'.

She dug the back door key out of a flowerpot, unlocked the house, and smelled its emptiness. Mice had been in the cornflakes. A potato had gone bad, sprouting white feelers under the low sink. The bread in the crock was mouldy, a jug of milk in the larder solidly curdled. Dead asters stank in the front room.

Although she had been away less than two weeks, the little house smelled damp and sad. When she came back from London, she would light fires and open windows, and start her winter project of painting and distempering and making flowered curtains and chair covers, after she bought some chairs. A bit on the quaint side, her family would say, and make a great pseudo-camping fuss about having a tin bath in front of the bedroom fire, and going to the earth closet with a torch at night. But the house was for her, not them. They would probably never come to stay, even supposing she invited them.

By the time the airship got back from India, she would have the house warmed and brightened for the famous supper party, or beer party, or whatever would transpire after the Morris finally came trundling home.

She locked up the house again and put the dog into the front of the Vauxhall, where he sat stiffly, like a tram passenger on an unfamiliar route. She put his basket into the back of the car, to keep him off her mother's furniture. On the floor under the seat, there was a bundled piece of newspaper. She pulled it out to throw it away, and felt that there was something inside, soft and limp and weightless.

She unwrapped the sheet of newspaper. Inside was a coil of tangled dark hair, greasy, not very clean, one end ragged, the other chopped.

Without thinking much about what she was doing, Charlie wrapped the hair up again and took it into the house. She went up to her room and looked round for a moment, weighing the bundle in her hand. Then she opened a drawer and thrust the bundle in at the back behind a jumble of shirts and pullovers.

At 6.30 PM, the R101 passed majestically over London on its trial flight.

Charlie and her mother and Bubbles and Bubbles's current naval officer and the cook and the parlourmaid and the housemaid and the distressed gentlewoman who came on Wednesday to do darning and mending were all up on the roof of the house in Fitzjohn's Avenue, as democratic as you please, since Mrs Lambert had this idea that servants were people, and had with her own hands helped to haul the cook up the attic stepladder and through the trapdoor.

The tall dark red brick house, turreted and gabled, blistered with bow windows, stood at the top of the broad hill where the cars changed up after the climb from Swiss Cottage and the coal carts shed the RSPCA trace horse. It was a splendid place to see the airship looming through the smoky twilight.

'We must have the best view in London!' cried the distressed gentlewoman, although the height of the roof gave her vertigo. 'I don't suppose there's anyone but us has as good a view of that mammoth creature.'

She buttered up the Lamberts, since she was not a very good darner or mender, and they were her last hope.

Charlie leaned against the sooty parapet at the edge of the roof, and watched the airship swim above the smokestacks of Camden Town like a slow mysterious fish brooding among the pillars and reefs of the ocean floor.

'The Zepps are coming!' her mother called out. 'Do you remember that night we put you under the mattress, girls? We thought our time was up.'

'I didn't,' Charlie said. 'I wasn't afraid,' although she had been terrified by the noise and the grown-ups' panic. Watching the R101, she imagined a door opening in the bottom and bombs dropping out of it on to Oxford Street and Tottenham Court Road. That would be the secret mission of the man who had taken her car. He was in there, his brown hands already turning the wheel that would open the trap and let the bombs come down.

She was beginning to believe that she would never see him again. The Cardington story had been a lie. She allowed herself to admit it. He was not in the crew photograph. He could not be on the airship. I don't know where he is.

When she had stuffed the newspaper bundle of hair to the back of the drawer, she had hoped to get rid of the thought of it too. But it had hung about on the edges of her mind, greasy, unkempt, inexplicable. Long hair was sold for wigs. It was not pushed under the seat of a car. Locks of hair were kept for sentiment. But not in newspaper, not in a tangled mass.

'You mean that you let him go off with your *vehicle*?' she could hear a policeman saying, in politer echo of her mother. 'I'm sorry, Miss. There's motors lost all over the country these days. If we was to go after every one reported missing, where would we be?'

But I found this woman's hair, you see ...

The airship turned and dwindled to the south, its lights moving steadily.

'Your coat!' Mrs Lambert stumbled in heels over pipes and roof vents and beat at the back of Charlie impatiently. 'You're worse than a child, leaning there dreaming against that filthy stone.'

The airship was out of sight now, only a tiny light on its tail seen, unseen, then seen again, like the first evening star.

'Show's over, ladies and gentlemen,' the sub-lieutenant said in an impresario voice. 'File out slowly. No money refunded at the box office.'

'Encore! Encore!' The gentlewoman gushed to him fatuously, because he might be the next in-law. The cook was descending on Mr Lambert's head. The tail light of the R101 was gone. The blue city dusk closed over the throb of the engines.

I don't know where he is. I don't know who he is. He lied to me.

H ehad lied, but not much. On Saturday when she got home to her cottage in the black Vauxhall, which she was beginning to drive as her own, since she did not believe she would ever see Mick the Miller again, Fisher's boy had added one more newspaper to the sodden pile he had been building outside the front door since Charlie went away two weeks ago.

The R101 was ready to fly that night. It would sail with eleven passengers and a crew of forty-three. There was a list of all their names and where they came from. There were pictures of the officers and coxswains and the engineers and the riggers. There was a picture of the galley staff with the chef in white and the stewards in tail coats. Slim and alert, curly hair brushed back, eyes bright on the camera, he had a napkin over his left arm, the hand flat on his flat black waistcoat. His name was Peter Clive.

They sailed away that Saturday evening on the flight that was to change the whole history of long-distance air travel.

Well, it did, of course, but not in the way they expected. After the R101, no more British airships were built. The R100 was broken up and sold for scrap. The R101 was made into pots and pans. The man who had invented the deadly things tried to hang himself. We saw no more dirigibles until the war, when the barrage balloons popped up in the air all over south-east London to trawl for Messerschmitts and doodle bugs.

I remember very well my first flying bomb. I suppose everyone remembers where they were and how they felt when the stale joke, 'Hitler's Secret Weapon' which they had been applying to the lame-brained and the inept since Churchill first warned us to expect something peculiar, suddenly materialized out of the June skies.

I went to work that morning earlier than usual. I had some cutting to do on an Air Vice-Marshal's speech that we were using in a news discussion programme. I was still at the BBC, although I had been trying, as we all did – the blind, the one-legged and the diabetic – to get into action ever since the affair started.

Terence Haig-Davenport, my local liaison with today's youth, who talks a lot about emigrating to California where the young are truly in power, instead of just acting as an illusory front for the old men who still secretly run this country, has declared himself in favour of burning his draft card, should one be forced on him.

When I asked him why, because I was curious to hear his opinion of Vietnam, he covered the fact that he had no opinion by mumbling that burning your draft card (or yourself) is what everybody does.

Were we silly then, who tried so manfully to get into our war? Now they kill themselves because they are called to fight. I remember feeling suicidal because I had not been quite old enough for my first war, and was not quite fit enough for my second. There were other people with small heart murmurs who joined up, or were called up. I was told, 'You're more useful where you are anyway. When you read a bit of news, people believe it.'

'Don't they believe it when Donald reads it?' Donald was a new announcer with a patched-up face who had come to us by way of an incinerated Spitfire and the French Underground.

'Well, yes, they do *believe* it, but there's not the confidence they have in you, after all these years.'

That was why if there was something ghastly to announce, like Tobruk or a cut in the jam ration (worse), it was often given to me, because I was a father figure, familiar in their homes and cars and workshops as their own breathing. If I could take it, they could.

So there I still was in 1944, walking to my work as morale builder for the listening British and for my secret audience in cellars and prison camps all over Europe, who risked death to hear my voice. As I rounded the prow of Broadcasting House, I remember one of the commissionaires was out on the pavement looking askance at the sky, as if he expected to see jackboots dangling from parachutes.

'Get inside, sir! Get inside!' He began to shout and scoop his arms at me.

'What's up?' I broke into a trot.

'They're sending them over without pilots. Get inside! There's thousands headed for London – they're sending them over without pilots!'

And I remember it was that hysterical phrase of his that brought fear to my mouth in an acid funk so that I had to swallow, and stand staring at him, trying to cope with this new and mysterious danger. The bombers had men in them. You could curse and shake your fist at them from underground, imagining them with cruel Teutonic teeth and glittering Eric von Stroheim eyeballs. But these were H. G. Wells impersonals, cheating, other-worldly, too weird. 'They're sending them over without pilots!' And then the drone that filled the air and made the weary stones of London vibrate.

'Get inside!'

The commissionaire and I pushed through the doors and were halfway across the lobby, racing each other for the stairs, when the infernal thrumming stopped. As we paused to take breath and congratulate ourselves, a policeman banged in from the street and yelled, 'Get down! When it stops, it falls!'

We all dived under a table full of pamphlets and recipe books for making cakes with carrots and soya flour, and the thing fell somewhere away beyond Euston.

That was the worst horror of it. The engine stopped. You knew it had to fall. For a moment that seemed an age, all movement froze, all breath was held, mouth open, waiting like a stopped film. It fell – on someone else – and you were glad.

After that first War of the Worlds day, when strangers stared at each other on the street in mute shock, we familiarized the monsters by calling them buzz bombs and doodle bugs and absorbing them almost rosily into wartime life, like Gobbles and Lord Haw-Haw.

Anti-aircraft guns were redirected to their range. Fighter pilots learned to pick them off without getting blown up themselves, and more blimps went up from quaint little sites on dumps and parks and commons, trailing steel tentacles like Portuguese men o' war.

I went with Charlie once to talk to the crew of a barrage balloon in south London. It was a reasonably boring job, winching the unwieldy blimp up and down, deflating it to a sort of billowing grey eiderdown or blowing it up like a tick on a dog to soar up silver with its mates in the midday sun.

Some crackpot at the Air Ministry had the idea that a little PT would be just the ticket to combat inertia, and for a short while, before the idea died of odium, Charlie had to visit a few test sites to see if she could raise any enthusiasm for arms stretch knees bend.

Desperate for fun, because it seemed at this time that D-Day had been not the end but only the beginning of for ever, I brought along a microphone to record the opinions of airmen and WAAFS, disturbed from the rustic peace of a July afternoon on Clapham Common.

I can't remember what the opinions were, though they were sure to have been along the lines of, 'Well, I don't know, it seems to me sort of daft, I means what are we here for, etc,

etc.' But I do remember Charlie sprawling on the grass in a very unmilitary way, squinting up at the belly of the blimp turning pink in the lowering sun, and telling me how she had stood on the roof at the crest of Fitzjohn's Avenue and watched that other gas-filled sausage nose over London with the hopes of England following it.

She did not tell me about Peter then. She did not tell me any of that until years later.

She kept the wireless on all that Saturday, as she had told him she would. In the afternoon, she went into Kingsgrove to collect her spare accumulator which she had left to be recharged.

'Thought you were never coming after it,' Mr Johnson said.

'I had an accident. Look.' She held up her hand, still thickly bandaged over the stump of her thumb. 'Lost the top joint.'

He peered, sucked his teeth, and told her the inevitable story she was to hear so many times from people who thought she had lost it by accident, not surgery, of the child/man/ soldier/uncle whose thumb/finger/toe was cut off by a saw/ knife/machine, and they picked it up and stuck it on again. Wrong way round was one of the few variations on this compulsive tale.

In the evening, she carried the heavy wireless set up to her bedroom. Dance music was interrupted to announce that the airship was over the English Channel.

'After an excellent supper,' the Commander had radioed back, 'our distinguished passengers smoked a final cigar, and having sighted the French coast, have now gone to rest after the excitement of their leave-taking.'

And there was Peter Clive, deft and concerned, as he had been over her poor martyred hand, bending over left shoulders with plates and vegetable dishes, bringing whisky on a tray, balancing easily against the slight roll of the ship to aim the syphon precisely.

'What cigars have you got, Steward?'

He brought a box to our distinguished passenger, lolling over the Channel, with the observation windows laying a path of light on the dark water under his rubbered feet. He struck a match for the sucking and the mumbling that meant the cigar was beginning to draw, then shook it out very carefully and buried it in sand, as a polite reminder that the bag above them was filled with hydrogen. Skilful steward Clive was not obsequious. He was attentive, without being sycophantic, performing his job with neat artistry. That was the kind of steward he would be.

But the hair. The long black coil of woman's hair. Since there could be a dozen harmless explanations, why must it lie in the hollow of her thoughts, as sinister as a snake?

Her oil lamp patterned the whitewashed room with spokes of light. The drawer by the wall held its secret there in the shadow. Where was the girl? Who was she? This was the nagging obsession. Hair cut from the live or dead was all the same. Hair cut last year or last week – there was no way of knowing, since hair did not die. A soft curl set in a locket looks just the same generations later.

Charlie went over to the dark wall and laid her hand on the drawer. She imagined her fingers opening the drawer, feeling among the clothes for the newspaper bundle, soft and limp, unwrapping it, holding the greasy hair. She dropped her hand. She did not open the drawer.

In the light at the other end of the room, she unbraided her own hair and shook it out, running her fingers through it, tossing back her head. Then she caught it strongly and pulled it to one side and tightened it round her neck.

His clean brown hands had strangled the girl with her own hair, before he chopped it off.

If Charlie should go to the police tomorrow (Sergeant Raikes at Sunday ease in the flint and slate station, curling notices of gun licences, smell of ink and urine), if she were to lean her elbows on the chipped linoleum of the counter and whisper, though no one else was there, 'I found this woman's hair, you see . . .'

If she was to go to Scotland Yard, and hear them tell her,

'Yes, there was this girl found in a ditch with all her hair cut off—' what then?

At Ismailia, the crowds are waiting at the foot of the mast, their faces turned up like pansies. Up on the mooring platform, the man with the coloured flags, the dignitaries in frock coats and medals. The quiet men in the background, mackintoshed in the broiling Egyptian sun.

The ropes are winched in. The nose of the airship opens. 'Excuse me, sir.' The quiet men go in first. No fuss. No scandal. The speeches and ceremonies proceed, and perhaps no one even notices when they come out with Peter Clive.

Charlie tied back her hair with a frayed piece of ribbon. She turned down the lamp and got into bed, and heard the dog come upstairs, as he always did when he smelled the smoking lamp wick. If she lay awake long enough, she would hear the stairs contract in creaks, step, step, step, as they did about the middle of each night.

By now, the airship must be over France. Did a steward sleep, or did he sit in the galley with his shoes off, drinking cocoa and waiting for the bells of our distinguished passengers? The Colonel wanted to know the time. His Excellency was sick. The Minister would like an aspirin.

She would take the Vauxhall to Cardington, if he did not come to her.

'Wait in here, miss,' the sentry says. He puts her into a bare little chamber like the waiting-room of a convent. Nothing to read.

Feet on a stone passage. He comes round the door with a questioning face, not knowing who it would be. 'Hullo!' His grin spreads. 'How's the hand?'

'I lost the top of my thumb.'

'Oh, I say.' She has forgotten how he spoke. 'Sorry about the car. I couldn't get away.'

'It wasn't that,' she tells him. 'It was – I found this girl's hair, you see . . .' Watching his face.

'Oh, that.' He laughs easily. 'Is that where that got to? A girl gave it me after she got a shingle. Stupid really. I was going to chuck it away. I didn't even know it was there.'

Or, after the flight, everyone would be given heroe's leave.

She would go to the address from the list on the newspaper page, already in twelve hours worn and creased from much unfolding.

His wife answers the door, with cold eyes.

Or his mother comes out bustling, hands wiped on apron. 'Peter?' The door opens wider. 'Come in, my dear.' A decent-looking girl at last after that slut with the messy hair.

'Who is it, Mum?' Coming down a dim passage, struggling into his jersey. 'Oh, it's *you*!' His brown head emerges. The grin spreads. 'How's the hand?'

'The giant ship,' the wireless had told her, before it shut down for the night with a hymn and the National Anthem, 'is due to return to her mooring mast on October 18th. It is expected that the Prime Minister and members of the Royal family will be there to welcome her home.'

If he did not come to her, she would go to him. 'I found this girl's hair, you see . . .'

JAMES (*loquitur*), as they used to say in the old nineteenth-century *Punch* jokes about children with hoops making precocious remarks to their mothers in Hyde Park.

The R101 crashed into the wooded field in northern France at the worst time of the whole week, as far as the newspapers were concerned. At 2 AM, the morning papers had gone to bed. There would be no evening papers because it was Sunday.

A survivor telephoned the Air Ministry from Beauvais.

'Hullo . . . Hullo . . . Speak up, old chap. I can't hear you.'

'We're down.'

'You're what? Where are you? Who's that speaking?'

'We're down, sir.'

'Good God man – *what*? Hullo . . . hullo, operator, I'm cut off.'

The *Sunday Express* put a special edition on the streets, but otherwise it was the BBC all the way. On a weekday, they would have had to honour their gentleman's agreement not to break any important news until the evening papers could come out with it.

Naïve. Amateurish, if you like, but looking back on it from the ungentlemanly sixties, it seems rather charming. And there was extra impact to the already shattering news about the proud airship, because it was the first time a really big story was broken to the public by wireless.

The newspapers were strong enough to keep the gentleman's agreement going right through the thirties. No news could be broadcast until 6 PM, except for world shakers like the end of the life of King George V ... 'peacefully to its close', and of course the September crisis of 1939 when Chamberlain broke the biggest news of all, though that was hardly news to anyone, for since we were already trotting around with gas masks, waiting bombs or rape according to sex.

I wish I had already been a BBC announcer on that morning of October 5th, 1930. It was John Snagge, proclaiming the disaster and its epitaph, 'They shall grow not old, as we that are left grow old ...' But I would have liked it to be my voice that Sunday morning that told Charlie to forget her dreams and plans and unformed fears. It was too late.

Of the fifty-four men on board the airship, there were eight survivors, six of whom lived.

Names were broadcast later in the day. Charlie heard them at Quentin and Bob's cottage, where she had gone for lunch, not because she wanted to, but because she always went for Sunday lunch, and Quentin and Bob were Darby and Joan in their set domestic routine and would not have it interrupted, even by disaster.

They did not know it was Charlie's disaster too, with emotions none the less intense for being self-induced. All they knew was that she seemed to have lost her chance of getting back the Morris. But she had acquired a black Vauxhall instead, which looked to Bob like a good exchange when he ambled down on his long loose legs to see why Charlie was not at 'End o' the Road' for shery-time.

'I don't feel well.' She put her head out of a window when she heard him whistling for her in the garden.

'Nonsense.' Bob was an amiable fellow with thick soft hair and a bland lack of conscience about leading a double life. His wife was drinking, but he thought she was quite lucky to have him during the week. 'You look your usual blooming self.'

'I'm not dressed.'

'Get dressed,' he said patiently. 'I'll commune.'

He wandered away round the side of the house, kicking at pebbles, picking off leaves and crushing them under his nose, bending to cup one of Charlie's few inadvertent flowers with a hand held as it would be under a champagne glass.

When Charlie came reluctantly down, her hair pulled through a rubber band, her head heavy with the ache of doom which would not leave her, he was in the yard at the back with his face inside the Vauxhall's engine. Not that he knew anything about engines, but it was the thing to pretend you did in those days before they became common knowledge to every small boy.

'Rather jolly motor.' He brought his head out of the bonnet and wiped his hands on a silk handkerchief patterned like the Union Jack. 'She'm a decent swap for poor old Mick the Miller, bain't er?' In London, he veered towards cockney. In Oxfordshire, he favoured what he supposed was the village vernacular, a mock-up of West Country and ectopic stage yokel.

He kissed her, or rather laid his cheek against hers, and his lazy eyes focused when he saw that her face was flushed and troubled.

'What be matter, choild? I say, this chap, he wasn't really a pal of yours, was he? Quentin told me—'

'No,' she said quickly. 'No, of course not. He was just a man – a man who rescued me.' Forlornly she showed Bob her hand, the stump of thumb taped over. He drooped compassionately over it, his mouth tender, clucking and murmuring as if it were a sick kitten. 'It's just so horrible to think of that thing going down like that, and the fire, and the people screaming.' Peter screaming. A human torch dropping out of the sky.

'Don't think on't, lass.' Bob took her arm and walked her off. 'And certainly not now. I never think of anything upsetting before lunch.'

'Don't,' Charlie said crossly, and pulled her arm away.

'Well, I'm sorry,' Bob said cheerfully. 'I didn't know it meant that much to you. I find airships a bit of a bore myself, and since they all blow up in the end, I can't see why everyone is so excited.'

'I'm not excited.' At the end of the short wall between her side lane and Gregory's barn, she turned on to the road without waiting for him.

'Perhaps he got away.' Bob loped up behind her in the grubby old tennis shoes he wore for being a country cottager. 'There were a few survivors.'

'There can't have been.' Charlie walked on with her head down. After a while she asked, 'How do you know?'

'Chap told me in church.'

Avid for integration, in a village which recognized permanencies slowly and weekenders never, Bob would bicycle down to the dead little church at the bottom of the neglected lane where the rectory mouldered, and iron bedsteads patched the graveyard fence. With the vicar's daughter and poor Miss Noonanby and Gregory's mother-in-law and occasional prim guests from the Big House, he sat in 'his' pew and listened to Mr Herriott speak of Love Thy Neighbour in literal, geographic terms (petty examples about washing lines and noisy wireless), and how much it would cost to fit new guttering.

'Friend of the Hammonds from town. Quoite a lovely gentleman. I don't know why they let themselves in for weekends with that dreary family.'

The Hammonds in their pedimented stone house in the railed park, with the walled kitchen garden and the ponies that regarded the peasantry through long eyelashes as the pudden-faced daughters rode mincing by, were so dull that their guests sometimes found their way to Bob and Quentin's cottage and stayed there as long as they dared, like truant children.

101

The lovely gentleman whom Bob had met in church was there for lunch, wryly professorial in hairy plus-fours and mountaineering socks with tabs below the knee. There were some people from Oxford, a poet, an actor, a burned-out genius with a paunch, a square woman who had once designed a set for Noël Coward, a boy who was writing an exposé of the University, as who was not, in the thirties.

Charlie knew them all, except the plus-fours professor. They greeted her chummily, as if a familiar dog had wandered through the door, and she went into the kitchen, as she always did, to keep clear of wit and esoteric jokes under pretence of helping Mrs Ram and Quentin with the lunch. Quentin was the busy one, neat-fingered, hospitable, tossing up his special salad. Bob was the lordly lazy one who lay back and was waited on.

Mrs Ram was making gravy with mushrooms and cream. No one made gravy like Mrs Ram. Nor soufflés, nor sponges, nor strawberry mousse. It came to her naturally, since she did not read or write. She hardly spoke either, but she was played up as a sort of rustic chorus in Quentin's articles. Mrs Ram says ... In the opinion of my Mrs Ram ... as familiar to his readers as the cat and the lardy cake and the whispering winter logs.

She nodded to Charlie without turning round from the saucepan, her flowered haunch enormous next to Quentin's slender hips as he chopped parsley beside her. He dropped the knife and came quickly to hug Charlie.

'You look a wreck, Charlotte dear. You shall have a drink at once. Here. Cooking sherry. Mrs Ram and I keep the best out here.'

The cooking sherry was another familiar allusion, although Mrs Ram had never touched a drop, and would not even taste her own trifle. 'Try this, pet.' He gave Charlie the sherry in a teacup, a kitchen tradition. 'You must be feeling unhappy for that poor man,' he said gently, but he had no more idea than Bob that the voice on the wireless, with its special BBC reverent timbre for calamity, had opened a cold chasm inside her, where banshees wailed about and wrung their hands.

'I don't suppose I'll ever get my car back now.' Charlie took

102

a swig out of the teacup and managed an abrupt laugh, so that he would not start to talk about the burning, twisting mass of metal and people which scarred the green geometry of that unknown French field. 'I was going to paint it royal blue with a red line, you know, and do my initials—'

The man in the plus-fours came into the kitchen on crêpe soles like lorry tyres, carrying pieces of broken glass. Charlie stopped talking with a little gasp and asked him, 'Is it true – what Bob told me – that you heard there were survivors?'

'A man at the Hammonds says so.' He looked at her more closely, seeing that she was strained and tense. 'He's been on the phone most of the morning. Insurance or something. My hostess was wild. She wanted us all for a woodsy walk. God, I hope someone did get out, though how they could . . . Went up like a torch, he said. There were local people who saw it hit and explode, but no one could get near. White hot. Melting. Most ghastly thing ever happened.'

She saw him fall clear, spread like a doll, then stagger up and run blindly across the field with his clothes on fire and his face black and smoking.

'If there were any survivors,' the Hammonds' guest said, tinkling the glass into the rubbish bin, 'I wouldn't give you much for their chances.'

Charlie found reasons to be in and out of the kitchen all during lunch, so that no one would try to make her talk, or notice that she hardly ate.

'Mrs Ram's Yorkshire! Come on, Charlotte, everyone eats Mrs Ram's Yorkshire.'

All hail Mrs Ram. At the end of the lunch, she would be brought into the doorway, an Epstein woman, arms folded under the huge front of her apron, enigmatic, not caring one way or another; but it was a fair paid job, and Mr Ram was bedfast.

'Our gal is well trained, don't you think?' Bob said to the plus-fours man, as Charlie cleared plates and dropped knives and spilled a glass of cider. 'Us keeps she in a shed at the bottom of the garden, us do, and only lets she out to wait on we.'

One or two people smiled and glanced briefly at Charlie,

without seeing her. Mostly they did not pay her much attention, Bob and Quentin's weekend friends, each listening to themselves. She was simply there, like the camel-saddle stool and the rosemary bushes that breathed in at the front door. After lunch, when they were playing the piano and talking about what they were going to do with the afternoon, although it was already dwindling into evening, no one noticed that she went to the other end of the long low room where Quentin's desk and bookshelves were and turned on the wireless.

She listened to the end of a church service, and looked at a magazine, and wanted to go home, but was too tired to make the effort. She had been awake on and off all night, sleeping with strange dreams and waking with a sense of excitement, sleeping again too lightly not to wake an hour later and pick up the same thoughts. The drawer by the wall held its secret.

When the choir climaxed in a shrill celestial shout and the news started, the announcer began to read a list of survivors of the R101 disaster. Charlie did not call the others over. She crouched by the set and held her knees, frowning, her jaw set like a pug. Eight names. Uncertain how many still alive. Cook. Disley. Eight names. Not his.

It was almost a relief. Now she need not think at all about it any more. She could pick up her life as it was before she put the leaves into the car and slammed the door. She could go home now.

'Goodbye, Quentin. Thanks.'

'Don't thank me, dear. You did most of the work. I say – you look rather wan. I knew those butchers at the hospital had done you no good.'

'I'm all right.' She went out by the back door without saying goodbye to anyone. They would not notice she had gone. She ran down the road, past the row of tilting old cottages on the right and the new pair of council houses on the left, which Mrs Hammond said were the beginning of the end.

At home, she quickly ran upstairs to get her purse and the folded page of yesterday's newspaper, put the dog in the car and drove away through Kingsgrove to the Lambert Arms and the London road.

When she had first read Peter Clive's address on the crew list, it had not registered with her that Wilton Crescent was an unlikely place for an airship steward to live – 79 Wilton Crescent, SW1. She did not have to look at the newspaper again. It was engraved on the tablets of her memory.

Still without much reasoned thought, she came into London by the Uxbridge Road, through Shepherd's Bush and across the Park into Knightsbridge. It was not until she turned into the graceful curving terrace, and parked the Vauxhall among the Austins and Daimlers that she realized her absurdity. Who lived here? Why had she come?

She went up the whitened steps and rang the bell by the high front door, still breathing fast and trembling a little from the impulse which had brought her all this way to see – who?

A quite small child in a red dressing-gown tugged open the door at once, as if she had been waiting on the other side, the heavy brass handle level with her head.

His daughter? Brown curly hair. Big toffee eyes. No stain of tears. Too young to be told, or even to understand.

'Where's your Mummy?' Charlie went down on one knee, but it was not that sort of child. She stared, and drew back perceptibly without actually moving her feet, so Charlie stood up and asked, 'Can I see your mother?'

Feet on the stairs. A nanny in a blue uniform dress with stiff white collar and cuffs. 'Who is there, Yolande? What are you doing down there? I called you for your milk and biscuits.' As the child ducked past her and ran up the stairs, she swatted at her automatically, without special aim.

The child screamed, 'I'll tell Mum-may!'

'Tell then,' said the nanny crossly, pushing back untidy straws of hair. She stood on the gorgeous carpet in the hall and looked at Charlie.

'I came about Peter Clive.' No use talking round it.

The nanny blinked, and worked her face as if she were too hurt to speak. She was about Charlie's age, skinny, with a bad skin and a small sharp red nose.

His wife? Charlie put out her hand. 'Mrs Clive?'

The girl looked puzzled. 'If you want Peter's mother, you must go to the basement door.'

'Oh yes, of course. I'm sorry.'

Been up to my mother's to get some winter clothes, he had said, swinging the big suitcase easily out of his car and into Charlie's. But he was coming from the north when he stopped to help her, driving towards London, not away from it.

The nanny had been crying. The acne on her cheeks was soggy and red. 'You can go down the back stairs if you like,' she said ungraciously, 'since Sir Henry and Lady Munsing are out.' She went with Charlie to the end of the hall and called down the turn of the narrow staircase, 'Mrs Clive! Someone coming down to see you.'

'She don't want to see no one,' a man's voice called up, and a spiky woman's voice said, 'Shut up, Gordon, it might be the papers.'

In the kitchen at the front of the house, half underground, they had not turned on the light. They sat like moles round a long table. On the pavement beyond the area railings, people's legs and feet occasionally flickered through the dusk at ceiling level. In the window, a shrouded birdcage swung like a suicide.

When Charlie came in, a man stood up and turned on the light. It shone bleakly under a flat white shade. The three others blinked at her, and the young man standing by the light switch, jowly, his hair sculpted in oiled crests, nodded at her in a surly way and said, 'How do.'

'I'm Charlotte Lambert.' She stepped into the kitchen, looking at them nervously, not knowing how to speak to them because they sat in the front row of tragedy. The young woman had her chair pushed back from the table, to accommodate a large and unbecoming pregnancy. Her face was pinched and petty, with false teeth in her twenties, top lips painted up into her nose, short dry hair tonged into ridges like a corrugated roof.

The two older people sat cramped with pain because they had lost their son. They looked up at Charlie without hope or animation, since there was no good news now that she could bring them. The woman was not cushiony as a cook should be, a floured scone, but spare as a street sparrow, sharp shoulders, quick hands, nothing much under the flowered apron bib, too gay for the occasion. No-nonsense hair was tugged up into a small doughnut riding the back of her head. A London face, at the same time childish and shrewd, with bright brown eyes like Peter's and cheeks veined red.

The man was slight, slope-shouldered and bendable where she was all quick angles. He had a whorl of silky grey hair brushed up in front and the sort of accidental nobility about his thin-lined face which might earn him the insult above stairs of 'Nature's Gentleman'.

The room was large and comfortable. A huge dresser along one wall was crowded with china and dozens of homely items, like knitting and old letters and one half of a set of teeth in a clouded glass, showing that this kitchen was also their home. In the wide chimney opposite, a heavy coal range gleamed with lamp black, a low fire showing behind its teeth. Copper pans and jelly moulds and Austrian spoons, which Madam brought back as a dubious holiday present for Cook, hung symmetrically above. A kettle murmured at the back. The sort of stove that would make continual pies and cakes and soups, with always some kind of stew or milk pudding maturing over-night in the warming oven, and Peter's mother opening the door with pretended impatience to bring out hot gingerbread men for clamorous children.

'I don't know why you came,' the younger man said to Charlie, in a voice that managed to be quite rude without trying, the tongue too thick for the mouth, the lips fat and fleshy.

'I came to say I'm – I came about your – about Peter Clive. I came to say I'm sorry.' Charlie spoke to the parents, and the pregnant girl said, 'What a cheek, disturbing people in their grief.'

'Nanny shouldn't have let you in,' the young man said. 'She's a bit daft, that girl. I don't see why Lady Mucking trusts her with the kiddies.'

'Not too daft to fancy your brother,' the girl said sharply. 'Serve her right, if you ask me, him getting killed.'

'How can you, Rita,' Peter's father said gently, but he winced as if she had jabbed him.

The mother told her sharply, 'Now you just stop being so down on people, because I'll not have it.'

The young man told Rita to shut her fat stupid mouth before he shut it for her.

A family row raged briefly round the table, the parents without heart in it, the brother from crude bullying habit, the girl because she was born quarrelsome. The subject matter was lost. It was just words bandied back and forth, domestic currency. Then they remembered Charlie, and the mother jerked her head and shaped up her mouth, and asked, 'What was it you wanted, miss? You've come on a bad day for us, I'm afraid. You must forgive us...' Her hands began to pull prongs out of her fiercely tidy hair and stab them in again in the same place. 'Must excuse...'

'But that's why I've come.' Charlie wished that she had not. 'You see, I knew Peter. Oh, not well,' she added quickly, as the mother and father looked up, as if just to say his name was to bring fresh hope. 'But he helped me once on the road, when I was in an accident. He was very nice to me. I kept hoping all day – I thought—' She looked at all their faces and found no help. 'I thought he might have been one of the survivors. Then when I heard the names this afternoon, and knew he – I just – well, I just came to this address without thinking. Just to say I was sorry to whoever was here. I didn't know it was you. I thought you lived in the country, somewhere north of Oxford.'

'Must have got the wrong party,' the brother Gordon said, leaning his oxen shoulders and the back of his oily head against the door frame, looking along his thick nose at her. 'Mum and Dad have been here for years.'

'Years too long,' added Rita, who had a genius for raising auxiliary grievances.

'Peter Clive. That's his picture, isn't it?' There was a photograph among the domestic jumble on the wide bottom part of the dresser. Peter in an open-necked shirt, with the sky behind him and the wind in his hair, laughing, showing his short white teeth.

'Sit down, miss,' his mother said. 'If you're a friend of my boy's, you're our friend too.'

'You don't know what she wants, Mum,' Gordon said, as

Charlie pulled out a chair and sat down with them, waiting with her hands clasped on the table, as if it were a board meeting and not her turn to speak. 'Everyone wants something, you'll find that. Even Lady Mucking.' He jerked his head towards the upper part of the house. 'So nice and kind. "We'll go out to dinner tonight, Cook. It will be easier for you." "Oh, thank you very much, My Lady, I'm sure." ' He did a rotten imitation of Lady Munsing and his mother. 'What does she care about Peter, except now she won't have to feed him on his time off? You'll see. Tomorrow she'll tell you she's asked ten people for dinner and it's soufflé and chicken à la, just as if your heart wasn't broken.'

'She's not like that,' his father said. 'You know she's not. She's been very good to us, Lady Munsing has. I don't know where we would have been last year when the works closed, if she'd not got me in at Jackson's. Jobs are hard to come by these days, as you should know.'

'Not rotten jobs like that,' his son said rudely. 'Anyone can get work if they'll sweep a machine shop floor and push the tea wagon. Bit of a come-down for a skilled fitter, I'd say. I'd have told her what she could do with it.'

His father gave him a rather sweet smile, and tapped his fingers one by one on the table, counting silently for patience. 'What are you going to do about supper, Nelly?' he asked.

'Supper!' Gordon was disgusted. 'How can you think of food at a time like this?'

'Well, it won't help Peter if we starve to death,' the father said sensibly. 'Come on, let's have some tea, at any rate. No doubt this young lady would like a cup. It will buck us all up.'

'I'll never be bucked up again, never.' Mrs Clive got up and stood with her face to the dresser, her narrow frame quivering with grief, the points of her shoulders hunched up to her ears.

'Come on, Nell.' Her husband went to her and put his arm round her waist. 'Come on, you've got more go in you than that. There's others in the same boat as us, don't forget.'

'I don't care,' she wept. 'I can't care about them. It was their own fault. Nobody asked them to take up that murderous thing.'

'Nobody asked Peter to go. But he had to. You know how he was, my dear. You know how he set himself at things, and who could turn him? I knew the day he told us he was joining the crew. I knew then. I told you, didn't I? I knew.'

'Oh yes, you knew. You always know,' Gordon said. 'That's such a help, I'm sure. It must be lovely to be able to say afterwards, I told you so, especially when it's your own son who's dead.'

'Don't talk to your father like that, young man!' This helped the mother to regain control, for the younger and the older couple never agreed on anything, even their common catastrophe. She busied herself with the teapot and cups, her movements smooth and time-honoured, her hands reaching by themselves for the tea canister, the old spoon in the front of the drawer.

'Please don't bother for me.' Charlie stood up. 'I've got to go.' Although Mrs Clive seemed quite composed again, she did not want to have to talk in front of Gordon and Rita, who would turn even a simple statement about the car into something highly suspect. But when Mrs Clive put a plate of cup cakes on the table, Rita said, 'I feel sick anyway,' as if that had done it. 'You'll have to take me home, Gordon. It's very hard on me, all this. I don't know how I stand it.'

'You're a fine good girl, Rita,' Mr Clive lied kindly, but she looked at him spitefully as she heaved her ugly fruit on to its feet. If she could have had a miscarriage on the kitchen lino-leum to show them that their grief for Peter was nothing to what the whole mess had done to her, she would.

Since she and Gordon were leaving, going out of the base-ment door with meaningless remarks like Take care, and See you when I see you, and Mind how you go, Charlie stayed and drank the tea. They managed to talk quite easily about the doomed airship, and about how proud Mrs Clive had been that her son was part of this cloud-age miracle. Mum, he had said, it's the dawn of a new area. About the drama of the wireless announcement, and how it had interrupted the hymns that accompanied her Sunday morning routine. 'The breakfast things were done, and Nanny's tray wasn't yet down, so I'd

110

started the potatoes and got my Yorkshire mixed. Dad was in the scullery shaving. Dad, I called. Dad, come in here, it's Peter. And he come, with his razor still in his hand, his face a sight. I'll never forget it, not if I live to be a hundred. I was standing right there, by the chopping board. I'll never forget it. Never.'

'It's terrible for you.' Charlie found herself able to talk freely and warmly, as if they were old friends. 'How can you bear it?' She saw again the huge dirigible swimming over the London housetops, lighted like a building, its engines safe and steady. It had looked so solid, the whole mammoth bulk of it, and yet it had gone up in a sheet of flame, like paper flaring and disappearing. 'I don't know how you can bear it.'

'I can't,' the mother said. 'He can. He's got more faith than me. He doesn't believe that people disappear for ever. I do.'

'I think you're both very brave,' Charlie said. Her second brother, the baby Teddy, had died of pneumonia when she was five. She could still remember her mother's hysterics, cursing the doctors, refusing to let her husband into her room, knocking over trays of food, hitting out at Charlie when she came offering her kitten, clutching Bubbles so fiercely that the child screamed and had to be taken away from her.

'I like you,' Mr Clive told her. 'I liked you as soon as you came in. I said, there's a girl I like. I always know, don't I, Nelly?'

'He always knows,' she said dutifully, her eyes lost and dreaming in the steam from the cup she held in her two hands below her flushed face, on which the sorrow sat more strangely than the sparrow pertness for which it was shaped.

'It was very nice of you to come and see us,' Mr Clive said.

'It was just on the spur of the moment.' She remembered now that she had run out of 'End o' the Road' without saying goodbye to Mrs Ram, buttering her famous scones. A cardinal oversight. 'I wanted to. But there was something else too that I had to tell you. It's a bit hard to explain, but when I had this accident on the road, I lent your son my car because his wouldn't start, and he was in a hurry to get back to Cardington. He left the Vauxhall with me, and so now I still have his car. It's outside the house.'

'His car?' They both frowned and looked at each other. 'But he hasn't got a car,' Mr Clive said. 'He's never had one. Talked about it a lot, of course, you know the way all boys are these days, but not on what they paid him. I hope there's some glory in this job, he used to say, because it's for sure there's not much money. He never had a car.'

'But he was driving it.'

'He couldn't have been,' Mrs Clive said, 'because he never had a licence, so that settles that.'

'But he was. A black Vauxhall. It's outside. He must have borrowed it from someone at Cardington. I suppose I'd better take it back and get mine, unless you want me to leave it here. What do you think I should do?'

They shook their heads, at a loss. 'I can't see why he would want to borrow a car,' his mother said. 'He didn't have a licence. I didn't even know he could drive.'

'We didn't know a lot of things about him,' her husband said. 'Leave it at that.'

And so Charlie left it, and asked no more questions.

'That's so.' Mrs Clive nodded at him. 'We didn't know about you, for that matter, Miss – er—'

'Please call me Charlotte.'

'He was away so much, you see, Charlotte, we never knew much of his life after he stopped going to school and left home. First in the hotels, then on the trains. On the Pullmans, he was. Back and forth to Brighton on the Southern Belle before he got this craze for the airship. We were in Belgrave Square in those first years, with Her Grace.' She made a respectful mouth for the Duchess. 'Then, when I got this post with Sir Henry and Her Ladyship, she said he could stay in the little room when he got his time off. So kind to him, she has been. She had the boxes moved out, and last Christmas, she gave him curtains and a spread. Always welcome, she said. He was very lucky. She's like that, you see, Charlotte. With all her wealth and position, she still thinks of others below her.'

Her servility was sickening, none the less for being simple and sincere, not sycophantic. It was easy to see why Gordon

112

was a scoffing radical. What had Peter made of it? How had he been able to stay in the Wilton Crescent house if his mother told him all the time how lucky he was?

'Such a nice little room, and all his own when he wanted,' Her Ladyship said. 'Wouldn't you like to see it?'

Impossible to say No to those eager eyes. Charlie wanted to stand in his room anyway, and see the bed where he had slept, and the things his hands had touched.

At the back of the narrow terrace house, where a knife machine and a boot rack stood archaic and a broken lavatory cistern flushed constantly, Mrs Clive showed Charlie a tiny room like a slot with a barred window looking on to a walled yard. There was not much more than an iron bed with the flowered Christmas spread, one corner curtained off for a wardrobe, a few souvenir ornaments on the mantelpiece over the blocked-off grate, a home-made bookshelf with half a dozen uninteresting books. It was impersonal and bleak. Mrs Clive had pasted the newspaper picture of Peter with the other stewards and the galley crew on to a piece of cardboard and laid it against the pillow with a bunch of flowers tied round with wool. Charlie found that she was crying.

'It seems a liberty.' Mrs Clive put a thin red hand on her arm. 'But were you, as one might want to put it, my boy's girl? I know you said you didn't know him very well, but perhaps it *was* more than that?'

She wanted it to be, and so Charlie said, 'Yes, in a way,' because she wanted it too.

Forty-eight passengers and crew died in the crash of the R101 outside Beauvais, the worst disaster in the short history of aviation.

On Monday, there were the newspaper pictures of the twisted skeleton looking like a giant fish picked clean, half in a wood, half in a field. No substance left of fabric or of flesh.

Charlie did not go back to work on Monday. She telephoned Mrs Baxter, who said, 'After your – erm, er – you must take every care.' Still embarrassed by the thumb, still talking about it with little hum hums, as if it had been a hysterectomy. Mrs

113

Fossick, she said, was holding the fort. Indeed, it was surprising how she had got back into the swing after so many years of retirement. She was managing splendidly, Mrs Baxter said, and hung up, leaving Charlie at the draughty hall telephone in her parents' house wondering whether she was trying to imply that she need hardly bother to come back.

'Where are you going?' Her mother was reading a tabloid greedily, searching for revolting details.

'Out.'

'With that mortuary face? You behave as if this man who stole your car had been your lover.'

'He didn't steal my car.'

'Where is it then? Don't *stand* at me like that. Stomach in, blackheads out. That's the way.' Charlie did not exhort her youngest juniors so childishly.

'Did you ever meet Sir Henry and Lady Munsing?'

'Once or twice. She's a bit of a parasite. He's a banker. Your father knows him.' That implied a bore. 'We went there to dinner once, and I sat next to a bishop. It was ghastly.'

'Why?'

No one but Charlie would ask that. Bishops were intrinsically impossible, without explanation.

'What did you have to eat?' She could imagine Mrs Clive, flushed and competent, with a pursed cooking mouth, getting the dinner away from the black iron range, Peter perhaps lounging in the window chair, hearing the titbits the maids brought down with trays from upstairs.' A Mrs Lambert there. Life and soul of the party, *she* is. You should have heard what she said to the bishop!'

'Don't be morbid. *I* don't know. It was ages ago. Reggie and Midge were there. She was huge with Weezie, and people too pointedly didn't look. It was that sort of a party. Do you know them?'

'I've been to the house.'

Her mother gave her one of her brilliant smiles, surprised and approving. Charlie tried to wipe it off by saying, 'I know their cook,' but her mother was not listening.

'It says here there are only blackened lumps of people left, so they're not going to open the coffins. Burned to a crisp,

114

it says. Your poor car thief won't need to roast in hell, at least.' She thought that was funny. Turning a joke about anything was one of her accomplishments, admired where it did not shock, the shock as pleasing to her as the admiration.

When Charlie went back down the stone area steps in Wilton Crescent, she was greeted like a family friend. Mrs Clive was up to her sharp elbows in flour, because, as Gordon had predicted, life must go on, and Lady Munsing had said in her thoughtful way that it was better to keep busy, Cook, and ordered veal and ham pie for lunch and scones and sponge cake for the Swedish Consul at tea.

Mr Clive had gone to work, because he had not thought of not going. After he left, an official letter had come. It stood like a bomb on the dresser, where Mrs Clive eyed it suspiciously as she slapped at the batter.

'You open it, Charlotte.'

'It's your letter.'

'My hands are all flour. You read it to me. I can't find my specs.' She had not got spectacles, but they were a good excuse.

The letter asked next-of-kin to give their consent to a public funeral at Cardington.

'Our people have always been buried at Epping.'

The victims would all be laid in a mass grave, since most of them could not be identified.

Blackened logs. Faces with no skin and empty eye sockets. Fat melted. Bones charred beyond humanity.

'This is only a formality. You'll have to say Yes.'

'You write the letter, Charlotte. You would do it better than me, and Dad gets back so late.'

'I can't write properly yet with this stupid thumb.'

'Draft it out then, there's a good girl, and Dad can copy it. He writes a nice hand.'

A housemaid came through the kitchen with a bucket of coal, her black stockings wrinkled, grimy cotton gloves on her hands, cursing.

'Who's this?' She stared at Charlie, writing in her new awkward style at the table in the window on a pad of paper

'As if we hadn't trouble enough round here today without inviting in all them bleeding reporters.'

'Miss Lambert is a friend of Peter's,' Mrs Clive said, 'so watch your filthy tongue, Alice.'

'Excuse *me*.' Alice turned up her eyes, as if she were already sick of the beatification of the dead, and slopped out to the coal cellar under the pavement. From the kitchen window, Charlie could see her broad labouring haunches as she shovelled and cursed, while feet trod above her head, clanking the coal hole cover. One pair was Rita's, coming to sit sullenly with Mrs Clive and drink tea out of a spoon. 'I dare say I'm not wanted then,' she said when she saw Charlie there, 'but Gordon wouldn't have me stay alone.'

One of the survivors was not expected to live. His family were called to the hospital in France. Other parents and wives crossed the Channel to be nearer what was left of their loved ones and to stand in blacks and greys among the black-clad French to watch the procession pass through the town square of Beauvais. Three battered survivors, still in their flying overalls, were already famous men, their heart-catching picture in the world's newspapers.

France declared a national day of mourning. King George V sent a message of condolence to Ramsay MacDonald. Ramsay MacDonald sent a message to anyone who would listen that he was grieved beyond words at the loss of so many splendid men, whose sacrifice had been added to that glorious list of Englishmen who, on uncharted seas and unexplored lands, had gone into the unknown as pioneers and pathfinders, and had met death.

Kings of all countries that still had kings sent royal sympathy. The Pope sent a saddened blessing. Charlie read it all to Peter's mother, who still could not find her specs. The ex-King of Portugal sent regrets. So did Mussolini, Burgomaster Max of Brussels and the Maharajah of Patiala.

'Ta ever so much for nothing,' Rita said through a clogged nose. She had a cold, somehow attributable to the disaster. Her doctor had dared her to take a cold before the confinement. She coughed and gasped and sniffed with her whole face instead of blowing her nose, and made the worst of it.

On Wednesday evening, Charlie met Her Ladyship, descending democratically after dinner to tell Cook and her Nature's Gentleman what Sir Henry had heard at the Club.

'They're calling it a crime not an accident,' she said.

Mrs Clive put a hand over her flat front and gasped. Her husband said, 'I knew. I knew it had to end like this.'

There were times when Charlie wondered if he might be a little off his rocker. When he said things like that in a dreamy drone, his fine nose went up like a prow, his lips parted, his puppy-blue eyes saw infinity.

'Er – yes.' Lady Munsing looked uncertainly at him, but he had shut himself away in his knowledge, his patrician face closed for business. She turned to his wife and resumed her high hectoring voice for talking to servant or foreigners. 'Sir Henry talked to a man from the Air Ministry. They'll never publicly admit it, of course, but he did hint that there were a lot of people who knew the flight was a mad risk, including some of the wretched devils who had to make it.'

'My Peter didn't know,' his mother said quickly, still holding the left side of her apron bib, but defensively now, not in shock. ' "It's the finest airship ever built," he told me, and those were his words. "The finest ever built." '

'Well, I'm sure he did, Cook.' Lady Munsing was a thin, rackety woman, a hangover from the jazzy twenties, who had married a richer, older man to whom she had given nothing but her bony body, two discontented children and a restless itch to be always somewhere else. Scotland. Paris. The Riviera. Sir Henry's hunting box. She rode foul-mouthed with the Quorn, used the Kingston bypass as a race track, and was learning to fly. A bit late in life, Sir Henry told her. One of his ways to keep her down was to remind her that she was forty. She wanted reckless youth for ever.

'I'm sure he did.' She smiled briefly and traced the key pattern on the linoleum with her long flat toe. 'But then, he wouldn't exactly know, would he? I mean, if you see what I mean. *Ça va sans dire*,' she tried out on Charlie, whom she could not exactly place. Of and not of the Clive milieu. What the hell was she doing in the kitchen?

'Oh, Peter.' Mrs Clive knew her place too well to weep now,

but her face was flushed and swollen with misery. 'What have they done to my boy?'

'They murdered him,' Lady Munsing said, without warmth. 'That's what everyone is saying.'

Charlie put her arm around the mother's waist, and found herself crying out to Her Ladyship, 'Why did you have to tell them this? Surely it's bad enough for them already?'

'You're a very rude young lady.' Lady Munsing's eyebrows rose above the lines she had pencilled for them. 'Whoever you are.' Not caring to be told, she turned towards the door.

'What are they going to do about it then?' Gordon, of course, butting in heavily. 'What compensation is coming to the families?'

'Don't expect anything from this Government.' Lady Munsing turned and dropped her eyes at him. They drooped easily, weighted down with mascara too black for her short wiry hair, which sprouted like sphagnum moss from a low Grecian band. 'The country's ruined, you know,' she informed him chattily.

He sneered, but only with his face, and only behind her back as she turned away again. He was only a small bullying seditionist. After the revolution, he might trample on the bodies, but he would not be first in with the knife.

'I'll have breakfast early, Cook.' Her Ladyship said from the door. 'So will Nanny and the children.'

'Yes, my Lady.' Mrs Clive had somewhat recovered now, making movements with her hands to start looking busy again.

'We're going to Leicestershire. I thought it would be easier for you poor things.'

'Don't tell me she wasn't going to Leicestershire anyway.' Gordon stuck out his thick tongue towards the sound of her feet escaping smartly up the stairs. He sat down heavily and picked his teeth with a match. He, like his parents, had remained standing through the visitation. So had Charlie, to show she was on their side against Upstairs.

'You shouldn't have spoken up like that,' Mrs Clive chided her, maddeningly tolerant. 'She means well, poor lady.'

'She doesn't. My mother was right, for once. She is a parasite.'

'Oh no, you don't know how hard she works on that committee for the East End Hostels Ball,' Mrs Clive told her earnestly. 'On the go morn till night, weeks before and weeks after.'

'Spending the profits on lunches and gin,' Charlie said, and she and Gordon guffawed, for once in unison.

Tomorrow, the coffins with the bits and pieces of people in them would be at Westminster mortuary, before the lying-in-state. A gentleman in a bowler hat and shoes you could comb your hair in, had come soft-voiced, clearing his throat as if the whole thing were his fault, to ask the Clives to be there for identification of personal belongings found in the wreckage.

As a key man in the sales department of his organization (ie, traveller in cheap jewellery), Gordon could not go with his parents. Rita could not go in her condition, though she would not have gone anyway. The mere word mortuary turned her.

'I'll come with you.'

'Will you, dear?' They clutched at Charlie like a floating spar. They were so tired. People like the man in the bowler hat and mirror shoes, and the newspaper reporters and photographers, and the Munsings, and the men in the machine shop who held their mugs under the tap of Dad's tea urn for a penny had offered them sympathy and help and a certain inquisitive awe, since they were central actors in this national drama, but nobody had seen how tired they were. Charlie felt young and strong and dependable, as if Peter had given them into her charge and said, 'Take care of them for me.'

She went home on the Underground to Hampstead station, and a man sitting opposite her raised the evening paper from his lap to show her what bloomed in his open raincoat. Walking home, a drunk grabbed her arm and asked her where she was going. A woman was sobbing against a wall, while a man stood by and watched her helplessly. London was full of small curious things, but Charlie was part of the national drama.

Her father called to her when she came in. 'Where have you been?'

'To the flicks.' She was not going to share the drama with her family, to be stripped into fishbones like Miss Perrott's chestnut leaves. I say, our Charlie's got it bad. I thought you hardly knew this unfortunate young man. Don't get your picture in the papers, that's all. It will be too hard to explain.

'What are you going to do about that car of his?' He had come into the hall from his study below the arch of the wide staircase, rubbing his eyes, heavy glasses in one hand, a pen in the other to show he had been working, not asleep.

'I don't know.' She wanted very much to tell him that it was not Peter's car, but she could not get those words out. The black Vauxhall lurked always in the wings of her mind, as unnervingly as the newspaper bundle of hair lurked at the back of the drawer in her bedroom.

She did not want to bring it forth and talk about it. She did not want to drive the car any more. Mrs Clive would not let her leave it outside the house in Wilton Crescent, because of Sir Henry's Daimler rolling in and out with speaking tube and silver flower vase. The Vauxhall was sitting at the top of Fitzjohn's Avenue, sinister now and full of mystery. Where did it come from? Who had pushed the hair under the seat? Whose hair? Whose car?

'You can't keep it here,' her father said. 'It's part of his estate. You must take it back to Cardington tomorrow and get the Morris.'

'Oh, Daddy, I can't.'

'Then I will.'

'You can't. I mean, I'll do it. I really will. Let me wait until after the funeral. I don't want to go up there and have to talk to people. It's all so horrible.'

'It's a bad business. Funny, in the war, we used to read of thousands of men being lost, but we were numb, like insane people sitting round the walls of a cell. The figures meant nothing any more. This thing's shaken everyone because it seems so futile. Yet it isn't half as futile as men chucked out against the barbed wire like a handful of gravel. In fact, it isn't futile at all if it adds something to what they know about flying.'

'Why do they have to fly?'

'Why does anyone have to do anything? The sky's there. People have been trying to launch themselves into it since they lived in trees.'

Standing in his rather grand square hall among the potted ferns and high-backed chairs and small expensive bits of statuary, he looked short and mild and friendly, the area round his eyes pink and vulnerable without his glasses.

'Daddy,' Charlie said. 'I'm worried about something.' She wanted him to put his arm round her, or take her hand. If he had touched her in some way, she could have told him about the car, and about the sad tired people in the basement kitchen, and her own sadness, haunted by this shadowy fear.

But when he said, 'Want to tell me now, or will it keep?' he turned away and put his hand on the carved pineapple knob at the bottom of the curving banister.

'It can keep.'

The tall clock with the months and seasons on its face began to strike.

'Goodnight then, dear. Come up soon.'

'Goodnight.' Through the banisters she watched him walk neatly up the exact middle of the red stair carpet as he did every night when the clock was striking eleven, pausing, as he did every night, on the landing with the round stained-glass window to take his watch from his waistcoat pocket and check it with the clock.

Soon Charlie followed him up to the room which had been hers before she bought her cottage. They kept it ready for her so that she could come and go. You can only keep children by letting them go, Mrs Lambert said. She was wrong. The longer Charlie stayed away, gym mistressy, bucolic, the harder it was to return to her room waiting too confidently, towels laid out and not a speck of dust.

She had slept in this room before she went to the training college. It was schoolgirlish, with team photographs, books about horses and dogs, holiday photographs all teeth and droopy wet bathing suits under the glass of the dressing-table.

Her thumb was hurting. Now that it was healed but still tender, she wore a yellow chamois fingerstall on it, tied round her wrist with white tapes. The distressed gentlewoman who came to do mending had made three of them for her out of housework gloves. She took it off. The stump looked disgusting, new skin puckered, shiny and red, pale dents where the

121

stitches had been. She was learning to write with the stump sticking up, the knuckle of her middle finger doing the work of the pad of the thumb.

At the bottom of the leather handbag which she swung on a shoulder strap like a telegraph boy, Peter's handkerchief was crumpled up, unwashed, stuck together with her own blood, hard and black. She took it out and wrapped it round her thumb, sitting on the edge of her low bed, nursing the hand in her lap, as she had nursed it in the lap of her wide pleated skirt in the grass by the side of the road. Poor Charlie. Poor Charlie. Mad as a hatter. I told you. There was a man once ...

Through the dark fields of Kent, the train came, carrying the dead. They were to arrive in the early hours, sneaking quietly back to the city over which they had sailed, all lights blazing, only two weeks ago.

Charlie put away the handkerchief, put on the thumbstall, tying the tapes with her left hand and her teeth, and went downstairs to the tocking clock and the narrow patches of coloured lamplight through the glass panels in the front door.

By the kerb outside the garden wall, Graham Brodie's car was parked in front of the black Vauxhall. In the car were Graham Brodie and Bubbles, twined together on the front seat, lips glued.

Charlie bent at the knees to look at them through the window, and saw, beyond the back of Graham's head, her sister's eyes wide open and quite divorced from the kiss, roving idly, rather bored. When the eyes saw Charlie, they narrowed under a frown. Graham murmured in pain as Bubbles jerked away, his hand still grabbing at her breast. The top of her evening dress was down to her waist, her breasts rounded and white under the street lamp, the nipples unperturbed.

Coolly, Bubbles sat there without pulling up her dress, and made a face at her sister on the pavement. Graham turned his head, but Charlie had stepped to the back of the car.

'Who's there?'

'Some dirty old man watching us.'

'This is hell. Let's go up to your room. The house is all dark. Come on, darling, don't you want to?'

122

'You know I do.' Her Jean Harlow voice, huskily artificial. Though Charlie could not see her, she knew her face would be a doll mask, her body an exquisite cold fake. If anyone ever got up to her room – and Charlie did not think they had – it would be practically necrophilia.

It was too late for a taxi, so Charlie started the black Vauxhall. She crashed into gear and jerked ahead. In the window of Graham Brodie's car, she saw Bubbles's face under her disordered cloud of hair turning to watch her go. A hand with a cigarette in it flipped her a careless farewell.

Although the arrival of the train from Dover had been planned for a time when few people were about, Charlie found a huge crowd in the road at Victoria, pressing under the archway to the side platform where the Southern Belle usually came in.

Charlie had two advantages in crowds. She was tall enough to see over heads, and strong enough to push her way through. Not all these people were mourners. Some of them had come to stare at the faces of those who mourned. Some, obsessed with a tragedy which seemed their own, had come to stand quietly in tribute. Some because it was spectacle of a kind, and they liked to know everything that went on in London. Some had come because they saw a crowd and joined it.

Charlie manoeuvred her way to the front, inside the echoing station where milk churns rang and a train hissed out its steam. She stood behind one of the policemen who was keeping the people back from the platform gates. His helmet was over his eyes, the strap across his moustache like a gag. Opposite her, a group of men in frock coats and top hats stood with suitable faces, communicating with each other in grave nods, or murmuring behind their hands. The Prime Minister looked like an undertaker. His daughter stood beside him with her feet planted squarely side by side in blunt strap shoes.

Nobody in the crowd spoke, but awareness of the train spread in a wordless shifting movement before its light was seen or its engine heard. It drew in very slowly, as if its burden was too heavy. Hats came off. A little group of weeping women, humped in dark coats, were taken through the gate to a passenger carriage at the head of the line of baggage cars.

People craned ghoulishly forward to see how they greeted the few survivors, and a man behind Charlie said in his throat, 'The Lord giveth with one hand and taketh away with the other.'

As the women came back through the gate with the bandaged men, the crowd tried to stare without staring. Two of the women were still crying, noses stoppered with handkerchiefs. One little one looked bewildered, as if she had only been told what to do this far. The men's faces were expressionless. The bandages on a head, an arm, looked like stage props, put on for effect. Policemen moved between them and the people as the forlorn little groups stopped to shake hands with the Prime Minister and some of the frock coats.

What did they say? Congratulations. Thanks. Such an ordeal . . . All in the line of work, sir.

Was it supposed to be an honour for the Prime Minister or for the survivors? I met Ramsay and a couple of cabinet ministers. What do you think of that, Ethel?

The baggage cars were opened, brightly lit, and the squad of airmen lined up on the platform began to carry out the coffins to the waiting tenders. It took a long time. There were forty-eight coffins. Draped in Union Jacks, they passed before Charlie at shoulder height. The faces of the airmen who leaned a cheek against them were mostly quite young, a tongue tip protruding, pimples, a jolly face made solemn.

It was over. The policemen began to move the crowd away. 'Come on, miss,' the policeman with the gagging helmet strap said to Charlie. 'There's nothing to stay for. Have you got someone there?' He nodded towards the street, where the tenders had driven away and the crowd were spreading out across the road, walking under the first light.

'Yes.'

'I'm sorry.' What was he thinking? Wife? Sister? Girlfriend? His eyes were a Dutch blue and his moustache was ginger. He put his hand on her arm to turn her out of the station. Now she must walk to where she had left the car, drive home and go through the tocking lights and shadows of the hall to her childish bed to lie there until Millie rattled the curtains back on their big painted rings, already damp under the arms and cross, because Charlie was the same age as her and still in bed.

'Can you help me?' she asked the policeman.

'I expect so, miss.' He smiled, and sniffed his chin strap higher under his nose, waiting to direct her somewhere. But she told him about the black Vauxhall and how she had come by it, and asked him what to do.

He watched her while she explained, his eyes moving back and forth under the helmet peak as if he were reading a page. 'That's done it,' he said when she stopped. 'Now I'll have to take you to the station about this, and it's long past your bedtime.'

Charlie was tired enough not to mind being treated like a child. At the station, she fell asleep in a chair while they were writing a report, and since she must now leave with them Peter's car which was not Peter's, she was taken home in a police car, a hammer-headed milk pony the only one to see her arrive.

On her pillow was a note from Bubbles.

'I don't care if you do tell Mummy, but in case you do, I'll tell her you're up to something, whatever it is.'

Next day she went with Peter's mother and father to the mortuary and stood about awkwardly with the other relations of the dead, the men with armbands and black ties, some of the women with new black hats that sat ill. Mrs Clive wore last summer's sailor, stiff and shiny, with marks of the glue where she had taken off the daisies. Charlie had put her hair into a heavy bun behind the Persian lamb glengarry which was the most inconspicuous thing she could find in her mother's hat boxes. She had not asked to borrow it. She had not said where she was going. Her mother, who might have been upset by the rest of her involvement, would have enjoyed the mortuary part, and wanted all details.

The details were reasonably gruesome. There were no tiled walls and slabs and running sluices, as Charlie had feared, but the purple hangings, rushed from some church, splotched here and there with candle wax, were almost worse, and the flowers were heavy scented. The coffins were that terrible suggestive shape of a man with folded arms, cruciform, final. On each one was an aluminium nameplate, made from the same metal used to build the airship. There were names on fourteen of them. The rest were inscribed. 'To the memory of an unknown airman, who died on October 5th.'

Charlie walked with the Clives through the rooms where the coffins were laid. Peter's name was not on any of them. In a side room, they were handed a labelled parcel. The number on the parcel corresponded to the number on one of the coffins. Inside that coffin was – what? A leg? A piece of bone? Some part of Peter's body near which someone had found his bent and blackened silver cigarette case, the twenty-first birthday inscription still half-decipherable.

'If you would kindly identify . . .'

Mrs Clive did not say anything. Charlie could not look at her face. Mr Clive was staring at the cigarette case, his skin waxen, his nose blue and pinched at the nostrils, as if he were dead himself. He groped out towards Charlie as if he were going to faint. She gripped his arm, feeling that her fingers hurt him, and was able to nod and say, 'That's Peter's,' because she had seen it before at the side of the road when the cigarette had passed like a kiss between his lips and hers.

The first I knew of all this carry-on was when I saw Charlie at Westminster Hall at the Lying-in-State.

I had gone up to Westminster in my lunch hour, along with thousands of my fellow citizens to whom the disaster was both a national and personal catastrophe. It hit us all like the untimely death of a king, like an assassination, an outrageous cruelty that spoiled everything just when we were going so well.

Now, more than thirty years later, it's easy to see that the R101 was almost bound to crash somewhere between England and India. It was only a question of where. But in 1930, we had set such great hopes on this impossible blimp. It was our stake in the air age, at once invincible and mysterious, half god and half technology, like the first space capsule. When I heard that it was gone, on the wireless I had made out of scrap parts in my bedroom, I remember thinking, Oh no. Oh no.

I knew nobody on board, nor anyone connected with them. I had not seen Charlie since the Garfield Hall weekend, and did not even know about her thumb. I hardly saw her father in the drawing office, and when I did he never talked to anyone of anything but work.

And yet the loss of the airship felt like mine. I went downstairs in my pyjamas to my dauntless little mother, measuring tea into a pot with a face that counted every leaf, and told her, 'It caught fire. Everyone is dead.'

She said, 'Don't talk nonsense, James, it can't have,' which had been her instinctive reaction to anything I told her from the day I could speak.

But when Margaret came down and agreed with me (you two, always banding together), my mother began to dab behind her rimless glasses with the corner of the apron that she wore too long, to make her look a drudge. When the newsboys began crying the extra edition of the *Express* in the streets, she ran out and bought one, and stood by the gate of our horrid slice of house in Holland Road, dabbing her eyes again as she read, and talking to the neighbours and the passers-by, for everyone knew it was a national disaster, and all right to talk.

Hardly anything else was talked about all week, at work, at home, and in casual contacts with strangers in shops and buses and trains. So when Joey asked me about lunch on Friday, I said, 'I thought of going up to Westminster.'

He did not say, 'You're mad,' and stare as if I was a freak, as he usually did for any idea he had not thought of first. He said, 'I'll go with you.' We had to go. We could not stay away.

Nor could anyone else in London, it seemed. We came out of the Underground to find the pavements thronged with people, the roadway filled with cars and vans. Everyone had come to Westminster to see the dead, or to see those who came to see them. A police car with a loudspeaker was giving calm

127

directions just off-tone, so that you could not hear the words. Policemen on big-footed horses were directing traffic. The broad line of quiet, dark-clad people stretched beyond the Abbey far along the river. Joey and I had to walk halfway to Lambeth Bridge before we could join the end of it.

'We'll be late back,' Joey said.

'We shouldn't go back at all. Almost everything else has stopped. Even the BBC.'

'Not Lambert's.'

'I'm taking the afternoon off anyway. I'll work tonight.'

'Work tonight? You must be mad.'

'I need to keep my job,' I said smugly.

'I need to keep Lorna,' he said unhappily, pulling down the corners of his wide clown mouth. But he stayed with me, shifting from one stork leg to the other, for the hour and a half it took us to shuffle inside the doorway of Westminster Hall.

It had been sunny outside, but within it was dusk. From the steps, you could look down into that ancient stone chamber over the heads of the people in front of you to where the coffins lay under their Union Jacks, framed with flowers, guarded by men in Air Force uniform, heads down, eyes blank. The first shock was that there were so many. Forty-eight is not a big number, but in terms of coffins, and in peacetime, it was shocking.

At the bottom of the steps, the people divided like a stream round a rock, to walk past the dead on either side. Women wept. Men looked solemn, children bewildered. Some people stared very hard at the coffins all the way, as if they could see through the flags and through the wood to what was within. Some did not turn their heads. They shuffled past as if they were in a breadline or a useless protest march, and did not look at all at what they had come to see before they passed out at the other end of the hall.

Just before I was off the steps and on to the stone flags, I saw a little group of people come through a side door, ushered in by a tall official person who bent his neck to them like a civil giraffe.

VIPs. Parents. Wives. They were brought up to the start of the slow procession and filtered in a few places in front of me.

Excuse me. Thank you. The man in front of me took an exaggerated step back to demonstrate his sympathy for the creeping little group.

One of them was Charlie, in a dark blue coat like a school-girl, and a fur hat with a Scottish flash on the side.

I walked behind her all down the hall, trying to think about the dead and the tragedy of their sacrifice, trying to form a prayer for them, which became no more than a mechanical Our Father in my head. I felt I had wasted my hour and a half, because I could not give my proper tribute.

At the end corner by the RAF officer, the group was taken out of the line again. I stepped aside and touched Charlie's arm. 'What's this?'

'Oh, James.' She had been crying. She looked as distressed as the other women in her little party.

'Who are they?' I whispered.

'I'll tell you some day. Don't tell anyone.' She breathed against my face, her own brand of sweet healthy Charlie breath. 'Don't tell anyone you saw me here.'

'Wasn't that the old man's daughter?' Joey whispered when I rejoined him in the line going out. 'What on earth?—'

'Just a girl I know. Someone's sister.' In those days, going through a reasonably virtuous stage (it didn't last), I was very good at lying without technically lying. Later, after I married Bubbles and after that with the BBC, I found out that if you wanted to lie, it is more honest to do it thoroughly.

After what had happened at the mortuary, there was no question about whether Charlie should go to the funeral.

She could have Gordon's place at the memorial service. Even for the brief fame of a reserved seat at the front, he was not going to allow God that much advantage by sitting through a religious service, although since he boasted there was no God, there could be no advantage.

'You'll not even come to the grave then?' his father asked, 'and pay respects to your brother? What will he think?'

'Oh, come off it, Dad, for Christ's sake. Don't start that now. It's more than a person can stand.'

And so Charlie went to St Paul's in her mother's Persian lamb glengarry, and sat under the dome two rows behind the Prime Minister and Mr Baldwin. Mrs Clive saw the Prince of Wales. It gave her the strength not to weep until everyone stood to sing 'Rock of Ages', a guaranteed tear-jerker in that splendid place at the best of times.

As the hymn swelled up into the vaulted spaces, the tuneful dominating the tone-deaf so that the mass voice rose pure and beautiful, a pigeon flew down to meet it from the dome and out along the nave. Holy Ghost? the journalists were already writing in their minds. Peter, Mr Clive's mind said as he bowed his lean grey head.

'We humbly leave in thy fatherly keeping . . .'

On Saturday, Charlie went with them for the burial. They had been given the choice of walking with the procession from Westminster Hall to Euston, or riding in a Government car. Sir Henry Munsing, who had taken off for Leicestershire by train on Friday evening, to be out of the way before the streets filled with what the Press called mourners and he called idle gapers, had even offered the Clives the use of his Daimler, complete with chauffeur and carnations.

'Take it,' Gordon advised. 'You'll never get the chance to sit in it again.'

'I'll walk,' his mother said, her lips set tight, as if she were already footing it over the wood blocks. 'I've said I'll walk, and walk I shall.'

'You'll never make it with those veins of yours,' Rita said knowledgeably. Coming from a mother who had borne ten children, she was an expert on varicose veins and white leg and prolapses of all kinds. 'As well ask me to walk all the way.' She sighted forward and down to where she could not see her feet. 'With these legs I've got.'

Charlie wished she would have the baby and shut up about it, although that would be only the beginning of a whole new saga of moans – little terror . . . if you had my nights . . . you

130

hold him, Mum, he's like to break my back – until she got pregnant again and could go back to her swollen legs.

'I'm walking with Dad,' Mrs Clive said. 'I'll walk behind my boy.'

She walked between her husband and Charlie slowly, funereally, in the two-mile long cortège between the mass of silent people on the pavements. They had not massed like that since the coronation of King George V. On that glad occasion, they had grumbled and squabbled and annoyed the police and wondered if it was worth the wait. I can't see a thing. Some people are born pushers. If you go to the WC now, you'll lose your place and there'll be all that wait for nothing. Shut up your bawling, Arold, or I'll shut it for you.

Now they stood patient and tractable along Whitehall and the Strand, watching without expression the endless line of slow-pacing horses, each drawing one coffin on an Army wagon, the lorry loads of flowers, the bands in slow time, the frock-coated dignitaries, the whey-faced women walking in unsuitable shoes, the men of Mr Clive's generation marching with medals on their coats as if they were in a parade of the Old Contemptibles.

Halfway round the Aldwych, Mrs Clive said, 'My legs!'

'Bear up, Nelly,' her husband muttered out of the side of his set soldier face. 'You can't drop out now. Pick 'em up, dear. Left, left, hup, right, hup.'

She marched on out of step with him, her ankles beginning to turn over her best shoes. At the top of Southampton Row, she staggered and took Charlie's arm, her hand grabbing like a claw, her breath whistling through her reddening nose.

'You all right?'

'I'll manage, dear. Don't rush me.'

The tightly packed crowd stared at her along the Euston Road.

Once in the train she was all right. She sat in the corner and fanned herself with her black wool gloves, while her cheeks paled from purple to their normal flush. She was able almost to enjoy the journey. At every station, at Barnet, Hatfield, Stevenage, Hitchin, people were lined up on the platforms three or four deep, hats off, medals worn, ex-servicemen at rigid attention. All along the line, through the back streets and the suburbs, through the stubble fields of Hertfordshire and the acres of cabbage stalks and the great black ploughland of Bedfordshire, already turned for winter sowing, they stood in groups by the railway to see the funeral train come through. There were faces at all the back windows of the smoked brick terrace houses, small flags at half mast on bean poles in the strips of garden. Schoolgirls like Charlie's stood in uniform at the end of their hockey field, hair and coloured girdles blowing, screwing up their faces as children do outdoors, even without sun. Men with ploughs stopped their horses in silhouette halfway down a furrow. Men with tractors had climbed down and pulled off their caps to stand at attention beside them. At a bridge over a busy street, women were standing below on the pavement, pink sea of faces raised, children at their skirts forgotten.

Nelly Clive sat by the window, the black sailor tilted slightly askew from leaning against the glass, and watched the people all along the line. Now and then she bowed imperceptibly and half raised her hand without knowing she was doing it, like Queen Mary giving a muted royal acknowledgement.

From Bedford station, where the crowds were even greater than in London, they drove between thick rows of people like hedges down the road to St Mary's church at Cardington.

An enormous grave had been dug by the gate of the churchyard, lined with grass and flowers. Charlie and Dad and Nelly stood with the mourners at the edge of it, and watched as the coffins were carried down and laid in rows. Bombers flew overhead. Photographers took pictures. A newsreel camera mounted on a car peered above the dark sea of overcoats and bowlers and homburgs, which the men kept on as long as they could in the damp October dusk, with the Englishman's fear of something happening to his head. The band played 'Abide with me'. The flags on the coffins were strewn with rose petals. The great airship sheds and the mooring tower stood away beyond the trees.

'I am the resurrection and the life,' the Bishop said, but what was here to resurrect? Cremation might have been kinder, to finish the work of the hydrogen fire. Charlie stared into the pit of death and tried to make it mean something. But there were too many coffins. The carpet of flags and flowers was too impossibly wide. Beside her, clinging to her arm, her great handbag like a sporran, Mrs Clive was whimpering softly. Most of the other women were crying, and some of the men's faces were bloated with the pain of tears they could not shed.

The rifles cracked, the bugles sounded, and presently the people began to move away. If a man you loved was lying down there, how could you turn your back and leave him to be filled over, patted down, obliterated with earth?

'I thought it was a very nice service,' Mrs Clive said on the way home, tightening her lips and nodding her head once, as she did when a kitchen task was complete.

'You've got to say that for the British,' her husband agreed. 'They know how to put on a show.'

'How can it be nice?' Charlie asked. 'How can it help?'

Mrs Clive said, 'Don't ask me riddles.' She thought for a moment and then said, 'It makes you realize. It's true and you've got to put up with it.'

On to the next thing. That's it then, Charlie old chump. There was always nothing and there's nothing now. When she got home, she would take the newspaper parcel out of the drawer and burn it.

There, that's done; a chunk of the past recaptured. How long ago it seems – it was – and how naïve that the whole country should have got so worked up about forty-eight people dying in a dirigible, when there were so many bigger and bolder air crashes in store for us.

Most of those I have forgotten, but the R101 has come back very clearly. I suppose because my brain was young and muscular when I stored it away. I read about all the obsequies at the time, of course, and listened to the BBC announcer describing them in that pious, respectful voice I later learned to do myself for holocausts and fighters lost and passing of the famous. Because of the mysterious meeting with Charlie in Westminster Hall, and because of that picture of her that appeared in the Sunday paper, I was involved, and a lot of the funeral details stayed with me.

Before I wrote about Charlie and the Clives going through that somewhat farcical ordeal, I dug into the attic trunk of letters and photographs of people long forgotten, and found again that famous newspaper picture of Charlie at the graveside in St Mary's churchyard, Cardington.

She is standing in the front line of the group of mourners who are looking down into that swimming pool of a grave where the coffins lie so bravely shrouded, as if the Union Jack were an absolution. In the line of black trousers and black stockings, Charlie is wearing light stockings, and what you can see of her legs, which was not much in that year, is not pin-up material. Her legs were strong and muscular, but always nicely shaped. She is standing awkwardly foursquare in this picture, like a child's drawing where the legs come out of the corners of a torso.

The women in the group wear cloche hats, and long fur lapels on tubular coats. The men sport untidy moustaches and mournful hats, like a railwaymen's outing. Very period. Mr Clive is respectable in a straightaway homburg, overcoat very long, hands at sides. Mrs Clive is much shorter than Charlie, with an Eliza Doolittle hat and a neck-piece of nameless fur, the great black leather handbag inseparable as a diplomatic pouch. Charlie is taller than the other women in the front line. Her shoulders are square in a rather military coat with big buttons and a low belt. Her hair is drawn back from her face under the Persian lamb fore-and-aft. She is staring down at the coffins as if Lazarus arose there.

Folding the picture back into the original creases that Charlie made when she put it in the envelope with the other cuttings about the R101, I put it in my wallet and took it with me last week when I drove through Aylesbury to Cardington to see what the grave looks like now.

It is still a haunted place, even after thirty-seven years of plane loads of people falling incandescent out of the sky, and lighter-than-air only a stunt in comic period films. The land here is flat, and from miles away you can still see those two sinister great sheds. The mooring tower is gone, but the sheds remain, cocoons for a giant. When you see the sheds close to from the road between Bedford and Cardington, you realize how big the airship was. The ground crew man-handling the lumbersome thing across the field to the mooring tower must have looked like ants moving a pound of liver sausage.

'We saw it go off.' An elderly lady in a woollen hat and little boots was pottering with jam-jars in the graveyard. 'We saw it go off and I said to my mother, "It's not raising right." I said that. There was a lot thought the same, mind you.'

Of course. This event was no different from any other in the amount of people who were wise after it. Aside from Mr Clive, who fancied himself a seer, there were people all over England who said, 'I knew it,' although they had cheered its going, just as my lady in the woollen hat had probably cheered it away from Cardington.

HERE LIE THE BODIES
OF
48 OFFICERS AND MEN

WHO PERISHED IN
HM AIRSHIP R101
AT
BEAUVAIS FRANCE
OCT 5 1930

I stood in the place where Charlie stands in the picture looking down into the pit. It is neat grass and paving now, with all the names on a big stone tomb in the middle.

'We keep it nice and clean,' the lady said, making a house-proud mouth, bustling about on the stone rim picking up fallen leaves as if they were threads on her carpet. 'Does someone you know lay there?'

'Yes,' I said, because I did see Peter once in Scotland, and I know him, oh how well I know him, from Charlie. For a long time she would not talk about him, but much later, after we were married, it began to come out, painfully at first, then like a broken dam. 'Don't let me,' she would say. 'Stop me, it isn't fair on you.' But I let her talk. I have always been what they call a good listener (said in women's magazines to be the key to a successful social life, but not so, I testify). I draw thoughtfully on a cigarette and nod and don't interrupt. People kill themselves trying to think of intelligent interpolations, or comments about paintings when the artist starts turning them round from the studio wall, but a nod and a grunt will do quite well.

They hold a memorial service every year in St Mary's church where the R101 ensign hangs on the wall, torn and battle-scarred like the fairy flag of the McCleod at Dunvegan. The vicar keeps it going because it gets a few into the church, but nobody much comes any more. Half a dozen relations. A handful of dirigible enthusiasts. 'Buffs, they call them,' my friend with the jam-jars said. 'Bit different from the funeral though. I can see them now, tens of thousands coming over those fields like a sea. Broke the hedges and crashed through people's gardens. They trampled all over my mother's marigolds.'

It began to rain. It always rains in this county, some time between dawn and dusk. I got into the car and drove back towards Bedford between the brick villas and the cabbage fields and the sour phallic stalks of Brussels sprouts. These flat wet market gardening landscapes are quite depressing. I like Oxfordshire much better.

Back in my own countryside, I stopped in at Kingsgrove churchyard to see my Charlie, like polishing off all one's sick visiting in one day. I was glad to get home. It was a long day for me. I don't enjoy driving any more now that it is merely a grim business of getting from one place to another. In the old days of which I write, when there was no driving test and the twenty mile an hour speed limit had recently been abolished, it was a sport, and, as the Duchess said on her wedding night, much too good for the lower classes.

Rules were made for the other chap. The pedestrian was a serf, the policeman bloody impertinent if he put up a hand to you at crossroads. We howled about the new traffic lights, until we discovered what sport it was to race each other for the getaway. Proportionately, I suppose we killed about the same number of ourselves as we do now, but we had more fun doing it.

After I got home, I ate a piece of toast standing up at the drop-leaf shelf which serves as a kitchen table and went to bed early with a whisky and nothing else, which is one of the squalid things you do as a widower. You also wake early, askance at the long day ahead. With nobody breathing warmly beside you, you tend to get up and wander about with your pyjama trousers drooping, rubbing your unshaven chin and yawning toothless in a repellent way and making tea with a teabag in last night's unwashed cup.

Now I have more purpose when I get up and start the day. My disordered table is ready. My view waits all in place before my window, the shadows still long on the sparkling grass of Gregory's meadow. The elms are yellowing and the lone oak on the hillside drying into the brown it will wear all winter. The capped heads glide bicycling to school along the top of my old wall. Sometimes I put on a dressing-gown or an old jersey and am still there in my sagging pyjama trousers when the heads bicycle back at lunchtime. We have school dinners at the new secondary school in Kingsgrove, a shilling a throw or free if you are needy, but some of the village mothers make their children come home, in case anybody might think they were on the free dinner list.

Mrs Meagan caught me yesterday afternoon still not dressed when she stopped in with one of her lop-sided sponge cakes and some shirts she had ironed.

'What in all conscience has become of you now?'

'I was so busy, I didn't take time to go up and dress.' I wrapped my old camelhair dressing-gown more modestly round me and grinned up at her with my tramp's chin. I had my teeth in, because the bathroom is downstairs in this house, a damp and draughty lean-to built on at the back after the war.

'I'll make your tea,' she said, 'and you can clock off. Sufficient unto the evil is the day thereof.'

137

She asked me, as she always does, for she is cautiously interested in my literary efforts. 'What did you write in your book today?'

'Funerals. All this.' I stacked up a sheaf of long yellow pages.

Mrs Meagan then told me that all the writing people of her acquaintance (she only knows the Bring Good Cheer, Hold So Dear Christmas card woman) put it all down on a typewriter. I retorted that the reason all those writers in Hollywood are shut away behind closed doors is that they are secretly writing long-hand on ruled pads with stubs of pencils. She replied that this is what is wrong with American films, and made me an egg sandwich to show she'd won.

THREE

THE PICTURE OF Charlie at the graveside with Mrs Clive hanging on her arm started a furore that kept everybody busy that Sunday.

Charlie had gone back to the cottage after the funeral. As soon as her mother saw the Sunday paper, she sent her a telegram: RING ME. She didn't but Mrs Lambert's telephone rang so many times before she even finished breakfast that it was noon before she got up and dressed and went down to Reggie's house on Camden Hill to discuss the peculiarities of his sister.

'But she didn't even *know* this man.' She had said this ten times with varying inflexions, pacing the carpet in buckled shoes, too wrought to settle. 'She must be even madder than we thought.'

'Perhaps she knew him better than she let on.' Reggie was in shaky shape. *Call It Springtime* had closed, and rehearsals for *Cornish Cream* did not start for a month, and he had a croaking cold. When he could not perform nor even sing, he felt himself lapsing into the negative person he really was. To strengthen the shell, he accepted every invitation to appear in public, to declare this or that open, to present prizes at talent shows or choose a beauty queen. Only by constantly whipping up Philip Lambert could he keep Reggie going.

'Not our Charlie. I'm sure she's a – well, you know, I don't think she has ever gone all the way.' Mrs Lambert liked to think she called a spade a spade, but all she did was boldly approach the words and then shy round them like a horse refusing a jump.

'Have you had her examined?' Reggie asked gloomily. 'I wouldn't put it past you, Mother dear.'

Midge said, 'Don't talk about Charlie like that. It's not fair,' meaning it for both of them, but directing it at her husband, since she was still a little unsure of her mother-in-law, swashbuckling today in her outrage over Charlie, in a highwayman cape and big swooping hatbrim over one of her splendid eyes.

'Everyone in London is talking about her like *everything*,' Mrs Lambert said. 'I had Hilda Munsing on the telephone from Leicestershire for half an hour telling me Charlie's been in and out of her basement hob-nobbing with the servants all week. She didn't know who she was until the picture came out and someone staying in their house recognized her. Sobbing into the grave on the arm of the Munsing's cook. Oh, it's too weird.'

'*Pas devant la bonne*,' Reggie said. The maid was in the room with sherry.

His mother said, 'Never mind about *la bonne*. She's seen the picture too, no doubt. What do you think of Miss Charlotte being plastered all over the front page, Joyce?'

'I thought it was very nice, Madam. We cut it out and pinned it on the wall downstairs where we keep the ones they show of the Master.'

'Fame comes to Charlotte Lambert.' Reggie sucked into sherry with a pettish lip. 'There'll be an offer from Hollywood.'

'And in my hat!' his mother raved. 'Arm in arm with the Munsing's cook . . .'

At St Gabriel's, the photograph raised an even greater stir. By Monday, when Charlie went back to work, the girls had all seen it. In a trice they assumed her only boyfriend lay dead, and immediately labelled the picture 'Lottie's Last Chance'.

They pounced. 'What were you doing at the funeral, Miss Lambert?'

'A man I knew was killed.'

'A man I knew,' they told each other, rushing away to spread the news. 'Old Lottie's last chance. Talk about the irony of fate.' They pored over the picture in cloakrooms, under desk lids, in the lavatories. 'Lottie's Last Chance.'

Cara Miles was waiting by the side door as Charlie walked in at the gate and across the netball court.

'Where's Mick the Miller?'

'Oh – being tuned up.' She could not possibly begin to explain. 'I came by bus.'

'That was a lovely picture of you in the paper.' Looking up, with her mouth hanging ecstatically open, she was all teeth and wires. 'My mother and I talked about it. We thought you looked so sad. Did you lose someone dear to you?'

Charlie nodded. If that was what she wanted.

'Oh, it's terribly sad.' Cara was thrilled. 'I won't tell anyone, I promise I won't, Miss Lambert.'

But the girls knew already. 'Lottie's Last Chance.' They had known about her thumb before they ever saw the chamois leather stump. Lottie Four Fingers she was now, and ever shall be, world without end, amen. Could she hold a tennis racket? Would she be able to catch ye beane bagge? A cripple now, forsooth, that's what St Gab's had to come to.

Etty said, 'You do look a sketch, my dear, in that picture. Who's that ghastly old char you're with? You've got to tell me simply everything about it.'

There was a time when they lived together and depended on each other when Charlie would have told her something, at least. Now it was different. Etty was brusque and impatient since she had discovered that marriage was only the beginning of the story, not the end, as the magazines had told her. She set no more store by Charlotte's ideas. So Charlie only told her, 'It was just this man. I know his parents.'

'Don't tell me then,' Etty said, huffed. 'See if I care.'

Mrs Baxter, still nervous about the mutilated thumb, offered sympathy in this new loss and asked if Charlie would rather miss gym class, as if she had her monthlies.

It was a dual-purpose suggestion, because she had forgotten to tell Mrs Fossick that Charlie was coming back. When she went to the gym for the first drill class, Charlie found Mrs Fossick corseted into an ancient gym tunic, gnarled knees exposed, hairband low on brow, knotted legs groggy but resolute, a hole surreptitiously slashed in the side of her plimsoll to let the bunion breathe. The yawning early class, hitching up black stockings, snapping knicker elastic, watched fascinated as Lottie Four Fingers had it out with the Fossil.

During her brief resurrection, Mrs Fossick had somehow persuaded Mrs Baxter to let her start a programme of country

141

dancing. 'We owe it to dear old England,' Mrs Fossick said, matching gums with Mrs Baxter's vivid set.

Dear old England at the time was lurching into a Keep Fit craze. Politicians had recently dug up the recurrent idea that the country was going to pot and that the health of the nation must be brought back to what they imagined it used to be.

Dr Banting's name became a verb as the slimming fad caught on, the women weighed themselves into neurosis before and after every meal and took castor oil if the pointer flickered up. The carthorse herds who had trundled round the wood at the Holland Park roller rink became flocks who swooped and scrambled on the ice at Richmond and Westminster, and the sale of gored kilts went up.

Hiking in divided skirts, bowling greens and clock golf in public parks, sunbathing at George Lansbury's Lido by the scummy reaches of the Serpentine ... The country has gone amusement mad, huffed the retired colonels and epistolatory vicars. Motor-cars and talking kinema and mechanical music ... and now girls and men lie about half naked like herring on a griddle.

Country dancing was to be St Gabriel's contribution to the Keep Fit movement. All the staff would join in, and Charlie would prepare a programme for the parents at Christmas.

So twice a week after school, those of the staff and girls who had not managed to sneak away were herded into the gym to jog through 'Rufty Tufty' and 'Gathering Peascods' and 'Haste to the Wedding'. Mrs Girodias bashed out the repetitious tunes on the piano and Mademoiselle played a thin fiddle. The girls sulked and kicked each other on the ankles. Miss Perrott jerked like a drunken marionette. Mrs Baxter pranced knee-high in a purple toga. The only hope was that one of them would have a fit or a heart attack and the whole thing would be called off.

Late one afternoon Charlie was in among the weaving sets, turning them the right way, separating them like a boxing umpire, when Miss Northcote appeared in the doorway with a man in a belted raincoat and trousers well above his shoes. He carried a soft felt hat and was recognizable anywhere in that film-going age as a detective.

142

'Miss Lambert, please!' Miss Northcote's bass cut through the piano and the fiddle and the feet. Scandal. Thrills. 'Gathering Peascods' broke up in disorder, the pebbles of chatter stinging Charlie's back as she followed the raincoat down the corridor to the office.

Miss Northcote wanted to stay. It was her office, but as she began to lower her buttocks to the chair, the detective held the door open, so she had to push herself up again and say, 'I'll leave you to discuss this in private,' to show it was her idea and to make it look as bad as possible for Charlie.

Next morning, everyone was surprised and disappointed to find Lottie Four Fingers at prayers and not in gaol. No scandal then to stir the turgid waters of November. 'I lost a piece of jewellery,' Charlie explained. 'He was making inquiries.'

'You haven't got any jewellery,' Etty said. The girls told each other, 'Her nest-egg, put by for her lonely old age.'

The detective had told Charlie that the black Vauxhall had been stolen from the garage of a house near Birmingham. It had belonged to a retired Army officer. He was dead, and his family were in a lawsuit over his property. The house was empty. That was why the theft had not been reported. The car was now returned to its garage. And that, said the detective, looking at Charlie with official expressionless eyes, would have to be the end of that.

'Aren't you going to do anything about it?'

The detective spread his hands and almost smiled. 'Under the circumstances, no. Naturally, no.'

'But I—' Charlie frowned in front of the confused, bewildering images. Peter picking the lock of a garage in the dark. A suitcase full of loot. Peter on the run – no wonder he had never come back for the car. He knew it was stolen. He had stolen it himself. The coil of hair?

'But you see, I—' with her mouth open, she looked across Miss Northcote's desk at the detective, at ease in Miss Northcote's broad chair, his raincoat bulging out over the tight belt as if he had Miss Northcote's bosom.

'Of course, it's understood that you didn't know about the car. You have nothing to worry about.' He stood up, and the moment for telling him anything was gone.

'What was done or not done,' the detective said, 'is of no consequence now. He died after all,' he added without emotion, 'for his country.' He opened the door quickly and his face showed neither surprise nor disappointment at not finding Miss Northcote at the keyhole.

When Mr Lambert went to the airship works at Cardington to collect Charlie's car, he eventually found it behind an unused storage shed at the far edge of the field, one tyre flat and the number plates missing.

'What's the form now?' he said, with the owlish look that settled on his face when he thought of the Law. 'Am I supposed to report this to someone?'

He jerked back, putting up a hand to his bull's-eye spectacles as Charlie flared at him. 'Leave him alone! He's dead – leave him alone!'

And she herself was able now to leave Peter alone. Dead. Buried. Sliding farther away from her as the weeks went by. One day, allowing herself to conjure him up, she found that she could not even see his face. Just a vague image of vitality, brown skin, thick jersey, the ghost of a creature smell.

She never looked any more at the newspaper picture of him dressed as a steward. She never looked at the bundle of hair. She did not throw it away. She hid it more secretly.

High up her bedroom wall, at one side of the whitewashed chimney bricks, a tiny panelled door led into a corner cupboard which ran back to an angle behind the chimney. Tall as she was, she had to stand on tiptoe to reach round and push the newspaper bundle on to the brick and mortar rubble at the back of the cupboard.

She climbed back with relief into the unexacting rut of school, and her shut-away life in the cottage, pottering a little with distemper and paint, cobbling an unrectangular curtain, not achieving much, for she had a whole lifetime to feather her nest. She weeded out the duds and cripples and delinquents to form some sort of rickety gym team for the Berks and Bucks competition in the new year. She seeded a hockey team from girls who could at least be trusted to turn up on Saturday mornings for a match. She choked Mrs Baxter off putting ribbons and bells on the 'Rufty Tufty' dancers. She tried to start lacrosse, but the parents would not buy the sticks. Olive Bartlett came clumsily over a leather horse and sprained her wrist and told everyone it was Charlie's fault, so Cara took Olive's history essay out of the homework slot and burned it. Everything normal. Very soothing.

Charlie drove the bull-nosed Morris with two jerseys under her coat as the winter seized up into January frosts, the black Vauxhall gradually sliding off the canvases of her mind, like Peter's image. She did not worry any more about who had stolen it, nor why he had been driving back to Cardington from the north. Been to my mother's, he said. He could have been to the Munsings' house in Leicestershire. Always so kind, her Ladyship. She let him have old pullovers and blankets for his chilly quarters. He could have wanted not to tell Charlie that his mother was someone's servant.

She never told his family about the car. She hardly came to London. She did not see them until Christmas, when she took them a cake and had to admire Rita's baby, which had features twice too big for its face and sour milk stiffening on the front of its green woollen coat.

She had a glass of passable Madeira which Sir Henry had given Mr Clive – 'He never forgets us, doesn't Sir Henry,' as if they were the shoemaker's elves – and ate Dundee cake (her own set carefully aside to be preserved like a Chinese egg) off the floral tablecloth from Lady Munsing – 'Such a kind thought of Her Ladyship.' Charlie had dreaded coming back to this kitchen where she had shared their grief. But Peter's photograph had a gay holly spray on the corner of the frame, and when they spoke of him it was comfortably, without emotion, as if he were only away on a trip.

All went well until Dad Clive suddenly swivelled round to face the scullery and said quite quietly, 'Yes, it's there. It's there again, you see. Very nice that it should be, on this festive occasion.'

'Where dear?' His wife peered.

'On the doorknob again. Very distinct. Thank you,' he said to nobody.

'What is it?' Hairs rose on the back of Charlie's neck.

'Peter's face.'

'His *face*!'

'On the knob, dear. It etches there, you see, on that white doorknob.'

'I don't see it.' If she did, she would know she was as mad as he was.

'Do you see it?' she asked Mrs Clive, who did not answer that, but told her equably, 'All kinds and conditions of people he sees, does Dad. Shakespeare, Charles Dickens. He saw Field-Marshal Haig's horse once, and once he thought his late Majesty came, but I don't think so.'

'You mustn't doubt, my dear,' Mr Clive said gently. 'It's not kind when people take the trouble.'

'I don't think Edward VII would,' she said. 'Not on a doorknob.'

'Knock it off, you two,' Gordon said. 'It makes Rita nervous, and she can't feed the baby as it is.'

'I can if I choose. It's just that Trufood is more modern. Nobody feeds their baby any more.'

'Sheila Kay does.'

'Oh, Sheila Kay.' She was a well-chewed bone. 'She would.'

'Are you saying she's not a good mother?' Gordon lowered his head and jutted the prognathous jaw, greasy brow receding sharply into the oiled hair.

'I'm saying she's a peasant, if you like. Opening her blouse in my lounge. Sheila Kay...' Rita got up and went to where the ugly baby lay in a grandiloquent pram that had been lugged down the area steps and along the stone passage into the kitchen, and rocked it fiercely enough to produce a sour wail.

Dad was up and examining the doorknob. 'There, well it's gone, thanks to you two. Raised voices don't help, you know.'

When Charlie got home, she looked at all her doors to make sure that they had latches. No knobs. That night, she lay and stared through the darkness towards the little cupboard door. It had a tiny wooden knob, dark and rough, not a flat white porcelain surface like Lady Munsing's scullery door. But she wished very much that Dad Clive had not done that. All had been going well until he started about the doorknob. The next

146

day, she unscrewed the little wooden knob and threw it away.

School reopened with a talk from Mrs Baxter on waxing buds while a blizzard hit the windows, a notice from Mrs Rivett about cigarette stubs in the staff washbasins, and the atmosphere of hopeless ennui common to all spring terms.

Charlie was not in London again until the first night of Reggie's play, *Cornish Cream*.

Reggie was a young man about town who has inherited a farm in Cornwall from a dead uncle, Uncle Josiah, red and whiskered in a portrait over the fireplace with one eye which winked, a jape that was not hilarious, but better than the father-in-law's descending trousers in *Call It Springtime*. There were two girls, one a dairymaid, one the daughter of the local squire, and a young baritone with rolled-up sleeves and a lot of caked brown makeup. He works on the farm and resents Reggie and hits him – smack with the clapped hands – at the end of the first act, and catches him kissing his dairymaid at the end of the second act, and so does the squire's daughter from behind another flat of bushes, and – all right, no need to torture ourselves with the third act.

There were half a dozen harmless songs, one with words by Quentin, a chorus who doubled as villagers and weekend guests from London, and one very good number, 'We doan't want noa furriners here', with Reggie in a blazer at the side of the stage singing in counterpoint, 'This is my home. Here I belong'. It got an encore, and bravos from Mrs Lambert. She was apt to make an exhibition of herself at first nights, with a lot of jewellery and furs and loud talk in the foyer, which was why Charlie sat moon-faced, disguising her pride in Reggie and his melodious throat, throbbing and boyish in an open-necked shirt.

At the party on stage afterwards, she and Reggie's wife stayed in the background and made sour jokes about the rest of the cast. The actress who played the squire's daughter was a nutcracker who looked ten years older close to, but the dairymaid was a young newcomer, big-eyed and breathless with success and Philip Lambert.

'Poor thing, she doesn't know,' Midge said, 'that this is as much as she'll get from him. Kisses in public and Darling Rosalie, I'm *madly* in love with her!'

'Why are you always so calm?' Charlie asked. They were sitting with Quentin on a sofa at the side of the stage, their legs stuck out in front of them and their toes turned up like Dutch dolls, drinking champagne while the crowd seethed round Reggie and Nutcracker and Darling Rosalie. 'If it were my husband, I'd go in there and bash him. Here I belong or no Here I belong.'

'Because I know him.' Midge spoke in her quick, husky voice, staring at the points of her doll shoes. 'He's pretty safe. It all goes into his voice and his acting.'

'He doesn't act,' Quentin complained, 'and if your mother-in-law had had his adenoids out the proper time, he wouldn't even sing.'

'Well, you know what I mean.'

'I don't,' said Charlie. 'You've got children.'

'Oh that.' Midge screwed up her neat features. 'Anyone can have children. Even Quentin could, if he wanted.' In those fast, emancipated days, women still could not discuss sex with men, which was why homosexuals were welcome companions.

'Could you?' At last someone was going to tell Charlie some of the things she could never ask her mother, who had sneakily closed the whole subject years ago with 'Let's not be a bore about it'. But the promising conversation was cut off by the voice of Philip Lambert, starrily projecting. 'Needless to say, the only people who've not congratulated me are my wife and my sister.' Smart people with glistening witty lips turned to focus on them.

Midge got up neat and poised to kiss him, and said, 'I was saving it for home,' which sprung a nice cosy vision of them in bed together, and sucks to Rosalie. Charlie fell over her big feet and said something reasonably boorish, and heard Quentin tell a woman who came to sit down beside him that he had written all the lyrics.

Next day was a school holiday. Charlie and Midge walked in the Park with Weezie and Jojo, whose pretty names were Louise and Jonas. A magazine photographer who recognized Midge took their picture on a bridge over the Serpentine. 'Not me,' said Charlie, who had had enough of her picture in the paper. She was wearing a dark blue school macintosh and a beret, with two plaits fastened by rubber bands and her ox-blood golf brogues with great fringed flaps like turkey wattles. The photographer did not press the point.

In Hyde Park at that time, there had been set up a small bell tower with a carillon, which was destined for Wellington in New Zealand as a war memorial. It played in the Park for a while first, edifying the passers-by with 'Drink to Me Only' and 'Somewhere a Voice is Calling'. On Sundays, it played 'All Things Bright and Beautiful' and 'Land of Hope and Glory'. Through the windows at the top, you could see the man in his shirt sleeves with thin fluffy hair playing the clavier which rang out the tunes.

He was an old friend of Weezie and Jojo. When he started to play, they pranced at the foot of the tower, lifting their knees high, feet stuck out and hands like starfish, romping an antic dance in corduroy leggings and corduroy hats like basins. They made faces at the man in shirtsleeves, sticking out their tongues and pulling down the lining of their eyelids. He stuck his tongue out in return, and in a pause in 'My Hero', he made a long nose.

He made it at Charlie, who was gambolling with the children. They had raced ahead of Midge when the bells started to play, since she was not supposed to run since her pleurisy. She caught up with them, but the three of them ran from her again, shrieking and jumping and making car noises, Charlie a great ungainly child, swinging the littlest one high over the low rails along the paths, finally catching her foot on one and crashing to the ground with the children on top of her.

'You'll make a good mother some day,' Midge said, as they sat at the bottom of the Albert Memorial and waited for the children to run up the steps to cool their tongues on the smooth worn nose of one of the figures, which was a secret place for initiate London children to lick. 'I can't play with them roughly and Nanny can hardly pick up a pin.' (Charlie's and Barbara's Nanny, a bitching Uncle Tom who could lead no other life.) 'They love you being like a child with them.'

'A husband wouldn't.' Charlie reached her big brown hand

149

down to a dog who came to smell her own dog on her clothes.

'It depends who it is.'

'It isn't going to be anybody.' Charlie fondled the dog roughly, shutting her face against Midge. 'I'm through with men.'

'Already?'

Charlie was silent. She would never tell anybody, not even Midge. There was nothing to tell. In fifty years' time, when she was eccentric Miss Lambert, the witch of the village, with newspaper stuffed in the broken windows and the Monahan family crossing themselves as they hurried past her house at night, she would not even have a legendary past to explain it.

'In that case,' Midge said, 'if I was to die or something' – she laughed to carry it off – 'would you take my children?'

'What about Reg?'

'He could see them on Sundays. That's about all he does now. Would you, Char?'

'God forbid.' Charlie shied away from the emotion that underlay the small breathy voice. 'I've got a hundred rotters at the school to worry about.'

'Are you always going to stay at that school?' Midge asked, not disgustedly as the rest of the family did, but because she wanted to know.

'I suppose so.' Charlie got up as the children came hurtling down the steps at her, and caught them one in each hand, like cricket balls.

'Then I'll have to find you a man.' Midge reached her shoulder when she stood.

'Don't bother.' Charlie walked towards the road with the children, swinging their arms, dragging the little one almost legless. Outside the railings, Midge stopped a taxi going towards Kensington. Charlie walked off in the other direction, to Wilton Crescent.

Nobody answered the basement bell. It was twelve o'clock, the hour when Mrs Clive was always steaming and thrashing about with the lunch. Charlie had turned away and climbed the stone steps when the tall front door opened and the young nanny with pale hair and acne called down to her.

150

'There's no one here now but me and the children and Alice.' She was out of uniform, the same colour all over in an unimaginative beige dress, her hair sticking out as if she had spent the night in a hay loft.

'Who's cooking?' It was hard to imagine the house surviving without Nelly Clive operating the perpetually stoked range as deftly as the man at the keyboard of the carillon.

'One of the dailies.' She was a country girl, still blurred at the edges of voice and figure, even after a year of London with Lady Munsing. Charlie had scarcely seen her since her first visit on the night of the crash. She was an upstairs person, trays and messages carried back and forth by one of the up-and-down people like Alice or the parlourmaid. She hated Charlie, Gordon said, though he never saw her either, because she had been in love with Peter.

'But I hardly—' Charlie had begun when he first said that. She stopped, not sure what she wanted them to believe, and Gordon filled in with, 'Ho no, you bet, tell that to the Judge,' and other crude phrases of disbelief. 'No wonder that poor soppy girl hates you. She used to hang round Peter with the whites of her eyes all yellow, something sickening.'

Had Peter ever touched her? She looked hot and fleshy, as if she might smell.

'Where is everybody?'

The nanny did not come down the steps, nor invite Charlie in, so they shouted at each other from front door to pavement in the elegant crescent like women over a backyard fence in Houndsditch.

'Sir Henry's abroad. Lady M, she's up in Leicestershire for the point-to-points. Houseful of riding people, she has, so she's taken Cook with her, since the local woman isn't up to it all.'

'But Mrs Clive hates going up there. She doesn't like it in the country.'

'Oh well, that's her affair.' The nanny stared, without the capacity to visualize Nelly Clive chopping and stirring in a large raftered kitchen in the shires, with milk in cans and a row of top-boots along the wall.

'Is Mr Clive all right?'

'I dunno. He lost his job, didn't you know? Laid off at the New Year.'

'Oh, that's awful—'

'I dunno. There's thousands in the same boat, they say. He's lucky. He got something else.'

A tall spindly dog on a leash came between Charlie and the nanny, smelling at the railings, swerving to the lamp-post, zig-zagging the woman at the end of the leash as if it were exercising her.

'I wonder at him for taking it though,' the nanny was saying, her eyes close together, her shiny nose a spiteful little beak. 'Washing up in a prison canteen – there's some people would rather be on the dole.'

'Does he hate it?'

'I dunno. He only started this morning. I saw him go off though, when I was dressing Yolande for school. He looked as if they were going to lock him up and all.'

Poor Nature's Gentleman in a long wet apron, scraping fish-bones and gobs of fat and gristle that even the prisoners would not eat. Next Saturday, Charlie hurried back to Wilton Crescent and found him disconsolate, alone in the basement kitchen, reading the Sits. Vacant column which had been getting shorter as the country's days of hardship grew longer. He had been given his cards again. A trusty was to do his job. He was not wanted. Always the first to go, someone like you, Gordon had told him.

'Six months at the business school, that boy thinks he's Gordon Selfridge.' He put the long folds of chin in his hand and sighed, not at all his spry, gentle self, very dejected.

'Oh, I am sorry.' Charlie would have liked to bend and kiss him, but although he was her father's age, she did not like to without Mrs Clive there to oversee. 'Especially with your wife away. That's rotten.'

'There's many worse off though, Charlotte. There's many would be glad to have their wife in a place where she gets her food at least. There's many would be glad of one son in a good job and the other out of it all.'

'Don't talk like that.'

'Why not? His line of work – hotels, Pullmans, airships –

when there isn't the money to spend, it's the luxury trades are hit as hard as any, and rightly so. That was one reason Peter left the trains. It stuck in his throat to be bending over the table with the little pink lights on – Will you take buttered teacake, sir? – when he'd seen men marching outside Victoria who hadn't the price of a slice of bread, nor even a platform ticket.'

How strange it is that when you are writing, you constantly hear or read about things that relate to your theme. You are looking out for them, of course, but the fact remains that there they are, presenting themselves ready dressed, like film extras turning up for a re-make of *Ben-Hur* or *Quo Vadis*.

When I was in America after the war writing documentaries for radio and television in the days when they offered other fare besides galloping horses and suburban teenagers saying Gee Mom, every newspaper or magazine or conversation seemed to turn up a fact or an opinion about my current subject. And only last night, after writing about Mr Clive and the Sits. Vacant, I read in the evening paper that our unemployment figure today is over half a million, and that Edward Heath (Conservative Opposition leader, in case someone reads this ten years hence and hasn't a clue who he was) has called Wilson's government stupid, incompetent, weak and complacently extravagant.

Where have we heard all that before?

Ad nauseam, of course, from both sides, but specifically in 1931 when Dad Clive was only one of more than a million and a half unemployed, and Churchill called Ramsay MacDonald a Boneless Wonder, which got him left out of the National Government.

I also read last night some fatheaded complaint about there being fewer jobless women than jobless men, and where have we heard *that* before?

Again, *ad nauseam*, and again, I remember, during that dark year of hunger and dying babies in the mill towns and colliery villages, when women who worked to help their men or help themselves were accused of taking bread out of the mouths of those who had 'sacrificed careers sixteen years ago in order that those very same women, and their mothers, might sleep safely in their beds', and so on and so on.

We can laugh about MacDonald now, with his moustache which meandered off-centre like his rich Gaelic oratory, but he stood at the time in his silk hat and frock coat like a spectre at the death march of the hopeless, sullen men who shuffled down the Strand with combs and tissue paper and lay down across the doorway of the Ritz.

One and a half million unemployed. Big figures that don't mean much, because it depends on how many people there were to start with and how many of them were employable. Statistics can prove anything, as the statisticians themselves have proved. But when you consider that this enormous statistic represented something like one able-bodied man in four in South Wales and the North Country, then you have some kind of picture.

I was very lucky to be securely employed at Lambert's, as my mother constantly reminded me, implying that I would never have got such a good safe job, paying enough to hand her three pounds a week, if she had not had influence with the boss. Sometimes she talked as if the boss had been in love with her all those years ago when the Kitteredges and the Lamberts had been young couples together with small children. Perhaps he was. All I knew was that he had not much use for her in the days when she used to telephone me at work to say that I must leave before the shops shut because she wanted washing soda, or some such damn fool thing of a plebeian enough nature to carry a reproach of her low estate. He was a decent enough man not to hold that against me. He liked me, that was what made it harder to tell him I wanted to leave than it was to tell my mother. She merely bit her lip and said something crisp about making beds and lying on them. Mr Lambert looked at me with those bull's-eyes that could be shrewd, benevolent or inscrutable according to how the light hit his thick spectacles, and I saw that he was hurt. It was not so much my leaving him and the opportunities he had given me. It was my leaving the work, the darling dwellings, abandoning Alma Tadema Mansions in Hendon before I even saw my louvred cabinet doors in place.

Joey was disappointed in me too ('You must be mad') because we always lunched together and went to the Dog and Fox after work, he to get malt strength in his long body, I to put off going home. Also because he went to the cinema practically every night of the week, roaming the distant suburban houses with Lorna, and could see no future in wireless.

I could not tell either of them that it was not only that the silver-haired queen at the BBC had come through with a definite offer. It was Bubbles.

Dear Bubbles. I like her so much better now than when I was in love with the girl she was, shrill and spoiled, breathless with the excitement of being herself. She ran agog through the corridors of my youth, admiring her reflection in the mirrors of my dumb enslavement. In her middle age, comically baffled by her politician husband and the son she would never have for me, who spends most of his time in Bechuanaland, she is so much more lovable. But now, of course, I am not in love with her, as I was when she was so unlovable. Which is typical of the havoc sex will play with your emotional judgement. I let her spoil large chunks of my early prime, both before and after I married her. Every time I thought I could give her up, and forced myself to avoid misery by staying miserably away, she would have a free evening (impossible!) or a row with Douglas Brodie or whoever was on her books at the time, and look round for Old Faithful. Even without the row or the free evening, she would be aware that a small detail was missing from the landscape, and crook her finger to get it back in again.

She had to be out every night. It did not matter where, nor whether she was bored, but to spend an evening at home, except when her parents had a dinner party (and sometimes even then) would spell oblivion. If she had once sat down after dinner and read a book or sewed a dress, she might have liked it, but she was not going to risk trying. She had to be out every night, with a man or with a crowd. Some of her friends were very grand and went to all the big balls and soaked the night away in champagne at Ciro's and played miniature golf at the Kit Kat. Some of them were quite awful, even by her standards, but they had cars and went out to the Ace of Spades and the Spider's Web and Skindles at Maidenhead, and pushed each other in the river with great vulgar splashes and would fall asleep driving home rather than get home before first light.

Since her twenty-first birthday, Bubbles was becoming a little passée, with all those high-powered eighteen-year-olds coming along. Her parents had spoken once or twice about secretarial school (death!) or a dressmaking course (*nobody* does). Although her father was no threat, her mother had been known to put down a buckled shoe, so Bubbles was toying with the idea of marriage. Most of the girls she knew were getting themselves engaged to young men in Piccadilly wine shops, or hard-boiled eggs like Rags Montcalm. Bubbles was trying to pin the gallant young motorist Douglas Brodie to some serious plans. She went out with me a few times so as not to be there when he came blasting up Fitzjohn's Avenue with the throttle open and an exhaust like a comet's tail.

I was in a ferment. I finally got her to go with me to a juvenile cousin's birthday party at Cambridge. I got her into the room of someone who was out being sick in a quad somewhere, and went for it.

She was totally unsurprised, neither angry nor willing. I should have realized then that it was a lost cause to try and arouse her, but with girls who look like that, you never believe it, and I pressed on. I even got large areas of her undressed. She lay back comfortably on that undergraduate's bed as if she were taking an afternoon nap.

Her breasts were marbled globes of opulence. Her white silken thighs were not jammed together, but relaxed and unconcerned, which was worse. I remember calling her a bloody telephone pole, and climbing off her in great distress of temper and manhood. Someone else drove her home, and I went back to London on the milk train. Two days later, she rang me up at work as if nothing had happened.

So when my silver-haired friend offered me my golden

opportunity, I grabbed at the chance to get away from her world, away from Bubbles Lambert for ever. I would meet some spectacled secretary, Today's New Girl, more serious and intellectual than those Maenads like Bubbles who tore a rip-roaring swathe through the thirties with the excuse, much later, that they were a Lost Generation (see how the same old labels keep cropping up?) who were having a last fling before their elders plunged them into total war. Which was a lie, because none of them were bright enough to foresee a war, and they were all madly in love with Hitler.

I was so busy at the BBC and it was so fascinating to work in the new studios at Broadcasting House, like being in a sort of Vicki Baum play where everyone is at sea together in a world of their own, that I had no time to look for Today's New Girl. There were several of them about, some plain, some not, all rather disconcerting since they knew much more than me, and this was the first time I had worked with women on an equal level.

They were not like the girls I had known, who all had an ulterior motive, either sex or marriage, or some such conceit. These BBC girls, programme assistants, script editors, repertory actresses, looked you very straight in the eye when they talked, and moved their bright mouths professionally and smoked endless packets of Craven A.

As my discoverer had predicted over the grilled kidneys, I proved to have a good microphone voice. When I graduated to being allowed to announce things like Clapham and Dwyer and selctions from *Lvoe Parade*, I had an audience of millions. I saw them all. Old ladies sitting beside huge sets with speakers shaped like cathedral naves, watching the cabinet as if I were inside it, and nodding gratefully when I said, 'I'm sure you enjoyed that beautiful melody.' Small boys with crystals and cats' whiskers, thrilled when they got me clear. Schoolgirls mooning over homework. Families crouching round the wireless as they do now round television, doors bolted, blinds drawn, hoping no one would visit. I was in all their homes. I was in their lives, the voice of a friend, if not yet a name. I was no longer a nobody. I had arrived.

That was how Terence Haig-Davenport felt when they

played his record on the air a few weeks ago. They have never played it since, though I thought it was quite good. He rang me up when it came on, a sepulchral mystery voice, 'Hit that radio button. I mean like now.'

It was one of the Pigeon's dirges, derivative, repetitive, a non-song, with no ideas in the lyrics and one attractive musical phrase transposed in every direction Terence could manage. Quite good of its kind, but so much like all the others which assail my ears yet more frequently since the BBC won the battle against pirate stations by the brilliant stratagem of playing pop music themselves.

The disc jockey who was a friend of a friend of a man Terence knew lost his job when the old Severn ferry from which he was broadcasting closed down. He did not get taken over by the BBC, as some of his mates did. Emperor Rosko, naked to the waist under a marmalade fur coat – strike a light! I went to work in my best suit and old Wykehamist tie. Once when I said, 'Oh boy,' I got reprimanded by the governors. And no one has ever forgotten the night of Alamein when Alvar Liddell broke panting in at eleven-thirty to tell the people not to switch off before the midnight bulletin, 'because it's going to be a cracking good one!'

We thought *that* was unprecedented. Now they break into any programme to tell you if the Pope has a bowel movement.

That one mass airing, which Terence captured for eternity on his tape recorder complete with the announcement, 'A searing little number from a new duo' has whetted his ambition.

He brought me the tape last week, though he knows I have no machine to play it, but they carry it about in the Pigeon's handbag – Terence's garments all being too tight to accommodate more than cigarettes or guitar picks – like a sort of talisman, as people frame a theatre programme with their names as understudy, or the first pound note they earned.

'Am I interrupting the fountain of genius?' If I say Yes, he still comes in. He was outside my window anyway in a sort of suède jumper with the nap rubbed off like the back of a baby's head, and Doris in her chair on the path.

'Door's open.' After the bangs and grunts and cries of 'Steady as you go!' with which he directs his manoeuvres with the chair, he pushed Doris into the room where I had been working and smoking for two or three hours. It was stuffy and chilly at the same time. The fire had gone out. The ashtrays stank. Silted coffee mugs stood about on every flat surface. A plate and a soup bowl from whatever my last meal had been were on the floor by my chair.

'Bit of slum clearance needed here.' Terence tut-tutted about the room, picking things up, tipping out cigarette butts, crumpling a newspaper I had not read to get the fire going. Doris's chair won't go through the narrow passage to the kitchen, so he brings her in bits of silver and copper to polish. One evening she sat by the fire and darned all the old socks which Mrs Meagan has left because they have no mate and sang softly while Terence tonelessly mimed a guitar, his soft eyes vacant, head moving dreamily to babyish syllables, Ba *dump*. Be nee. Ba nee ta dee.

'You ought to marry again, Mr James,' he said last week. Mavwy, he says, Vevwy Gvwoovy. The pigeon is Dovwis. His mecca is Amevwica.

'Not I.' I stood up and stretched and turned my pile of papers upside down, for he is liable to hang over the table and look at them, mis-reading the words and then complaining that it doesn't make sense. 'What about you?'

He glanced at Doris, docile under the hair, her pale lips curved in the sweet half smile with which she accepts his decisions as tractably as her handicap. 'No time for that.' He stood up and threw a match in the fire, then threw the matchbox after it to ensure a blaze. 'We're going places. Fast. Getting that break on the air. Sitting there, listening to *me*. It made me understand. All this—' He swept an arm at the bleak December landscape beyond my walls. 'This is small stuff. Local shows, couple hundred kids in the dance hall, squealing girls in the works canteen. I mean, we're big here, don't mistake me, but when I listen to that tape and think of all those millions and millions of people, I think – I mean, well what are we doing here?'

'Got to start somewhere.'

'OK, but not stay. In your day, these things took time. No communications, see? But the way things are now, given the

159

breaks, you can get on the charts overnight. The Winged Pigeon.' He held his palms before his face and read it from an imaginary magazine, peering and frowning as if he did not read very well, which he didn't. 'We'll be up there. They'll know us. Everyone will know us, me and Dovwis. Crowds everywhere we go, screaming, beating on the glass at London Airport, and we don't even notice them. You don't wave, see. She'll be sitting there.' He squatted on air, put his head on one side and smiled like a child. 'Just like she is now, only she'll have a better chair.' He sketched it with his hands, square back, round wheels, his hands turning them, as she did. 'Real leather, all chrome, ball bearings . . .'

When he is acting things out, he is tense, full of exaggerated movement, pansy eyes sparkling as if a flowerseller had wet them with a laundry sprinkler. Then he relaxes, and says something quite naïve like, 'You think it's all silly dreams, don't you, Mr James? Like that book of yours.'

I ignored the insult, since he did not intend it as one. And I suppose he is right in a way. Perhaps Charlie's story is only for myself, not even for Julia.

'But you heard the broadcast. Do you honestly think we've got a chance?'

A question like that is a reminder of the poverty of his acquaintance. Why ask me? I'd be the last person who would know. But the blokes and birds at the laundry, the toady dance-hall manager, the teenage hangers-on with coruscated skins and sagging lips, they don't really know either. His father is a disappointed man with an acid stomach who sits in front of the television set and belches. He doesn't know. Or care.

I said, 'I thought the record sounded pretty good. I'm no expert, but – well, it sounded like all the others they play.'

'Like the others.' Doris nodded, satisfied, but Terence said, 'That's the point. We're not like all the others. Look at us.' He spread out upturned hands, glossy head back, offering himself. 'Look at her.' He offered me Doris, hands folded on the rug over her knees. 'Who's ever had a gimmick like that?'

'Connee Boswell,' I began. 'Flanders and Swann . . .' but he had never heard of them.

'So don't say we're just like all the others.' He brooded,

thumbs in pocket slits, hair swinging round his chin like scimitars.

I ventured to say, 'Why don't you try for something a bit more positive? A stronger lyric, something people can really listen to, not just emotionally, but making them see pictures in their heads of excitement and drama.'

'Dvama?' He sneered up his squashed nose and left his mouth agape on the question.

'I mean with more in the words. That song.' I nodded at Doris's handbag. 'It's touching, but what does it give you? Face in the crowd. Who am I – a couple of clichés repeated. There are thousands of people who feel like that, so why rub it in?'

'You don't know anything about it.'

'All right, but you asked me. I'm only suggesting you should try something more positive. Tell people life is all right. They know it's not, but you could tell them.'

'Got any whisky?' Sometimes you think he has not heard a word. He got the glasses and the whisky and the sweet sherry I keep for the Pigeon and Molly Dryden the headmaster's wife, and after a little large talk about a man he knew who knew the floor manager of some swinging television show, more to keep face with himself than because he thought I would believe him, he wheeled Doris off into the starlight and left me with the ruins of my evening's work.

Why do I tolerate him? I even like him. Why? He stimulates me more than other people I know. I don't go to London much these days, and the local people – Henry Clay, the brewery people with their useless swimming pool, Mollie and her husband and the rest of them up at that crank school which used to be the Big House – they're pretty boring and predictable.

Terence is unpredictable.

Did I say unpredictable? That is an understatement which is going to need elaborating.

I've done no writing for two or three weeks. I went up to London for my sister Margaret's birthday, got ill and had to stay there. Bumpkin that I am, I caught some kind of London germ, like a South Sea Islander exposed to measles for the first time. Good Margaret nursed me, with damp sponges like old ladies' laundry, in her spare room that has never quite shucked off the hot smell of her daughter. The dachshund was always on my bed, licking itself.

I was quite wretched. Also a nuisance. It was the holiday, and Margaret and John had planned to stay with their son in Carlisle. They could not take me and could not leave me. Margaret would not put me into a hospital, although I've heard it's quite jolly there at Christmas, with the nurses climbing into bed with the private patients and everyone drinking ether.

Margaret does not like her son's wife, so she did not mind missing Carlisle, but John minded. He came into my room morning and evening and said, 'How are you, old fellow?' though he's three years older than I am, and looked at his watch as if it would tell my temperature. I heard him outside my door arguing with Margaret about my condition. I heard her say, 'He happens to be *my brother*.'

When I was better, Margaret insisted that I go to My man Brock at Thomas's as Charlie's mother would have said, to have a thorough examination.

I drove in from their outer limbo, had lunch with Reggie and walked through Trafalgar Square and across the bridge. London was full of thighs and hair. The girls looked like Robin Hood in little tunics and boots and brightly coloured tights. Reggie, who has never progressed far from his original Peter Pan collar, marcel-wave type of leading lady, says they look ludicrous, but I think they look very sexy and marvellous. He is disgusted with the handkerchief skirts his daughter wears, but with tights, it's far less indecent than those draughty cami-knickers Bubbles used to wear, as I recall.

Discussing girls during the examination with old Brock, whom I have known for years, he said, 'Why don't you use that thing while you still can?'

I said, 'Can you tell I don't?'

He said, 'Yes,' and I, being still in my innermost fibres constrictedly British, was too self-conscious to ask how.

Any shortness of breath, nausea, headaches, cramps, buzzing in the ears? ... One has them all, of course, but I am passed fit, with the usual futile admonitions to smoke less and go easy on the gin.

Driving home on the viaduct of the M4 over what used to be our super raceway of the Great West Road, I looked down and saw the crenellated parapet on the roof of Chenonceaux Keep. *She non so* to postmen and tradespeople. The ground floor of one wing seemed now to be a showroom for motorcycles. Rows of them were drawn up on the broad paving outside, where Mr Lambert had once put tubs of bay trees, chained to the wall and violated by dogs. Crowded in by newer buildings, advertising signs, the road roaring above, the whole block looked small and brown and dingy. I gave it a nod, for I felt like that too. On the road between Henley and Stonor, someone had squashed the back end of a small animal – a squirrel or a stoat, it seemed, as I charged past it, involved with the guilt of its slaughter. It lay curled on its side, head bowed, paws praying, humbly accepting its death.

Back at the cottage, feeling my age and more, I was visited by Terence late that night. He had come two or three nights before, and gone away to shoot himself because I was the only friend left and he thought I had sold up or pegged out at last.

Did I say unpredictable? Lord, he is that. He came tapping at a back window after I was in bed. When I creaked down the stairs which complain like awakened sleepers, and opened the kitchen door, there he was in the yard with the Winged Pigeon, and she was not winged at all, but standing on two good legs!

He snapped his fingers to her, and she walked in over the sill with her hair hanging forward so that I could not see her face.

'There's something funny here,' I said, sharp as a needle, although I had been asleep. 'What the devil is going on?'

'Keep cool,' Terence said, though he himself was more nervous than I have seen him since that first night when I caught him in the room with Charlie. He was pasty pale. His eyes were bruised with greenish-brown shadows. His hands were nervous, touching kitchen things, running through his hair, for once limp and greasy, grabbing my dressing-gown sleeve to keep me in the room. 'Where you been, Mr James?'

'In London. I got ill there.'

'Yeah, that's right. You do look rough.'

'I'm cured,' I said impatiently. 'Explain about Doris.'

'Well . . .' They had the nerve to smile, he and she, glancing at each other as if they had been clever. 'Got to have some gimmick to get by.'

'You mean, she never—'

'Fooled you, didn't it, same as everyone.'

'Don't they know? Don't they know at the laundry?'

'I told you. She irons sitting down. They do these days. It's not the bad old days of slavery, you know,' he said with that irrelevant righteousness that makes me want to knock his shaggy block off.

I still could not believe it. Even though she was standing up in a short plaid skirt and white woollen socks, Doris was still tiny and frail as a cripple. She had the air of a cripple, hurt and accepting, like the run-over animal.

'Pretty good act, eh?' His eyes were shameless enough to look for my approval.

'Why stop now?' I asked disgustedly. I wanted to shout at him, Get out – get out! Don't ever come back!

'Oh, I dunno.' Terence slumped his shoulders forward, hands hanging, eyes empty. 'Don't seem to be no point no more. What's the point, carrying that great girl about if they're not going to listen? Saturday night, I wheel her on.' He did not even have the spirit to make the movements with his hands, just spread them hopelessly. 'Half an hour, we make music for them, and those kids never even stop dancing.'

When I was his age, in the days of Carroll Gibbons, Harry Roy *et al*, you were supposed to dance, not cluster and listen as they do now, intent as primitives round a saga teller. I remember the beginnings of that at the Streatham Locarno with a BBC telephone hook-up, and I was there to announce the numbers. *It Ain't Necessarily So* – ridiculous from my eloquent larynx – and the floor was three-quarters empty because they were all thronging round Cab Calloway. It was the first time I had ever seen that happen.

'Well, you don't even care,' Terence said, before I could decide whether I did or not. 'Come on, Dovwis, we'll get no help here.' He grabbed her hands. He is not tall, but she is much shorter, like a child. Her legs unveiled at last are rather stiff and shapeless. They were better under the rug.

'What on earth can I do?' He is impossible in his righteous demands. He has never had much out of life, so why does he behave as if he expects the moon? 'Don't blame me if you're a flop. I can't help you.'

Then he told me why he had really come. Why he was so upset. Why he felt too rotten to bother with the sick gimmick. He had been caught housebreaking.

'Never took nothing.' He turned on me eyes of wounded innocence, though I had done no more than draw a breath to speak. 'But I was in there all right, having a look round their lyeberry. I'm not going to deny that.' Oh noble Ben Japp! 'I couldn't explain that in court. They don't listen anyway.'

'Go on,' I said sternly. I had not felt the upper hand of him like this since I had him pinned like a starfish to my broken french door.

'Got remanded to Assizes. This person I know up the Estates who's got it all at his fingertips, he says fifty quid, since it's my third time up.'

'Go on.'

'Or three months.' He did not look at me.

'You'll have to sell your car.'

'Whose car? I've only made three of the payments.' He walked to the cupboard at the other end of the kitchen and began to take lids off canisters, although he knows where I keep everything.

'Will you help us?' The Pigeon's little hand was on my sleeve, her hair tossed back, her pale patient eyes unblinking. It was the first time she had ever asked me a direct question.

'Yes,' I said wearily.

Terence spun round from the cupboard. 'I told you he was all right,' he said, as if she had denied it.

'Yes, you told me, Ben.'

'Tevwence.'

'Terence.'

'I should have turned you in that first night you broke in here,' I told him. 'Look where it's got me. You try to help someone and they end up sucking your guts out.'

But he had stopped listening. Relaxed against the shelf, his body fluid in the tight white trousers, sharp boots tapping, toe out, toe in, he had started his toneless guitar miming. Suddenly Doris began to sing. Her voice rose in my tiny kitchen. She sang, 'I'm so in love with life. I run, I jump, I fly. I run through the world with the song of my heart in my mouth. My hair flies up like wings to meet the sun.'

'What's that?'

'My ironical bit. I wrote it last week when we was so down.'

'You wrote it – words and music?' It was lilting and joyous.

'Yeah.' He leered at me so rudely that I thought he must be lying. 'I'm creative. I told you.'

'But it's nothing like the other stuff.'

'Oh well.' He apologized. 'We was smoking pot, you know.'

'Doris too?'

'She does everything I do.' He turned his wrist up to mime the guitar again, left hand fluently fingering air.

'Drugs are for dreamers and fools. The world is my drug and my life and my youth and my leaping heart.'

In that surprising way, without seeming to draw breath, Doris's voice came gushing out of her mouth like fountain water. I suddenly had an inspiration. I took her by her frail shoulders and dumped her in the kitchen chair where Mrs Meagan sits with my newspaper and does the crossword before I can get at it. I dragged the roller towel off the door and wrapped it round her knees. 'Now sing!'

Up to now in the wheelchair she has sung these sick agony songs, as sad as her condition (*erratum*: pseudo-condition). The contrast between the pitiful little cripple with the useless legs and that soaring voice rejoicing of running and leaping was irresistible. I could understand how Terence, carrying her about, pushing her chair, brooding over her like a mother, had almost come to believe in the deception himself. I almost believed. I was genuinely moved.

'Keep her in the chair,' I said. 'But sing of joy. It's good.'

166

He shrugged. If you found the key to the universe and handed it to him, he would receive it with a shrug. He is only enthusiastic about his own ideas.

'I really like it.'

'You would.'

I should tell him to go and stuff himself. I should let him go to gaol. But if he did, and lost his job, it would probably be *me* who would have to support him.

Of course I have lent him the fifty pounds. And of course I have rung up the son of an old friend of mine who is a producer of popular television rubbish and abased myself to solicit an audition for the Winged Pigeon.

'Don't let them do one of their dirges, Ned,' I told him. 'Try them on the other kind. It's the contrast between that crippled child and that joyous lilting voice...' I practically vomited over my shoes talking to him, but it's my only chance of getting any of my money back, and as Mrs Meagan so rightly said when the price of cream went up and I told her to stop bringing by weekly half-pints, choosers can't be beggars.

After he got dropped from the prison kitchens, Mr Clive could not find another job. He walked every few days to the labour exchange to save the bus fare. 'Shoe leather comes higher,' his wife told him, sharp with worry, for his stoicism seemed like lack of enterprise.

'There's others worse off than us, Nelly,' he would tell her. It was true, since she had a job and they both had a home, but she would bang down a pan or a tea caddy and cry, 'Don't *tell* me that! You're driving me demented with your pump water talk!'

'I'm on her nerves,' he told Charlie equably, as one might say I'm on a diet, or on the wagon. 'Though it's worse for me to have to see her be the breadwinner.'

Although he had done skilled work for years before the machine shop closed down, he would not have been too proud to take any job he could find. But there was nothing. When a vacancy came up, there were dozens of men after it, most of them younger, with small children. When he went for an unattractive job as nightwatchman at a warehouse in a shifty dockland neighbourhood, he found that five hundred had already applied.

'Five hundred nightwatchmen. That would cut down the population a bit.' That was Gordon's level of humour.

'Don't be so vulgar.' His wife puckered her whortleberry mouth and covered the baby's ears.

'Don't keep on at Gordon all the time,' Mrs Clive said. 'He's been a good husband to you, and kept a roof over your head and food on your table in these difficult times.'

'Unlike Dad?' Rita was pregnant again. Her giftless face was puffy, her eyes like a pig.

'Say that again, young lady—'

'Don't you hit her, Mum. She's carrying.'

'Don't you dare raise a hand to your mother, young man.'

A family row flared like a paper match and sputtered quickly out, since Mr Clive was too dispirited to make more than a token contribution, and the parlourmaid came charging through the door with her knee, crashed down a tray and said, 'She will have it that the steak is raw and it's to go under the grill again.'

'And you can tell her what to do with it, and all,' Gordon said as she banged out again. The parlourmaid was not a Bolshevik like Alice, but a high-nosed woman who was called by her surname. It did not enrage her to have to carry the steak down instead of sending it back in the service lift and yelling down the hatch after it, but she was not going to stand in the kitchen and wait while Cook had it under the grill. Not with that family of hers lounging about as if it was a bottle party.

Charlie was not there, but she heard about it later, along with other anecdotes that began, So there I was, shelling peas to go with the lamb, or basting my duck, etc, etc.

They all had a look at the steak and Gordon cut off a strip. 'Delicious.' Grease lay on his lip 'What's the matter with Lady Mucking?'

'It's her steak,' his mother said from the stove. 'She can have it how she wants it.'

'All she wants is to give you extra work.'

'Well, I am in her employ. I am under her roof.'

'Oh shut up that cant, Mum. You ought to get out, you know. It's degrading to be a servant.'

'I've always been in service, Gordon, you know that.'

'More fool you.'

'Why wear yourself out waiting on people who aren't fit to wait on you?' Rita aired her favourite theme. 'You look awful, Mum, really you do.'

'I feel all right.' Mrs Clive patted hair, waistline, thin red cheeks to make sure everything was still there.

'You're run down,' Rita insisted, since she was not well herself in these early weeks. A small upheaval in her stomach brought bile into her mouth. She sampled its quality briefly before she patted her lips. 'Pardon me.'

'Mum is very strong,' Mr Clive began, but Rita put her eyebrows in the air and said, 'I'm surprised at you really, letting her be used like a work horse.' Mrs Clive said, 'Don't you speak to Dad like that, young lady,' and they were off again on a tow-row-row which came back inevitably to Gordon's 'It's degrading, this job. What's your mother do, Mr Clive? She's a cook. Oh – reahlay?' There can't have been anyone in wholesale jewellery who talked like that. 'I mean, it's not very nice in my position.'

Mrs Clive put the steak on the shelf of the food lift, hauled on the rope at the side and touched the buzzer to let the parlourmaid in the dining-room know it was on its way.

'You ought to send up your notice with it,' Gordon grumbled on like a dormant volcano.

When Lady Munsing announced that she was taking his mother up to Leicestershire again for the visit of the Duke and Duchess, he erupted. Without telling his parents, he got himself let in at the front door by the slow-witted nanny (neither Alice nor the parlourmaid would have admitted him) and went storming upstairs to the drawing-room.

'I told her.' He came heavily down to the kitchen, flushed and breathing heavily through spread negroid nostrils. 'I told her straight. It's not right for my mother to work so hard. She don't like it in the country, and I'm not having her used so familiar. I told her straight. See what she makes of that.'

What Lady Munsing made of it was to give Mrs Clive two weeks' notice. She was quite pleasant about it. No recriminations. Just the sack. Lovely, she was. So kind, Her Ladyship, I don't know how I shall have the heart to leave her service.

She wrote a beautiful letter of reference and put an advertisement on the front page of *The Times*. 'Say what you like, Gordon, but you couldn't want fairer than that.'

'*Lady Munsing wishes to recommend her cook. Reliable. Excellent plain and fancy cooking. References.*'

Gordon and Rita were furious. 'Got you out of a life of slavery and you want to sneak back in again.' Dad's face hung like a coat on a nail. Though times were desperate, he did not want her to get a job before him. In the acrimony and indecision the two weeks was up and the new cook coming in, vast and powerful with elbows like knee joints and forearms like Jack Dempsey, and the Clives had to go and live in Gordon and Rita's flat in Edgware. There was nowhere else to go.

That worked out as ill as might be expected. Rita announced 'spotting', although she stayed in bed half the day and let her mother spring clean the flat and do all the cooking and shopping while Dad wheeled the baby to the labour exchange. Her doctor dared her not to take better care of herself. If every foetus clung as securely as Rita's, there would be no miscarriages, but she threatened to lose the baby five times a day, and when Dad saw Peter's face on the doorknob of her broom cupboard, that was it.

'I'll unscrew the knob if you like,' he said obligingly, but Rita was retching into the baby's chamber pot.

Charlie, who though clumsy at things she tried to plan, had quite a little gift for turning up at crucial moments, came trudging up the stairs that very evening. 'You must come and stay with me.' The thought flew into her head, and she spoke it.

'That will be very nice, I'm sure.' Rita accepted for them.

Charlie drove them down to her cottage. They moved into the other bedroom, with the doorknob of Rita's broom cupboard, which Mr Clive had managed to unscrew in the confusion of departure.

Mr Eldredge's ulcer had taken him to hospital at last. With a whole stomach, he had disliked his job as village postmaster. With half a stomach, he and Florrie were off to his sister at Bognor. A notice was up in the front room of his small pink cottage on the village street. 'Vacancy for Sub-postmaster.'

Mr Clive was not surprised when he applied to Oxford and got the job. He was not conceited. Just unsurprised.

With the position went the chance to live in the thatched cottage for two and six a week, and a salary of some hundred pounds a year which included the rent of the dark little front room for post office business.

The cottage stood back from the main street, on one side of the village triangle of which Bob and Quentin's 'End o' the Road' was the apex. Mr Eldredge had been a neat man, for all his groans and peppermint sucking. The bricks of the low front wall were newly pointed. The wooden gate was very white. The path that led between the tidy pansies was free of weeds. The front door was painted shiny green, with the post office sign above it. In the side window, there were two small slots, one for letters and one for postcards, which all fell into the same box on the other side. Anything larger had to be taken inside, but most people would rather go in anyway. A visit to the post office was a small event of the day. A chat with the postmaster a chance to exchange weather forecasts, agricultural opinions, physical symptoms and news items of married children moved away.

Mr Eldredge's forecasts, opinions, symptoms and family items had all been gloomy. Mr Clive was the best thing that had happened in that village for years, with a gentle smile and a friendly bit of chat for everyone and peardrops in a drawer for the kiddies.

The chest of drawers that stood partly across the front room was the post office. The fireguard stapled to the public edge protected the heart of His Majesty's Service, the green cash box in the middle drawer. At night, Mr Clive unlocked the drawer with the keys at the end of his watchchain and took the cash box up to bed.

Mr Browning from the Head Office in Oxford had been there at the start to explain about stamps and savings books and postal orders and Old Age pensions, and how to change the date stamp which could convert a line to Maud into official mail with King George's head neatly obliterated. He showed him how to count the words in a telegram and how to use the telephone. Except for the one at the Big House, it was the only one in the village.

It would have been unthinkable for Mr Clive to go upstairs at Wilton Crescent, whether Sir Henry and Lady Munsing were there or not, so he had never learned to telephone. He was still nervous of it, even after Mr Browning from Head Office had pronounced him ready for business and gone back to Oxford in the little red van. When the telephone rang, Mr Clive cried, 'Nelly! Nelly!' as if it were a new-born infant that was her affair. When he had a message to send, he made her lift the receiver and ask Mrs Foreless in Kingsgrove exchange for Oxford Telegrams. He would have made her read the message too, but she had lost her spectacles.

When a telegram came in, he would call to his wife to mind the cash box and would spring to his red post office bicycle and dash away like Dirk and Joris with clips on his blue serge trousers to farmhouse, cottage or rectory.

He was happier than he had been for years. At night he slept more peacefully than he had since he lost his son, with the tin cash box under a floorboard. On the days when HM business was slow (every day), he worked in the long narrow garden at the back, and tended the chickens he had bought from Mr Eldredge. He acquired a stray cat and two puppies someone was going to drown. Raised a country boy, he had not been able to keep animals since his wife was in London service. He fed birds. He gave names to all the Rhode Island Reds. He was negotiating with a man in Ewelme for a nanny-goat in kid. He cared for the flowers and vegetables with the same concerned face that he would bend to the merest furry caterpillar, lifting it on to a leaf from a wrong situation on the doorstep, raising his foot high to bridge the line of ants who crossed the beaten earth of the path like well-drilled pedestrians. He had found a couple of derelict hutches at the back of

172

the shed at Charlie's place and was talking of rabbits.

'That's going too far.' Though Mrs Clive had been miserable in Edgware, she was not nearly as happy as her husband. Leicestershire had been bad enough with its mud and its archaic stove and its vast stone distances between kitchens and pantry and larder, its nowhere to go on your time off, and no time off because the house was always full of people ravenous from blood sports. But at least the Munsings' hunting seat had been a civilized big house with running water and electric light and a flush toilet for servants. Here in her thatched cottage which Quentin, rushing to buy stamps because he could not wait to view the new faces, assured her was almost unbearably period, she was dubious about many things.

The floors downstairs were stone tiles set right on the earth. She put on an extra pair of knickers when she found that out. Lamp wicks had to be trimmed every day and the black cleaned off the glass chimneys. Work like that she did not mind, but she hated the swinging patterns that the lamp made on the low ceiling and the smell of the bedside candle after she snuffed it. She still put out a hand automatically to the light switch inside each doorway, and it gave her the creeps to find nothing there. She thought she would put her hand on the soft warm flesh of someone waiting by the wall in the dark. Her hostility towards the earth closet in the back garden was limitless. Dad, who had done this for years as a boy, willingly emptied it in the pit down by the compost heap at the end wall, but every visit was a penance to his wife. The mere sight of the cracked wooden seat and the shovel in the box of ashes was enough to bind her.

Rats ran under the thatch at night.

'They're having a party,' Mr Clive said soppily. 'Just look at old puss twitch his whiskers.'

'If that animal comes on the bed, I'm putting it out of the window.' His wife hunched the quilt round her small red-veined ears, her thin plait of hair tied with pink tape from the Sundries drawer. The thatch would let water, she knew. She kept a dishpan in the bedroom, quite disappointed when she did not need it in the spring downpours.

A Londoner, a cockney, a city woman with noise and smells

173

and soot in the very marrow of her, dust and bustle and quick gritty repartee in her motor nerves, she did not like the country. Although she had not liked the staff at Wilton Crescent, there had been life there, morning tea sessions, feet on the stairs. There had been the tradespeople incessantly at the back door, personal friends whose lives she knew. She had knitted a pullover for Sainsbury's man at Christmas, and saved chocolate paper for the silver ball of the greengrocer's daughter. When Peter was killed, one of the Harrod's drivers brought her a plant.

Here in the country, the baker's horse and cart came twice a week and the travelling grocery once a week, if that. Milk was collected in your own can from Gregory's farm. The churns were out in the dairy and you helped yourself from a dipper, because Gregory's wife was too busy to come out unless you wanted cream.

With Mr Clive pottering over his accounts or scattering grain to the hens with biblical sweeps of his arms, Nelly Clive was mad for company. The Kingsgrove bus stopped at the village corner twice a week, and she was always on it. She spent all afternoon looking at the shops and pricing ribbon and woollen goods in Noble's London House, where the buttons and hooks and eyes and needles were kept in drawers with paintings of the wrong contents outside. 'Darners are in beads dear, you've been here long enough to know that.'

She made more trips than necessary to the little village shop at the side of the White Hart, with the excuse of a pair of shoelaces or a packet of custard powder to help Mr Clive along with the stewed rhubarb. But Mrs Hathaway, who crouched there like a Beatrix Potter woodland animal, had nothing to talk about even if she could have heard. She nodded and peered and sewed up her mouth and gave the wrong change and poured a bagful of Kreem toffees when you asked for treacle lumps.

It was quite hard to make friends with anybody in the village. They were not unfriendly, but they were in no hurry to get closely acquainted. They had all the time in the world. Their slow difficult lives, an endless unresolved struggle with the weather and the land and archaic wages were enough to handle without trying to match chit-chat with Mrs Clive's quicker tongue.

Friendship was something they did not often think about. They had their loyalties. People were either there or not there. If they were your neighbour, you chatted every day and baked a cake for a death or brought round broth and a basket of eggs for sickness. Many of the villagers were related to each other and intermarried, families weaving in and out of families as cousins got each other pregnant or a grandmother who had buried two husbands took up with a third she had known all her life.

There was not the discrimination that friendship implies. But what they scored in tolerance over a townee like Nelly, picking and choosing who to like and who not to like, they lost in the special intensity of finding and holding a friend.

Charlie was her best and only friend. She often went down there for tea when Charlie came home from school in her gym tunic and brown stockings. She would do some sewing or ironing for her, and tell her tales of life in service and things about Peter as a little boy.

'If he had not been taken,' she said once, head down, darning on a wooden mushroom with close-held lips, 'would you have gone with him?'

'Yes. Yes I expect so.' Charlie had never told them that her involvement with their son had been all on her side and all imaginary.

Mrs Clive enjoyed her visits 'down Lambert's,' but Charlie's cottage was not much better than her own, with no inside toilet or lights or taps, and the velvet dark hushing the fields and hedges as if the world stood still under the stars. In London you never had to see the stars.

'Brr-rr,' she shivered, wheeling out her bicycle to the side lane, its lamp wobbling yellow. 'It's just like the country.'

'It *is* the country.'

That was the trouble.

Then one day Mrs Hammond from the Big House came into the post office. 'Good day, Mrs Hammond. How are you keping, madam?' It was just like old times, because she was gentry enough for Mrs Clive's taste with a porkpie hat with a little feather in the brim and a pair of corgis on a double leash. Dad was off delivering a telegram about Mrs Cartwright's new grandchild. 'So she's had it at last. That poor woman *will* be relieved. Take over here, Nell, while I pedal down instantly.'

'Will this be enough postage?' Mrs Hammond asked pleasantly (just as if I was anyone).

'Where's it going, madam? I can't see without my glasses.' Mrs Clive fumbled, terrified she might have to figure out postage for abroad.

'Oxford. It's an advertisement for the *Oxford Mail*. I'm going out of my head trying to find a cook before the Easter holidays.'

Everything swam before my eyes. Mrs Clive had heard the expression, but never knew what it meant until now. The little front room spun round her and she had to grab at the edge of the chest of drawers before she could summon the strength to say weakly, 'Cook? Would you – would you consider, madam—'

Mrs Hammond was so pleasant, so easy to talk to, and a lady who knew her own mind. It was all fixed up there and then, the letter to the *Oxford Mail* unposted, though carrying a penny halfpenny stamp, which upset Mr Clive some days later when his wife found it in the Pensions drawer and threw it on the fire.

He was already upset, of course, about her job, but Nelly did not care. She bicycled off every morning in a hat to the grey stone house in the railed park on the Wallingford road, back to cook Dad's lunch after she had served the Big House meal, and back again six nights a week to do the dinner. It was no longer just like the country. It was just like old times. She had light and water and an Eagle cooking range and a kitchen-maid and a flush toilet and an employer on whom to pin her sights, like God or monarchy.

The coming of the Clives had made a difference in Charlie's life too. Before they moved from her house to the post office cottage, Mr Clive had been painting and distempering for her and running up shelves, while his wife ran up curtains and

176

chair covers in peony chintz from Noble's London House. She had taken the whole bolt of cloth because it was marked down, so Charlie had to buy another chair at an auction to give her something else to cover.

Dad helped Charlie to dig and prune and tear out the jungle of years to replace it with neat plants which he handled as solicitously as the insects he encountered. When he told a sweet william, 'I think you'll like it there,' it should have been whimsical, but he did it whether anyone was there to hear him or not.

'My dear, what's happened?' Mrs Nixon the doctor's wife, coming in a pony cart to reconnoitre the sick and the hapless people like Charlie, was amazed. 'It used to look as if you were only camping here on the way to somewhere more exciting.'

'I'm going to eke out the rest of my spinster life in this house,' Charlie said.

Mrs Nixon haw-hawed. 'Oh *you*! Young and attractive as you are, you're going to make a wonderful wife for some lucky man.' Charlie had heard her say this to dried-up roots like Miss Noonanby and Ethel Herriot who had gone a little mad being a perpetual vicar's daughter in the unpatronized church at the end of the tree-wet lane. 'You silly goose, who's going to notice your thumb?' Charlie had forgotten that they did.

There were nights when she panicked quietly, wide-eyed in the dark with the dog at her feet, seeing herself like Mrs Fossick, gums and belly braced, knees locked with calcium, clapping the beat for 'Rufty Tufty' from generation of girls to generation. Seeing herself like Ethel Herriot, mad and manless. In the morning she was Charlotte Lambert again, waking to the pleasure of her new curtains, greeting the smell of new kitchen paint as she went barefoot downstairs.

At school lunch, she bored the girls at her table with stories about her kitchen linoleum and the flounce on her bed. She had never been interested in domestic decoration before. Now she found, as some women never do, that no one else is interested either, unless it is their own.

Cara Miles was interested. She would slide up to Charlie after netball practice, yanking at her stockings and screwing up a running nose. 'Oh, Miss Lambert, did you buy the cushions?' or 'Have you painted the dog kennel yet?' So after the Clives moved out of the cottage, and lino-laying and painting revealed itself as less fun without someone to exclaim about it at intervals, Charlie let Cara come out on the bus at weekends to help her with the house and garden.

They were painting the outside woodwork a soft blue grey. Cara did the work on the ladder, showing her knickers, sluicing down paint on the bushes and plants.

'What if life was only weekends, Miss Lambert? My mother says it ought to be. She doesn't like school any better than I do. But if she taught me herself, they'd put her in prison.'

'Why don't you like school?'

'Nobody likes me.' Lips drawn back over her outsize fettered teeth as she reached to slap paint on a wooden gutter, Cara was able to state a truth with a detachment that would escape her as she grew older.

It was not only being so wet as to be in love with Lottie Four Fingers that damned her in the eyes of St Gabriel's. She liked her parents. She liked her mother. Had even said so before witnesses at the basins in the hockey pavilion.

Because she was a bright child, idiotic enough to try for good marks, she had recently been moved up to a higher class. In this class was the famous Set, some half-dozen world-weary girls with more bust than brain, who turned to the door and said, 'My dear, *look* what's crawled in!' when Cara came to take her place among them.

They did not wash their hands of her. Generous as they were, they gave a lot of their valuable time to converting this poor innocent brat to the right and true.

'I've seen your mother. She wore an old apron and her hair was all on end. What was she doing out on the common in that apron?'

'She was picking mushrooms.'

'Oh you poor child. And what did *you* do at the weekend?'

'We went for a walk. There was a goose for dinner, and my father played cards with us by the fire. My mother found some birds that fell out of a nest. I helped her feed them.'

A chorus groan. 'And still she lives to tell the tale.'

'Oh shut up.' Cara kicked out. At first she was fiercely loyal, but there were so many of them, and they were big and busty with red lips and staring eyes and thick curtains of bobbed hair while hers was drawn back, fine and pale. They began to break her down gradually, first by snorting and turning away and leaving her out of their talk and jokes as if she were too juvenile. When that did not crush her flat enough, they began to take more trouble.

'I'll psychoanalyse you,' said the one who had heard about Freud. 'When you go home tonight, you must stop looking at your parents through a clouded window and see them as they really are.'

'They're all right.'

'Aha. They've psychoanalysed *you*. How disgusting. No wonder everyone hates their mothers.'

'I don't.'

'You do. You've got to let yourself admit it. Get it out of your system like pus.'

She did not tell her mother. How could she, since to her eternal shame she had allowed herself to look at her with the girls' eyes and seen that it had been unfair of her to have a baby when she was forty. Seen that she looked old and weird in that sacking apron she loved with the big pockets full of millet and strange pebbles, with her basin cut hair and her serene way of treating people as if everyone loved life as much as she did. How could she tell her mother that this was not so and that she herself had no right to her illusion, looking and behaving as she did, too differently from everyone else's detested mother?

'What's the matter, pet? You're not usually so moody.'

'I'm not. Well – I've got my friend.'

'I had to tell her that.' But this was wrong too. You never tell your mother.

'How disgusting. She's too old to have it anyway.'

Once, Cara would have asked her mother. Now she could not. She looked in the drawers in her room, and reported at school. 'She does, so there! I found the things.'

'Look child, have you never heard of a woman keeping the

179

blue hair ribbon she wore as a girl?' sneered Olive Bartlett.

'Ah – memories,' sighed Avril.

The bus down Ashton Hill to Kingsgrove was escape, a rattling ambulance to safety. At Charlie's cottage she could talk about the mother she used to know before the girls disfigured her. Usually they did not talk very much. When Cara said, 'Nobody likes me,' she did not have to tell Miss Lambert why, because Miss Lambert did not ask. They painted and hammered and laid stair carpet and ate with their fingers things that other people ate with knives and forks. Soon they were going to get some car paint and do over Mick the Miller with a red stripe and red spokes on the wheels.

In April of that year, an official inquiry into the R101 disaster yielded the enigmatic statement that with the weather stormy and the airship unready, only reasons of 'public policy' actually sent her off. This neither increased nor lessened the bitterness of people like the Clives. Like everyone else in the country, they already knew that someone had played ducks and drakes with the lives of their husbands and sons.

The anticlimactic whitewash of the inquiry was in and out of the news quite quickly. But not long after there began to be rumours, uncorroborated stories in one of the dailies, that a medium had been comunicating with some of the ship's dead officers and learning ghastly details about the tragic flight.

'I notice they only communicate with officers,' Charlie said bitchily, eyes close to the newsprint in the soft yellow lamplight.

'Catch them conjuring up a man with an oil rag,' Nelly said. 'Much less a steward.' She and Charlie smiled at each other, in league against gullible Dad.

'You mustn't joke about things like that, dear,' he said. 'It's not nice.'

'It's not very nice to lose your son. It don't bring my boy back, does it? It don't bring him back to me the way I want to see him, with his bright eyes and his lovely hair and his comical ways.' She began to cry. A tear fell on the cat in her lap and it complained and jumped off.

'If you could bring him back, would you?'

'Don't be daft.' She blew her nose and scrubbed at her eyes, mouth drawn open on a choked breath. 'I'd give my right arm to wake one morning and know it was all a dreadful dream and him alive.'

'I don't mean that. I mean – like it tells in the paper. I mean, if a man would come back like that and talk to someone he never knew, wouldn't there be a better chance yet if it was his own father?'

'You shouldn't believe everything you read, Dad.' Mrs Clive had recovered. The cat jumped back in her lap. 'Dratted thing.' It always went to her.

'Wouldn't there, Charlotte?' He leaned forward to make her answer. 'If I was to try, would you sit with me and try to talk to Peter?'

'No.' Charlie shivered. She looked quickly over her shoulder, all round the walls of their stuffy little sitting-room.

But Mr Clive was not to be put off. Peter's face had disappeared from Rita's doorknob (they had to take his word for that since they had never seen it), but a few other faces had come and gone. The Kaiser on a whitened stone by the path to the hen-house. St Francis again, a regular, in the shallow water at the bottom of the stone sink, just before it ran out and took the saint with it.

He had no reason to suppose his powers had left him with his change of job and scenery. He could still, on his day, see things about people. He saw that customers were going to be ill.

'Why don't you tell them?' Charlie asked.

'It's against the Law.'

He stopped a stranger in the street in Wallingford on market day and told him he was going on a journey.

'That's right,' the stranger said calmly. 'I'll be going to see my mother next week at the infirmary.'

After Mrs Hawkes went out of the post office, he called back to his wife in the kitchen, 'There's gastric trouble in view for *that* party.'

'Poor soul.' Mrs Clive clicked her teeth. 'That will be bad luck with the wedding coming on.'

181

The story in the paper had set off an old dream. For a long time he had wanted to try his hand at a seance. There didn't seem to be much to it, by all accounts.

'Come on, love, you won't mind it a bit.' He coaxed Charlie as if he were trying to get her to the dentist. 'Come on, Nelly. I want to try. I want to try and talk to our boy.'

'Oh don't!' She clutched for his arm, but he had already pushed himself nimbly out of his chair and gone to sit at the round table which stood in the corner of the room, with a thick fringed tablecloth and a photograph of Sir Henry Munsing going to the Palace in knee breeches to get the CBE, with Lady Munsing brittle in aigrettes.

'I'm off.' Charlie got up too and called to her dog.

'Well. I didn't think *you* would let me down.' Mr Clive was sitting at the table, arms prone on the green cloth from elbow to fingers as if he were playing Up Jenkins. 'I thought you were supposed to be so fond of Peter.' His face could droop as piteously as a child's if he were disappointed.

'Come on then.' Mrs Clive slid the cat off and went to sit with him. 'Come on, Charlotte, if he wants it.'

He was so pleased to get their cooperation that he did not see that he was being humoured.

'Oh, all right.' Charlie sat down heavily on a wooden stool. Her dog went under the table and licked the wax on Mr Clive's bootlaces. 'How are we going to start?' she asked grumpily. 'I want to go home. Some people who aren't civil servants have to go to work early, you know.'

'This is what they do.' Dad had seen a film where a dead child came back in a nightdress and reconciled her quarrelling parents. He threw back his gentlemanly head and began to breathe through his nose, lips chiselled shut like a corpse, a slit of eye showing through half-closed lids.

'Are you all right, dear? You look very queer.' His wife got up to carry the small lamp over, but he motioned it away.

'Turn it down,' he said without opening his eyes. 'It's not dark enough. Now try, both of you, try very hard. Think very very hard about Peter.'

Mrs Clive snapped her eyes shut like a doll. She obviously was not going to try. Charlie stared at the wallpaper which sprouted a trellised pattern of rosebuds and violets and thought about Peter in his thick white jersey. She did not think too hard, because the back of her neck was already pricking, even though this was only a joke. Mr Clive did look very strange, with his tombstone face and the snoring breaths as he intoned. 'Are you there? Is anyone there?'

'Only the bailiffs,' Mrs Clive muttered. Charlie laughed, and Mr Clive brought down his head and opened his eyes, annoyed.

'I'm not playing, ladies,' he said. He got his head into position again.

'Why are you breathing like that?' His wife stood up and put a hand on his forehead. 'You're not taking a fever, are you? Last time,' she told Charlie, 'he went near a hundred and four and I had to strip off his clothes and wash him all over with soda water.'

'Oh, it's hopeless. You don't want to try.'

'Yes, yes I do.' She sat down with a bump, like a child playing musical chairs.

'It won't work. You've not the right attitude.'

'Perhaps you did it wrong the first time. Come on, dear. Try again.'

'No, it's no good. You don't believe. You don't believe in me.'

'I do. Wasn't I the only one believed when you said Nanny's wart would go away on Armistice Day?'

'Did it?'

'Hush, Charlotte. But I believed, that's the point to bear in mind.'

'But you think all this is a joke. I'm serious, Nell. Don't you want to try to get in touch with your son?'

'No!' She mouthed it at him, very cockney. 'I won't play such games with the memory of my Peter. It's blasphemy.' She banged back her chair against the wall, fell over the cat's bowl as she floundered to the lamp, turned the wick the wrong way, knocked over a set of fire irons and swore her way out of the dark room with Charlie's dog barking after her.

'You see how she is.' Mr Clive got up to light the lamp. 'It's no use trying with her.'

183

'It's no use anyway. Give it up. Peter's dead, you know.'

'No one is dead. They wait. What if they are waiting some-where there?' He pointed over his left shoulder. 'What if they wait for us to call to them and we never even try? You help me, Charlotte. Let's try without Nelly. She's afraid to open the old wounds by letting herself think about where Peter might be now. Just you and me. Not here. I'll come to your house one evening when she's at work.'

'I don't want to.'

'I thought you cared about Peter.'

'I did, but – why does it have to be at night?'

'They always do it at night.'

Half afraid, half joking, she finally agreed to a night the following week when Nelly Clive would be safely involved at the Big House in a birthday supper for the elder daughter with the dullest adolescents from miles around.

'I'll bring a picture. Perhaps something he owned.' He pinched her arm like Olive Bartlett planning a classroom rumpus. It was a conspiracy between them. His eyes were bright and fevered. Charlie felt quite bad about leading him on in his dementia. 'Have you got something? Didn't he give you something of his own?'

'His handkerchief. I have his handkerchief.' She was whispering too. Without saying goodnight to Mrs Clive, she slipped out like a spy into the silent street where the curtains were all drawn and the village shut away into itself below the sleeping hills.

When it was time for the seance, she put a cloth on the dining-table, set two chairs face to face, and brought in the best lamp in the hope that Mr Clive would not want to operate in the dark.

In the two days since the first fiasco, she had realized how silly it was, but as the darkness gathered on this evening she began to feel uneasy. Three or four times she went out to the gate to see if she could see Mr Clive's bicycle lamp coming round the corner by the White Hart. Back in the room, she rearranged the furniture, poked up the fire, tried to coax the lamp to burn brighter without flaring.

When he finally arrived, he caught her unawares as she

184

came back from the shed with another log, materializing suddenly inside the house, as if he had come out of the woodwork.

'In here, I thought.' Although it was only Dad Clive in his familiar dun cardigan and rounded boots, she was as nervous as if he were an abortionist. She led him to the front room. 'Would you – shall I make some tea?'

He waved the suggestion aside, frowning at the room from the doorway. 'This won't do. This won't do for my purpose,' he said as if he had been doing it all his life. 'I'll just have the candles, if you please, and a screen in front of the fire. Thank you. Thank you.'

Charlie hurried to take the candles from the mantelpiece, drag out the fire-screen, pull out his chair, as if she were a conjurer's assistant in high heels and a naughty swimsuit. He was quite different. In the two days, he had been creating some persuasive new images of himself. He rubbed his hands as if he were going to play a concerto, and sat down with such an air that if he had actually had coat-tails to flip he could not have done better. He motioned Charlie to the seat opposite him and looked at her gravely.

'Are you ready, Charlotte?'

'Are you *sure* you want to go on with this?'

He nodded. 'I feel it's right. I feel that I know now perhaps why you were sent to us.'

'I had Peter's car—' Desperately she tried to keep the conversation banal.

'In some way,' he went on, ignoring her, eyes veering towards each other, slightly fanatical, 'it seems that you are necessary for the contact. Isn't that so?' He threw the question briskly back over his left shoulder, like salt.

'Stop that,' Charlie said. 'There's no one there.'

'Not yet. But I think there will be. That is what we're here to find out.' Out of his coat pocket, he drew a small package wrapped in tissue paper. He put it on the table and unwrapped it carefully. Peter's silver cigarette case, blackened and battered relic.

Charlie drew in a breath. 'I'd forgotten about that.'

'Perhaps Peter hasn't. What do you have, Charlotte, my dear?' he asked more kindly, more like his proper self, bending forward to smile at her, with the madness softened out of his eyes.

From the sleeve of her pullover she took the handkerchief, still dirty and stuck with blood. 'Perhaps he hasn't forgotten this either.'

Mr Clive stared for a moment at the crumpled handkerchief on the table between them. Then he said, 'All right. Now turn out the lamp. Put the candles here, on either side of me.'

In the yellow wandering candlelight, shadows moved in and out of the deep grooves on his face. His nose was sinister, his eyes unblinking.

'Why did he give you the handkerchief?' he asked, assuming the monotone that he could only imagine from the film, which had been before Talkies.

'To wrap round my thumb.' Charlie kept her voice practical and brisk. She was not going to give him any leeway.

'Wrap it round there now.'

'There isn't anything there.' But she put the handkerchief over the stump of her right thumb and held it there, thinking that the other hand that held it was Peter's hand, covering her own, warm and alive and reassuring. She shut her eyes in a half dream for a moment, then opened them and jerked up her head, blinking at the candle flames, for Mr Clive had begun to moan.

'Oh – oh,' he went. 'Ooh – ooh,' like children playing banshees in sheets. His eyes were closed, his head tilted back so that the cords of his neck stood out like the bones of a bat's wing. The underside of his long chin was lit, and his nostrils, and the roofs of his eye sockets. The rest was shadows, shifting and changing as the candle flames moved in the small draughts of the old cottage.

He whimpered a little, then smiled briefly, then pulled down his mouth and pinched his nostrils to draw in a long sniff of breath. Charlie waited for him to exhale, but it did not seem to come out anywhere.

'Are you there?' he asked, in his usual voice. 'Is anyone there?'

If there is, I'll scream, Charlie's thoughts gabbled.

'Pe – ter. Pe – ter.' The chant descended chromatically. His

186

face worked through a series of expressions, exaggerated by the weird light. Under the sparse lashes of his slitted lids, his eyes appeared to be rolled back. For a ghastly moment, Charlie thought he was really in a trance. She wanted to run, but was glued to her chair, her hands holding each other tightly on the table with the handkerchief between.

What would happen? He suddenly came slumping forward out of the shadows and crashed down on to the table with his head on his arms, sobbing and stuttering. 'It's no good – it's no good! Oh, Peter, Peter. Oh my God, my *God*!' His fist beat the table in front of his head. His narrow back and shoulders were like a sack thrown down.

Charlie had jumped up to pick up the fallen candle. She put out a hand to him, but drew it back. You could not touch despair like that.

She lit the lamp and pulled away the fire-screen and stirred up the logs. She poured out some cherry brandy and brought the glass to the table.

'Come on,' she said. 'Come on, Dad dear, don't cry.'

'Is that you?' He groped out a hand without raising his head.

'Yes. Yes, I'm here.' She took his hand and he clutched her painfully. She stood by him, holding the glass of cherry brandy, and her thoughts roved over a world of images, impressions and unrelated things until his sobbing eased and then stopped.

He let go of her hand and sat up. 'I'm sorry,' he said. He looked about a hundred and two. 'I shouldn't have done that.'

'Better not to meddle with things we don't know about,' Charlie said, but he meant the tears, not the aborted trance.

'Here.' She held out the glass.

'What is it?' He sniffed. 'No thank you, dear. You know I never . . .'

'Medicinal,' she said. 'Do you good.'

But Mr Clive would perish, if brandy were his only hope. He shook his head so smugly that after she had drunk the cherry brandy, she asked him sharply, 'Were you shamming?'

'I don't understand.'

'Moaning and all that. You scared me.'

187

'I didn't mean to. I don't quite know what I did. I don't know what happened.'

She still could not understand whether he had been deliberately faking, or self-deluded, or genuinely on the way to some kind of psychic experience. He did not seem to know himself.

'Nobody came anyway,' she said.

'And yet, you know, there did seem to be something—' He turned his head to his left shoulder again, then turned right round and looked for a long time at the door. There was no knob, only a wooden latch and slot. See something on *that* if you dare, Dad Clive!

'There was something wrong . . . It was you, I think.'

'Me? All I did was sit there and let you frighten me to death.'

'You didn't give yourself a chance. You were holding something back.'

'Oh stop it, Dad. That's quite enough. Come on, it's late. I can't stand any more and your wife will be home from the big orgy.' She went to the door and shooed him out. 'Where's your bike?'

'I walked. I didn't want anyone to see me coming here.'

'You could trust 'em to think the worst.'

He was shocked. He was very prudish, Dad Clive was. He walked off down the garden path with his head up, and did not swing round at the gate to salute her goodbye before he turned on to the path at the top of the bank, his profile and the upper part of his body moving rigidly along the top of the wall like a toy on a string.

Poor man. His tears had been genuine, at least, whatever the rest of it. Charlie should have walked home with him, but she was still angry because he had told her, 'You're holding something back.'

Dark and secret, the coil of a woman's hair lay beneath all her thoughts of Peter. How could Mr Clive know? He couldn't. He was guessing. Trying to explain away his stupid failure. No one was ever going to know. She should have burned the hair that day of the funeral when it all was finished and final. If she went up and got it now and pushed it in between her incandescent logs, it would flare up and frizzle

188

away to nothing in a moment. She saw herself doing that, like seeing yourself swing your feet on to the cold morning floor and wash and put on your clothes, but you are still lying in bed, with it all still to do.

Take a pull at yourself, Lambert. Take a hold of yourself, old chump.

For several days after Dad's secret visit, she was quite nervous. She despised herself for this. She had never been afraid to live alone, never had a moment's unease in this dear house. But Dad had unsettled her. He would unsettle anybody with his moans and faces. It was not fair of him to involve her in such antics. If she were not so loyal to her promise, she would tell his wife about it and get him properly told off, and put a stop to doorknobs and St Francis and all the rest of it.

'You are in a state!' Etty laughed because she jumped when Etty came suddenly up behind her and slid a hand round her waist. 'Who did you think it was – a man? You hoped.'

Since she had the baby and her marriage seemed to be going better, Etty had taken on a repulsive tendency to drag in sex at all times. Some mornings there was a juicy air about her of 'Guess what I've been doing?' as if nobody had ever done it until Etty and the solicitor discovered it in High Wycombe.

'I'm finished with men. I told you.' Charlie had eventually told her about the humiliation of Cousin Alaric. In the end, she had to tell Etty most things. Not because she wanted to, but because Etty dragged them out by the suction of her persistent curiosity.

'That was a century ago. No wonder you're in a state.'

For the first time since childhood, Charlie was not liking to go into a dark room without carrying a light. She made the dog go upstairs before her at night. At this time, she began to have half-formed delusions of somebody in attendance, not quite behind her, just out of range of the corner of her eye. She would spin round to catch the shadowy presence – a coat on a hook, the edge of a door ajar.

One night, the dog barked at an owl. When she went into the kitchen, she thought she saw a man's face outside the window, gone in an instant.

It was minutes before she could make herself open the back door just far enough to let the dog out. He rushed away, barking insanely at the owl.

She did not lock up her cottage when she went to school. Nobody locked doors in the village. When she came home one evening she found that a thief had been in her house. Things were moved, drawers left slightly open. Upstairs, a box of summer clothes under the bed was not quite pushed back.

She drove to Kingsgrove and told the police. The sergeant came and beat about the bushes with a stick, and poked at dozens of different people's footprints in the muddy yard, and the hoofprints of Mrs Nixon's pony.

'Never had a burglary round here since I can remember, and that's been ten years. What did he take, you say?'

'Nothing.'

'Well, that's all right then. I'll say good day, miss, and thank you for the tea.'

After he had gone, Charlie went up to her room and opened the little corner cupboard. There was a dusty narrow shelf at the side before it turned back behind the chimney bricks, a fingerprint in the dust. She stood on a chair to reach far round and feel down into the rubble, touched the newspaper bundle and pulled it out.

The hair looked just the same. Why didn't it die?

FOUR

WHEN DOUGLAS BRODIE went to Australia to sell racing cars, Bubbles Lambert pretended that he had asked her in vain to go with him, and only I knew that he had not.

She sobbed out her rage on my faithful tweed shoulder. She had done this to me before. It was one of the things I was good for, like a fur mat or a shaggy dog for a scolded child to cry on.

It was not only that he had run from her ('I was sick of him anyway, having to stand in the rain at Brooklands while he whizzed by in the Bug'), it was that he had run to Australia, which of all places on earth, simply did not exist.

I comforted her as best I could, and got in a bit of a feel while I was at it. None the wiser for my experience with her in the college bedroom, I was encouraged, since she did not fight me off, to tell her that I loved her. Had always loved her. Was the only man who had ever loved her as she deserved to be loved.

'Honestly, Jamie?' She took her head out of my coat and looked at me with surprised round eyes. Not a tear in sight. She cried dry.

'Oh yes.' I even repeated it, which was blaspheming Eros, for love and Bubbles were two quite different commodities. I then completed the sacrilege by asking her to marry me.

There were several reasons why she said Yes. She did like me, I'll give her that, and since she did not know what love was, she could not miss it. She was twenty-one and I was thirty, and her rebound from the young bounder Douglas Brodie aimed her naturally towards an 'older man'. I was also progressing at the BBC, and had recently been promoted to announcing, with an increase in salary. I had finally got away from Holland Road and was in a flat of my own in the Finchley Road, whither Bubbles had run to me with her tears. Scores in the game of youth are significantly swayed by whether you live at home or away.

Added to all that, Bubbles wanted to be engaged. There was a series of advertisements running at the time with romanticized portraits of betrothed Society girls. 'She's Engaged. She's Lovely. She Uses Ponds.' Muzzy Rugg-Gunn and Bobo Watts had been recently featured, hags whom no amount of face cream could salvage. So Bubbles said Yes to me, and made the loveliest advertisement they ever had. They ran it in twice as many papers as Bobo Watts, whose father was an Earl.

Charlie was at our engagement party in the Fitzjohn's Avenue house. Reggie came after the theatre with some of the cast, including the new ingenue, who was tougher than Darling Rosalie, and more disenchanted. She and Reggie quarrelled about a new song that had been put in to bolster the start of the sagging third act. It was her song, with Reggie being sung at for a change, which gave him a taste of the medicine he had spooned out to so many glazing-eyed, gently swaying leading ladies who had to wait until the last chorus to burst in, breath to breath.

Reggie went to Midge for comfort and she was very nice to him. She was the only genuine Good Woman in the family. Deep though my devotion was, and is, to Charlie, you could never call her that.

Bubbles shimmered and dazzled and drove me quite besotted by the winsome show she put on for the benefit of people like Bobo Watts and her vacuous Major, and various ex-boyfriends who were no doubt drily amused by the fatuous smile with which I received her caresses and the kisses she blew across the room.

Charlie was Charlie, her hair in two coiled mats over her ears with wisps of the ends sticking out, and paint under her fingernails. She left early to go back to the country.

Her mother said, 'I don't like you going back to that empty shack, not after what happened. She had an intruder, our girl did. Charlie had an intruder, everybody. Did you hear about it?'

Nobody said, 'Do tell,' so Charlie could leave, ridiculing her mother's fears quite irritably, to quiet the knowledge that she would throw the dog inside her cottage door and say, 'Go get 'em!' to flush out the nervous shadows by his barks and scampering.

'I thought you were staying the night.' Her father took off his glasses, which made him look like a snubbed baby, with pink rims to his eyes and a twitch in the lids. 'I'm lunching everyone at Sunningdale tomorrow.'

'I can't, Daddy. I promised Cara we would paint the car.'

Her mother frowned. 'You shouldn't encourage that intense child. It's not healthy.' Since the publication of *The Well of Loneliness,* Mrs Lambert was spotting lesbians everywhere, like spies.

I went with Charlie to start Mick the Miller. Nursing my wrist, I leaned over to kiss her. It was a warm spring night and she had the tattered top down, billowing untidily behind her head. When I kissed her cheek, her skin was fresh and cool, tight as an apple. Bubbles's cheek was a flat plane, furred with powder. The pores in the corners of her nose were small craters already.

'Goodnight, Sis,' I said.

'Are you really going to marry her?'

'Don't you want me to?'

'I want you in the family, but I thought it was just one of her tricks.'

'You're jealous,' I said as a joke, but it came out sounding cruel.

'Jamie! What the hell are you doing?' Her hair an aureole, a golden halo (you have to use clichés to describe the Pride of Ponds), Bubbles was posed in the front doorway in a dress with a Mae West silhouette, and I went to her, obedient, slavering.

Sunday was the start of Summer Time. Charlie and the child worked the long day in the yard, wearing boys' grey flannel shorts with snake belts, sleeves rolled up, whistling, laconically companionable. The relationship had levelled out from the peaks and depths of hero worship into an open-handed comradeship more casual and normal than Cara could have with her mother. Mrs Miles was serene and beatific. She never argued or raved or nagged or whipped up a domestic crisis out of a lost sock or a muddy footprint. It was usually her footprint. Charlie shouted at Cara if the child annoyed her, and Cara shouted back. She could not do that with her mother, who would lift a finger and say, 'Hush, there's a blackbird somewhere,' or 'Listen to the jays giving the alarm about cats.'

When Cara spilled water inside the car, Charlie yelled, 'Look what you're doing, you clumsy clot!'

'Grown-ups always expect children to do things they don't do themselves.' Cara had been aware of this for years. 'If you make a bosh shot, it's bad luck, and I'm not supposed to scream at you.'

'You're only a silly kid.'

'I'll grow up. I'll learn to be rude to children. I'll ask them potty questions – how old are you? How do you like school? – and not listen to the answer. I'll walk into their own house and not speak to them. I'll correct them when they stammer. I'll start telephoning while they're telling me the plot of a film.'

Working all day, they covered most of the car with a bright blue paint which made it look like part of a fairground ride.

'You can come back with me after school,' Charlie said, 'and do the red bits. It will be light longer, and if you don't mess about and gas all the time, we can finish it.'

They never did finish painting Mick the Miller, because of what happened after that.

When Charlie had taken Cara to the bus, she lit the lamps and sat down in her unbecoming flannel shorts to read the Sunday paper.

About two weeks ago, a pair of adventurous boys, exploring a ruined farm on the edge of Whittlewood Forest north of Buckingham, had fallen through a rotting well cover into an old cistern, some kind of underground tank or root storage, and found pieces of a dead body wrapped in newspapers. Now there were more details about the gruesome discovery, jostling the Cup Final and the forty-million budget deficit for front-page prominence.

When the boys explored underground, they had found a small leather trunk fastened with two straps in a corner under a pile of refuse and rotting leaves. There was a picture of the two boys, grinning in school caps, not yet grown to their teeth. In the trunk they had found the arms and legs of a woman and part of what had once been her head. After checking the relatives of missing persons, the remains had now been identified, through some trinket, as those of Miss Elizabeth 'Bessie' Hunter, of 114 Calshott Road, Birmingham, missing since September, 1930, from the home of a Mrs Thomas Dexter in Doniston St Mary, where she was employed as a maid. There was a blown-up snapshot of a gipsy-looking girl sitting on a railing in a cotton dress, with a lot of black hair and a raffish grin for the camera; Weston-super-Mare pier in the background. The Home Office pathologist was of the opinion that the woman had been dead for about seven months. There was also a photograph of the small leather trunk.

Cold, logical, Charlie surprised herself by the calmness with which she was able to reckon back to the weekend at Garfield Hall, the last weekend in September, seven months ago. All right. Peter was dead too, so there was nothing to be done about it.

Nothing to be done except to know for sure. That seemed to be the important thing that Charlie had to do. Next morning, she took the dog and the fish to Quentin, telephoned Mrs Baxter, who did not hear well on the telephone and thought she was saying, 'I can't win' instead of, 'I can't come in today,' and took a train from Oxford to Birmingham to try to find out whether the hair of Elizabeth Hunter had been chopped roughly off.

On either side of Calshott Road, brown brick terrace houses stood flush with the narrow pavement, watching each other across the street like men and girls at a village dance. Small windows, a whitened doorstep, flat roofs with clusters of chimneys whose odd-shaped vanes and turning funnels were the only variants of the street.

It was a poorish dwelling place, but not busy and neighbourly. No children played in the street. Housewives in aprons and hairnets stood at doorways to receive the baker instead of going out to his cart. Curtains and great plants in fat containers like chamber pots blocked the view in and out of the ground-floor rooms. Every window of every house had an ochre blind drawn exactly halfway down, cord and wood acorn hanging dead centre.

There were no cars at the kerb. A bicycle with a butcher's basket, propped neatly. Motorcycles covered with tarpaulin. A few small tradesmen's vans in which the roundsmen had come home, since it was dinnertime.

When Charlie knocked on the door of No 114, varnished with an artificial grain, a man came to open it with a napkin in his hand, jaws working.

'Mr Hunter?'

He nodded. He was a big man with stooped shoulders like a bear. He had taken off the collar of his shirt. His trousers were held up with a thick belt like a – like a strap round a leather trunk.

'I'm sorry to bother you.' She had not thought out what she was going to say.

'We've done eating our dinner,' he said, as if that were the only thing on his mind.

'May I talk to you? I'm a reporter for the *Oxford Mail*.' Fated to barge in on parents of the violently dead, Charlie remembered Gordon calling up the back stairs at Wilton Crescent, 'She don't want to see no one,' and Rita arguing. 'It might be the Papers.' People would always talk to the Papers.

'Come in,' the man said ungraciously. He turned and went ahead of Charlie, since he was too bulky to step to the side of the dark narrow hall and let her pass.

Mrs Hunter was in the back room with a white cloth on a small table, and sauce bottles, cruets, pickles, jam, a pot of tea under a cosy made to look like a crinoline skirt with a doll's china body on top.

It was an everyday scene, and the Hunters behaved in an everyday way. They did not seem excited or upset by the gruesome tragedy. They were even quite hard. Charlie took out a pencil and an old envelope to look as if she were taking notes, and they answered her questions with a certain flat bitterness, getting in digs now and then about their murdered daughter.

'No, we didn't report it for quite a time after she went missing. Old Mrs Dexter carried on, because she was left with only her companion, but she'd been off before, Bessie had, with some man or other. Don't expect me to go chasing after her skirts,' Mrs Hunter said to Charlie, as if the girl were still alive, and out of favour.

'Amusement mad, she was,' the father said. 'Man mad. We couldn't do nothing with her.'

'Did she have – one particular friend? A man, I mean.'

'She had dozens, don't ask me. Asking for trouble, and trouble she got.' He did not need to add Serve her right.

A pounding on the door admitted a policeman with a red neck above a tight collar, who had come with a message from the Inspector.

'Who's this then?'

'The Papers.' They were neither annoyed nor pleased with Charlie. She stood with the corner of a sideboard jammed into her back while they sat and sucked at their tea and did not offer her a cup.

'Now then, now then,' said the policeman automatically. 'You can't come bothering people in their time of sorrow.'

Charlie was more distressed than the Hunters. Glandular lumps ached the sides of her neck. She could not swallow down the tightness of her throat to ask them anything about the body. *Part of the head.* What did that mean? She saw one staring eye. The skull full of teeth that had grinned with such bravado at Weston-super-Mare.

She left the house with the policeman. As they went out, two skinny young men in grubby raincoats came down the street, one slung about with a big box camera, genuine reporters. Mr Hunter let them in as laconically as he had let Charlie out, and banged the door behind them.

'Are you on the case?' Charlie asked the policeman, who was a friendly sort, red-cheeked and merry-eyed, the life and soul of the foundlings' Christmas party.

'I might be.'

'I wondered if you had seen the body.' Charlie managed to get the words out hoarsely past the constriction of her throat.

He shook his head. 'You don't want to think about things like that, love,' he said.

'I have to get details. I mean – I'm supposed to find out things like whether the hair had been cut off. Long hair, she had, you see . . .'

'I'll tell you one thing.' The policeman looked up and down the street and then lowered his voice, just as avid for horrors as he thought Charlie was. 'They're saying at the station,' he said, 'that the top of her head was blown right off. Just this bottom part of the skull, they found, with bits of black hair stuck here and there, all chopped about where he'd hacked her up. I didn't see it, mind, but that's what they're saying at the station.'

She had locked her house before she went to Birmingham. When she got home, she could not turn the key in the back door. She looked and saw that the keyhole was slightly distorted, as if someone had put in a screwdriver or some piece of metal and tried to turn the lock.

Although most of the days were windy and grey, with big sheets of cloud storming up across the hills, more like hockey weather, it was now the summer term, so it had to be cricket.

To encourage the flagging enthusiasm of the girls, who hated it even worse than hockey, because it took longer, Charlie let one of them umpire, wearing layers of sweaters and linen hats discarded by bowlers and batsmen, and played herself to show them how it should be done.

Cara Miles was the only one who was as keen as Charlie had to be. One spidery, one solid, they galloped about the field, telling each other, 'Good shot!' or 'Fielded!', and running to change sides at the end of the Over, pushing and clucking at the loafing girls with bits of long rank grass in their mouths.

After she had been to Birmingham, Charlie did not speak properly to anybody. She walked in a private cloud, and the girls told each other that since it could not be pregnancy, it

must be the change of life, brought on prematurely by demon-
strating the backstroke in the Wycombe Public Baths, whither
crocodiles now slogged through the rain every week with
rolled-up towels, because it was the summer term.

When she was not at school on Monday, Cara, obsessed by
the job in hand, was afraid she had stayed at home to finish
painting the car without her. Although they were casual and
close at the cottage, they could not be at school, especially now
with Charlie hardly speaking to anybody. She did not even
speak to Cara, though the child hung about like a news photographer trying to sneak a shot of Garbo. There was no
'Fielded' or, 'Good Try' at cricket practice. Charlie stationed
herself in the Deep Field and let the game go to pot by itself
in a welter of squabbling and swung bats and wildly hurled
balls. It was only by mistake that Caroline Mutch swiped a
ball to the boundary, the weight of the bat swinging her body
round and round and knocking down her wicket. The game
broke up in shrieks and yells like Derby Day, as everyone fell
on Caroline with backslaps, knocked her to the ground and fell
into the wet grass themselves, legs in the air like puppies. Two
of them took the opportunity to slip away while Charlie loped
after the ball, which had rolled into the long grass at the edge
of the field by the road.

Beyond the fence, a shabby man in a battered hat stood
watching her. Charlie bent for the cricket ball, and looked up
into his eyes.

'You're dead.'

He shook his head. He did not say anything.

'I saw you dead. I saw your coffin. I was there when they
buried you.'

He shrugged, and put his hands down into the pockets of his
rough jacket, kicking at a tuft of grass with a boot that looked
as if it did not fit him.

'Who was it then?'

'Bit of somebody else?'

'They couldn't identify people.'

'That's what I reckoned.'

When he smiled, his short white teeth were the same, and
his lips were long and responsive, but the skin round them was

drawn back to hollows under his cheekbones. It was like seeing him ten or fifteen years older. His eyebrows and the front of his hair must have been burned away. The eyebrows had grown back sparse and paler, with a ragged gap in one where a white scar cut through. His hair under the punched-in old hat was still thick and brown, but it grew farther back on his forehead, less boyish. The bright brown eyes by which she had known him had lost the richness of their lashes. He had a stubble of gingerish beard round his chin. He looked gaunt, beggarly, haunted, a man who had walked among the dead.

Charlie hung on the wire fence like an ape, staring at him. 'You got away,' she said stupidly.

'A water tank burst above me. It made a gap in the flames for long enough to kick a bit of the window out.'

'But then why did you—'

Cara was windmilling towards her. 'I'll help you find it! I'm coming, Miss Lambert!' sputtering her excuse to get close to Charlie again.

Peter pulled down his wretched hat and turned away.

'I can meet you in an hour,' Charlie said quickly.

'Not here.'

'Walk on the road towards London. I'll come in the car.'

Cara was upon her. 'Here I come, Miss Lambert!' – and she turned and ran back with her to the disintegrated game.

He was wandering slowly along the side of the road like a tramp, hands in the pockets of his sagging jacket. When she stopped by him, he tugged at the car door, remembering its vice, and sat down with a sigh on the lumpy seat. She did not know what to say to him. She drove on, aware that he was watching her. She was wearing her blue gym tunic with her cricket shoes and her white sweater with the school colours at the neck. Her hair lay down her back in long pigtails.

'You look like a schoolgirl,' he said.

'So I've been told.'

'Where are we going?'

A secret place. 'That church on the hill at West Wycombe. The mausoleum. Nobody goes there.' He was a ghost. She would take him to a ghostly place.

They left the car at the bottom of the hill and climbed up through the long grass and bushes. Breathing easily, she was ahead of him at the octagon of open stone arches, weird burying place of the Dashwoods. He trudged up in his clumsy boots and leaned against a column, looking down the hill to where the long straight road ran into the town, gathering houses as it went. Charlie stood a little apart, not knowing what to do. When he had recovered his breath, he said, 'Come over here.' He took her hand. His hand was hard and rough, not clean as it had been before. He looked for a long time at the stump of her thumb. Charlie hated people to look at it.

'That was a funny day,' he said.

'If you hadn't come, what would have happened to me?'

'You might have been better off.' He spoke rather roughly, with the careless accent of a man who belonged to no place.

She did not want to be afraid of him, but she pulled back her hand and said breathlessly, 'Let's go inside the church.'

She went quickly ahead of him across the grass to the medieval church at the crest of the hill. Poised on a slender shaft at the top of the square bell tower, the crazy gilded ball sailed above the Chiltern landscape, a hollow sphere for orgies or trysts or secret huddles of Cavaliers. A tangle of different legends clung about it.

It was cold in the church. The stone and brasses gave off an empty bitter breath. Peter and Charlie sat in the very middle of the church, as if the pews in front and behind could protect them. He did not want to talk, and she could not. He sat as if he were very tired, with his hands between his knees, turning his old hat round and round by its shapeless brim, his eyes staring at nothing, like a homeless man on a station bench, waiting for dawn.

I wanted him alive. I wanted it all to be a dream. I am sitting next to him. My elbow is against his jacket. He is alive, that's all.

He is a murderer. She looked at his brown hands and tried to force herself methodically to think what they had done. She dragged her mind inwards to the point of truth, then let thought snap quickly away into the outer vacuum where there was only sensation. If they could sit like this in the church for ever, there would be no need to think.

The only things that Peter said were, 'I'm hungry,' and 'I'm tired.' Charlie wanted to throw her arms round him and tell him that she would feed him, give him rest. He had been sleeping in barns and haystacks. He dropped out small bits of information jerkily. He had done odd jobs, begged from housewives, trod out a pair of boots on the road south. He had been working on a factory site near Belfast. Jack Morgan. Casual labourer.

Why? If they could just go on sitting here, she would not have to ask him.

A sort of verger came into the church. They sat in silence while he pottered about for a bit before coming up to them very pleasantly and asking if they would like to visit the golden ball.

'Oh?' Charlie had to jump her wits back in again. 'Oh no. No thank you.'

'Well, I thought. Most folk who come here come for that. Quite a landmark, you know.' If he thought they made a strange pair, one an overgrown schoolgirl, the other a tramp, he did not show it.

Peter looked up at the man with a smile on his thin stubbled face. 'Thanks very much,' he said. 'I'd like to go up there.'

The verger took them up through the tower and across a platform where bell ropes slanted through the floor, to climb a steep rickety stair which spiralled up in a corner space no wider than a man.

'The Hell Fire Club used to come up here to play cards and drink in the ball, they say. But I always say if they didn't come down sober, they must have broken their necks.' The verger's chuckle went with the joke, repeated for every sightseer.

Peter and Charlie stood in the wind on the small platform round the base of the hollow ball. A tiny gold knob from a distance, from close below it was about six feet across, unstable on its slender neck, a giant child's fabrication of papier-mâché, patched in gold leaf. The verger climbed up the steps at one side of the neck and braced himself there to lift the

202

leaden trapdoor, which opened up and out. They looked up at his legs, trousers tensed to the calves by the wind, the dim interior beyond his shoulders, above that the golden curve of the globe, racing across a sky of tempestuous clouds.

Charlie looked at Peter and saw that he was trembling.

'Let's go down.'

'No,' he said, still looking up. 'I've got to see if I'm still scared of heights.'

'Are you?'

'Yes.'

She moved closer to him, and he gripped both her arms. 'I'm all right if I don't look down.'

'Help yourselves.' The verger came nimbly down and Peter turned Charlie to the steps and pushed her up them, following so close behind that she fell through the trapdoor opening and landed on her hands and knees inside the ball.

It was a wooden framework, musty smelling, with narrow benches round the sides, just room for about six people to sit with heads bent, backs curved to the wall.

The verger called up to them. 'There's someone down there to see me. Take care. I'll be back to get you down.'

Charlie looked out and saw a foreshortened man get out of a car far below. Small portholes gave views of the straight thoroughfare to High Wycombe with traffic like toys, the western road by which they had come, turning away round the long shoulder of the hill, the green meadows and the tops of trees along the valley to Risborough.

Below her, a bird flew. 'Look,' she said, but Peter pulled her down. They sat hunched on the bench, knees side by side, leaning forward, as if they were waiting to be shot into space.

'I can't look down.' Peter's hands were still shaking a little, plucking at the worn cloth of his trousers "We're down!" someone yelled. The lights went out everywhere and the floor tipped up. I saw the trees rush up to me and the earth was smothered in flames and the flame was the ship. Everything was burst open, red and screaming with fire. I knew we were all killed. The water soaked over me like oil. I fell into the rain and I ran in the rain, my clothes were burning. I fell into a swampy place and rolled about. I thought I could still hear people screaming. I thought I had gone mad.

'That's why I ran away,' he said quickly. 'I couldn't think. I couldn't remember who I was. I couldn't remember anything. That's why I can't go back, don't you see, because I can't be the same man again.' He talked rapidly now, stuttering, to try to make her believe, and yet she thought that all the time he knew that she did not believe him at all.

Did he guess how much she knew? He knew she had the dead girl's hair. That was what he was looking for. That was why he had come to find her. He is a murderer. Why doesn't he kill me? He put his hands on her fiercely and she thought, He could kill me now.

Instead, he bent her back away from the overhanging framework and kissed her very roughly, beard cutting her, eyes staring yellow like a lion. He dragged at her clothes. The golden ball spun through the sky as his hand found her breast tenderly, his hand, his butcher's hand.

How can I ever show this to anyone? How can I even show it to Julia? Certainly not to Julia. What shall I do, Charlie? She inhabits my head so busily now, but does not tell me what to do.

You can believe that the dead communicate with us through thoughts and dreams, just as easily as Dad Clive believed in his doorknobs. But you can't prove that the thoughts and dreams are not products of the living brain, any more than you can prove that God puts ideas into your head. If He can't speak without using your brains, how can you prove that the ideas are His not yours?

Dad Clive used to believe in spirit writing. When the eldest Jaffry child wrote a book that summer, he held it in his lap in a darkened room and then came forth to announce that it had been edited by Sir Walter Scott. Subsequently the manuscript got burned by mistake in the perforated dustbin he used as an incinerator for secret memoranda from Post Office Headquarters, so no one ever knew.

How much does Charlie want me to tell?

'My dad a killer?' Julia will leer up one side of the mouth she lards with leucous slug's trail lipstick as if she were a teenager. 'Yeah. Oh sure.'

But there are two other people to think of. Gordon and Rita, who still live at Cowley Centre, retired to ten pin bowling and Bingo. I have not seen them for years, and did not like them when I did. But they have children. Their children have children. Like Julia, they might fancy the joke, 'My great uncle was a murderer.' So I think I shall not give any of them that pleasure. They probably wouldn't believe it. I didn't at first. Even when Charlie cried to me, 'He's killed once—' I did not really believe her. And then he was dead and a hero. *Jack Morgan, a Gallant Death* on the headstone the locals put up. How many people get their names on two tombstones? How many die two hero's deaths, for that matter? I asked a lawyer once what the police would do if a man who was gallantly dead came under suspicion of some unsolved crime, years and years later.

He said, 'It would be kinder not to tell them. They've got enough live crooks on their plate already.'

'Would they start another inquiry?'

'What for? You can't have a trial without a suspect.'

It was not until years and years later – about twenty-five years later, after we were married and back in the village, that Charlie began to tell me bit by bit who Jack Morgan really was. She wanted to show me the coil of black hair, but I would not let her.

It was odd of her to keep it all those years, and odder of me to keep it now. It is still in the place where she hid it more securely when she brought Peter back to this cottage after that session in the golden ball at West Wycombe.

It was a weird place to have such a session. It is even weirder now that the tourists have taken over the whole outfit and they have opened up the Hell Fire caves and started a museum with souvenirs and teas.

I took some boys there from the school that the Drydens run

up at the Big House. The school is called New Hope, although it really should be called Last Hope, since that is what it is for some of the boys.

They are neither fish nor fowl boys, not completely retarded, but not able to cope with an ordinary school. Some of them can't read properly. Some cannot concentrate, even on a game of cards. Some of them have broken homes and wretched histories of drunken fathers or psychotic mothers. Some of them have brilliantly successful parents who would not allow a slow child to fail. And they had better be successful, because old Dryden charges the earth.

Some of the local people, like Henry Clay who is trying for a Conservative candidacy on a Clean Up Oxon platform, and Mrs Nunn the antiquarian in Ewelme, talk about the school as if it was full of lunatics who will break out and rape everybody. I suppress the obvious retort that you would have to be a lunatic to rape Mrs Nunn. Mrs Meagan, who does a bit of sweeping through at New Hope, says that it is full of hot red Communists, but that is not true either.

The boys who are dependable are allowed to wander into the village and buy things at the new Mini-market which has replaced the old sweetshop at the White Hart, though it does not stock much more than Mrs Hathaway did. I have got to know a few of them. Some are about nineteen or twenty and doing twelve-year-old work, but most are ordinary boys with a bit of bad luck. Two of them, who walk across my back garden on their way to the Kingsgrove road, I have got to know quite well. Their parents never come to see them, so I take them out sometimes.

I took them to West Wycombe. You can't climb up into the ball now. They can't get anyone to open the trapdoor, and they had to take away the steps because they had the ball regilded ten years ago and people wrote their names all over the gold leaf.

We went into the caves, past a machine that sold iced lollies, through a turnstile like a public lavatory, and into the honeycomb tunnels that an early Dashwood excavated for the dual purpose of building up the long straight road for his guests and giving work to the local unemployed. After the Hell

Fire Club broke up at Medmenham, its remnants came to West Wycombe and had a few orgies in the caves, 'tis said.

And said now by the tape-recorded voice of suave Sir Francis Dashwood, which follows you like a bad conscience down the horrid white galleries. My boys yelled and gibbered like mad monks and chased each other and chased some girls who were there in trousers so tight they must have to shave their pubic hair. In the inner cavern, an old geezer in knee breeches who looked rather like me leered at a doxie's waxen legs. Although by all accounts in those days they didn't waste time leering.

'Oh, Miss Lambert, please Miss Lambert.' Cara Miles lurked outside the gym, flattened against the wall in an attempt at camouflage.

'What?' Charlie had walked on round the corner of the corridor before she realized the child was tagging after her, and stopped.

School was like a dream now. She went through the motions of drilling and coaching and bowling leg breaks to faltering girls in the nets, but she was scarcely aware of what she did, until she could wake from the stupid dream of the day and run for her bright blue car.

'Oh Miss Lambert, please Miss Lambert, you did say we could finish Mick the Miller.' Cara tugged at her stocking tops, took the end of her hair in her mouth, did everything except look at Charlie. 'You did say we-we-we could do it after school.' She had taken to stammering sometimes, since one of the girls had said, 'No wonder you stammer with all your repressions.'

'Well look, I didn't *say* that.'

To the old Charlie, Cara would have shouted, in a whisper, for the dadoed walls of St Gabriel's had a thousand ears, 'You *did*! Why isn't it lying when grown-ups do it?'

207

To the new, bemused Charlie, who used to shout at her man to man, but never snub her irritably, it was difficult to mumble, half turned away, 'Then what – about Saturday?'

'No, no, we can't. I'm – I'm going to be busy. I've got a lot to do.' Charlie began to walk on, bouncing a little in her gym shoes, the walk that Cara watched and knew. 'We'll do it some day.' She looked back and smiled. 'I promise.'

'Some day.' Cara refused the smile. 'I promise.' She stood where she was until Charlie rounded the corner and the magical essence of her was gone from the dull green corridor.

After the verger had flushed them out of the golden ball – 'Hulloa, up there! Is anyone at home?' – Charlie had driven Peter back to the village after dark. It was the first time since the seance that she had not minded going into her empty house at night.

'You were here, weren't you?' she said to Peter. 'Looking through the house.'

'Why should I?' He went in ahead of her and waited while she lit a lamp in the kitchen. He stood looking round as if he had not seen it before.

'I had to get a new lock, after you tried to get in again.' Charlie showed him the new key, but he did not look at it. He put back her plaits behind her shoulders and held them there with one hand, forcing back her head so that she thought her neck would break. His face covered hers hungrily, devouring, her reason sucked powerless into a vacuum, deeper and deeper. She did not feel the pain in her neck until he let her go. She staggered, staring at his face, wolfish in the shadowing yellow light.

'Let your hair loose,' he said.

Upstairs, her black hair falling over her breasts and shoulders, she whispered, 'I never . . .' She wanted to tell him that she was afraid, not of him but of herself – still she sat on the bench outside the mullioned window and heard them laugh at her – that she would do something wrong and he would leave her in disgust.

But he would not talk to her at all. It was very rough, not tender. She screamed and he said, 'Shut up,' and held his calloused hand across her face.

'That was almost rape,' he said afterwards. 'So now you know the worst.'

'I don't care.'

'It gets better.'

'I don't care. I don't care what you do to me. You can do anything you want.'

'You're insane. Do you always say that?'

'Nobody ever did anything to me.'

'I know that.' He laughed with a sort of beastly triumph, mocking seduction. After he had first kissed her, he had seemed to be growing stronger, draining her into himself.

'Peter.'

'Yes love.'

'You killed that girl.'

He did not answer. The room was quite dark and she could not see his face. He lay very still, and after a while he said, 'How do you know?'

'I found her hair in your car.'

'And gave it to the coppers?'

'I've never told anybody.'

'It was an accident. They all say that, I suppose. It was an accident, you see.' He began to tell her things quite calmly in the darkness. If only she had not said, 'You killed that girl.' If only he had denied it. If only he would not tell her. In some way it could not be true.

'I was fooling with the gun – pointing it at her and she was jeering and laughing in that way she had. She died laughing at me. I was fooling with the hammer to cock the gun. It was stiff and my finger slipped. It blew off the top of her head. Her brains and stuff were all over the wall of that old shack. You know what I did?' From his voice, she could hear him smile. 'I went mad. I didn't know what I was doing. She was still propped on the bench and I tried to scoop up her brains and put them back in her skull and I was screaming at her, "Don't die!" But she was dead, you see.'

Charlie whispered, 'The hair . . .'

'I chopped it off. When she told me she'd got this chap's baby, I called her a whore and I grabbed her by that long mucky hair and got my knife out.' He made a harsh cutting sound at the back of his throat. 'So now you can run to the police.'

'They think you're dead.'

'That's why I ran when I found I wasn't. Now I'm dead. You saw me buried.'

'Why did you come back?'

'I read in the paper they found the trunk. I knew you had her mucking hair. I knew you were the only person in the whole world, the only person in the world ... I came back to get Bessie's hair.'

After he was deeply asleep, Charlie took the hair out of the little corner cupboard in the dark, watching the bed to see if he stirred. She took it downstairs and hid it in the bricks of the thick chimney built against the back of the shed for the old stone copper. The copper was cracked, part of the rim fallen away. No one had boiled clothes in it within memory. The chimney ran up behind it from the fire space underneath. Kneeling down, she thrust in the newspaper bundle, then with a stick she managed to push it quite far up the chimney. Reaching forward, her head against the stone side of the copper, she wedged bricks tightly across the chimney opening, so that he would never find what he had come back from the dead to get. Because once he had found it, then he would kill her too.

He stayed hidden during the day, and every evening she drove home in a panic that he would be gone. He slept most of the day, and at night he ate and drank and made love to her brutally and passionately and tenderly. She looked back in wonder at the awkward gym mistress virgin Charlie, exorcized at last by the rebellion of the flesh.

They made the other bedroom into a sort of a sitting-room, so that he could stay upstairs while it was light. Charlie met Mrs Nixon in Kingsgrove. She said, 'I came by to bring back that book while you were at work, but the house was locked up and the curtains drawn. You shouldn't draw those curtains on the south side, dear. They'll fade shockingly.'

'I bought a new rug. I don't want the sun to fade that.' That was the sort of talk Mrs Nixon understood.

'Why haven't you been over to supper? You don't look yourself, with those eyes.'

'I've lost a bit of weight.'

'Not banting, I hope. You must come next week. The early peas are ripe.'

'I'd love to if I can. I'm working on a textbook for students at Physical Training schools.' Charlie was using this to explain why she was not seen at Quentin and Bob's for lunch, or in the village hall for the touring players' production of *Under Two Flags*, or in the Clives's thatched cottage for evening chats, and visits with Dad's chicks and ducklings and kids and cucumbers and the various other forms of life he was propagating.

The Clives were the danger. It tore at her heart to see Peter's picture on the top shelf of the cakestand with the little pitcher of fresh flowers. To hear Nelly say, 'I baked a rhubarb pie today for Madam. Peter's favourite, I told her. Mum, he'd say, there's no one can make pastry like you. And Mrs Hammond said, "You must be very proud of him. He died for his country." "Of course," I said. "That's the way we try to look at it, madam."' To listen to Dad throw a remark over his left shoulder once in a while and smile or look wise, as if he had an answer. Peter's face was on the lime-washed glass of the cucumber frame again.

How much longer was it possible to keep the secret? And because it seemed to be possible, Peter began to get bolder. At night he came downstairs. If the dog barked, or feet crunched on the road, he could escape up the stairs which led out of the sitting-room.

Dad Clive slipped down one night when Nelly had a dinner party. Peter was in the outhouse at the end of the path (he used a chamber pot by day and emptied it at night), and Charlie had wandered out to look at stars. Peter was halfway back down the path when his father materialized noiselessly out of the night and stood like a shadow in the dark doorway. Peter kept very still by the hedge until he heard Charlie stumble over a stone and her voice. 'Peter ... Oh, goodness Dad, you frightened me! I thought you were a ghost.'

'You saw something?' Mr Clive grabbed her arm eagerly.

'I thought—' She tried to steady her voice. 'Just for a moment, you looked like someone else.'

'You see, it is possible.'

'Oh no, I didn't mean that. Come through to the front room where there's some light.'

Peter never used the other downstairs room where she and Dad had sat for the seance, so that there would be somewhere to take a visitor, with no risk of his beer glass or his cigarettes, they were a different brand from Charlie's, and he had taught her to be cunning, neglecting no detail. They lit a lamp in that room while they were sitting in the other behind drawn curtains, so that if a neighbour's child came to tap for a loan of sugar, he would tap at the lighted window.

'You want to sit again with me?'

'No, no, Dad, come on. It isn't good for you. Let's not talk about it any more. Look, I'll play you a gramophone record.'

She tried to humour him out of his spiritualist mood, but he could be stubborn in his gentle way. He sat in the same chair at the table, and said, 'I'm waiting, Charlotte.'

When she refused to sit opposite him, he got up stiffly and went to the door quite piqued. 'Some day when you've passed on,' he told her, 'you'll be waiting for me to call you. Well, perhaps I shan't call.'

'You'll be dead before me,' Charlie said, for he really knew how to get on her nerves.

'O-oh no. O-oh no.' He smiled. 'He shall come as a thief in the night, you know.'

When he had gone, she ran out into the back garden, but could not find Peter anywhere. She looked for him, calling softly. She was going back into the house when his hand fell on her shoulder and stopped her heart in a rush of terror.

He pushed her into the house and slammed the door. 'You bloody stupid bitch.' His brown eyes were cold with anger. 'How did he get in?'

'I can't stop him. Peter, someone's bound to see you in the end. It's not safe for you to stay here.'

'I've got to keep an eye on you, Charlie.' In his indeterminate accent, neither urban nor rural, her name was almost Charlay. 'I don't trust you, girl.'

His anger was cold. Hers flared red hot. 'You're mad!' She threw a spoon, whatever it was, the first thing to her hand, and shouted at him. 'You're raving mad to think you can get away with it. There must be people who know you knew that girl. They've probably told already. You'll be caught in the end. Someone will see you.'

'I don't know.' He fingered the beard which was growing in soft and brown, ran his hand over his bony forehead and cheeks. 'I don't look like I used.' It was true, although rest and food had filled out some of the gaunt hollows.

'It's mad to live like this.' She turned away because she was beginning to cry. 'You can't be invisible for ever.'

'That's why I've got to have the hair.' He stood behind her. They were the same height. He talked into the black cascade of her hair, which she had to wear loose when she was with him.

'Why don't you kill me?' She put her hands over her face and her breath, full of tears, filled the hollow of the palms, hot and damp.

'Because I don't know where it is. You're going to give it to me.'

'No.'

'You will in the end,' he said. 'I can wait.'

On a Sunday morning, opening her eyes in the darkened bedroom, she saw Peter awake and watching her.

'It's my birthday,' he said.

'Many happies.' She had bought presents for him. Another jacket, whisky, a dressing-gown. She had buried all his old clothes on a disused dump among old wheels and bedsteads. All the money she earned was going on food and wine and shoes and clothes for him. A new wireless. Books he wanted – 'Get me a book of stories about the sea. Bring me another Edgar Wallace.'

Last week she had to ask her father for a loan to pay the rates on her house.

'You don't have to pay me back, my dear.'

'Yes, I must.'

'That puts you in debt. I'd rather give it you than have you be in debt.' One of Dudley Lambert's apothegms was that he had never owed a penny in his life.

'So what say for a birthday treat I put on dark glasses and we go to London?'

'I've got to go out with your father and mother.'

'You can't. It's my birthday.'

'That's why I've got to go.'

'Where?'

'To visit your grave.'

After the loss of the airship, a memorial fund had been started for the families of the dead men. Because of the Depression, not much money was raised, and most of it was spent on the stone tomb over the grave at Cardington, whose foundations were being laid when Charlie and the Clives went there with potted plants.

'Working on a Sunday?' The tears which had crimsoned Nelly's cheeks as she gripped Charlie's arm on the same spot where they had stood at the funeral like swimmers at the edge of a pool, ebbed when she saw this extravagance. 'I never gave leave to spend my money on overtime pay.'

Because the newspaper appeal had been signed by a lady of title, she had contributed to the fund, although it was giving money to herself.

'You'll whistle for any return on *that* money,' her husband said sadly, 'for there'll be none ever distributed, you wait and see.'

'Are you saying that as a prophecy, or because it's common sense?' With Dad forecasting at all hours, Mrs Clive liked to know where she stood.

Since the seance project had fallen through, because Charlie would not cooperate and you never heard of anyone having a seance all by themselves, Mr Clive had gone back to seeing, stimulated by something he read about Mrs Woodruff, the famous clairvoyant.

About a year ago, she had been at a dinner where a government official had publicly insulted his own wife.

'Here's to you, sir.' The outraged 'Woody' raised her glass. 'May you descend in the flames of hell!' Shocked, the whole room listened, and heard her add in a whisper, 'As you will, within three months of this night.' The man was one of the passengers on the R101.

This was the sort of story that mightily appealed to Mr Clive. Inspired, he 'saw' the assassination of the Chancellor of the Exchequer by a waiter at a banquet. It was only with difficulty that Nelly dissuaded him from going up to London to stand outside the Mansion House and shout, 'Beware!' when Philip Snowden arrived.

He saw the foaling of Honeywell's cart mare, right to the anticipated day. He said to Mrs Hawkes, writing out a telegram on the chest of drawers, 'Excuse me mentioning it, but a smear of cowdung would get rid of that wart on your finger.'

It did! Snowden still lived, but Mrs Hawkes's wart had not let him down, and he was encouraged to 'do' Quentin and Bob, who exclaimed that nothing so exciting had happened to them for years, and invited a crowd of friends to see them being seen.

Whether Mr Clive did have a small gift of clairvoyance, or whether he was only lucky in a few noteworthy guesses among the wild shots that went unremembered, no one could ever decide. He could not be accused of faking, since he believed so sincerely in himself.

He told Bob some things about his wife and children which he could have known if he kept his ears open in the post office, nerve centre of local information. But Bob, in his slow, grinning way, was amazed.

'Tis a right miracle, Postmaster dear. Thee has told oi things us never knew we'mselves.' Everyone drank quantities of cider from the keg in the scullery and Mrs Ram was at the stove, turning out girdle scones like a maniac.

She brewed tea in a special pot for Mr Clive. 'A clairvoyant neither drinks nor smokes,' he chided a foaming tankard. Nor eats meat, he had also read, but he liked a nice roast, and Nelly's braised veal.

Head up, nostrils wide, inhaling his success, he returned lightfoot to Mrs Clive, who was inclined to disapprove of Quentin and Bob because gentry did not belong in thatched cottages, but in big houses like the Hammonds, with draughts and endless distances to carry trays.

'I was a great success, my dear. I don't like to say this' (a favourite prefix to a statement he was going to enjoy) 'but they do put you to shame in the strength of their belief.'

Quentin wrote a piece about him for the *Morning Post*: 'Saying Sooth in an Oxfordshire Village.'

Most of the local people read it. 'Let's see what our Quentin has to say for himself this time,' half amused, half possessive. It was *fun* to have a real live author in the neighbourhood. Our Tame Scribe, he was introduced at garden parties and bazaars. He bought a pair of plain glass spectacles at Woolworths so that he could blink owlishly at the White Elephant stall.

After he had written 'Saying Sooth', it was Dad Clive who was the lion. Mrs Hammond started it by asking Nelly to persuade him to come and sit in a tent at her fête, dressed as a mystic.

'I don't think he would do that, madam, no.'

'Well please find out at least, Mrs Clive. That's all I'm asking.' The garden fête at the Big House was her event of the season. People and food were shipped down from London. Her daughters were forced into their *Quality Street* costumes. Mr Hammond took to the hills with dog and gun. Guests tried to remember from year to year what the date was likely to be, so they could avoid that weekend. Nelly Clive and the other servants, run ragged on preparations, had been fed up with the fête for weeks, since Madam talked of nothing else and had even asked Mr Herriott to pray for sun, since she did not go to his church to pray herself.

When Mrs Clive told her husband, 'I said I didn't think you'd do it,' he said, 'Why not? Those who have something to give should not be close fisted.' He even consented to wear a brocade turban, which sat low on his narrow head, but a burned cork moustache he jibbed at. 'With all due respect, Mrs H, this is not a pantomime.'

He also jibbed at taking fees for clairvoyance.

'But it's to raise money for the Africans.' Mrs Hammond made a special visit to the post office with dogs and brogues, busy as she was.

'I don't like it, madam. Don't like it at all.'

'Come, don't be so stubborn, Mr Clive.' She had one of those high, carrying voices with which Englishwomen go round Harrods saying, 'That isn't what I had in mind at *all*.' It carried to Mrs Clive at the washing line and she hurried in, afraid that Dad would forget his place and Mrs Hammond, who had influence in the County Seat, might get him sacked from the post office and then where would they be?

'You explain to him.' Mrs Hammond turned to her thankfully, like a lawyer greeting the nurse of a senile testator. 'If he doesn't charge a fee, it's robbing the Africans, don't you see?'

'I've got nothing against the black people . . .'

'If you don't charge, they won't think it's worth anything.' Nelly Clive could often make logical truth out of a confused conversation.

He agreed on condition that he never touched a penny, which turned out to be quite a disappointment to his wife, since he was such a success in his turban that other people started to ask him to appear at fêtes and socials and charity bazaars. He developed quite a profitable line by telling people a few things they knew already and then saying, 'Give me another two bob and I'll tell you what's to come.'

He 'saw' obvious things like pet dogs and journeys and children and minor illness. If the sitter began to look too sceptical, he drew in a breath with lips like the mouthpiece of a trumpet and said, 'I'm not allowed by Law to tell you what I see,' sending them away far more disconcerted than if he had told them that they would be run over by a bus next Tuesday.

Dead serious, he got away with it because it seemed that if the whole thing was a fake, it would have been done much better.

'My dear – it's the *postman*!' If you had not been done by Mr Clive, you were not in the swim. When the Jaffry children got up a concert in the village hall, they had Dad in his turban as the star feature of the programme: The Great Clivurkha, Sage of the East. It was quite a little excitement in this quiet village where nothing ever happened.

No one had ever been as glad of the quiet nothingness as Peter and Charlie. He could get out of his prison at night.

They could escape in the car unseen, Peter crouched down like a fugitive until they were away from places where anyone might know Charlie. They went to dinner in Oxford and sat in the cinema with their hands on each other's legs like everyone else. One weekend, Charlie told Quentin she was going to London, and she and Peter went to Wales and took a room in an inn by the river, Mr and Mrs Jack Morgan their name.

'Your mother drove down to see you yesterday,' Quentin told her when she went to collect the dog. 'I thought you were with her.'

'I told you.' Charlie did not even blush any more, as she used to for smaller futile lies. 'I stayed with a friend, in Kent.'

'You said London.'

'You have to go through London to get to Kent.'

'Don't mind me, sweetie, but if you're having a bit of a thing, do let me in on it. Everybody tells Quentin everything.'

'Don't be an ass. There's nothing to tell.'

Her love was so consuming that she was not tempted even to hint. Commitment grew with secrecy. Intoxicated, toxic with love, Charlie could forget for days what he was. What was he? An accidental killing did not make you a murderer.

'If only you had gone straight to the police!'

'Shut up with that.' He would never talk about what he had done after the girl was dead. He would say something to make her laugh. When there was no tension of danger between them, they laughed and were so strangely happy, wandering the darkness as lovers.

Sometimes at night they roamed about the village, slipping into the shadow of a wall or a tree at the crunch of weary boots or the swinging rays of a stable lantern. Sometimes a boy and girl came by, but most of the young ones had gone away. There was no work here, nothing to do. Boys like Fred Gale's son Arthur, who used to do odd jobs for Charlie until she told him not to come round any more, sat on gates, or threw stones at rocks, or left a parcel outside an old lady's door, knocked, and ran to jerk it away on a piece of string.

Arthur, who was more ambitious than the other urchins, used to hang about the village street outside the post office, in the hope that Mr Clive would open the door and call, 'Here lad, nip down to Dodd's Farm with this telegram and I'll give you a penny.'

He would go straight to the post office from school. 'Any grams, Mr Clive?'

'Not now, but there will be. I sent one off for the vicar this morning, so he should be getting an answer about his poor mother's operation.'

So Arthur, having nothing else to do, would sit on the wall and kick his heels until Oxford Telegrams rang through. 'Good afternoon, Mr Clive. And how is everything out in your fair countryside?'

'Mustn't grumble, Dot.'

'Keeping you busy, then?'

'Can't complain.'

'My sister says she saw you at Milton Fair. It was ever so nice, she said.'

Mrs Clive still sighed for London, still took the bus to the shops or the train to Risborough on her day off, but Mr Clive had come into his own in Oxfordshire. He bought a cinnamon corduroy jacket and cap. He was a famous man.

Dad Clive and I have a thing in common here, because I too in my time have been much in demand at fêtes and Christmas bazaars.

In the early days at Broadcasting House, we were announcers without names, all pulling together in this jolly gentlemanly effort to stem the lapping vulgar tides of mass communication that we knew in our hearts would eventually swamp our esoteric little isle in Portland Place.

But during the Second World War, when invasion was the bogey and nuns in jackboots spotted in every tube train from Ongar to West Ruislip, someone came up with the idea that we should read the news under our own names so that when the enemy stormed Broadcasting House, our friends the public would not be fooled by a German news reader pretending to be one of us.

That seemed almost as ludicrous as taking away signposts and the names of country stations. One imagined a Conrad Veidt style Nazi: 'Ach, just ass I thocht – Byvay to Leedul Messing on ze Vold,' or: 'Zees ees ze zeegsoglokneuss.' They were still making films with characters who talked like that, even during the war.

It did actually happen, however, in radio stations in Holland and France, so the idea was justified, although some people always regretted the passing of the old sportsmanlike anonymity. A disgruntled MP complained in the House that all the newsreaders sounded alike anyway, names or no names, so they hired Wilfred Pickles to shut him up.

'This is the nine o'clock news, and this is James Kitteredge reading it.'

... Marshalling yards at Hamburg ... Enemy aircraft were over this country during the night ... But the most exciting part of my war was reading the news on the European service, trying to give the thousands of secret listeners enough hope to hang on. The Home news had to be flatly accurate, without any slant or opinion. The news we read to Occupied Europe was accurate too, but lit with more optimism, to keep endurance alive.

They listened to us at the risk of death. They listened in cellars and in shuttered back parlours, with Nazi officers in the café across the Square. They listened in attic hide-outs, in the caves of the Maquis, in the stone cattle byres of French farms, where a British airman crouched under the hay. These were our unknown audience, but we knew that they were listening.

We were beginning to know a lot about our listeners at home. Now that there were names to write to, we were getting fan mail. People had a favourite Voice and would write to it, send it snapshots and black market tea, fall in love with it, believe only the news it purveyed.

Like my colleagues, I had several regulars. A woman in Croydon who thought I sounded like her lost brother. A doctor in Sudbury who wanted me to announce that Hitler was dead.

A girl in Dawlish who was going to have a baby. Sometimes we would get letters from people who had figured in an item we had read, protesting that it wasn't so. At night, because the lady who ruled on the pronunciation of unfamiliar place names went off duty at seven, we would get telephone calls from Indian colonels complaining that we had not produced the name of some Burmese village in the local fashion.

With a name, I was a personage. I was James Kitteredge, invited here and there to make speeches and open sales of work and present prizes at schools and Boy Scout jamborees. I was so charming I sickened myself. I was that charming James Kitteredge, he's just as delightful as his voice, and scarcely a mail came in without at least one letter that concluded, '... finances will not run to an emolument, but we can assure you of a warm welcome.'

Towards the end of the war, as tired as everyone else with being that charming James Kitteredge and fire-watching and playing backgammon in the ARP wardens' post at Swiss Cottage, I used to write back and tell them I could not support a wife and children on a warm welcome. Which would have been true if our premature child had not died in the hospital incubator and I had not divorced Barbara in 1943.

'You should have let her divorce you,' Mrs Lambert said. 'That wasn't very gallant of you.'

I pointed out to her that it was Bubbles who had been sleeping with all the American colonels, not me. You could say anything to that old girl, right to the day she died. I used to stay with her in Wales where she retreated with Julia and Reggie's motherless children, while he was master-minding concert parties for Ensa, since they would not let him sing. We were good friends, even better after I unshipped her youngest daughter, for she always said that Bubbles had made me suspicious and morose.

'She disappointed me.'

'I could have told you she would.'

'Why didn't you?'

'I was glad when she married you and not one of those questionable creatures like Doubles Brodie. You weren't a prize, but at least I knew your parents. That sort of thing used to matter to me then. Funny how the war has made us all much nicer.'

It did, I think, especially women of that generation. It was not until they had to start doing their own cooking and housework that they discovered that their famous 'servant problem' had been all of their own making.

Charlie and I went back to the village to check on her cottage, which was full of Landgirls in green jerseys and gumboots. They cultivated everything for miles round except Charlie's garden, bossed the Italian prisoners who worked with them, and carried on with the American airmen at Chalgrove in a way that would have delighted democratic John Hampden, whose monument stands there at the corner of Chalgrove Field where he was mortally wounded in battle for the rights of commoners against King Charles I.

Mr Clive was still at the post office, surrounded by notices about Careless Talk, and growing carrots and potatoes in his flower garden and raising rabbits which he refused to sell for food. Mrs Clive was off in a canteen somewhere. 'Too much for her legs,' her husband told us, 'but she likes the money and the men give her their sweet coupons.'

When we went to see Mrs Hammond, we found her much nicer and much happier than in the days when Nelly cooked rhubarb pie and great roasts for both lunch and dinner in that vaulted stone kitchen that never got the sun. She still wore her cashmere and pearls, and she still had that voice, but she was busy and real and had ruined her nails beyond caring.

The Big House was a billet for a small training unit of some kind, who lay about the park on their stomachs like Red Indians and kicked in the bottom panels of the doors, so the Hammonds had moved into the servants quarters, where they seemed to be more content and comfortable than ever before. She gave us tea off the Rockingham china in the maids' sitting-room, and she and Charlie had a lovely chat about pounding soya flour with butter and what could be done about dried egg.

Not that Charlie knew much about what you could do, except eat it in the mess hall of the WAAF training camp. After her mother agreed to take Julia, then about eight, to Wales,

Charlie, alias widowed Mrs Morgan, joined the Air Force as a physical training instructor. She lived in a very dreary billet in Gloucestershire for almost four years, reverting gradually to her early St Gabriel's days, so that by the time she was de-mobilized, she was a forty-year-old Charlie old chump with a big stride and a loud laugh and a muscle-bound waist, and I had to feminize her all over again before I could marry her.

I should, of course, have married her in 1931 instead of Bubbles. If it had been I who kissed her in the butler's pantry at Garfield instead of Cousin Alaric, how different her life would have been! Much duller, for one thing.

But in those days, it was Bubbles, Bubbles all the way, and when I stood there at the altar of St Paul's Knightsbridge with the cleaners' ticket visible at the back of my morning coat, I felt my heart would burst with joy and pride. It wasn't my heart, of course, but at that age one still does not know the difference.

Charlie was there, in gloves and a hat, looking simply – radiant. There was no other word for it, although those who knew her used it with some surprise. Even I, in my rapture, noticed that she looked somewhat different. Her eyes had a dark depth to them in which there swam a sort of light – a radiance – how describe the splendid secret that Charlie's eyes concealed?

She was properly dressed and she seemed to have lost some weight. That is to say she stuck out and went in at the right places, instead of being rather thick all the way down as she used to be. Or was it only that she was moving like a woman for the first time in her life? Even her hands were more grace-ful. She kept on her gloves, since she had no pockets, and drank quite a lot of champagne. We all did. When she kissed me goodbye she was a little tipsy, lips moist and warm. She put her arms round my neck. 'Darling James.' Although I had Bubbles just ahead of me in a pink suit the colour of straw-berry ice taut over the delectable ball of her bottom, I re-member thinking with the fraction of my mind that was still sane, 'Some man somewhere is doing rather well.'

Of course I was not the only one who thought that. When an awkward, unfeminine girl suddenly blooms, everyone cries, 'A man!' as though it could not be merely the discovery of the joy and beauty of life. Which is a nice little compliment to men in general.

After we got back from the honeymoon, where things went better than might be expected, in case anyone is interested, Mrs Lambert telephoned my wife to discuss the wedding which had set Mr Lambert back the annual rent of at least three flats at Chantilly Mansions, and of course one of the first things she said was, 'What did you think of Charlie?'

The family had not seen her for some time. She was making the mythical textbook the excuse to stay away from London. 'Charles writing a book – that's a good one!'

'I think she's got a man somewhere,' I heard Bubbles say from bed while I was shaving. To her mother's obvious question, she replied, 'God knows. I only hope it's not one of those ghastly yeoman farmers in canvas leggings. It's a man though.'

Well, I could have told her that. But of course none of us knew who or why, nor could ever guess in ten thousand years what had happened to our beloved gym mistress.

Beloved g.m. and I had been married about five years before she began to tell me the entire and honest truth, which I am now retailing for Julia's sake and am going to seal in a casket and drop in the old underground tank where the boys found Bessie Hunter's body, or some other such macabre spot.

In about -956, the R101 Memorial Fund finally paid out, so sucks to the Great Clivurkha and his false prognostication. The Clives had passed on to where Dad could now take his turn at materializing on doorknobs. The lady who now had the post office on a card-table in the front hall of her council house gave their letter to me. 'Your wife used to know the Clives, didn't she?'

Charlie was working at the rehabilitation centre, so I opened the envelope and found a money order for £19 9s 9d which I cashed and spent on a present for Charlie, so she could not send it on to Gordon.

It was that evening when I gave her the present that she began to tell me some of the incredible, terrifying things about Peter. I asked her, 'Why didn't you go to the police?' Charlie was so law-abiding in later years. If we'd had any income worth mentioning, she would not have let me fiddle the tax.

'I thought he would kill me. He would have found me somehow and killed me.'

'You could have brought the police to surround the house before he could get away. Why didn't you do something like that?'

She made several half excuses like police never listening, the story too fantastic, and then she said at last, 'Because I was blindly in love with him.'

He used to torment her, force her to listen to things about the dead girl. He laughed at her sometimes and said, 'You're not as good as Bessie.'

He would sit downstairs and drink. Charlie would hear him go outside, thrashing about and falling over things. He came back. He always came back. With the light burning itself out and the wireless still playing downstairs, she would hear the latch of the door at the bottom of the dark stairs. He stumbled up to her, and then it would start all over again.

'Drive me mad, she would. Tease me, torment me with that mucky hair. She used to drive me mad. I can see her laughing at me, laughing through all that hair hanging down. Even when I cut it off, she still laughed. Why don't you laugh, Charlay? Why don't you laugh like she did?'

'Stop it, Peter. I—'

'All that hair...' He grabbed Charlie's hair, twisted it round his hand and dragged it round her neck, holding it so tight against her throat that she clawed at his face, choking. He loosed his hand suddenly and let it fall all over his chest, pulling Charlie forward and burying his head in her hair. 'It's like hers,' he whispered. 'It's just like Bessie's mucking hair.'

One day after school, Charlie turned away from home and

drove to High Wycombe to the hairdressing salon of Mr Canigliano Stoker. He sat her in a booth and gazed at her in the mirror, his hands caressing her hair as if it were the coat of a silken dog.

'Are you sure?' He had sad eyes and a small uncertain mouth. He stood on his toes, because Charlie was too high and the mechanism of the chair was stuck. 'It seems a pity after all these years. Never had it cut, you say?'

'Never.' Charlie did not look at him in the mirror. She kept her eyes on her grim face.

'Of course it shows it, split ends and so. But a little shaping—'

'I want you to bob it.'

'Not that I couldn't get a good sale for it, mind. Black hair is worth more than blonde, if I'm not being personal, because Italian girls don't cut their hair like the Swedes do.'

'Please hurry. I haven't got much time.'

With her eyes shut, she felt him cut off the whole mass of it at once. He went away, and when he came back, she opened her eyes and said, near tears, 'I look awful.'

'No, no, we have to trim and shape now and so.' Tiptoe, he worked with comb and smaller scissors, shaping her a round head with the smooth black hair painted down over the ears, clipped into the back of her neck.

'I think it looks very very chic. I think it was a wise decision after all.'

I want my hair. I want my hair back. I want my moonlight hair that tumbles o'er his breast. She stared round-eyed at the doll of herself. She had done a terrible thing that could never be undone.

Stiffly, when he had brushed her off, she got down from the high chair and turned her head to him on its cold neck. 'Where is it?' she asked, like a mother who must see her dead baby.

He brought it to her like a severed limb, tied at both ends . . . her long black hair.

'What will you do with it?'

'We shall make a braid to go over the top of the head like so.' He twisted it lightly and put it for a moment across his head, appraising seriously in the mirror.

'I used to wear it like that.'

'Very chic.' That was of no interest now. 'I'll make you a price for it.' He weighed the hair on his upturned palms.

Charlie nodded at what he suggested, stuffed the money into her purse without looking at it, and drove home, tears rolling over her cheeks and down her cold naked neck.

By the time she reached her cottage, she had recovered bravado. She unlocked the door and banged in, calling in her hockey-field voice for him to come and see her. He could say what he liked. She didn't care.

But he said, 'It's lovely!' and took her in his arms very tenderly and nuzzled all over her face and neck.

'Don't you think I look like a muffin?'

He told her she was beautiful and desirable and that he had loved no other woman, nor ever would.

'You aren't going to have the chance of another woman,' Charlie laughed, feeling marvellous.

'I might get sick of you.'

'And if you do, I'll turn you in and they'll hang you.'

When they were like this, they could make any grisly joke. She could say anything to him. Everything would please him. They could say crude terrible things to each other and laugh and fight and drive the car to the top of the hills in the dark and sing and roll about on the sweet chalky turf.

They went up there tonight and ran about. The lightness of her head was funny. She hung it down, no soft warmth fell forward. She ran her hands through the short nothing and left it sticking up in the air to make him laugh. He caught her leg and pulled her down on the grass, and said, 'I'm glad you did it. I want to get rid of her. I'm afraid.'

'Peter, Peter, she's dead. I'm here. I'll keep you safe.' She tried to hold him like a child, but he pulled away.

'Listen. Listen to me.'

Lying on the short turf of the hill with the bushes black and silver and the moon inspecting the white wheat-fields below, he began to say things to her that he had never said before.

'I've got to tell someone,' he said. 'And there is only you.'

'I don't want—' she began, but he put his hand over her mouth.

'It's what I want.' His moonlit mouth was saddened by the beard. The bright amused eyes were narrowed, looking within himself. 'I want to tell you what happened.'

'I don't want to know.'

'This is what happened. It was like this, you see. It started like this. I had Sunday off, the last Sunday before the flight. That was before the oil cooler kicked up and we had to wait. It was pretty nice weather and I was fed up staying with those people in that house in Shortstown where I lodged, and trying to keep the man's wife off my neck.

' "Come on a picnic," she said. "We'll go to the river, just you and me." She had those terrible spots all over her face, you never saw anything like it. But it didn't set her back.

' "No thanks," I said, loud enough so her husband could hear she'd offered me something and offer her the strap. "I got better things to do."

'Sunday one of the fellows gave me a lift to Bedford on the back of his bike, and I got a train to Birmingham and then a bus out to this little town where Bessie took care of the old lady. Well, she didn't exactly take care of her. She had a companion for that, a poor sort of flattened out niece or something who was hoping to benefit by it, only she never had the guts to put weed-killer in the old lady's tea. Bessie used to joke about that. She used to say she was going to ask the niece for a half share of the proceeds if she put something in the chicken broth. Bessie did the cooking there, and what cleaning she fancied. A terribly sloppy girl, she was, like a gipsy. Half mad, I used to think sometimes. I couldn't do anything with her. She used to laugh and dance about and play tricks on people. When we were both at the hotel in Birmingham – I was in the kitchens, portering and cutting meat and things like that – she used to leave pots of water on top of doors, tricks like that. Once she put a dead mouse into the soup.

'She wouldn't really have poisoned the old lady, of course. That was the way she talked. I knew she had a half-day Sunday. When I walked into her kitchen and surprised her, she dropped a whole trayful of china, she was so glad to see me.

'There was this beautiful sort of heath, you see, that ran

right away for miles and miles at the end of the lane from the house where she worked. You could go for miles along a valley and over the top of the hills and not see anybody but the sheep. I used to walk with Bessie there, and shoot rabbits sometimes.'

'To eat?'

'Don't be daft. I wouldn't touch rabbit meat. But you can sell 'em. I had borrowed a shotgun from one of the riggers on the ship, and his thick crew sweater.'

'I remember it. I remembered the smell of it, long after you died.'

'The rigger died, poor sod. His gun's at the bottom of a canal. We wandered off quite far. I didn't shoot anything, but we went into an old sort of shed, a shepherd's hut, whatever it was, and it was when we were in there that Bessie told me, "You needn't come up here again. I'm not going to see you any more."

'Just suddenly like that. All the time out on the heath, she'd been just like she always was, and I couldn't understand this now. She teased and sulked and played up a bit, and finally told me she was pregnant.

' "God," I said, "I'm sorry kid." See what a nice boy I was in those days? "I'll stand by you," I told her, though it was the ruin of a lot of my plans and dreams. When the airship was in regular service, I would be roaming the world from end to end. I could marry anybody. Become anybody. But here I was in that smelly sort of hut, where things had died, telling her, "I'll stand by you."

' "Promise?"

' "I promise, Bess."

'And then she laughed. She'd looked so serious and worried, her mouth down, running her hands up into her hair, all tousled about with the wind. And then she doubled up laughing, clutching herself.

' "What's the joke?" I was getting angry.

' "It's not your baby."

'She began to taunt me. She was so brazen, standing there with her hands on her hips and her hair hanging over her face, telling me to guess, guess, tormenting me. She was so bold ... I jumped at her and grabbed her hair in my hand, and with the

229

other I got out my jack-knife and chopped it off. Sort of sawed it off. It made a sound like hissing – snick! I pushed her away from me and stood holding her hair in my hand. 'That's what they did to the French girls in the war," I told her, "when they went with the Germans."

'I called her a whore and a lot of other things, but there was nothing you could do to shame her. She shook her ragged-looking head and kept on laughing at me, and teasing.'

'She sounds mad,' Charlie said. They were lying on their stomachs, plucking at turf, not looking at each other. 'She must have been mad to go on teasing to make you angry when you had a gun.'

'She knew I'd not have hurt her. I didn't really like shooting the rabbits even, she knew that, just liked the feel of the gun. She had nothing to be afraid of. She was sitting on a bench against the wall with her head back and her mouth open, laughing. I was perched on the corner of a sort of table across the hut with the gun on my knee. I was fooling with the hammer. It was stiff and needed oiling. I took a pull back on it to see if I could cock the gun, and because it was stiff my finger slipped, you see, and the gun went off.

'The top of her head was blown right off. It was like a – like a – like when you take the top off an eggshell. Brains and blood and stuff all over. I told you. I went mad. I yelled at her, "Don't die!" I was trying to scoop the stuff off the wall. One of her eyes was open. The other was shot out.

'I went out of the hut. I didn't know what I was going to do.'

'Why didn't you go to the police?'

'I couldn't. I was mad with fear, can't you understand? All I knew was I had to do something so nobody would ever know what I had done. I ran – ran and walked, it seemed like miles – and I came to a spooky house outside a village, with ivy up to the roof and great dark fir trees looking in the windows. There didn't seem to be anybody about. The garden was all strangled with weeds, and the lawn like a meadow. I busted a window in the garage door and got this black car out and drove back along the road to where a cart track turned off that ran by the hut. She was still sitting there, propped up somehow, with her skirt up and her legs apart, her face sort of black, her skull like a broken china cup.

'I couldn't pick her up. I mean, I was strong enough, but I couldn't do it. Yet I could do the other. Now all these things were like as if they happened to someone else, you see. I've tried to explain to myself how I did it, who it was that did it, but it was like standing off and watching myself do the things I did next.

'I had started to cry when I got back to the shed and saw her still there, and couldn't pick it up and put it in the car. All of a sudden, I felt I was calm as ice, and very clever. I drove back to the empty house. On the workbench in the garage I had seen all kinds of tools someone had used for carpentering. I took a saw and a chopper, a knife. I took some old newspapers from a big pile under the bench. Under there too was some old luggage and boxes. There was a tin chest with the name Major something painted on it in white, and a sort of little leather trunk. I put all that in the car, and I went back for the last time to that accursed hut.

'After, I set fire to it. There were some papers left. I dipped them in the petrol tank and started a fire.'

'Why didn't you set fire to it at first, when she—'

'Look, it's no good asking me *why* I did any of it. I'm telling you what I did because that's all I know. On the road south, I dropped the tin box into a canal. It's stuck in the mud somewhere. They've never found it. I was going to send the other in after it, but when I went back to the car, there was a lorry coming towards me in the distance, so I drove on. I thought anyway, the farther I get from where I killed her, the safer. And every time I saw a likely place, I thought No, go a bit farther, like people do when they want to find a place for a picnic.

'I'd read about them finding a dead baby in a suitcase in the tunnel under the line at Oxford Station. I thought of leaving the trunk in the cloakroom there, like they do. I didn't know what I would do. I kept off the main roads and I was just driving along as if I was going to drive off the edge of the world. Then I met you.'

After a moment, he laughed shortly and said, 'Funny, isn't

it? I mean, life really is funny. I was a fool to stop, of course. I should have let you rot there. But after I'd helped you, I was even fool enough to think of how it could be when I came back with your car.'

'Why didn't you?'

'You mad too? I wasn't coming back. When I stopped by that ruined farm and had the luck to find that place to get rid of the trunk, it was then I realized about Bessie's hair. It was late by the time I got back to Cardington, so I ditched your car and tore the number plates off and trudged in through the gate and said I'd walked out from Bedford.'

He turned to look at her and smiled. 'You were a nice sort of girl. You were different to people like Bessie and the girls I'd had. They'd have screamed bloody murder if that with their thumb had happened to them. You seemed sort of – true. And I was sorry I couldn't come back. I started being sorry about everything then. Not standing apart. I came back into myself and saw what I had done.'

'Were you afraid? I knew where to find you.'

'You know, it was funny. I think the reason it all seemed like a dream and not happening at all was because I really knew at the back of everything that nothing mattered any more. There was a lot of us felt that way, though we didn't talk about it. We just swaggered a bit more, and made out the whole thing was a bit of a lark. Because we had this feeling, you see, that the ship would go down.'

Standing at the mirror in the morning, Charlie said, 'Dogs have got more sense than people. They won't look at themselves in the mirror.' She gave her short hair a couple of bangs with the brush, and watched it fall absurdly into place.

'I know why you cut it off.'

In the mirror, she could see the bed, and Peter propped on his elbow behind her.

'I told you. To stop you torturing me.'

'It was because you haven't really got Bessie's hair.'

'How would I know about it if I hadn't found it in the car?'

'But you threw it away, or burned it.'

'I hid it.'

'Show me then.'

'Haven't you found it yet?' She knew he looked for it when she was out. 'I'll show you, if you like.'

'Go on.'

'Oh no, you won't get it. I'll lock you in the house and stand outside and show it to you.'

'*Your* hair. Why did you never offer to show me till now, after you had yours cut?'

'Damn the hair – what difference does it make?' She turned round to him angrily, hating him and wanting to hurt him. 'I could tell them about it. I could tell them about the leather trunk. Don't forget I saw the trunk.'

'You couldn't prove it.'

'They'd believe me.' Hating, they played a hideous game back and forth.

'I'd tell them what a liar you are.'

'They'd believe me against you.'

'Because you're a lady?' He called her something foul. 'I'll tell them what you are.'

Now she did not know whether he believed she had the dead girl's hair. She did not think he knew either. He did not look for it any more. She did not find brick dust in the fireplace, her clothes disarranged, chalky fingermarks on the door of the little cupboard where he had reached back to search in the rubble behind the chimney.

They talked a lot about getting away, made plans for how easy it would be to start life somewhere else where they were unknown. Australia. The West Indies. How does a man get a passport under a false name? They stayed where they were and watched each other. Gave to each other everything but trust.

She missed whole days at school, or got there late because she did not want to leave him. The third form were delighted, because their first class was gym, a barbaric arrangement through which they grumbled and yawned sour morning breath.

Mrs Baxter was less pleased, but trying doggedly to be fair.

She gave her old iron pills to Charlie, and carved her an extra slice of beef at the staff table. She said she had always thought Charlie might be anaemic, and that cutting off her hair had robbed her of her last strength, like Samson. She added a rather nasty innuendo about some people who were *not* a very good advertisement for the Keep Fit programme.

'You mean Mrs Fossick?' Charlie was quite rude now that she did not care about the job or the school.

Her bobbed hair kept St Gab's in conversation for days. Lottie Four Fingers was getting chunks of herself lopped off bit by bit, like the Death of a Thousand Cuts. What would go next? Some said she would be hamstrung and never run the length of a cricket pitch again. Frances Parker knew a boy whose mother had one bosom bitten off by a milk pony, and the doctors had to cut off the other one to keep her on an even keel.

Miss Perrott was quite disappointed. 'Your hair was your best feature, I always thought. You won't catch me falling for these modes.' She waggled her nested head over the staff-room tea-tray, and Etty, who had had her hair shingled long ago into an Eton crop that already dated her, said, 'Lottie's was worth selling. There was some point to that.'

It was bad enough at the beginning of the winter term to see the same old faces turning up for one more year, with a few new ones here and there who did not look as though they would stay the course. It was even worse by the last weeks of the summer term. Most people's nerves were on the point of collapse, like desert wanderers who drop in their tracks within very sight of the oasis.

In spite of the iron pills and extra meat, Charlie was flagging more than anyone. 'We've got to get you married,' Etty said. 'There's nothing else for it.'

'Who to?'

'*I* don't know. I simply can't understand why some man hasn't fallen for you already. Honestly, I don't think you're so bad looking,' she said, as if Charlie had denied it. 'In fact, without all that black seaweed hanging round your head, you're really quite a smasher. I can't think why I didn't see it before.'

Etty was too stupid to detect that the bloom on Charlie had not been induced by Mr Canigliano Stoker. She did not see far beyond herself. If marriage was the thing for her, then it must be for everybody.

With the right man, of course. 'In marriage, you see' (she was a great authority on marriage), 'there always has to be one who gives more than the other.'

Charlie thought she was going to boast of her ample giving, but not a bit, it was the solicitor who gave and she who took, sitting back with her feet up while he cooked the supper and telephoned his mother to ask – no, tell – her to keep the child all night as well as all day.

'And then, you know—'

Charlie tried to sidle out of the cloakroom, but Etty was between her and the door, buttoning the twenty-five buttons on a frock coat very very slowly.

'– with the baby out of the way, we're more relaxed.'

At first, marriage had not been all that it was cracked up to be. But the solicitor had bought a book. They read it to each other at night. 'My child is going to be taught all about sex as soon as he can understand. Mother-in-law is always clucking to him about his diddly. No, no, I say, you must call it penis.' And so on and so on.

'I like your hair, Miss Lambert.'

'I don't. I liked it the way it was.'

A while ago, Cara would have said, 'Oh so did I, but I mean, I like it now too.' She knew better now than to hang round Charlie and spray compliments up at her through her teeth and wires. Her love for Lottie Lambert was one of the things the girls in the Set jeered about. Through their diligence, she was being steadily dragged down towards their level – or up, as they called it.

'I do believe our baby's growing up at last. Hope for everybody, chaps.'

To get their favour, since it seemed she could not now have Charlie's, Cara was beginning to join in with charges against her parents, half vaguely true, half made up to the fashionable pattern. Her mother was more interested in her stupid animals than in her. Her father's suit was five years old and his hair

235

was grey. One of his patients had died of puerperal fever because – she had overheard two ladies whisper in the waiting-room – he was too old-fashioned to let women have babies in the hospital.

Soon it got out of hand. The others used it back at her – 'We know you're miserable at home too' – until gradually she was no longer sure what was her own invention and what was half true. She was wretched among Olive Bartlett and the Set, because for all her masquerade, she still could not truly accept their debased values and their rejection of love as a reason and a force. She was wretched with her parents, who could not understand why she had grown so pert and prickly, why all the close family things like bed time kisses (with her mother half-way up the stairs, she heard Avril's voice, 'She kisses you goodnight? Icky') must be rejected. Could not understand, because she would not talk to them, how the security of this child was being corroded by the dreary clamour of the second rate for what they thought was independence, for freedom from the 'tyranny' of home.

Everything she had loved was out. Off the menu. No bloody good. She had a pony. That was baby stuff. She had loved her deaf white cat. The Set was very neurotic about cats. They were neurotic all round, and got claustrophobia in lifts. If the pork was slightly pink, they made sneering noses and said, 'Nobody is going to make me eat that.'

Lottie Lambert was outer than out, and Cara's love and pride in her a buried thing that she must not even let herself acknowledge. But Charlie was her only hope, and the memories of their painting days a small light that had not yet gone out.

It took her two days of thinking of nothing else to get up her courage to drop back to walk with Charlie at the end of the crocodile from the swimming baths to the bus stop.

'Would – would next Sunday be a – I mean, I don't want to be in your way. If you don't want the wheels done, I could garden. I know how to prune. My mother—' She blushed and looked ahead up the line to where Avril minced, tied in at the knee, moving the same arm and leg forward together.

'It needs it.' Charlie laughed. 'Mr Clive planted all that stuff, and now there's more weeds than flowers.' She would not let Dad Clive come down with string around his trousers and his pet hoe. She said she liked the garden to look natural, and he said, 'It takes all kinds.'

'Then Sunday?' The light flickered brighter, was ready to shine, but Charlie said, 'Not this one. Next week perhaps. Let's make some plans. In the holidays there will be lots of time.'

'Lots of time,' she said to Mrs Jaffray. 'I'd love to come and see you all in London when I can.' In ordinary times, she would have been friends with Ann Jaffray. She would have liked to go to their weekend house full of children who sailed bathtubs on the duckpond and played gangsters with the village boys and walked to Kingsgrove with wastepaper baskets on their heads to see what it was like to be blind. Ann became one of the dangers. Rangily nordic, she loped down with dogs and children, calling, 'Come on, Charlotte, we're going to the river to swim. We're going to see some puppies at Christmas Common. We're going to the cinema.'

'Can't you keep the bloody woman away?' It was becoming more and more difficult for Peter to stay hidden. 'We've got to get out of here. I feel like those rotten fish.' The goldfish bumped their snouts against the side of the little tank. Peter put his face against the window and looked moodily out at the evening rain. Always a back window. Only at night.

'I'll tell them next week,' Charlie said. 'I'll give Mrs Baxter my notice when I get my money next week.'

About that time, I met Quentin at a gala night for the five hundredth performance of *Cavalcade*. Bubbles wore a gold thread dress I didn't like.

'Penny a look.' She pulled the cleavage lower.

'I can see them any time for nothing,' I said sourly. If she was a topless waitress in California today, you would swear they were full of silica gel.

Quentin spoke to me while we were in the breadline at the bar to get our gins and lime. I knew him slightly. Everyone knew everybody in those days when there were not so many people doing things. Now half the world is in what they call the communications industry, though if I understand the situation correctly, all they have done is make it more difficult for people to communicate by the normal processes of speech and writing.

'How's young Charlie these days?' I asked him. 'We haven't seen her for ages. She hardly ever comes to London.'

'She's gone all *hermitty*.' Quentin laid emphasis on words as if he were laying a jewelled orb upon a satin cushion. 'I don't think country life is good for her. I went down to collect her for lunch last weekend and she rushed out of the house and practically shoved me out of the gate into the road. "What's the matter, rejecting your old friends?" I asked her.

' "Why can't anyone in this village leave anyone else alone?" was her reply. It's being a spinster is doing it. I'm afraid,' Quentin fussed, the most spinsterish of all in a mid-night-blue dinner jacket and shoes like a woman, dabbing at the pink tip of his nose with a silk handkerchief full of eucalyptus.

Talking of the communications industry, Terence Haig-Davenport came in unheralded (he never outgrows the sneak-thief approach) and read over my shoulder while I was correcting this.

'Are you writing a story about me then?'

'I didn't know you could read.'

'Doris can.' He is really quite literate for an illiterate. I have lent him a few books. Paperbacks, because he throws books away when he has read them. 'Shan't have no more use for that then.'

Doris was off her legs again. When I asked why, he stuck his thumbs in the armpits of a braided Edwardian waistcoat and said, 'Got to pvweserve the bloomin image.'

'You don't mean—'

'I mean.' He went for the bottles like the old hand he is

238

around my house, and we toasted the Pigeon, while she smiled shyly and drooped her head – she can't blush – and sat in the chair where he had perched her with her little sandalled feet two inches off the floor like a child in church.

They had taped half a dozen songs for a teenage television programme which comes on at what Terence calls peak viewing hours. They have even been paid (no mention of my fifty quid, now in the coffers of the clerk of the court, but I bide my time).

'You've got to get a set, Mr James.'

If I had the money, I almost would, to view this marvel. Doris sounds delightful in my little house. I would like to hear how she sounds with all the technical advantages of a studio.

'Of course.' Terence can look down and smile shyly too. 'I had to persuade them to let us work with our own kind of material.'

Oh Ned, you are an unworthy son of my friend, your father. Have you fallen for the dirge routine?

'It's the contrast, I explained to them, between her being a cripple like you see, and singing of running and leaping and flying to the sun.' With his knees jammed together and his sharp boot toes turned in as if he was a paraplegic, he raised his arms and swayed about like a rooted flower reaching for the light. 'I must say, they were very much impressed, weren't they, Doris?'

'Yes. But it was his idea in the first place,' she conceded to me. Although she acts a fantasy, she is more honest than Terence, who can make himself believe anything.

'Who cares who thought of it first?' (He would have, if it had been him.) 'It's the start. It's our break at last. After this, it will be the record companies, more TV – a slot of our own even. We can go anywhere, me and Dovwis!'

'Why don't you go to the altar?' I inquired mildly. They had been living together so single-mindedly for so long, they might just as well be married.

'It isn't like that these days.' He explained to me patiently. 'You like a bird, she likes you – it's all more honest and natural, you see. Very different to what it was in your day.'

'Yes. We didn't talk so much about it.'

239

But Terence had stopped listening. Like a politician, when he has said his side of it, he switches topics. There had been talk of a trip to America. ' "The Winged Pigeon Flies In" – I can see it now.' Ned's director knew a man on the Coast who was wild for new British groups. Did I know anyone in New York who might help them?

I had told him how I went to America in 1952, when television did not want my fifty-year-old face and I did not want the dead duck that it had made of wireless. I lived in New York for a meagre two years, writing scripts for documentaries, working on series dialogue. I even did a stint with a soap opera, 'The Pollocks of Hungry Hill', about a family who ran a roadside restaurant – 'Dad, Dad, guess what! An automobile that looks like that stolen Cadillac just pulled into the parking lot!'

Terence had not taken much notice of my uninspiring tale, until it might benefit him. He was very much on his toes today, snapping his fingers, jingling cash in the pockets of his white jeans – how does he get it out in a hurry for a bus fare, let alone get it in? – pouncing from idea to idea, missing nothing.

'Then how about your daughter? She's a contact.'

'I haven't got a daughter.'

'The fat lady who was here the night you and I first met' (it might have been at a formal dinner). 'Vevwy hystevwical, I thought, but it's the time of life.'

'She's only thirty-six.'

'That's what I mean.'

'My stepdaughter. She wouldn't know anyone. She went over as a doctor's wife. After her divorce, she floated about – all sorts of jobs I never knew existed. All sorts of men I didn't want to know. She works in a bar now on Cape Cod. Bare feet and beads.'

'You mustn't worry about that,' Terence said kindly. 'What's her name again? When we get over there I'll look her up, see if she can give us some leads. There's a big demand for talent in those summer places. I met a boy who'd been a singing waiter. Fifty dollars a night. We could perch Doris on a bar stool.'

I gave him Julia's name and address, because (a) he'll probably never get to the States and (b) why prick his bubble? Julia can do that herself.

Mao Tse-tung Meagan says that some people were put into this world to help others, which reminds me of Etty and her solicitor doing the washing up with a towel tied round his striped office trousers. Quotes from Mrs Meagan keep seeping in like sewage through the broken walls of my narrative; but she is in and out of here more frequently since I was ill, and is about the only quotable person I talk to.

Dinner the other night with Henry Clay at 'End o' the Road' restyled 'The Firs' for less reason, with a wing added and a bright new thatch too clean and clipped, left me with no impression at all of what we talked about. There were eight of us, and we talked of anything but politics, since Henry did not get the nomination. He talked of his daughter who wins prizes at the horse shows, which would make people like the Hammonds whirl in Kingsgrove cemetery where they have been burying our people since pond water started to leech into the graves of the abandoned village church. When their daughters went to shows, hacking over the road where the Clays' shiny trailer now rolls, common people were not allowed to win. Unless they were genuine farmers' children, which didn't count.

I am getting worse than Quentin and his Mrs Ram with my quotes from Mrs Meagan, except that mine are true and his were mostly made up to flavour his articles. He is still making people up, the old darling, although of course he's been out of journalism for years. It's novels now, rather short because he gets tired, slightly Gothic, about the peasantry in Suffolk where he now lives. Although they are meant to be in the sixties, with a few topical allusions to make sure, he has them living and talking as they might just possibly have done about thirty-five years ago, and gets his nieces to tell him the sex parts.

He has a niece with bowlegs and hair like Rapunzel who says witty things, and since there is no demand for his thistle-down articles any more, he writes letters to newspapers about modern youth, quoting his niece (one worse than Mrs Ram), and using the particular to prove the general, as he always did. He never did become famous, but he makes enough to keep himself in good wine, and he has outlasted many people who burned more startling and bright. If you have never made a sensation, you have nothing to live up to.

FIVE

THE TRUSTEES OF St Gabriel's did not like it, but Mrs Baxter insisted on handing over the pay envelopes herself every month. 'Just,' said the Chairman of the Board, trying to make a dry joke of it, 'as if banks had never been invented.'

'You'll allow me my methods.' Mrs Baxter always wore her purple dress and the brooch with the lock of hair and the picture of her dead mother to board meetings, to make them feel sorry for her. Her mother had been dead for years, but it was no strain to feel sorry for Mrs Baxter. 'If there is anything you don't like, Madam Councillor, Reverend Silcock, Gentlemen, you have only to say.'

Having already said, and got nowhere, they let her retain the little ceremony of summoning each member of the staff to her office in turn, Laura McNaughton, volunteer runner since it got her out of Arithmetic, nipping round to the rooms with whispered messages.

'Mrs Baxter wants to see you.' She was really a Miss, but she called herself Mrs, like a cook.

Charlie was hanging on the wall bars with her legs straight up and her short hair flicking the floor. She somersaulted neatly down. 'Keep on up those ropes, girls, and if you get to the top, hang on till I get back.'

Groans and wails from despairing monkey figures sagging and struggling halfway up the hawsers.

Mrs Baxter always gave you your envelope as if it were a bonus, not your earned wages. 'I'm glad to see you looking a little better, dear,' she said, since Charlie was still red in the face from hanging upside down.

'I was going to tell you—' Charlie got hold of her pay packet before she said this. 'I've got to leave the school.'

'You mean you won't be coming back with us next year? That *will* be a disappointment.' Under the orange hair, thoughts flubbed and floundered. Mrs Fossick? Might die on

243

the job. A new bouncing girl who would want all sorts of modern equipment?

'I mean I have to leave *now*. Right away. I'm sorry, because I—'

She really was sorry, but Mrs Baxter gave her no chance even for that. 'How can you leave before the end of term? The drill display, the swimming regatta, the country dancing festival – I've ordered all the ribbons! How can you do it to me? It's only a few weeks more – how *can* you?'

Charlie couldn't. She dragged back to the stranded monkeys, shuffling ideas round and round in her head, worrying about how she was going to go on, what was going to happen.

It was becoming more and more difficult to lead this strange double life in the village. She had not felt like a cheat at first. Now she had grown to see that she was a cheat and a traitor. But only Peter mattered.

Months after the crash, the shock of such an enormous disaster was only just loosing its numbing hold on Mrs Clive. She began to want to talk about Peter a lot, and cry sometimes to Charlie, looking over his things and the memories she kept of him. She showed her his blue jacket from the days of the Southern Belle, with the attendant's badge woven in gold wire, and his number, one ninety-eight. She had a photograph of the train at Eardley Sidings with an X over the frosted kitchen window of one of the cars and his writing below: 'Princess Patricia behind King Arthur Class engine, Sir Blamor de Ganis.'

Gordon and Rita came down for the day with a heavy hanging face (Gordon) and a huge rather pointed stomach (Rita). The Baby Austin was sold and Charlie had to fetch them at Nettlebed because they had got on the wrong bus. The jewellery firm was closing down because of undercutting from abroad. Gordon was doing a little jobbing for a friend, but it would not last. What then? Cocky enough when he was secure, he was collapsing like a lump of dripping in the sun, whining outdated old Socialist saws about fat capitalists and the rights of man.

'Though what rights has a man got but what he works for?' his mother said when they had gone. 'Soft, this generation.

244

Good thing his Dad didn't carry on like that when he was laid off.'

'Seek and ye shall find,' Dad said. 'I kept on seeking.'

'And I found.'

'I'm not sure that's anything to boast about, Charlotte, the way things are turning out.' He was in a huff today about the post office, because the Inspector had found him two pounds and eightpence short on his pensions money and he had got to make it up by selling some hens. Since he would not sell any chickens for killing, it was taking time to raise the money. Mr Browning from Head Office had been round in the van, although it was Saturday, and caught Dad in his braces in the yard with yesterday's date stamp unchanged. 'I've a mind to offer Gordon the job, and retire.'

'On what?' his wife asked uncharitably. 'He wouldn't take it anyway, the hours it demands, and the paperwork. He wants it all for nothing, Charlotte. He's always thought he was owed some reward just for being so clever as to be born. My Peter now, he'd go after what he wanted. When he was only a little boy, he'd set his heart on this or that and save and scheme for it. He got his first job when he was only fifteen. Pageboy he was, a marvel. Went on through the hotels and restaurants and set his heart on the trains, set his heart on the airships ... while Gordon was laying with the quilt over his head, and a life's work every morning to get him out of bed.

'Peter was the one. My Peter was the one. If one of them had to go,' she wept to Charlie, 'why did it have to be him?'

'The Lord giveth and the Lord taketh—'

She rounded on Dad, quoting automatically without meaning to offend. 'Don't tell me that! Do you think it helps to tell me that the Lord is cruel?'

It was very hard for Charlie to bear.

She went to Cardington with Mrs Clive, and when they came back, it was Charlie who cried. She cried to Peter.

'To see her bending down to pull a piece of grass out of the stone, as if she was tucking you into bed – Oh God, I'd give anything, anything if only I could tell her and see her face!'

'And see her face when the judge put on his bit of black cloth and they led me away out of the dock?'

'Are we going to run all the rest of our lives?' She lay in his arms, crying silently without tears, limp with misery.

'I seem to have been running ever since I picked myself up soaking wet with my clothes on fire, and saw the hell I'd come out of.'

'Don't, don't—'

There was a panic horror that would never leave him. Sometimes he woke in the night screaming and begging for help, choking through a fire.

'The air was all sucked away by the burning gas. It was red hot, a vacuum, and I was choking, suffocating, I don't know how I burst away. And then after I'd rolled in the swamp – my skin was like fire – I ran and ran, I don't know where I was. I went through the woods and across fields. I ran and stumbled on because I knew it was my only chance. I wandered about – weeks, it seemed like, but perhaps it wasn't so long. I begged like a tramp, and stole some clothes. I got to the coast and in a café there were some Irish sailors from a freighter. I took a rowboat in the dark and climbed up the ladder on the hull and got in among the cargo. If they'd found me at Belfast, I'd have given myself up, told everything, I was so beat. But they didn't, so I went on, running and hiding.

'Don't cry, Charlay.' He held her tightly. 'Don't be sad, darling. We'll be safe. It will be all right.'

It was usually she who had to comfort him like that, when he was angry with fear, or bedevilled with the little prison of the cottage. Sometimes he sat silently with his hands hanging between his knees, staring at his hands, turning them restlessly over and over as if they were haunted by what they had done.

After the first stories, with pictures of detectives looming through the rain round a kind of tarpaulin tent they had put up over the place where the body was found, there was not much in the papers about the 'Arms and Legs Mystery'. All decent murders have to be nicknamed to make ghoulish headlines.

The police, getting nowhere, were not giving out negative reports. There was nothing to lead them to Peter, dead or alive, but he made Charlie go back to Birmingham to try to find out what was happening.

The Hunters were not there. Gone to her sister in Rhyl for

their nerves, said a neighbour in Calshott Road when she came to her door with a mop and saw Charlie knocking.

'It was a bit of a strain on their characters when it came out at the inquest that Bessie had carried on like that with so many men. Even her employer didn't know who she knew and who she didn't. Too simple, the poor old lady, in any case.'

Thank God she was. Thank God.

'And the gormless kind of companion she had looking after her, she was daft enough to have chopped poor Bessie up herself, in Mrs Hunter's opinion.'

Conscious of Peter driving her – Didn't you talk to anyone, didn't you find out anything? – Charlie went on into the town and found a reporter in the newspaper office who had worked on the Arms and Legs murder.

'I'm with the *Oxford Mail*,' she told him, aware that she did not look it. Girl reporters had tailored suits and spectacles and nicotine on their fingers to show they were doing a man's job. 'I was up here when the investigations started, but we don't seem to have heard much lately. Aren't there any new leads?'

'Not much, dear. Fingerprints, of course, you'll have known about that, but none of them on file. Footprints. What does that prove? It was a man did it.' He grinned. 'Any one of three hundred and sixty-five men, by what I hear.'

He told Charlie who was in charge of the case, and she chugged the Morris along to Buckingham, but never got past the sergeant behind the desk. When she offered herself as the *Oxford Mail*, he said, 'Let me see your credentials.' He leaned a patient hand on the counter, and she pretended to look in her bag.

'I forgot my card.'

'Forget your head next,' he said indulgently, as if she were his six-year-old daughter.

'Can't I talk to Mr Hicks?'

'Sorry, love. Come another day.' He showed his pipe-rotted teeth briefly. 'Come up and see me sometime,' he quoted listlessly, again as if she were his child and he in the habit of communicating with her through tired old family jokes and worn-out catch phrases.

There were other murders. Other sensations. A woman

strangled herself in bed, trying out a new slimming exercise. A picnic party was attacked by a bear. Another pair of legs was found in a suitcase at King's Cross, the torso turning up at Brighton. The Arms and Legs were never in the headlines, though a few odd news stories appeared from time to time. A forensic opinion that the murderer had some rough knowledge of butchering. The police were seeking the whereabouts of a certain sailor who might 'help them with their inquiries'.

'That means he did it, poor bleeder.' Peter crumpled the paper and threw it into the cold summer grate in the upstairs room. 'He'll stay out of their way.'

'*You* did it!' Who was going mad?

'I *told* you that. What if I only read about it and made it up? Any time there's a good murder, they have a dozen cranks confess to it.'

For a wild moment hope flashed. Blacked out. 'The hair—'

'What if you made that up too?' His lips moved towards a smile that was not in his eyes. 'Perhaps we are both making everything up and this is only a nightmare that hasn't happened. Yet.'

Sometimes he watched her like a cat at a mouse hole. She could not leave him and he would not leave her. They had gone too far together. They must be damned or saved together.

Mr Clive did not go to Peter's grave with Nelly and Charlie. He was still hoping for communion with those who had passed over, standing at the edge of the valley of the shadow, hallooing over to the other side. So he was off cemeteries, not having solved, or even faced the problem of how a person could be over his left shoulder and in the ground too. He sat in a tent on the lawn of Swyncombe rectory with his turban over his eyes and a succession of hands in his, sceptical, unsure, gullible.

He made one pound nine – half price for Major Breen whose left arm had gone at Arras – for the widowed mothers of unemployed machinists, which was more than his wife and Charlotte had done, gallivanting over the countryside and killing chickens.

'We didn't kill any chickens.'

'But what did you do for your country in these desperate

times?' Dad had made one pound nine for his country, which made him feel especially noble, as he could have put the money towards his deficit at the post office, which would not count as prostituting his gift for gain, since the gain would be the Postmaster-General's.

The Postmaster-General and the other members of Ramsay MacDonald's last Gadarene government were sliding rapidly towards their Crisis. In the 'Great Betrayal', model for any future Socialist acts of collaborationist non-Socialism, the dole was cut by twenty per cent to a howl in the House almost as anguished as in the mill towns and pit villages, where the great gaunt army of unemployed were slowly starving.

Ramsay MacDonald 'intended to do some thinking'. Meanwhile, he hoped that the country would 'give every example of indomitable British spirit in the face of difficulty'.

'He can whistle for that,' Mrs Clive said. 'It was all used up in the Great War. The common people will never be like that again. If there ever was another war, you'd see the rot set in. They've gone soft, that's where it is.'

'Soft – on the dole?' Gordon sneered his ugly lippy laugh. 'Demoralized, more like. There's thousands have never known what it is to work for a living.'

'There's some don't want to.'

'I suppose that's meant personal,' Rita flounced at Nelly. 'Thanks ever so.'

'You shut your face,' her husband told her.

The Government passed a motion in the House favouring the solution of the unemployment problem, as if that in itself were a solution.

'I could pass a better motion than that in me Mum's privy,' Gordon said.

'That's enough of that.' Nelly Clive did not allow such talk. 'They're doing their best, I suppose.' She had heard on the wireless that six unemployed miners had sent the Prime Minister a fifteen-shilling postal order to help reduce the Budget deficit. 'Do you think it would encourage the poor man if I sent him a box of eggs?' She wanted anyone in authority to be infallible. She would have made a good Roman Catholic.

'You can send him a box of chicken droppings from me.'

Gordon sat heavily in his father's chair with the carpet seat, picking his spaced-out teeth with a nail. He and Rita and the cross-eyed baby had come to stay. The friend had turned them away. People he had dealt with in other firms were not interested. There was nothing in London. No work. No flat in Edgware. No car, no pride, no hope.

They had arrived one evening – 'Just at teatime, and I only had two kippers!' – and announced that they had come home.

'Home! This isn't your—' Mrs Clive swallowed. 'Of course, my dears. Of course you come to us.'

'It so happened that my mum was laid up with her chest again,' Rita said defensively.

But since they were here and the taxi was sent away, there was nothing to be gained by war, so Mrs Clive swooped on the baby and exclaimed with sincere joy at its hideous face, laid it instanter on the kitchen table to be dried out, and generally hustled about to see what could be done to make them all welcome.

There was no room for the three of them under her thatched roof, so they took rooms on the corner with Mrs Hardcastle, whose husband was dead and children far away. Mrs Hardcastle would not feed them, and one look at Rita had warned her not to offer her speckless kitchen, so they were up at the post office cottage all the time, Rita's bulk almost wall to wall in the small kitchen, the baby screaming every time the telephone rang, so that Dot from Telegrams asked, 'What do you do, Mr Clive, torture the poor innocent mite?'

Dad had tried to teach Rita something of what went on behind the post office fireguard, so as to give her something to do at least, since she liked the country even less than Mrs Clive, who was gradually coming to terms with it. She would do nothing but push the baby up and down the village street – not even round the triangle for a change of scene – in high heels her doctor had forbidden, because she wanted to stumble and totter to show what she thought of the gritty road to the eyes who watched behind the curtain corners.

After a half-hour dissertation on stamps, she shrugged and said, 'Well, I'm sure I don't mind helping you out if you've something better to do.'

'It's to help you, not me.'

'Selling twopence happorth of stamps and a four-shilling postal order isn't my idea of a morning's fun, thank you very much.'

She was hopeless. They would welcome the birth of the second baby, if only to get her out of the house for a week.

If Mr Clive did leave her while he cycled off with a telegram, she would antagonize anyone who came into the post office with her adenoidal stare and her air of great offence, as if a penny happorth stamp were offal. The customer would find an excuse to come back the next day especially to say, 'I missed you yesterday, Mr Clive. Your daughter-in-law doesn't say much, does she?'

With the help of Mr Hammond, who shot over the land of a man who knew the engineer, Gordon got work on the new Benson bypass near the river. He was disgusted because it was a labourer's job, but it was the first work there had been for men like Arthur Gale's father, who had been bicycling eight fruitless miles to the Labour Exchange every week for months, and sometimes thirteen miles to Cowley to hang about with the other dog-eared men outside the employment office of the Morris works.

It brewed up to an argument one night in the tiny public bar of the White Hart, where the tables and chairs smelled like sodden old beer barrels. There was a scuffle. Someone was knocked down, not by Gordon, who swung wild and cowardly. An elbow went up and knocked his lip against his teeth.

He slouched across the road to Charlie's house and banged on her locked door. 'Help! Lemme in!'

'Go away. You're drunk.'

'I'm hurt, girl. I'm bleeding.'

Peter had escaped up the stairs. She opened the front door to the scented night and saw Gordon reeling on the brick path, hand to his mouth, sticky dark smears on his fingers. She had to take him in to the kitchen sink.

He was hurt, but he was fairly drunk too, so after she had washed his mouth with pump water, she unlocked the back door and tried to push him through. Like a bull, he stood and swayed, looking at her through a half-closed eye, his greasy black hair curling like the poll of a Black Angus.

'Get on home!' She pushed at him. She even kicked him with a slippered foot. He turned and lurched back to the front of the house, a hand on each wall of the narrow passage, leaving smears on the rosebud paper Dad Clive had hung. She got between him and the sitting-room, standing with hands and feet braced in the frame of the doorway so that he could not go in.

'I've got nothing against you,' he said thickly, swaying in the hall, jutting down his forehead like a lowbrow baboon. 'We always got on all right, you and me. So come on, give us a piece of what old Peter had. Stupid sod, he's dead and burned all up, and what do you do for fun, Fatty?' He put his hands about her unprotected waist, ran them upwards and lurched inaccurately to kiss her with a slobbering mouth that was bleeding again. She tasted his blood. She hit out and kicked. He lost his balance and she got the door open and sent him reeling out into the night.

She went quickly to the door at the bottom of the stairs to call softly up to Peter. He was just behind the door, crouched on the turn of the stairs, shivering.

'I'll kill him. If I wasn't dead, I'd kill him.'

She dropped beside him, and he kissed Gordon's blood on her lips. 'I've got to get out of here. We've got to get away.'

The greengage tree, whose ancient roots heave at the turf of the front lawn and make it difficult to mow, is in blossom against a pearled sky. The clump of beeches on the Danish hill which look black in winter have gradually grown lighter as spring surges up the hill towards them in a riot of wet green and white. The hedges froth with hawthorn flower. The children are out of school for Easter, and shout down the road beyond my wall at all hours, instead of their routine clocking back and forth.

More cars go by. The sixties have discovered the glories of Nature. Our chalky lanes and hills, pancaked with starry yellow and white flowers, have always been there, but now they are discovered. 'Never knew there was so much *real* country so near to London!' What do they expect it to be – plastic? Motorcycle helmets go by my wall like peeled hard-boiled eggs.

It was so beautiful this morning, fresh and sunny, with all the obvious things like blackbirds, and the musky smell of pinks, and swallows dive-bombing me as I came through the door below the place where they are renovating their nest, that I went out to mow instead of sitting down to work. The greengage tree makes it impossible to do a neat job on the left side of the lawn. Every year Charlie and I used to discuss whether it would give us more pleasure as firewood. Then like a dog wagging its tail and licking your hand as you take it sadly to the vet, it would open tenderly into blossom – a pure fancy dress, because it never sets to any fruit.

Charlie said that when she first came to this house she used to pick greengages, but that may have been a fantasy, because of everything being better in the Old Days. She used to say things like, 'That rose used to bloom right up to there, great cabbagey flowers pushing in at the window.' Lovingly, she always assured me that she had never been completely happy in this house until she lived in it with me, which was nice to hear and I was glad to believe it. But I know that before Peter came back from the dead, and after too, she loved this little place very intensely. She must have hated the thought of leaving it. She knew they could not stay. The house was the old life, the safe life, the becalmed half life when she had been big bumbling Lottie Lambert without a plan in the world more ambitious than painting a door or entering a team for the drill display.

Now their plans grew bolder and enthusiastic. As soon as school was over, they would lock up the house, give the fishes to Arthur, take the bristly little dog and go . . .

To Scotland, they planned. Charlie had never been there. As a child, if you did not go abroad and get foot and mouth disease on the Belgian coast or diarrhoea in the Mediterranean, you had not had a holiday. From Scotland to Northern Ireland. Eventually smuggle their way across the border to the South. Peter would get a passport somehow. There were always people. They could go anywhere! They would go to the West Indies. They would find an island. They would run a hotel in Canada, or tramp about on tennis rackets in Labrador. They hugged each other and planned their life as adventurers. They never thought of themselves growing old together, flopping down tired in some deadly place because it had running water and electricity and was only two minutes potter from the shops. They would roam the world with delight. Mr and Mrs Jack Morgan, immortal.

A telephone call from Mrs Lambert to the post office brought Rita down heavy-foot, content to bear bad tidings.

'Your sister-in-law has been taken very sick. You've got to go to London.' She stared and tried to see beyond Charlie into the house. 'And please tell them they're not supposed to use the GPO for private calls.' She would know that. 'OHMS,' she said nastily, and picked her way back down the path, her ankles turning genteelly.

Peter refused to stay in the village alone, so they went together to London, and Charlie left him in a Paddington hotel room that smelled of railways, with a frieze of hanging dirt round the top of the wall above the reach of a lazy swabbing hand.

Charlie went to Fitzjohn's Avenue, where the family were gathered for a crisis dinner. They looked unhappily at each other over lamb cutlets with onion sauce, and made redundant suggestions of what should be done now and what should not have been done in the past.

I know, because I was there. One of the family now, calling Mr Lambert Father, as Bubbles had done since she decided at fourteen that Charlie sounded silly calling him Daddy at nineteen. I felt rather silly calling him Father, because he still felt like my boss. But he was still very nice to me, and he told me that evening that he was glad I was one of them now, to help in time of trouble.

'Anything I can do, sir . . .' If I had stayed married to Bubbles, I might have degenerated into the family MC, invaluable at weddings and funerals, like the man in the first act of *Sleeping Beauty* who gets his hair pulled out by Carabosse.

Midge had sat up in bed that morning and before she could say a word, blood had gushed from her mouth while Reggie slept beside her.

It was TB. 'That old spot of trouble on the lung flaring up – bit nasty that.' Umphie Sears was no scaremonger.

In those days before miracle drugs, there was not much you could do except wait it out under a red blanket in some cold and bracing spot where everybody had the same disease, which was much more depressing than the varied symptoms of a hospital ward. Because Reggie could not keep popping over to Switzerland, Midge was to go to a windswept barrack on the Yorkshire coast. For how long? 'That's up to the bug, my dear. Bit tricky, yes.'

The children could stay at home with Nanny and the maids for a while, but when Reggie went on tour with *Cornish Cream* at the end of the month – what then?

Someone had stopped him saying, 'This has all come at a ghastly time, right in the middle of rehearsing the new cast' before he could get further than looking as if he were going to say it. But they could not stop him saying, 'Well, do you want me to give up the part then, let everybody down, is that what you want me to do?' as if the crisis of poor Midge were more theirs than his.

They did not even ask Bubbles to move into the Camden Hill Square house with me (carting me along like a hatbox). I would quite have liked it, for she raged around our small flat as if she had been brought up at Blenheim. Everyone knew she did not like small children. That was another of the things I had not known before I married her.

Charlie was the obvious person. It was the end of term. She was footloose. She could go with Nanny and the children to the bungalow at Cromer where their spades and shrimping nets awaited them, and ineradicable grains of last year's sand.

She sat across the table from me, vivid with her short glossy black hair and high colour of embarrassment. 'I don't see how I can.' She looked in vain round the family faces for help. They were not stony. They were relaxed with confidence in

255

her, which was worse. 'I'm going abroad, you know.' She had already tried to pave the way of her escape. A holiday in Europe. She might get a job and stay. It had evidently made no impression. 'I told you about it. It's all fixed up with a friend.'

'What friend?' Bubbles asked, implying amazement that she had any.

'A mistress at school. No one you'd know.'

'Obviously.'

'You'd put that before Weezie and Jojo?' Her mother frowned. 'I can't believe it, Charlie.'

She saw herself and Midge sitting on the steps of the Albert Memorial, with a stray brown dog licking her hand.

'If I was to die, would you take my children?'

'God forbid.'

But she would have, then. Six months ago. A lifetime ago.

'Don't you understand?' Her mother shook her head with a patient smile, as if Charlie were a child who could not learn. 'Being without their mother is bad enough for them already, without losing the security of Cromer as well.'

'I never liked Cromer.'

'It's not for your pleasure.' It was spelled out for her. Her duty. Average common decency. 'It's for the poor darling children. Nanny can't do a thing except mend vests and bake apples. She won't even step *on* the beach.'

'I know. I know all that, and I'd love to go with them, but—'

'You mean you'd rather go poking round Chartres Cathedral with some schoolmarm in pince-nez and a raffia hat?'

'She isn't like that. She's quite young.' The lie grew deeper.

'She or he?' That was Reggie. He lowered his sparse eyelashes at his sister and made a purse of his mouth that showed precisely how unromantic it was without make-up. It was typical of this family that even a first-class dramatic crisis degenerated into mediocre bickering.

Apple fritters came, and coffee and brandy, just like any night. It would be harder to stop them coming than to consume them obediently. Everyone wanted them anyway. When the maid had gone, the arguing started again, and ended, in the way it had so many evenings when Charlie was an adolescent, by her crashing her chair into the fireplace and rushing from the room in tears crying, 'I can't stand it any more!'

Her mother went after her, in the way she had so often, and found her in her room sitting on the edge of the bed with her shoulders hunched and her hands gripping the mattress in the way she had sat so many times when she had ten nail-bitten fingers to grip with.

'I'll go to Cromer.' Mrs Lambert stood by the door. She was not the cuddling sort of mother. 'I'll get a girl from Universal Aunts and send Nanny on holiday.' Although she had wished Nanny on to Midge as a family heirloom, she could not stay in the same room for two hours with the woman herself. 'It is a man though, isn't it?'

Charlie nodded miserably. There was more chance of them understanding that than the mythical schoolmistress, with or without pince-nez.

'Anyone we know?'

Charlie shook her head.

Her mother did not ask, 'Are you going to marry him?' She sensed that there was something going on here outside her ken of Charlie.

Her daughter looked up and saw in her mother's face something unexpected. Wonderment, yes, for who would have thought it of Charlie old chump? But a tinge of – not quite admiration – envy.

Mrs Lambert had married at twenty-two. Although she had sat for several pictures besides the Yellow Dress, her father looked more like a stockbroker than an artist and his studio was as spruce as the clean sky-lit office where I had drawn my doors at Lambert's. She had never modelled without her clothes or even had tea with anyone who could possibly be described as 'bohemian'. The few young artists whom her father chose to help had to buy or borrow a suit and tie before they came to his house.

In those days, although young people carried on in the normal way, their parents either did not believe it or pretended not to believe it, which made a far bigger 'generation gap' than the one they boast of now. Now a mother gives her daughter contraceptives for Christmas. In the early thirties, they cried, 'She would *never* do anything like that!' or sobbed, if it transpired that she did, as heart-brokenly as if they had discovered she was a criminal lunatic.

Mrs Lambert did neither. Ahead of her time, though sheltered, she neither condoned nor condemned. She envied.

For this reason, and because she was going to see Midge tomorrow, Charlie came downstairs and played Racing Demon until Reggie stopped the game because he had bottom score, and went to bed in her own white room with the school pictures and china dogs.

When Bubbles and I got home, she found she had left without her handbag. She was the only beautiful woman I have ever known whose handbag was not a fifth limb, shrieking like a mandrake if it was separated from its owner. Bubbles was surprisingly careless about hers. My jacket pockets were always weighted down with second-string lipsticks and powder compacts. Tonight, the key of our flat was in her bag, and I had not brought mine.

Our neighbours were having a party, so Bubbles went in and joined them while I went back to Fitzjohn's Avenue. I had a key to that house. I let myself quietly in to the wide hall where mauve and blue light from the windows beside the door changed the colours of the rug in odd-shaped patches. The house was very quiet, the measured clock like drops of water. Everyone was in their rooms.

I crossed the hall into the drawing-room. Without turning on the light, I found the beaded satin bag among crushed cushions. I was just at the door again, when I heard the tiny squeal of a hand on the banister at the top of the stairs, looked up, and saw Charlie.

There was a broad polished banister in that house. I had never seen her come down those stairs except sliding side-saddle, landing with a thump on the rug and taking off for a room or the street all in one movement. She had even come down that way tonight, after her adolescent retreat from the dining-room. Swish – thump – and a defiant bang and bounce into the drawing-room. 'What's the game? I'll play.'

Now she was not only walking down, she was creeping. She

looked so stealthy that I slipped back into the shadow of the door until she had reached the bottom, crossed the hall and let herself noiselessly out. Gone for cigarettes? A run round Hampstead Heath? She could not have looked more secret and intent if she were going to meet her lover.

'What are you going to do in the hols, Miles?'

St Gabriel's was not normally a surname school with people saying, 'Hard cheese, Magnusson', or, 'Sit next to me at Assembly, Carker-Hughesdon', but the Set had taken to doing it to Cara – 'the Miles kid' – in case she felt too integrated.

'Oh, *I* don't know.' Cara made her new face, a sneer, a pulled lip, but her features were built for spraying eagerness, not ennui. 'If my cousins come, we may hire some horses and go on a riding trek.' Once long ago, Miss Lambert had talked about going too. 'With saddlebags.'

'Oh, my God.'

'If two women have babies when they're supposed to – one's the vicar's wife—'

'Oh, shut up.'

'My father might take us to Brittany for a week. With my uncle and aunt and the twins.'

'Boys or girls?'

'Girls. One lost all her hair. She has a wig and she can't swim or stand on her head.' The twins were lifelong sharers of many agreeable holidays, but she had to add, 'Isn't that icky?'

'Oh, lousy luck, Miles. How *wet*!'

At home, her parents offered each other the stock reassurances. Only a phase. She'll come out of it. Difficult age. Her mother could not understand how Cara had lost her happiness, and tried with all the old steady charms to woo her back. But Cara did not want to gather flies for abandoned fledgelings, did not want to swish bare knees through soaking bracken in the woods that skirted their hill, did not want to bake bread or play cards or be read aloud to in the fading light in their secret grassy place against the fallen tree.

She fought against happiness, and at last her mother turned in her dipping skirt, sleeves rolled up over bare scratched arms, and fought back.

'I'm not going to let you change!' Her outdoor face blazed hot and strangely angry. Her blue eyes were fierce. 'This isn't you – I'm not going to let you *be* like this!'

'How do you know what I'm like?' Cara blazed back. 'I'm not your child.'

'What do you mean? What on earth are you talking about?'

'I know I'm adopted.' The Set had decided for her that this could be the only way she could have come by such impossible parents. 'You should have told me sooner. It wasn't fair, you should have told me.'

'But you're mine.' Her mother gripped the bony arm with her strong hand. 'I gave birth to you.'

Cara felt sick. She tried to pull her arm away, but her mother held her, staring into her eyes with a desperate flushed face.

'You couldn't have.' She heard her own cruel voice. 'You were too old.'

With a cry, her mother dropped her arm and ran away. Later, her father, who had never hit her, came to her room with a leather belt.

Outside the door, through her shrieks and sobs, she heard her mother tell him, 'That's the worst thing you could have done.'

And yet, buried somewhere within her where her real self lay imprisoned, there was the knowledge of a pure truth in what he had done. Somehow with all the wrongness, it was the only right thing. She would die rather than admit it.

'He hit me.' She hastened to tell the girls at Break, capping their regular Monday stories of drunken quarrels and mothers' boyfriends pinching them.

'Let's see.'

'No.' There was nothing to see. He had not hit her very hard, and only twice before he drew in his breath with a gasp and went out of the room.

'He hit her.' They hailed Avril, dawdling from the cloak-room.

'What for?'

'Nothing.'

'That settles it.' Avril unleashed a deep fulfilled sigh. 'You owe them nothing.'

'What am I to do?'

'You'll probably just stick it meekly out. Yes, Mummy, no, Daddy, like a stupid clod.'

What am I to do – what am I to do? Cara ran through the bottle-green corridors like a dreamself, with staring eyes and rasping breath: Somewhere round some corner, Miss Lambert would catch her outstretched arms and hold her tight against her gym tunic. Oh, save me!

Through a window of the gym corridor, she saw Miss Lambert walk quickly through the rain across the netball court. Cara ran out to the yard where she was bending to the starting handle of the Morris.

'Where are you going?'

'I'm taking a half day. It's too wet for games.'

'Take me with you.'

'I can't. You're supposed to be at lunch.' She tugged at the starting handle and then looked up. 'What's the matter, Cara – are you in trouble?'

Cara shook her head. 'Take me home with you,' was all that she could say.

'Oh, come on, it can't be as bad as all that, whatever you've done.' She puffed and grunted at the handle. 'You go on back and face it like my good brave girl.'

The car shuddered into mediocre life. Miss Lambert ran back and jumped in to race the engine.

'Chin up, kid!' She waved from the car and jerked ahead. She waved again as she turned out of the school gate, but Cara had gone.

They did not find her for three days. She had walked and wandered and been given a lift by a man in a lorry who thought he was taking her home. She was found roaming somewhere in the Midlands, soaked through, her shoes in shreds, the tight hand of pleurisy on her breath.

Waking after a long sleep, she told her mother as much as she could put into words. Some of it she could neither understand nor explain to herself. Mrs Miles came to Kingsgrove on a bus and walked the two miles to the village to find Charlie.

'Quite flushed and queer, she looked when she came in the post office, dust all on her shoes and the bottom of her skirt. I said to Dad after, "Did I do right, I wonder, to direct her to Charlotte's house?" She looked like a gipsy.'

Charlie looked out of the upstairs window and saw her walking up the path with her eyes fixed on the house and her mouth set in her pleasant sunburned face.

She had seen her at school. She knew who it was. She ran down and brought her into the house, too upset at the sight of her to take her usual care to check for traces of Peter in the downstairs rooms.

Mrs Miles wore a faded cotton dress and a cardigan that stood up in a point behind her neck where she had hung it on a hook. Her yellow-grey hair was cut in a childish bob. The dog came up to her and she bent to stroke it without taking her eyes off Charlie in her dressing-gown.

They both stood, while she told Charlie what she had heard from her daughter.

'Those beasts.' Charlie looked just to the side of the blue eyes. 'I know what some of those girls are like. They can be really vicious if they think they can get away with it, and poor little Cara was younger—'

'I didn't come out here,' the mother said, 'to tell you about the girls, though I wanted you to know everything, since everything seems to have passed you by.'

'I knew she wasn't very happy this term, but—'

'Because of you! The girls – she wouldn't have paid any heed to them if she'd had some strength behind her. She loved you, don't you know that? She loved you and you let her down. That's what I came out here to tell you.'

Mrs Miles did not shout at Charlie hysterically, because she was a calm slow person who could go through even a scene like this with a sort of dignity that did not come from poise or pride.

'She still loves you,' she told Charlie, 'because that's what she's like, but she's not to see you ever again, even supposing you tried to make amends.' They were both aware, had been aware since they came into the room, of Peter's jacket on the back of the straight chair by the desk.

'I'm sorry,' Charlie said at last. 'I didn't know—'

Mrs Miles went to the door and then turned and stood with her hands clasped, kneading her brown hands, her peaceful face very troubled. 'What have you done?' she whispered. 'Oh, what are you doing?' Tears clouded the clean blue eyes. She went away down the brick path, her short hair and her loose cotton dress blowing out behind her as she turned into the wind and hurried away down the road.

'Who was that?'

'A woman I know.' She did not tell Peter any of it. There was no point.

Two nights before Charlie and Peter were planning to leave, the village was rocked by the most exciting thing that had happened there for years.

At the end of the empty puddled lane, the church and the rectory mouldered by a dark pond. Three centuries ago, a manor house stood here in its rich farmland. The pious family had built the little church and square cold rectory in thanks to God for their crops and cattle. Disasters came. Young men were lost in war. The house burned down. Now the land was divided between other farmers. Only a tumbledown barn and the corners of ruined walls showed where the manor house had been, but the church and rectory still mildewed at the end of the lane, Mr Herriott and his daughter with them.

It was an epic Sunday that saw a dozen people in church, unless it was Christmas or Easter, when the Hammonds came with their servants, and even Quentin stood up to drown out Ethel Herriott's quaking contralto. The organ had died long ago. Bob Rickett the cowman pulled a single bell on a Sunday morning to summon nobody, but the rooks were in the other bell frames and a peal had not been rung within memory.

Ethel used to play the small harmonium which smelled of rotted leather, until the joints of her fingers seized up into

263

strange attitudes. Dad Clive could play half a dozen of the more defeatist hymns, but at his own whim, not the vicar's. Mrs Hardcastle played when it was not too cold, and occasionally a musical guest from the Big House took over, and talked about it for the rest of the day, because it had been a quaint thing to do.

Mr Herriott could have played, but he had to conduct the service, gaunt as a vulture, his stringy neck holding his head high above his surplice, bloodshot eyes bulging like a victim buried in the desert sand. He preached very personal sermons about the village and its inhabitants, which was why they did not come. If any of them did, he belaboured them for the absence of the others.

At Evensong, he was sometimes alone with Ethel, battling the drip of her nose winter and summer. Then he would stay afterwards and play the harmonium for himself, with only one lamp lit at the end of the melancholy church. The slitted light glowed faintly on the dark surface of the pond as if it came from under water. The music flew weird into the tall waiting trees. Only a gang of boys on a dare or a girl with a lover's safe arm around her would wander down that lane at night.

On this extraordinary evening, Mr Herriott had played for an hour after supper, then locked up the church, written a page or two of his memoirs and gone to bed. He did not know how long he had been asleep when he woke with a shock and sat up with his white hair on end, his heart going like a dynamo.

He went to the window and looked across the pond to where his church squatted in the moonless night. Shadows moved on the roof. He knew what they were doing.

Nevertheless, after he had put on his coat and his Wellington boots and slipped through the long churchyard grass, unlocked the door by feel with the big iron key and stepped inside the church, he called querulously up towards the roof, 'What are you doing up there?'

With this fair warning, the men got safely away with half the lead from the church roof which was already stripped and rolled up in their lorry.

Episode over, and only the tracks of the lorry in the soft gravel of the lane, Mr Herriott went back to bed as quietly as if he were a thief himself. The one thing was not to have Ethel shouting through the house, stabbing the air with those twisted hands. He was too excited to go back to sleep, so at first light he cycled into the police station, and soon the church lane and the village was swarming with men. Two in uniform and a detective from Wallingford called at all the houses to find out if anyone had heard or seen anything during the night.

Charlie and Peter knew nothing of the sensation which had spread magically through the village even before Mr Herriott came back with the police. There was a knocking at their front door before they were awake. Peter got out of bed and knelt close to the wall by the low window, squinting down sideways at the edge of the curtain.

'God damn you, Charlay.' He turned, crouching. He looked as if he would spring at her and choke out her life.

'What is it?'

'You should know.' Still crouched, he looked quickly right and left, not knowing what to do.

'Are you there, miss?' There was no mistaking the sergeant.

'Oh my God.' She pulled on a dressing-gown and ran down. They could be all round the house. The only thing she could do was talk to them, keep them away, stop them coming inside. They would kick in the door with their great boots and storm up the stairs to where Peter crouched like an animal.

Fumbling, she unlocked the door and shot back the bolt. There were two of them, the sergeant and a man in plain clothes.

'Sorry to disturb you, miss.' The detective had a casual car-salesman manner, his hair slicked wetly back, his club tie too bright, his smile at Charlie's bare feet and red dressing-gown too confidential. 'Just like to ask you a few questions.'

She shut the door and came out, pretending to blink up into the morning sun, which had not yet come through the mist.

'Don't catch cold.' He looked at her feet as if they were her breasts.

'What do you want?' She should be standing with her back against the door and her arm through the iron bolt slots, like the picture of a girl remembered from a childhood book of saints and heroes.

'Little bit of bother down at the church.' The detective's eyebrows went up. You and I, of course, see it as comic, though it's drama to the peasants.

Charlie felt her face grow red. She knew it must have been flat white before. 'No ... no, I heard nothing. No lorry. Nothing unusual ...' She could hardly speak to him.

'Good day, miss, and thanking you. Better get something on.'

They went at last, and Charlie rushed upstairs and hurled herself at Peter. 'Oh, thank God, thank God! It's all right, darling, they—'

'I heard.'

Charlie was panting. Her heart was hammering in a pulse below her chin. 'Oh God, at first I thought—'

He held her stiffly. 'So did I.'

When he said that, she realized what he had said at the window. She had been too terrified to take it in. Now she remembered.

She got up and went downstairs. She went into the kitchen and started to do ordinary things. She let the dog out. She put a pan of water on for tea because the handle had come off the kettle, took butter from the stone slab under the window in the store cupboard.

He came down in a pair of slacks, bare-chested, his bare feet coming noiselessly up behind her on the stone floor. 'Where's the tea?'

'Get back upstairs. They may still be in the village.'

'I said, where's the tea?'

The kitchen curtains were drawn. She lived most of her life now with the curtains drawn, like the people on the village street whose front parlours had not ever seen the sun. Still tense and wary, he lifted an edge and looked out. The dog was whining to come in, but he said, 'Leave him out there. At least he barks.'

'He wants to come in.'

'Oh, he's in the plot too, is he?' He dropped the curtain and stood leaning against the primitive stone sink, his hands in his pockets, a cigarette on his lip, the split eyebrow screwed up against the smoke.

'It isn't funny,' she said. 'It isn't funny at all that you thought upstairs that I—'

'Got a fright, that's all. Pounding on the door – "Open in the name of the Law!" A man's liable to say anything.'

'Not if he hasn't been thinking it. How could you think that about me, Peter? Don't you trust me?'

'I don't trust anybody.'

'I trust you.' She came and stood in front of him and put her hands on his skin. 'I didn't at first, but now I do.'

'More fool you.' He did not take his hands out of his pockets and put them round her.

'At first,' she said, standing very close to him with her eyes closed, 'I was afraid of what you would do to me, because of what I knew. I was afraid that if I let you have the hair . . .'

'Ah yes, the hair. If you trust me now, Charlay, why don't you give it me?'

'I want to forget about it. I don't want either of us to see it ever again. When we're gone from here, we'll forget everything. We'll start again, and be safe.'

'What makes you think I'm not safe here?' he asked casually.

'You know you're not.'

'Because you still might turn me in, isn't that it? You've not quite decided you want to live with a murderer for the rest of your life. That's why you want to keep Bessie's hair, isn't it?'

She dropped her hands from him and turned away. 'I've got to go to work.'

'Oh no.' He threw his cigarette into the sink and grabbed her. 'You're not going anywhere and leave me alone here. That's a plot too, I suppose. You'd rehearsed that dear little conversation with the coppers so I'd not jump out of the back window and run for it.'

'Let me *go* – I'll be late.'

'You're not going, darling girl. You're going to stay here where I know what you're doing.'

'I don't understand you.' Desolate, she went limp in his grasp and he let her go. How could he think these things of her? She had always known that she was more in love, but did

267

he not love her at all? Had he never? Was that why he had first made love to her – to trap her, sink her, drown her?

If it was like that—

'I can't go on with you,' she said.

Anger rushed into his scarred face. 'I'll kill you too!' She backed against the other wall. Tin plates and saucepan lids clattered on the flagstones.

'Go on then, tell me you're going to leave me. Go on, tell me. Tell me you can't stay with a man who's done what I did.' He had her trapped against the wall, between the table and the side of the stove where the pan of water was boiling away over the noisy paraffin flame. 'You can't stay with a man who shot a woman's head off, who slashed her up and butchered her and had his hands all in the blood and muck – tell me!'

He snatched the pan of water from the stove and held it in front of her face. Steam swam in her eyes. Scalding water fell on her bare foot.

'Tell me you can't. Tell me you've got to turn me in. All right, but before you do, you'll have this water in your darling face and then who'll want you? I've taught you how to want a man. But when I'm done with you, no other man is ever going to want you.'

Her lips moved, but said nothing. He held the pan steady, so close that the hot edge burned her chin. She watched the scalding water in horror.

'Tell me, Charlay.'

With an effort as great as a corpse thrusting aside its grave-stone, she brought up her hands and pushed pan and water across the room, scattering them both with stinging drops, then ducked and ran through the house and up the dark stairs. She lay on the bed and heard the stairs creak, step by step slowly, as he came up to kill her.

She lay on her back and watched him come towards the bed. He put his hand on her, and she shivered.

'You're ready for it, aren't you?' he said. 'It's always best after a fight.'

It seemed like a judgement for her passionate sin that the dog ran away one night when they were camped in a field, and though she searched and called as long as Peter would let her, the dog did not come back and she never saw him again.

'We can't go – Peter, I can't leave without him!'

'Get in the car.'

As he drove away, she strained backwards to see the field, the hedge where they had slept, until they turned a corner. She did not even know exactly where they were.

Looking at the map, she saw that their road would not take them far from the sanatorium where Midge was.

'I wish I could see her. Look, it isn't far. Don't you think we—'

'You're not on a picnic,' he said. 'You're leaving your family. It's goodbye to everything. There's only me.'

'I know. I know that.' She had faced it by not going back to London to say goodbye to anyone. She would write – some day, from somewhere. She would tell them something. Never the truth, but something they could think about.

'I would like to talk to Midge.' To be able to share even only a hint of her secret guilt with someone she loved. And Midge would never tell. 'I think she's going to die.'

'So you'll tell her the whole story. "It won't matter, because she's dying." He imitated Charlie's thoughts unnervingly. 'And then she'll call the police. "Hullo. Hullo. You remember that terrible Arms and Legs case they never did solve . . ." '

Midge did die, of course, slipping quietly away a few years later, wept for but not painfully missed, because she had been away from her family so much.

My hand is stiff from disuse like an outmoded lawnmower. 'A little holiday from work,' Mrs Meagan indulged me. But a holiday is not much use when you feel like that. Stomach this time, and various other small disorders related and unrelated. Not a lawnmower, but a hulk on a reef, breaking up.

I took a few days in bed, but got up in case Margaret got

wind of it by jungle telegraph and came to nurse me. I've been mooning in the garden in the first blessed warmth, lying about in my sagging old chair, and thinking about the old days.

They don't seem all that far away. In my soul, if that is what you call the self that floats like a foetus within this rotting body, I don't feel any different from that slender young man in his thirties in the thirties, stuck with Bubbles, but basically convinced that life was a good idea.

I lay in my chair with my hand in the sweet warm grass and I thought about the death of poor little Midge, which was about the same time as the death of my baby. I don't think of it as 'our' baby, since Bubbles never wanted it. She had made all sorts of excuses since we were married. Time to play (I was far more interested in work, and she'd been doing nothing but play since she was born). We couldn't afford a child (true, but her father forced an allowance on her which I did not want). Women should refuse to bear babies in protest against the threat of war. (She had heard that suggested by a women's pacifist group, but being herself too young to remember the last war and too silly to expect the next, she was one of those people who could fluff off even Abyssinia by calling Haile Selassie Highly Seductive and giggling at his beard.)

I did what is known as slipping one over on her one night when she was a bit drunk. She carried the baby healthily but not happily. She would not share my joy, although she could not dim it. My daughter was born prematurely – I can't blame Bubbles for that; she did not ride the bumps of Exhibition Road in a three-wheeler – and died in an incubator three days later.

My wife got some subornable doctor to say that she could never bear another child, and after that we began to grow steadily further apart until the divorce. The war brought her all sorts of new men. The Americans were *the* people in town to sleep with. I don't believe she enjoyed the actual sleeping all that much. She was a mental nymphomaniac and liked the idea of adultery.

I would have liked to have children. By now I would have grandchildren and they would tease me and have the grace to try to make me over as if it were not too late, as Reggie's do with him. He is much happier with his grandchildren than he ever was with his children.

My children would be nearing forty now. They would take me to the theatre if I never asked, 'What did he say?' and have me to stay in warm country houses where there was lots of gin, because it would be too uncomfortable for them here in my bachelordom.

All I have is Julia. I had a rare letter from her the other day. She has heard from Terence Haig-Davenport. After he and the Pigeon burst on to British television screens – with some success, I'm bound to say – an American agent half promised him a brief airing on one of the curiously old-fashioned shows which they seem to have filched from Saturday Night at the Palladium. Nothing else is promised, either half or whole, but Terence and the Pigeon are mad to go to Amevwica. That is to say, he is and so she is too, as his left leg might be, tagging along perforce. He asked Julia for names of bars or clubs where they might perform this summer.

'Who does he think I am?' she ended characteristically. Someone who might help him, I suppose.

I saw two of their appearances on television here. I could not go to anyone like the Clays or the Drydens at New Hope School and say that I wanted to watch a programme called *Teenagogo,* so I went to the Meagans and sat with them there in their immensely comfortable room where the huge set dominates all, as the great wireless cabinets used to in the days when my voice came out of them.

They live in the end Council house, by the grace of somebody or other, since the Council has been trying to turn them out for putting chestnut paling round the garden instead of the regulation two foot fence or hedge.

'If you want me to be a public spectacle,' Mrs Meagan told them, 'then move somebody in next door who won't want to see everything that's on my line.' (Are my shirts and pyjamas making a scandal then?)

'The beholder is the eye of evil, Mrs Meagan,' they said.

The neighbours actually don't mind the fence, because they can go upstairs and see over it. It is the Council who minds. Not because the fence is unsightly, for Mr Meagan has grown creepers quite artistically over it, but because they cannot stand to lose a point to their vassals.

Dick Meagan is an easy-going man who works at a Kingsgrove garage and drives a taxi for them on request. He brings the taxi home at night and takes his wife for jaunts in it. They took me out after I had been ill and did not feel like driving.

They are very good to me. We all had a glass of wine and watched *Teenagogo* with some pride. Mrs Meagan has seen Terence and the Pigeon once or twice at my house, or on the road in the little white car which now, since fame, has a pair of wings painted on each door.

The songs were good. His melodies are uncluttered, but the electric guitar was too loud – perhaps because he is slightly deaf? He told me the songs were recorded first, and then mimed, which makes it even cleverer of the Pigeon to look so endearing and spontaneous. She wore a white dress with a white rug over what I cannot help thinking of as her crippled legs, and a white band in her hair which did not impede its fall. She sat in a new white wheelchair. No wonder I have never had a smell of my money. Terence wore a white sort of thing that could loosely be called a suit, in that it had a jacket and trousers of no style recognizable to me.

I was very proud of them. Everyone else on the programme sang the old plaints and morosities (What jeremiads will they have left if the bomb does drop?). When Doris's joyous song soared away from her open mouth and ceased on a pure high note, halfway to the sun, there was an astonished pause like the beginnings of a gasp, and then the young studio audience broke into a tempest of shrieks and squeals, and the Meagans and I found ourselves clapping foolishly, as if Terence, grinning moistly over the Pigeon's head with his hand on her fragile bare shoulder, could hear us.

Julia also said she had a letter from a Mr Arnold Macklin with some questions about her mother. She wanted to know what this was all about, which was really why she wrote to me.

This Arnold Macklin is a journalist who has been bothering me these last two weeks like the kind of large fly which can't find its way out of the open half of the window.

It seems he is writing a series about unsolved murders. So the Arms and Legs Mystery, about which a certain amount has been written already – all speculation – is a natural choice.

He is a very tall man, with a tiny head on the top of his long thin neck, and legs that run up into his waist. He looks like those paper games we played at Garfield Hall, where you draw a section, fold over and pass it on, and it comes out either with no neck or thighs, or else too much, like Arnold Macklin. He favours perfectly round glasses on top of all this extra length, Glen plaid trousers and polo neck knitted shirts which show his nipples.

If I had known what he was after, I would not have let him in, but when he mentioned Charlie, I thought he might be something to do with death duties, since you can't judge by clothes any more these days. He was snugly in my only good chair with a gin and tonic before he told me what his mission was. My instinct was to throw him out, but a second bell told me I had better try to find out how he connected Charlie with the murder, and quash it then and there.

I kept calm, so he would not know that he had shocked me, and invited him civilly to speak. He told me that he had tracked down a woman who had once been a friend of Bessie Hunter. They had worked together in the Birmingham hotel. At the inquest, she had given evidence about the various men of Bessie's acquaintance. Those she knew about, at any rate, a long enough roster in itself. Now in her mellow and foolhardy years, hypnotized by the Open Sesame word 'Press', she had confided to this Macklin that she had not mentioned the name of Peter Clive at the inquest, since he was killed in the airship and nobody's business.

Much as I detest Arnold Macklin, I have to admit that he is a painstaking man who follows every lead, and will grow grey in the service of this magazine series if he carries on like this with all the cases. At Cardington, he found a retired member of the reserve watch of the R101 who had known Peter slightly. Together they went to the public library and studied the old pictures of the airship's crew, and the pictures of the funeral. This man had been there as a sort of usher, and had spoken to Peter's parents. So of course in that famous photograph of the mourners round the grave, he spotted the Clives, and Charlie between them taller than both, with her Persian lamb glengarry and planted young legs.

He then unearthed Peter's Wilton Crescent address, tracked Lady Munsing to a nursing home in Gerrard's Cross where her body is *kaput* but her brain still working, and through her traced the Clives to this village.

I have put all this down while I remember it, so that if he starts using it on Julia as proof against her mother, I can be ready to refute it. The Clives, of course, are dead. Gordon and Rita had the good sense to bang the door of their Cowley semi-detached in his face, which is what I should have done with my detached. Back in the village, Old Faithful finds Arthur Gale the telegram carrier, whose dash and enterprise has taken him to the top in masonry and cesspools around these parts.

'Do you know who that is?' He has a photostat of the famous picture.

'Why that's Miss Lambert. Mrs Kitteredge, as she was.'

So he came bothering me, and I am really very angry about him, but Mrs Meagan says that is the worst thing for me. She turned off the television when the news came on, because I saw de Gaulle. So I am trying to write Arnold Macklin calmly out of my system. A catharsis which began, I am happy to record, by him banging his head hard, very hard on the doorway as he went out.

I was so angry at that point that I had actually pushed him towards the door too fast for him to stoop.

'How well did your wife know this Peter Clive?'

'I know nothing about it.'

'But she was at his funeral. Didn't she ever talk to you about him, Mr Kitteredge?'

'Look here, I won't be cross examined. You have a damned impertinence barging into my house and trying to stir up all sorts of lies.'

'But it's a matter of history. It's the pure facts we're after.'

'You don't care whose life you ruin for a quick read.'

'You don't seem to understand. These articles are going to be very big. I already have a publisher interested in bringing them out later in book form.'

'Get out,' I said. 'Get out of my house. If I did know anything, which I don't, I wouldn't tell you.'

'But the public has a right to know the facts . . .'

That was when I shoved him towards the door and he practically split his skull open. He pretended that it had not hurt, but I watched from the window and saw him weaving on the path, so I am hoping he won't come back. He writes, but I don't answer.

'Tell him nothing,' I have written to Julia. 'He is an impostor and a madman who is trying to get money out of you.' That will keep her mouth closed.

They drove on, up into the Highlands, camping one night, staying in a comfortless hotel that was no more than a pub, one night in a bed and breakfast cottage at the side of the road.

Charlie had drawn out what money she had. Later, she would sell her house. They had enough to live on for a while, and as soon as they were somewhere safe, they would find work.

'Where are we going?'

'I don't know yet.' After his weeks of imprisonment, he just wanted to travel on. He knew enough about engines to keep the Morris going. It boiled over on hills. It leaked oil from its sump and air from its tyres, but Peter patched it up. They were near Inverness, south of the loch when the gearbox went. A grinding crunch, a smell of hot metal, then nothing, the gear lever waggling obscenely, like a broken arm.

'This will take longer.' Peter's teeth grinned white through the smears of oil as he wriggled out from beneath the car and wiped his hands on the back of Charlie's slacks. Nothing bothered him now. He was gay and casual. She was not afraid of him. She let herself be carried along into the blind future, keeping the past closed away, laughing with him in the present, loving him because she could not help it.

They were on the outskirts of a collection of houses and shops and churches. More than a village, not quite a town. There was a garage which had once been a stable. There was still a smithy at one end, where a draught horse was being shod.

The blacksmith was the garage owner. When he had finished the horse, he went back with them and towed the Morris on an old rope into his barn, where bits of cart harness still hung among the gaskets and fan belts, and the dry ghost of old manure hovered behind the more urgent reeks of oily metal.

He could rebuild the gearbox, but he would have to wait for parts. A week. Two weeks. Even this did not bother Peter. They might as well be here as anywhere.

They took two rooms in a stone house near the water where a draper's widow let out rooms to fishermen and motorists. They had a bedroom and a sitting-room for five shillings a week, and Charlie was allowed to cook their meals in the unfriendly kitchen where smoke from the range rushed back down the chimney into what she was stirring. Mrs Donald was a grim, hard-working woman, wrestling with mattresses and slop jars, who was as close-lipped about the business of others as about her own. It was not unlike the inn in Wales where they had spent the weekend as Mr and Mrs Jack Morgan and rejoiced in being unknown.

It began to rain the day after they arrived. There was nothing to do. Peter walked often to the garage to see if the spare parts had arrived. Sometimes he stayed to work the bellows and watch the blacksmith shape the shoes out of iron bars and nail them on.

'I think I could shoe a horse if I had to,' he told Charlie. 'Let's go to Argentina.'

'Let's go to Iceland.'

'We could pick fruit round the Great Lakes and then work our way south through hotel kitchens.'

'I think I'll have a baby.'

'Not yet.'

But she was not sure.

'We could go to Detroit and drive a new car for them that was going somewhere exciting.'

When it was damp, Mrs Donald lit a fire for them and they spent a lot of time in their rooms drinking wine and looking at an atlas and telling each other what their life was going to be.

There was nothing else to do. They did not want to fish. It was too cold to swim, and Peter did not want to swim because Charlie swam better than he did. He would not do anything that she could do better, like climbing trees or vaulting fences or rowing a boat. On that first day when they met by the roadside, he had told her admiringly that she had pluck, that she was a good sport. Now if she moved too athletically or took a running kick and sent a clod flying or hurled a stone far out into the loch as if she were fielding in the deep at St Gabriel's, he told her not to be so bloody sporting.

After they had been there a few days, the Simons arrived in an ancient Lancia tourer with fishing rods strapped to the sides and baskets and gaffs and flopping thigh-length boots like amputated legs piled in the back with their daughter Missy. They were after trout. They put on rain capes and sou'westers and set off through the driving rain with the windscreen open because there was no wiper, to spend whole days in their waders and come back with baskets of fish, which Mrs Donald had to cook and Charlie and Peter had to eat.

Missy could not go with them in the wet because she was asthmatic, and as it was always wet, she was always in the square stone house with the dripping yew trees, reading or doing jigsaw puzzles, or knocking on the door of Mr and Mrs Jack Morgan's room and calling, 'Can I come and be with you?'

She was fifteen years old, with long red hair flopping on her back like the tail of a chestnut mare, freckles that blotted out her squat nose, square little teeth that sat on her bottom lip, and pale-lashed eyes that watched too closely. The youngest of a much older family, she was a solitary child of unseen passions, one of which surfaced to attach itself to Charlie and Peter. Especially Peter.

She was a great nuisance. Charlie was sorry for her, but Peter was not. 'Get rid of her,' he said, 'before I kick her pearly teeth in.'

So Charlie hinted to the parents, 'Missy was with us all day today. I cooked lunch for her and we played cards and when the rain stopped we went for a walk and I took her for a row in Mr McGregor's boat. She was with us all day.'

'What a nuisance for you,' they were supposed to say. But Mr Simon approvingly nodded his inanimate profile which dropped in a straight line from hairline to chin like a Greek god, but not so attractive, and Mrs Simon, who was the wide-striding weathered matron that Peter would never let Charlie become, said, 'We've been so glad the child has found someone to keep her company. She's devoted to you, you know.'

But Missy was less a child than a young woman, with thrusting breasts and pale parted lips that trembled slightly like fruit on the fall of ripeness.

Charlie was faintly repelled by her, but the still painful memory of what she had done to Cara kept her from rejecting Missy.

'Tell the kid to stay away,' Peter said irritably when the familiar voice called outside their door.

'I can't,' Charlie said, but when Missy came in, she made an effort to say, 'I'm going to be busy today. You'd better find something to do.'

'I'll help you. What are you going to be busy at?' She put her arms round Charlie and kissed her. Charlie stepped back from the pushing breasts, and Peter said, 'That's enough of that, kid. She's not your mother.'

'My mother doesn't like to be kissed.' Missy swung her hair. 'Charlie does.'

'She doesn't.'

'I've seen you.'

'Not by you, I mean.'

'Yes she does. She told me.'

'You've been told to clear out, young lady,' Peter said. 'So get out and stay out.'

'Oh no.' She swaggered across the room, swinging the cheap kilt Charlie had bought for her in Inverness in the days when she was trying to encourage what she thought was a shy and lonely child. She stood in front of Peter's chair with her hands on her hips and her pelvis stuck out. She was not deliberately provocative. It came to her naturally. 'Charlie and I are going to the shop to buy currants and candied peel and then we're going to make you a wonderful big cake, aren't we, Charlie?'

'Oh all right.' There was nothing for the poor child to do if she said no.

'As a surprise?' Peter did not look at her.

'You've spoiled it by finding out.' Missy pouted her flat pale lips. 'Come on, Charlie, don't let's waste time with *men*.'

With the age she was, and the turmoil of her glands, it was not long before she began to be very aware of Peter. She began to be very pert with him. Once he slapped her.

'That was a mistake,' Charlie told him.

'Silly kids get spanked.'

'She doesn't think she's a kid.'

'You're jealous!' He hugged her very tightly. 'Oh, I adore you for that. You're jealous of any woman I even speak to, even Mrs Duncan. Listen—' He whispered. '*I felt Mrs Simon through her waders!*'

The spare parts for the Morris gearbox had at last come rumbling up from Oxford on the train to Inverness.

'We'll be leaving in a day or two,' Charlie told Missy, trying not to sound too glad.

The freckled face fell. Real tears sparkled on the sandy lashes. The ripe mouth trembled, pulled into a square. She cried like a child, standing up with face exposed, stomach out, toes in.

Would she run away like Cara? Throw herself under a bus? Into Loch Ness where she could not swim? To console her, Charlie took her in McGregor's boat across the little bay of the loch to the cottage where the old lady sold teas with scones and cake. On the way home, Missy clamoured to row, but she was all legs and arms and snagged oars, so Charlie pulled them into shore. Missy left her to drag up the little skiff and ran across to the house to find Peter and tell him that she had rowed all the way home. Charlie found her sitting on the arm of his chair, flipping his tie and giggling. Their heads turned together as she came in, as if she were the intruder.

The blacksmith had been kicked by a horse and could not work on the car at once. He would not let Peter try it, since he had grown possessive about Mick the Miller, standing so long in the clutter of his garage. He had polished the brass and touched up Charlie's paintwork and mended the torn talc at the back where the dog used to stick out his bristly nose at pursuing cars.

Restless, with departure in sight but out of reach, Charlie did not know what to do. The Simons had gone to the Isle of Skye. The thought of a whole day and evening with Missy led her to say to Peter, 'Let's go to Inverness on the bus.'

'And do what?'

'Wander. Look at shops. Go to the cinema. Eat.'

'You go. I can't be bothered.'

'What's the matter?' He was usually the one who could whip up a jaunt out of nothing exciting. 'Don't you feel well?'

They had walked a lot in the soft wind and rain. His skin was brown and his bright eyes had clear golden lights in them, but he took her hand and said, 'I don't know. I get the hump sometimes. You know that. I get to thinking.'

'About me?'

'Only good about you.' He kissed her hand. 'You've got a hand like a boy, do you know that, Charlay?'

'Come to town with me.'

'Not on that bus. You go. Here!' He pulled some money out of his pocket. It was all her money, but he kept it. 'Buy a bit of steak and a bottle of champagne.'

'Won't we have to have supper with Missy?'

'We'll have supper in bed. With the door locked.'

That was how I met Charlie in Inverness. I was coming out of my hotel and she was walking up the street with a brown paper bag and the rather puddingy expression she wore when she was alone and unobserved.

'What on earth are you doing here?' We both said it together.

'I thought you were in France,' I said.

'I'm going. I came up here first. I've never been to the Highlands.' She laughed and shook her hair back and began to ask me about the job that had brought me up there. She listened quite earnestly as we walked up to the hill, to keep me talking about myself.

Although the big Loch Ness Monster excitement did not start until about 1933, people had been seeing things in that suggestive stretch of water since the days of Robert the Bruce. Just recently, a Scottish listener had told the BBC that two maiden ladies who were neither mad nor drunk had seen something very strange, and I was up there to investigate whether there was enough in it that we could use.

We were experimenting with short news features at that time, a sort of forerunner of what today's personality commentators do, except that we did not have the researchers and writers to do most of the work. And there was no 'I heard James Kitteredge say'. It was 'I heard the wireless say', as if the set had voiced its own idea.

Actually no one voiced anything about the maiden ladies of Drumnadrochit. They lost courage when I suggested a visit to the Aberdeen Studios, and said, 'Och away, there's naething to tell.'

I saw them again a few years later when the Monster ballyhoo was really on and Inverness full of reporters and zoologists in knickers. They wanted to talk then, but so did dozens of others, and they had lost their chance of thunder.

Charlie was headed for the bus stop. I was going out to the loch, so I offered to drive her to wherever she was staying. She began to say that it was too far, that I would never find my way back, that she liked the bus. So I had to ask her in a brotherly way, 'Have you got a man there or something?'

When Charlie blushed, it was like the sun coming up very huge and glowing over an eastern hill. The colour spread from her neck up the bluff of her chin, into her wide cheeks and right over her eyebrows to her forehead, to disappear under the short black hair which flopped on her round head like a boy.

'Good luck,' I said, or something absurd like that. We had all known for ages that she was up to something. I was too busy to worry about it, and whatever it was, it had done wonders for her looks.

'Tell me some time?'

'Mm.' She kissed me with her warm blushing lips and jumped on to the bus with a flick of her well-sprung legs.

Bumping back in the bus with the steak and the bottle of champagne, she thought about getting back to Peter, and all the many evenings she had driven back from the school and thought about getting back to him. With her brother-in-law so close, they would have to leave the moment the car was ready. Away from danger, away from Missy, away from everybody who could grasp into their life.

'Mind how you go!' Mrs Clive had called to her as she ducked under the post office thatch and went out between Dad's alyssum and lobelia, planted in patterns like a miniature public park.

Dad had not taken much notice of her departure for a long holiday abroad. He had been disenchanted with her ever since she had refused to be his psychic partner. 'Send us a postcard,' he said, because it was quite nice when a piece of mail in the red van was for him.

But Nelly had looked sad. 'Mind how you go!' She waved from the green door. 'Come back safe.'

'See you soon!' This year, next year, some time, never ... Charlie bounced a little ruefully in the bus, a woman in history, who had thought the world well lost.

Peter was not in the house. Nor was Missy. Mrs Duncan did not know where they had gone. The blacksmith had not seen Peter. No one knew where either of them might be.

Charlie waited. It grew dark. A wind got up in the lake and blew some rain against her window. Mrs Duncan refused to worry. She shrugged her pointed shoulders and said, 'You'll see them back for their supper.'

But at eight o'clock, she came upstairs to ask, 'Will I call the police?'

'No!' Charlie jumped up from the chair by the window. 'Wait. It's all right—' She went out and ran down the road to the telephone box at the crossroads.

The waiter came to my table as I was finishing dinner to tell me that I was wanted on the telephone. Charlie was in a state of what sounded like barely controlled hysteria. She tried to tell me something, but all I could understand was, 'Come out here. Please come and help me.'

She told me where she was. After I had found someone to unlock the hotel garage and move the large car they had shunted in behind mine, I drove fast through the rain to the place she described.

She was waiting for me outside with a scarf round her head and a man's raincoat. Light came from the windows and open door of the house behind her. A big old-fashioned car squatted in the puddled drive. People were moving about.

She leaned into my car. Her eyelashes were stuck together. Rain was running off the front of her hair down her nose into her mouth.

'He's gone,' she said. 'I can't find him anywhere.'

'Who?'

It was a logical question, but she said angrily, 'What does it matter? He's disappeared and so has that girl. Something's happened to them. They're hurt somewhere. Nobody knows where they are. Oh, James, I'm so afraid—'

I have to admit that I thought the same as everyone else, although none of us voiced it at first to Charlie. The man seemed to be known as her husband, so I pretended I knew him. Jack was his name. Jack Morgan. If he had walked in at the gate between the sodden firs, I would have half slaughtered him for doing this horrible thing to Charlie, terrified and alone in this draughty grey house of sounding doors and feet.

As we went in, the girl's father came out in a silly sort of macintosh hat.

'I'm going to phone the police,' he said woodenly, 'whatever you say.'

'Oh please. I don't think you—'

'I don't care what you think. It's the only thing to do.' He splashed off in galoshes and Charlie began to cry.

I took her into the house. The girl's leathery bulky mother was in the hall, and the landlady, and some other lodgers, and a few hangers-on who had got wind of trouble. They were all talking at once, but they stopped as we went through, and looked at Charlie as if she had done some terrible crime.

I took her up to her room, a married people's room, with a man's things everywhere about. There was a bottle of champagne on the dressing-table, and I asked her if I should open it.

She shook her head. 'We'll open it later, when Peter is back.'

'I thought his name—'

She threw herself face down on the bed and moaned, 'Don't, don't . . . those awful people . . . don't let them, James . . .' and other half-formed cries of despair.

The police came after a long while, unhelpful, a bit cynical. They told us more about what they could not do than what they could. They insinuated some chill reason into the distraught house. It was obvious what they thought, although the girl was so young. There was no need to say it.

Because Charlie could not bear to stay in the house, I drove her about purposelessly half the night. What did she expect to find – his corpse mangled in a ditch? Shadows on the blind of a hotel room? When we got back, she clattered up the uncarpeted stairs and flung open her door. I saw her face as she stared at the empty room, blank and finished.

There was nothing we could do but wait. Charlie slept for a while. I sat by the bed and watched her tossing and murmuring. Towards first light, she fought out of sleep in a panic, sat

284

up and looked at me as if she did not know me.

'He's killed her?'

'Come on . . . it's all right . . .' I leaned forward to stroke her hair, and made soothing noises. I thought she was crazed with anxiety and dreams.

'But if he's killed once, he—' She put the back of her hand in her mouth and stared at me in terror, biting her hand. Into my troubled mind, swirling with fears I could not properly understand, there came a glimpse of the outrageous alien thing that possessed her. Then her eyes closed for a moment and she let out her caught breath on a sigh, and her face became secret.

I kept her secret. I had no right to know it. No one, not even I, need have ever known about Peter, because he was already dead. A hero.

After they found McGregor's boat drifted upside down into the reeds beyond the wooded promontory, they began to drag that part of the loch. When they found them, the girl's hands were still locked round his neck, as she had dragged him under.

It is still painful to write about these things. It was agony at the time to live through them with Charlie. She behaved well. She suffered the buffets of Mrs Simon's hoarse apologies in a sort of stoic impersonal way, as if she were a post. I was the hysterical one. It was I who got into a fight with the news photographer. There was a man from the Humane Society talking about a posthumous medal. I told him what he could do with it.

NOTE FROM ARNOLD MACKLIN

The curious thing about this whole story is that Julia gave it to that bloody little guitarist after Mr Kitteredge died. The little creep came to the cottage to say goodbye before he went to America with his girl friend, who was later exposed, legs and all, and was run out of a hotel in the Adirondacks for false pretences.

He found Mr Kitteredge's sister sorting his meagre possessions.

'Where's Mr James then?'

'He's dead and what's it to you?' You can imagine the dialogue.

'I was his best friend,' the boy says, hoping to get something out of it. He tells her that he is off to the States on an extensive tour (two TV dates lined up and a spot in a third-rate club in Las Vegas that was closed down before he ever got there). He adds that he will visit Julia, meaning to swank. He has not seen how she lived then.

They have cocoa or some such fool thing, and the sister unbends far enough to tell this unlikely character that Mr K left his stepdaughter nothing. Except there is this thick brown folder with her name on a torn old label, half smudged out.

The sister has not looked at it. It is tied up with string and she minds her business. Will the boy Terence take it over to Julia? He will. By devious routes too depressing to think about, he fetches up eventually at Provincetown on Cape Cod, where the unprepossessing Julia waters the Bourbon in a dark tap-room where the bar is made out of the side of a boat.

She rejects the big brown folder unread. 'I don't want it.'

'But he worked on it for months and months. Pathetic, it was.'

'Why should I want it? You can have it. Chuck it off the dock, I don't care.'

She didn't care much about anything, as I found when I

tracked her down and got her to talk by telling her that Mr Kitteredge had been willing to help me.

She didn't care what she said, but she wasn't much help, since with a slob like that you can't tell what's true and what isn't. But she did tell me that her stepfather had been writing a story, and she gave me a vague idea where to look for Terence.

I found him playing the guitar in an off-season club farther down the coast. His discredited bird had left him some time ago for an engineering student somewhere in the Middle West where their money ran out. He had read a bit of the book where he was a success on television, so he was glad to sell me the manuscript, partly for vanity, mostly for money.

It's clear that if Mr Kitteredge had lived, he would never have shown it to Julia. If Julia had read any of it, she would never have given it to the guitarist.

But the public has a right to know the facts.

There are some facts I've dug out that even the omniscient Kitteredge didn't know. He never took out the bricks in the chimney of the old copper in the shed and looked for Bessie Hunter's hair. I did.

There was nothing there. Newspaper does not disintegrate in thirty-five years. Nor does human hair. At Masada, they found a woman's long plaited hair nearly two thousand years after she was killed. My guess is that Peter had found Bessie's hair and destroyed it. So it wasn't only the hair that bound him to Charlie. It wasn't the hair at all.

It's very sad, really. Vevwy sad.

Monica Dickens
Kate and Emma 70p

Kate is sixteen, a victim of cruelty, neglect and poverty.
We meet her in a London court 'in need of care and protection'.
Emma is a bare two years older, daughter of the presiding
magistrate. A girl with a comfortable background,
with a mind of her own.

Between these two an enduring, if turbulent, friendship is struck as
Emma toils doggedly not only to lift Kate out of the mire,
but also to make sense of her own life and love . . .

The Listeners 70p

The enthralling story of what happens when people at the end
of their tether contact the Samaritans . . .

In this deeply felt, absorbingly told novel, Monica Dickens
not only vividly portrays three would-be suicides,
but also the Samaritans themselves.

A story in Monica Dickens's inimitable style — salted with humour
and inspired by love.

You can buy these and other Pan books from booksellers and
newsagents; or direct from the following address:
Pan Books, Cavaye Place, London SW10 9PG
Send purchase price plus 15p for the first book and 5p for
each additional book, to allow for postage and packing

While every effort is made to keep prices low, it is sometimes
necessary to increase prices at short notice. Pan Books reserve the
right to show on covers new retail prices which may differ
from those advertised in the text or elsewhere